Nyght & Daie

Part 3:
When Nyght and Daie Collide

PAUL W. GIBBS
ILLUSTRATION BY VICTOR GUIZA

SonWright Books

Glossary

Sun-cycle: One day

Moon-cycle: One month

Sun-mark/mark: One hour

Moon-mark: One week

Season: One year

Land-mark: One mile

Blessed Day: Birthday

Handbreadth: Three inches

ONE

The sun was high in the sky, but even after so many seasons, Hanna still would not look at it. As she hung out the linen, she kept her eyes and mind on her task at hand. It is what she has done for as long as she can remember.

She was going on twenty seasons. It was three seasons ago that Papa passed away. It was just two seasons ago that Mama had also left the world. Before she died, she had the boarding house placed in Hanna's name, so she was now the owner and operator. Because she had been working there since she was a young child, she had no problem with running it on her own. However, she did employ another woman to handle the cooking for the guests and to serve the meals as well. This allowed Hanna to take care of all the other duties without having to associate with the people staying in her establishment.

Hanna was alone, but she was not lonely. Everyone she had ever known that was close to her was now gone so she spent a lot of time by herself, which was the way she preferred it. She rose in the morning and took care of all the chores she had been doing for the majority of her life. She had been doing them for so long that she did not even have to think about them. Her body went through the motions, allowing her to keep her mind on not thinking about the way her life had turned out.

After she finished hanging out the linen, Hanna went downstairs to her small office. The one Papa used when he took care of the boarding house. She sat down at the desk and began going through the ledger. Papa had shown her how he managed the books not too long before he passed away. After he died, Hanna figured he knew on some level that he would not be around for much longer, so he taught her how to handle the funds so she could take them over one day.

After Papa died, Mama continued to help run the boarding house, but with each cycle of the sun, with each cycle of the moon, Hanna saw her spirit dwindling more and more. When Mama did pass away, Hanna had already hardened her heart, so she was prepared for the last person she had truly known to leave her.

Her days consisted of the same routine. She woke before the sun rose, she did her chores, she went over the books, she went shopping for any supplies she or the boarding house needed, she then did more chores, she then went to bed, to start over again when she awoke the next day. She ate her morning and evening meals in her bedchamber; her midday meal she took in her office. She led a very routine life.

If she did happen to see one of the guests, she was always polite and thanked them for staying at her establishment, but she spoke those few comments without putting any thought into them because she had done so for so long.

When she went shopping for supplies, which was the only time she left the boarding house, she was always polite and greeted anyone who greeted her. She always said thank you to the shopkeepers she dealt with, and the people delivering the supplies that she could not take with her, but it was a routine she had been performing for a long time with no true emotions.

Hanna was over nineteen seasons old, closer to twenty, and even though she did not show it by her outward appearance, inside her heart was the same as her life, empty.

As Hanna sat at the desk looking over the ledger, there was a knock at the door. Since she knew who it was, and what she wanted, there was no need to say anything so she continued with what she was doing. Right after the knock, the door opened, and Elisa, the woman Hanna hired to prepare the meals for the guests and herself, walked in.

Elisa was in her late sixties. She had never been married and had no children. Both of those aspects were a big factor in Hanna hiring her to work at the boarding house. She figured that since the woman did not have any family then she would not be bringing anyone around. When there were fewer people around, Hanna liked it all the more. She did give Elisa one of the rooms in the boarding house but that was so the woman would be available to prepare all three daily meals. Hanna did not provide her with the room because she wanted company.

Elisa walked into the room and brought the tray she had prepared for Hanna's lunch. When she made her way over to the desk, she sat the tray down, and Hanna did not hesitate to speak the same statement, the same one she gave every day, "Thank you, Elisa." She said it politely and even meant it, but it was obvious to Elisa the words had no feeling.

"You're welcome, ma'am," Elisa said, then turned and left the room. She knew there was no need to try to say anything else to her employer. She had tried when she first started working at the boarding house, but she soon realized that the woman she worked for wanted to keep their relationship strictly professional. Elisa understood, having worked with several people through her many seasons, but now the elderly woman was working for someone who had not seen twenty seasons and it saddened her. Elisa had never married nor had any children. It was her decision, and she was happy with it, but when she looked at Hanna, she saw a person who had stopped living long before she ever began to live.

It did not take Elisa long, after she had started working at the boarding house, to see that her employer had closed her heart and would not let anyone in. It saddened the elderly woman but there was nothing she could do about it; she was only the servant.

Hanna ate her lunch while looking over the books. The boarding house would never be a place to make anyone wealthy, but it supplied Hanna with enough income that she did not see a problem in maintaining the place for many seasons to come. There were always people needing a place to stay, and when the city put on one of its four seasonal festivals, it brought in so many patrons that she boarded out every room she had available. Since the festivals lasted for a moon-mark, the boarding house did enough business during those times to make up for when business was slow.

Even when Mama and Papa ran the place, they never lived a life of luxury, and even though Hanna did not want to either, she could not understand why Mama and Papa always seemed to be happy. Not only to Hanna and her mother, and not only to the patrons who stayed at the boarding house, but they also seemed to be happy being with each other.

Before Hanna and her family moved to the city, she had already learned that not everyone who called themselves a friend was truly one. When two men murdered her father, she learned that someone could take away the ones she loved. As she watched her mother's health dwindle over the seasons before she died, Hanna learned that losing someone you love could kill you just as a knife. When her mother passed away, Hanna learned that no matter what you may think, everyone always leaves you. When Colton went away, she learned that even if you do not call a person a friend, when they leave, it will still leave a hole in your heart. When Papa and Mama passed away, Hanna learned that there was no meaning in life. A person is born, and they will die. Everything in between is just a lie, because in the end, we are all alone.

Hanna had no problem with being alone. The one thing she did not realize was that in being alone, she never realized that she was lonely. A person has to allow themselves to accept others into their life, even if they are only there for a season. When the time comes that the person leaves, the one remaining needs to fill the hole of loneliness with someone else. Hanna did not. She sealed the hole up to make sure no one could ever get inside.

Hanna finished her lunch and then closed the ledger she had been reading. It was now time for her to go out to a couple of the shops and arrange for the delivery of some of the supplies the boarding house was getting low on.

She walked out of the study and went into the kitchen where she saw Elisa working, "I will be out for a while," she said, and waited for the standard reply.

"Yes, ma'am," Elisa said.

Now that she had informed Elisa that she would be away, she simply turned around and walked through the boarding house to the front door. She then went out into the well-populated city but took her emptiness with her.

When she had turned sixteen, Hanna blossomed physically. She was always a beautiful child, with her golden hair, but when she began to show signs of womanhood, she became even more alluring. This did not go unnoticed by many of the young men in the city. There were a few gentlemen, some Hanna's age, and some even a bit older, who had noticed her walking through the city. During many of her walks, an admirer would try his best to acquire the name of the beauty who had captured his heart, just after seeing her for but a moment.

Hanna was not impressed by any of her admirers and not one even came close to acquiring her name from her.

Some of the men would not take no for an answer and even went as far as finding out all they could about the new love of their life. They found out where she lived, and even her name. With a couple of those young men, when Mama was still alive, she was more than helpful in trying to give the callers as much of a chance as possible to make an impression on Hanna. Mama knew that she would not be around forever and she did not want to see the girl she had helped to raise be alone after she was gone. There were very few things Mama had failed at, but that particular task with Hanna was one of them.

Every so often, a more persistent admirer would

try a little harder than others to make an impression on the young woman. Hanna did her best to ignore all the attention she received, and in most cases, the young man finally gave up and went off to look for another true love. On those rare occasions when the man was willing to show her that he was the man of her dreams, Hanna would finally grow tired of the devotion and simply say to the man, "I have no use for you." This statement usually came just before the front door of the boarding house slammed in his face. It was not so much the words that put off the admirer, it was the emptiness in them. The young man might have walked away with a broken heart, but at least he would not quit looking for his true love. Something the woman who rejected him never thought about seeking.

Now almost at twenty, Hanna was still one of the most beautiful women in the city. If a stranger, who had just recently come to the city, were to ask one of the many men who tried to get to know her, just who that vision of loveliness was, they would receive the answer, "That one is so cold, not even the hottest of fires would thaw out her heart."

To Hanna, she was just being herself. To others she was empty. Soon the men in the city stopped trying altogether because they knew they had no chance of warming her heart. Hanna had been so unaffected by the attention men would show her, that she did not even realize when they had ceased altogether.

Hanna walked into the shop and waited until the owner finished with the customer he was taking care of. While waiting, she looked around to see if there was anything she could use that was not on her list of items. This was something she would do whenever she would wait, but since her needs were little, the items she had decided upon earlier would suffice.

"What can I do for you Miss Hanna?" the shop-keeper asked, happy to help one of his regular customers.

"I have my list ready," Hanna said and handed the piece of parchment to the man on the other side of the counter. "Can they be delivered within two sun-cycles?"

The man looked at the list and was sure he would be able to meet the young woman's request. He then looked back up at Hanna, "I will have them there with no problem at all," he said and smiled. Hanna had been coming to his shop even before she took over running the boarding house. She would come in, give the list of supplies she needed, and then leave. The man had always thought the young girl was just quiet and shy and eventually she would grow out of it; but after all these seasons, every time she came into his shop, no matter how big of a smile he gave her, she would not return one. Now that she was older, she still had the same look she had when she was younger. As if she was doing what she was because she knew no other way. He had even thought about trying to arrange a meeting with her and his nephew but decided he would prefer his nephew to find a woman who would make him happy, not someone who looked as if they never had a happy moment in their life. "Will there be anything else you will be needing?" the man asked politely because he was always nice to his customers.

"No, that will be all, good day," Hanna said and turned to leave.

"And a good day to you as well, Miss Hanna," the owner said, and as he watched her walk out of his shop, he could not help but feel sad about how someone so young had given up on living.

Hanna spent the rest of the afternoon going to the different shops and giving the proprietors her orders for the supplies she needed. She only took an outing like this once a moon-cycle. That way she did not have to spend more than one sun-cycle out in the city for a long period of time and away from the boarding house. The place she had decided to remain until the day came when she would leave the world.

As she walked through the city, she might stop and look in one of the shops that she did not need supplies from. However, when she exited, she had not purchased a single item. She might have been curious at something she had seen, but before the curiosity changed to a desire to have the item, Hanna had already told herself she did not need it. To her, all she needed were the basics. The least amount of material items was all she required because possessions were just like people. They were either taken away or destroyed, so there was no need to become attached to something that would someday be gone. It was what Hanna believed.

It was going on the fifteenth sun-mark and as Hanna was walking down the street she felt as if someone was watching her. Every so often, she would turn around and see if someone was following her. Since she did not see anyone taking an interest in her, she decided she had been out in the city too long and it was time for her to go back to the boarding house. She had a couple more stops to make but after that, she would return home. Even though she wanted to head home at that very moment, the thought of having to come out another day bothered her even more.

She made her way to the last shop she had planned to visit and just before she went inside, she lingered a bit longer than she needed to just to see if what she was feeling was accurate or if it was her imagination. Since she still did not see anyone, she decided that she was just paranoid and that it was all in her mind.

On her way back to the boarding house, she passed a certain building, although she made sure she did not look in its direction. It was one of the temples of the Creator. Just one that the local citizens would attend, not the big one closer to the upper levels of the city. Not the one Colton had gone to so he could study to be a priest.

Whenever she would pass the temple, Hanna felt a pull in her heart, but as strong as it pulled at her, she pushed it back down with more force. There were times at night while she slept that she dreamt of Colton. On the morning afterward, she made sure she put more effort into performing her chores. Chores were always something Hanna had, and she knew that no matter how long she lived, they would always be there for her. Not like people.

When she returned to the boarding house, just before she entered, Hanna turned and looked behind her. She moved her eyes over every bit of the scene in front of her, but she did not see anyone watching her. People were walking on the street in front of the boarding house, but all of them seemed to be going about their business, and not a single person was looking her way.

Hanna took one more moment to look around then went inside. As much as she wanted to place the locking bar across the door, she could not. The guests staying at the boarding house would be coming and going throughout the day and they would need to be able to enter. She decided that what she was feeling was because she had spent too much time taking care of her errands and it caused her to be a little flustered from being around so many people. She did wonder why she had never felt like this before.

She opened the door to the kitchen and saw Elisa working on preparing the evening meal. "I am back," Hanna said, and usually she would wait to hear some reply from the woman, but this time, Hanna let go of the swinging door, and walked to her study. Once inside she closed the door and went over to the window. Since it was on the side of the boarding house, when she looked outside, she could not see the street in front of the building. She did her best to see if anyone was watching her because even when she had entered the building she still felt as if someone was.

Not seeing anyone, Hanna pulled the curtains together and secured the middle of them tighter, trying to make sure there was no space where someone could see into the room or her. She then went over to the desk, but instead of sitting behind it, she paced back and forth in front of it.

She did not know why she felt the way she did. It was not as if someone was just watching her, it was as if they were preying on her. That if they were to get close enough, they would go out of their way to cause her harm.

All of a sudden, she thought about her father, specifically his murder. The local authorities even had a good idea of who had killed him, but since they had left the city, and unless they were no longer alive, they were still out there in the world. She had not thought about what had happened to her father since her mother had been alive. Now with bringing up the memory of his death, Hanna did not like being in the room alone.

She walked briskly out of the room and went into the kitchen. Normally, she would not go into the kitchen while Elisa was working, but with the way she was feeling, normal, was not part of her world.

When Elisa noticed her employer standing at the door, she stopped working with the dough she had been kneading to make into biscuits, "Is there something you wish, ma'am?"

Hanna could not think of an answer. In the time Elisa had come to work for her, if she did need something from the kitchen, Hanna would walk in, take what she needed then leave, not saying a word to Elisa. Now she just stood in the doorway, and from the way the elderly woman was looking at her, she was going to have to either answer the woman's question or turn and leave. She did not like the second option. "I thought I might give you a hand with preparing the evening meal."

Both women were surprised at what she had said. Hanna, because she had never offered to help the woman before, and Elisa for the same reason.

Hanna was the one to move first. She walked over to the small window and looked out. Since this one only showed the view of the back of the boarding house, she was sure no one was watching her. That is unless they were hiding in the relief shack, and even though it crossed Hanna's mind to go out and check, she decided it would be better to stay in the kitchen. "What are you preparing tonight?" she asked.

Elisa had not gone back to working the dough. It was obvious the young woman was acting differently. Not only about offering to help, but she seemed as if she was somewhat distracted. Elisa was still only the servant, so she had no place to pry into the way her employer was acting, or even about her offer to help in making the evening meal. Elisa went back to what she was doing and answered Hanna, "The chicken quarters are in the pot in the hearth boiling now. Once I have the dough prepared, then I will start preparing the vegetables to add to the chicken."

Hanna looked over to her right and saw the vegetables sitting on the counter. "I will see to them," she said and went over to begin the task. When she reached the counter, as she picked up the first potato, she felt the feeling again as if the eyes of someone were on her. Only this time when she turned to see if she was correct, she saw Elisa had stopped working and was staring at her. Hanna could see by the look on the woman's face that she thought there was something wrong with her. She turned back around, picked up the small paring knife, and started peeling the potatoes.

Elisa went back to working the dough, and not staring at her employer any longer. However, Hanna still had the feeling as if someone was watching her, just not the person in the room with her.

Hanna helped her mother in the kitchen from the time she was able to walk and hold a spoon. She had helped Mama prepare the meals for the guests at the boarding house, and even though she had not cooked a meal since Elisa had taken over the duty, Hanna fell back into the routine with no effort, since it was just another chore, and chores were what made Hanna comfortable.

When she finished cutting up the vegetables, she went to the cooking pot hanging over the fire, removed the lid, and stirred the water to move the chicken around. She saw that it was still too early to add the vegetables so she covered the pot and went off to do the next item in preparing the meal.

Since Elisa was taking care of the biscuits, Hanna decided she would start preparing the dough for the next meals. When Mama and Papa ran the boarding house, they would purchase their bread from the bakery. When Hanna took over, she decided that she preferred to have the bread made at the boarding house. She told herself that it tasted fresher, but deep down, even if she would not admit it, she did not like going to the bakery because it reminded her of the trips she would take with her mother.

When Elisa saw Hanna begin to work at the table in the center of the kitchen, along with her, she wanted to tell her employer that she did not have to help, but since she was only the servant, she remained quiet. Elisa also thought that what Hanna was doing was a good thing. Maybe she had finally come around and realized that her life did not have to consist only of doing chores and going over the ledgers of the boarding house. If that was what was happening, Elisa did not want to say or do anything to scare the young woman back into the little hole she had made for herself and lived in.

While Hanna worked with the dough, she still had the feeling someone was watching her. As much as she wanted to go to the window in the kitchen or go back to the front door and look outside, she felt more comfortable staying in the room with Elisa so she would not have to be alone.

The more she concentrated on making the bread, the more she began to take her mind off the feeling. She and Elisa had never worked in the kitchen together, but even though this was their first time, they were able to move around and take care of their task without getting in the other's way. For Hanna, it was just a way to not be alone. For Elisa though, it felt as if she had a daughter to cook and bake with.

As they continued to work, Hanna took another look at the boiling chicken quarters and saw that it was time to add the vegetables. She brought the bowl over, poured the contents into the cooking pot, and gave it a good stir to mix the vegetables in with the chicken. When she stood up from leaning over the pot and turned around, she saw that she was alone, and cried out, "Elisa!" Since she had frozen right where she had been standing, she had not moved when Elisa came running back into the room.

"What is it, ma'am?" she asked with concern, standing in the doorway.

Hanna had to force herself to get her breathing under control before she could answer, "Noth... nothing. I was just surprised when I turned and you were not here."

As much as she liked the way Hanna had participated with making dinner, Elisa could tell that there was something wrong with the young woman. She walked over to where Hanna was still standing by the fireplace. "Are you alright, ma'am? Is there something wrong?"

Hanna looked at her, turned her head to take a quick look at the window, and then put her focus back on Elisa. "I'm fine, just a little startled is all."

Elisa was only a servant, so it was not her place to contradict her employer's statement, but she still felt that maybe Hanna was not being totally truthful. "Perhaps you should go and take a rest before dinner." Elisa thought that was the best way to speak to her employer and state in a kind manner that maybe she was not well. "I will finish with the evening meal, and then I will serve yours in your bedchamber."

The thought of being alone in the upstairs room made Hanna even more nervous than when she had turned and saw that Elisa was not in the kitchen. With her bedchamber on the second floor of the building, she would have no way to get away from the person watching her. As soon as the thought came to her, she realized that she had never even seen anyone watching her, and she had no need to worry about trying to get away from them.

Hanna decided that the best thing to do was to continue to help Elisa with the evening meal. It would not only take her mind off what she was feeling, but being around someone else would make it more difficult for someone to come after her. Once again, Hanna did not know why the thought came to her, but when she went over to the table to continue to work, she made sure she had a knife within reach of her right hand.

Elisa was confused about what to do. Her employer had told her that she was fine, but it was obvious that there was something going on with her. Since she was only the servant, it was not her place to say anything, so she went back to work.

Just before the chicken and vegetables finished, Elisa positioned the pan of biscuits close to the fire so they would be ready at the same time as the rest of the meal. It was now time for her to set the table. She had not even exited the room before Hanna called to her, "Where are you going?"

This time, Elisa thought she heard fear in the words of the question. She turned and looked at her employer, "I must set the table in the other room." She waited to see if Hanna wanted her to do something else, but when she gave Elisa a nod to let her know she understood, Elisa walked out of the kitchen, but not before giving the young woman one more concerned look.

Hanna did not know what to do. She looked around and saw the meal cooking over the fire, which she knew was not ready. She finished with the dough for the bread for the next two days, so there was nothing else for her to do. With no chores to occupy her time and thoughts, her mind had nothing else to do but think about the feeling she had that someone was watching her.

She stayed in the kitchen for about ten more breaths, then ran out to go and help Elisa. She burst through the door so quickly that if Elisa or anyone else had been standing next to it, it would have knocked them to the floor.

The dining room was just outside the kitchen, so when Hanna exited it, Elisa immediately saw her, as well as the worried look Hanna had on her face. She was about to ask her employer if she was okay, but Hanna could tell that the question was about to come so she walked the rest of the way into the room and went over to the small table next to the wall where the plates and silverware were. Since Elisa was placing the plates on the table, Hanna took the forks, knives, and spoons and began setting them next to the plates Elisa had already sat down.

After Hanna placed the second set, she could tell that Elisa was looking at her. When she looked at the elderly woman, Elisa quickly turned her head and put her eyes back on what she was doing. Hanna then realized the reason Elisa had been watching her. She looked down at the set of utensils she had just placed and saw that they were not in the proper order. She looked back at the first set and saw their placement was haphazard. Having learned from her mother, as well as Mama, Hanna knew the proper way to set a table, but she had not done so. Elisa had noticed it as well, but since she was only the servant, it was not her place to correct her employer.

Hanna readjusted the silverware in front of her and then went and redid the set she had first placed. As she walked around the table, following Elisa, she had to concentrate to make sure she set the table properly.

When she finished, Hanna took a last look at the table and counted the placings. There was a total of four, one for each guest staying at the boarding house. What she said next was even more surprising to Elisa. "I will take my dinner in the dining room tonight with the guests."

Elisa heard what her employer said, she just did not believe it. Ever since she has worked at the boarding house, Hanna has always taken her dinner in her bedchamber. It was the biggest room on the upper level and there was even a small eating table, so Elisa did not think anything about it when Hanna had told her that she would have her morning and evening meals in there. Now, she had just said she would be dining downstairs with the guests. Elisa was sure that there was something wrong with her employer, but it was not her place to say. "Yes, ma'am. I will set another place for you." She moved off and grabbed another plate.

Hanna was right behind her setting the utensils

down. She then turned around and grabbed another plate and another set of utensils. She then walked to the far end of the table and placed all the items down. She looked up and saw Elisa staring at her and could tell she wanted to know what the setting was for. "You will be joining us for the evening meal as well."

Elisa had spent the last fifty-four seasons of her life working in boarding houses and inns, as well as being the house cook for well-to-do families. In all those times, she had never eaten a meal with the people she cooked for. She now decided it was time for her to speak to her employer about dining etiquette. "It would not be proper for me to dine with you or your guests, ma'am. I am only a servant."

Hanna was not upset with what Elisa had said. She had never eaten with the guests when Papa and Mama operated the boarding house. Since they were the hosts, they could choose to eat with them or not. Hanna, and even her mother and father when they were alive, had taken their meals in the kitchen, so even though Elisa spoke the truth, at the moment, Hanna did not care. She went around the table toward Elisa. "Since this is my boarding house, I will decide what is and what is not proper."

"Yes, ma'am," Elisa said quickly to let Hanna know she meant no disrespect.

Hanna continued to walk into the kitchen but then realized that she was alone once again. She walked back into the dining room and looked at

Elisa, "Are you going to help me with the evening meal or just stand there?"

Elisa came out of her confusion, "No, ma'am, I mean, yes, ma'am. I mean that no I am not going to stand here, and yes, I will help you." Elisa, still confused at what was going on, quickly stepped past her employer, and even thought that it would be best if she did not join her employer and the guests for dinner. She was only a servant, so it was not her place to say.

The evening meal was interesting. Not the food itself, but the atmosphere.

Four guests were staying at the boarding house. Two men were passing through the city of Maridian, each of them on business, but not together. The last two guests were a man and his wife in the city for the woman's third cousin's wedding. Since she was only a third cousin, they were not related close enough to obtain an invitation to stay at the family's mansion.

Hanna sat in the chair at the end of the table closest to the kitchen door. The two businessmen sat to the left of her, and the couple to her right. Elisa sat at the opposite end of the table from Hanna, who made sure she kept an eye on everyone to make sure she could see if someone was watching her.

When she decided to dine downstairs this particular evening, she did so because she did not want to be upstairs by herself. Now sitting with four strangers, and her cook, she felt as if maybe she had overreacted; nevertheless, she remained down-stairs. The reason she had insisted on Elisa joining as well, was because she wanted to make sure that everyone staying in the boarding house was in her view. At least now she could see the people there were not watching her in a way that made her feel uncomfortable. That is with the exception of Elisa who did not take her eyes off Hanna for the entire meal. Hanna figured the woman was just acting that way because of the way she had been acting herself. Yes, even Hanna had to admit to herself that she was acting differently.

Throughout the meal, the guests conversed on a variety of different subjects and even tried to include their host, but when she simply gave a one-word response to the questions asked of her, it became obvious to the guests, that even though she had joined them for the evening meal, their host was not a sociable person. Or if she was, she could use some work on her social skills.

With the way she was acting, it was no surprise to Elisa when the guests left the table sooner than they normally would. All four of them declined dessert, which made Elisa a bit agitated because desserts were her specialty.

When the guests left the dining room, Elisa began clearing the dishes and was surprised when Hanna immediately began to help. "Ma'am, I am thankful for the assistance you have given me with the evening meal, but I can take care of the cleaning.

24

I am sure you have other things to attend to." She might have been only a servant, but even Elisa knew the host should not be cleaning the table. Even though Hanna was the one to clean out the relief shack as well as taking care of all the other chores at the boarding house, it was the fact that she had never helped with the meals, or the removal of the dishes, which let Elisa know something was wrong with her employer.

Hanna thought for a moment but decided that she did not care what Elisa thought. "Two of us can do it quicker than one," Hanna said, then walked into the kitchen with the dishes she had collected. When she noticed Elisa was not with her, she called out, "Are you going to help?" Elisa grabbed the remaining dishes and joined her employer.

It did not take long to clean the dishes. The water to wash them had been set over the fire while the evening meal was taking place. By the time they finished in the kitchen with everything, it was only going on the twenty-first mark of the night. Two marks earlier than Elisa had ever finished since the time she had started working at the boarding house.

While they were working side by side, they had the work to occupy them, so they went without speaking to one another. Now that the work was complete, the only thing to occupy them now was awkward silence, something Elisa brought to an end, "Well, I should turn in now." As soon as she had finished speaking, she could tell that Hanna wanted to say something, so she kept her eyes on her employer and waited. Since she did not say anything, Elisa did, "Goodnight, ma'am." She then turned and walked out of the kitchen.

Hanna was able to stay in the room by herself for two breaths before she quickly caught up to Elisa.

They both headed toward the stairs and as they passed the sitting room, Hanna saw the two businessmen sitting and chatting. Since she did not really know either of them, Hanna decided she would continue to follow Elisa up the stairs.

When they reached the top floor, they both had to walk down the hallway and turn the corner to where their rooms were. Elisa stayed in the room where Hanna had before Mama and Papa passed away. When Hanna took over the boarding house, she moved into the bigger room once belonging to Mama and Papa. The two doors to the two rooms were no more than three paces from each other. When Elisa stopped at her door and Hanna moved to stand on the outside of hers, she looked back to where Elisa was standing, it seemed as if the two doors were on opposite sides of the world. Hanna knew that it was now time for her to be by herself, something she was not pleased about.

"Ma'am, is there something else you need before I turn in for the night?" Elisa asked because she could see that her employer was still acting strangely.

Hanna wanted to say that she did not want to be alone but forced herself not to and berated herself when she had thought of it. Being alone was what she preferred. "No. Goodnight, Elisa."

"Goodnight, ma'am," Elisa said, gave one more look at her employer then entered her room, closing the door behind her.

The door shutting was the loudest noise Hanna had ever heard, and now she was alone in the hallway. She thought about knocking on Elisa's door but did not know what she would say when the woman answered. She decided that if she got into her room, she could lock the door, and then she would be safe.

Once inside, and once she secured the door, Hanna lit a candle. She looked around the room to make sure she was alone. As she was doing this, the thought came to her that if someone was hiding in her room, she had just locked the door, locking herself in with whoever was in there with her. Those types of thoughts ran through her head as she continued to inspect every corner, every shadow, and every place someone could hide, including under the bed.

After her thorough inspection, she realized that even though she had been feeling as if someone had been watching her, from the time she had been shopping, until now, she had not seen anyone. Now secured behind a locked door, she thought about how silly she must have looked to Elisa and the guests. She would not be surprised if all four of them checked out tomorrow morning and Elisa resigned.

Hanna put those thoughts out of her head as

well. Normally, she would not be going to bed so early but with the way she had been acting, it took a lot out of her, and so she was ready to turn in. Just before she climbed into bed, she looked out the window in the room. This one faced the front of the house and she was able to look down into the street.

Once again, she did not see anyone and decided that she was imagining everything. Besides, she was just someone who ran a boarding house. There was no reason for anyone to take an interest in her. With that thought, she climbed into bed but left the candle lit on the nightstand by the bed, just to keep the darkness away. She then rolled over to try to get some sleep. At least that was what she wanted to do. It never even crossed her mind that she had gone to bed wearing the same clothes that she had on during the day.

TWO

hen she arrived in the lands to the west, Nyght had mixed emotions. She had enjoyed the two moon-cycles it took to cross the great waters and loved to go up on deck and stand at the prow when the sun had left the sky. As the ship rushed across the waves, she listened to the noise of them breaking against the hull, as well as the smell of the salt, and the feel of the spray on her skin. Nyght had never felt freer in her life. Even though she knew her calling was to be an assassin, if she had to choose another path for her life, it would be to take to the sea and never leave it.

Once *The White Squall* made port in the coastal city of Carto, she immediately headed to the Assassin's Guild House. Since this was the port where most ships coming from the east used, the Guild had built a house when they expanded their territory to grow with the world.

She was not known to the local Guild, so a coded letter, given to her by the High-Masters of her own Guild, granted her admittance. The letter stated who Nyght was, regarding her being an assassin. The part about her being the Ruler of the entire Assassin's Guild was not part of the message and Nyght did not mention it either. Both Nyght and the High-Masters thought it would be best to keep that information to the Guild Castle alone. Since she had the letter, and it was in the code of the Guild, the ones operating the house had no trouble acknowledging that she was one of them.

She only remained at the Guild House for a sun-cycle. Just long enough to obtain the supplies she would need for her journey in fulfilling her assigned contract. The letter did not state what her task was, and she did not tell the members running the Guild House, but since they were very efficient at their jobs, they made sure that when she left, Nyght received everything she needed to ensure that she would be successful.

When she rode out of Carto, she headed west. Her target lived in the city of Millbury, and from the information the local Guild House gave her, it would take her a few moon-marks to reach her destination. Even though she knew she would have to remain in these lands for the next three seasons, she did not want to wait to begin.

As she traveled, Nyght began to enjoy the freedom she had when she was younger. She had spent most of her time in the woods hunting. Even when she lived in the city, she still would have preferred to remain in the wilderness where others did not surround her. When she had lived in Sarzanac, she did not have the luxury of the woods. While in the city, even though she spent most of her time alone, especially when she was killing rats on the ships, she still felt trapped. Being alone in the wilderness was freedom all on its own.

When she thought about it, she had not felt that way during the four seasons she spent at the Assassin's Guild. She had never called it or any other place "home," but the Guild was the only thing that came close to the word.

Nyght continued to travel at night. Even with her cloak wrapped around her and with the hood pulled down over her head, she still did not like the sun touching her skin. When she was at the Assassin's Guild, she spent very little time outside. The most she ever spent was when she attended the funeral of Esteemed-High-Master Wraith. Whenever she was outside, the clouds blocked out the sun so much that it did not bother her. There was always an overcast, and even though she could still feel the sun above her, she was able to tolerate it for the short amount of time she was outside.

The Guild House in Carto had supplied her with a tent, but the first time she used it, she felt too confined and decided she would prefer to sleep under a tree and cover up with her cloak to block out the sun.

Even though she had no problem with seeing at night, she was surprised at how well the horse the Guild had supplied her was at seeing in the dark.

She did not have to keep an eye out for anything in the horse's path that could cause it to stumble. The horse traveled in the dark with no problem at all.

While traveling when she was younger, and when she was in Sarzanac, she had seen horses. She remembered Selby had offered to pay for her lessons, or even teach her himself since he had learned how to ride, but she saw no need for it at the time and declined the offer. When she thought about that moment, she quickly pushed it away. It was something from her past and did not pertain to her now. She felt the same way about Selby. When Moon blessed her, right before she entered the Assassin's Guild, Moon also gave her the knowledge of how to ride a horse. There were many battles where a warrior would have to fight from the back of a horse so Moon made sure she would be able to as well.

She had not been in the woods since she was twelve seasons old. She had spent over three seasons in Sarzanac, and another four at the Guild. For over seven seasons Nyght had not had a chance to spend time in the wilderness, but when the time came, even though this wilderness was on the other side of the world, she had no problem falling back into her routine.

She traveled during the night, but a couple of marks before the sun rose, she would find a place to make camp, then if she needed to, she would hunt for her food. The Guild in Carto had given her enough supplies to last her for at least a moon-mark, and since there were towns, villages, and cities between Carto and Millbury, she would have plenty of opportunities to purchase more supplies when needing them. However, that was not Nyght's way.

After making camp and taking care of her horse, she would go out hunting. The first time she caught a rabbit, she felt the thrill as she had when she hunted before. When she had lived in Sarzanac, she purchased the food she needed, except for the occasional rat she would fix for a light snack. For Nyght, there was something about the kill she made when hunting for food. She was the one who supplied her needs without buying it from someone, or someone providing it for her, as the Assassin's Guild had. Hunting in the wilderness made Nyght feel alive, and she knew that if she had to spend the remainder of her life in the woods, it would supply her with all she needed.

When she came near the town of Maridian, she had not planned on staying or even entering it. However, as she moved closer to the city, Nyght felt something she had never felt before. There was something in the city pulling her. Something she could not resist. Something which filled her with hate.

As she looked at the city off in the distance, she struggled within herself with what she was going to do. Part of her wanted to continue on and make for Millbury. She was not even halfway to her destination and she did not want to change her plan. As she sat on her horse and looked at Maridian, she could not ignore the feeling that there was something in the city she needed to find, needed to destroy. She did not know what it was. Not only was this her first time in the lands to the west, but also her first time even seeing the city before her, so she did not know why she felt as if something was pulling her toward it.

There were only two more marks before the sun came up. Normally, this was the time she would find a place to make camp and sleep through the day, but the pull was too strong, so she urged her horse on, heading straight for the city of Maridian.

The gate she passed through was on the east side of the city. There were guards posted at the entrance, but they did not stop her to ask any questions. Nyght noticed that the two guards standing at the gate did not take their eyes off her as she moved toward them, and they kept looking at her as she rode by them and passed under the portcullis. Even though the sun was not up yet, she had placed the hood of her cloak over her head before she reached the gate and kept her head bent down. The guards might have been able to see part of her face if they had taken any interest in the one entering the city. If they had, Nyght was sure they would have the same reaction as all the other people she had met since she arrived on this side of the world.

She had very little contact with people right after Moon had changed the color of her skin. In fact, the very next day she entered the Assassin's Guild. Assassins are trained to keep control of their emotions, so when they saw Nyght for the first time, they did not reveal their surprise at seeing her pale white skin.

When she had once again seen Keyota, the young woman had asked what happened to her. Since they had known each other before, the question was not so surprising. When she walked onto *The White Squall*, the crew members who got a look at her could not hide their surprise at seeing the way she looked. On the voyage, she heard people talking about her. About her pale white skin and she learned that there were others like her, ones called Albus, a word referring to their white skin. The only difference between them and the one on the ship was that most Albus have pink eyes as well as white hair. The one sailing with them had deep black eyes and dark black hair. Nyght did not care what others said about her looks. When Moon made her skin to match Moon, she thought her skin was beautiful, and did so to this day.

The people in this land acted the same way the crew of *The White Squall* did when they saw her appearance. They were shocked, and even in the short amount of time she spent in Carto, there were some who pointed at her, especially children. When she did come to a place where people were, Nyght kept her hood up over her head, and let it fall across her face as much as it could. She did not do this because she was ashamed of the way she looked, she did this because she knew that even if someone saw part of her white skin, the way she kept it hidden would only make them want to stay away from her even more. Which was the way she preferred.

In Maridian, like most cities, there were always stables close to the entrances. That way, anyone who did not want to take their horses through the city, could leave them with a caretaker. Nyght made her way to the nearest one. Even though the sun was not up yet, the man running the stable was already attending to the horses.

Nyght climbed off the back of her horse and walked into the stable, holding onto the reins. "I wish to put my horse up," she said when the man did not turn around after she had entered.

As soon as he heard the words, the stable worker knew the person who had spoken was not from around the immediate area. He could tell it was a woman, but the accent she spoke with was thick. The man tossed the last bit of hay he had in his hands into the stall to his right, then turned to see to the customer's need. When he did, he saw the person standing at the front of the stable, holding onto the reins of her horse. Her head bent low enough so that he was not able to see her face, which did not matter to him, as long as the person had coin to pay. "It's three copper pieces for one sun-cycle. Five if you want your horse to be fed. Six if you want him rubbed down and brushed."

The Guild House had given her grain for her horse, but since she spent so much time in the wilderness, there were plenty of areas where the horse could graze. She still had some grain left, but decided she would keep it for her travels. "Feed and water will be enough. I will not be staying long."

The man walked over to his new customer and she handed him the reins. "Don't matter to me how long you will be staying. I'll be taking my fee upfront. You don't come back for your horse or pay for another day then your horse is mine to do with as I will."

Nyght did not put a single thought into what the man had said. She knew she would be back for the horse, but if for some reason she did not return to make another payment, she was sure the man would regret keeping her horse from her.

She reached to her left hip and pulled out her coin purse. She dumped some of its contents into her hand, counted out five copper pieces, and handed them to the man, who already had his palm up and out waiting to receive them. When he saw her pale white hand, he had to force himself not to pull his own hand back. She then turned to head back out into the city.

"What's his name?" the man yelled to her. "He will respond to me better if I call him by his name."

Nyght turned around, looked at the horse then gave her answer, "It is just a horse. Why would it need a name?" She then turned and walked out of the stable.

The man stood there patting the center of the horse's head. He had dealt with horses his entire life. Very few people would not give their horse a name. To him, it just did not seem right. As he lifted the horse's head and stared into its eyes, he spoke to it. "Well, your color is about as dark as night. Night doesn't seem to fit you for a name and neither does the word Dark, but there is a word that means dark that suits you, Stygian, so that is what I will call you." He then led the horse further into the building to find an empty stable. "Tell you what," he said to the horse, as they walked, "Even though she didn't pay for it, I'll go ahead and give you a rub down and a brushing. Would you like that?" The horse did not give any type of response. It was just as quiet as the one who rode it.

Nyght moved through the city. She had no idea why she was feeling the way she was and did not know what else to do other than to look for the reason she felt pulled to the city. Normally, she would have been taking her rest at this time of day but she knew she would not be able to until she found out what was going on.

She walked around the city and within a few marks, the sun was overhead. She kept her arms and the rest of her body inside her cloak, with the hood pulled up and over her head, and kept it bent down as much as possible. Since she was trying to find what was causing her to feel the way she did, she had to keep her eyes positioned to see ahead of her. This allowed the citizens passing by to notice her face and more than a few took in a quick breath at the sight of her skin. Some of them did not hesitate to move further away from the person with the pale white complexion.

Nyght did not pay any attention to the onlookers. Not even the ones who pointed at her or rushed away. She could tell that the people in the immediate area were not the ones causing her to feel the way she did, so she ignored them and continued to walk through the city.

Whatever was affecting her, she could not tell where it was, so she could only walk around hoping to come across it. Whether it was a person, a place, or an item, she did not know. After a few more marks and with no success she had to turn to another. *"Father,"* she thought to Moon.

"Yes, my child," Moon thought back to Nyght. Moon had sensed what the child was feeling. Moon had been waiting for this moment for a very long time, but Moon wanted to see what Nyght would do when she came across the one she had been searching for ever since she had entered the city, even though she did not know it. The only thing Moon was not happy with was the fact that it was day, and since Moon was on the other side of the world, Moon could not see what was going to happen. Moon hoped the child would wait until the night came so Moon would have the full and perfect view.

"Something is not right, Father. There is something here in this city that is pulling at me. But I cannot see it. I only feel it."

"What do you feel?" Moon asked, even though Moon could sense the emotions in Nyght. Moon wanted the child to take action. Action Moon wanted to have happened for so long.

Nyght answered Moon, "I feel anger, hate. I feel that whatever is pulling at me is something I must destroy."

Moon was very happy with what Nyght had said. "Then seek it out. Do not let it get away. You will find it. You will destroy it. You will kill it." Moon took a moment to let Nyght take in what Moon had said, then added Moon's final instructions, "You will do this for me. You will not fail me."

Even though Nyght did not know what was going on, she heard what her father relayed to her. "I will not fail you, Father."

"I know you will not, my child."

With what Moon had communicated to her, Nyght had no better understanding than she did before she called to Moon. Now, she knew Moon wanted her to seek out whatever was pulling at her and destroy it. She started walking again, more determined to find whatever it was and do exactly what Moon wanted her to do.

Even with the sun over her head, Nyght did not stop moving. There was no particular direction in which she was traveling, so she continued to walk through the city. Around the fifteenth mark of the day, she felt the presence of what she was seeking close to her. She did not know what it was, but she knew she had tracked it to where she was now. Nyght stopped walking to get a better bearing on where she needed to go.

As she stood stationary, she felt the presence move farther away from her. "It is moving," she said aloud but to herself. She decided that since it was getting farther away, it must be a person or something the person had. Then she remembered what Moon had told her, she had to destroy it, had to kill it. Being who she was, Nyght knew that if she had to kill whatever it was, then it must be alive, so she now was sure the thing she needed to find was a person.

She started moving again, and after going another two parcels, she turned to look to her left and saw on the other side of the street a woman, a woman with long golden hair. Just as Nyght was about to cross the street, she noticed the woman looking around. Not at her immediate surroundings, but as if she could tell that someone was watching her, only she did not know from where or by whom.

One of the lessons taught to her by Esteemed-High-Master Wraith was to never rush into a situation without knowing the reason you need to rush in to begin with. Nyght did not know what was going on. With herself or the woman across the street who had just entered the shop she had been standing in front of. Nyght looked behind her and saw an alleyway off to her right where she could wait for the woman to appear again. She moved into the alley and waited.

The woman with the golden hair was in the store for less than a mark, but when she stepped out, she looked around her. The thought came to Nyght that if she was able to sense the woman, then the woman might be able to sense her. She did not know how that was possible, but it would put them on even terms, at least to the point of being able to feel the other's presence. To Nyght, the woman was no threat to her.

The woman turned and started walking down the street. Now that Nyght had found what she was looking for, she would have no problem keeping her within sight, especially since the woman's golden hair was easy to spot in the crowd. She waited until the woman was a good distance away, but was still able to see her, then Nyght stepped out of the alley. She stayed on the side of the street she was on, the opposite one of the woman, then walked in the direction the woman had gone.

After a few moments, the woman once again walked into a shop. Nyght moved to the area directly across the street. There was no alley for her to hide in, so she quickly entered one of the shops. Once inside, she positioned herself just inside the place but still was able to see out the window, as well as being able to see the entrance to the shop the woman had entered.

"May I help you?" a woman spoke to Nyght as she came up to stand at her right.

Nyght turned her head and made sure the woman got a good look at her face. Nyght was not sure if it was the color of her skin, or her eyes that caused the woman to realize she had something else to do. As the woman walked away, Nyght quickly put her focus back on the shop across the street. She had only taken her eyes off the place for a breath, but Nyght knew that in a breath, a person could disappear forever.

To her relief, she saw the golden-haired woman step out of the shop, looking around once again. The woman then turned and walked down the street. Nyght rushed to the door of the shop but waited until the woman was further down the street before she stepped out herself to trail the woman once again who had somehow forced her to come this far into the city.

Before the woman entered the next place, Nyght saw her look around again, only she appeared to be doing a more thorough search of her surroundings. The woman then stepped into a house.

Nyght moved closer to the house but kept out of the direct line of sight to the windows. From where she was, she was able to read the sign posted at the front of the building, which read, "Boarding House." It was clear to the assassin as to what the place was, she just did not know what the woman was to the place. Was it where she was staying? Was it where she worked? Or did she even own the place? Nyght did not know the answers, but what the woman was doing in the place was not important.

Nyght had never felt like she did now. She had never felt anger toward anyone as much as she did this woman. There were a lot of people she did not feel comfortable about, but never to the point where she wanted to kill them, with them not having done anything to her. If they were a threat to her, then Nyght had no problem dealing with them, even if it meant ending their life, but not once did she do it with anger or hate, not like how she had been feeling ever since she came near the city and even more so when she set her eyes on the woman.

She looked around and saw the buildings behind her connected to one another, so there was no alley for her to hide in. Since the buildings did not appear to be open to the public, she did not try to enter them. Instead, Nyght walked down the street, away from the house the woman had entered.

When she reached the end of the parcel, she turned left and walked a bit more. She finally saw an alleyway and turned down it. She still did not find what she was looking for, so she walked back out of the alleyway and continued down the street. She knew she was moving further away from the woman, but she could not help that for the moment.

She finally found a building with stairs on the outside. She climbed them and when she reached the top, she stood on the small wooden banister at the top of the stairs. She turned around to face the building, crouched down, bending at her knees. With as much force as she could, she propelled herself upward. With the distance from the banister to the top of the roof, she was only able to grab the edge of the building with her fingertips, but for her, it was enough. She worked her hands to get a better hold on the ledge then pulled herself up onto the roof.

The sun was still out, and being on the roof of the building, it was even brighter and hotter on her. Nyght pulled her cloak around her as much as she could and made sure her hood was over her face as much as possible. She then started heading back in the direction the boarding house was located.

Like most cities, the buildings were built close together to utilize as much space as possible. Some of the building's outer walls were touching each other, so all Nyght had to do was step over the ledge. For the buildings with some space between them, she had to jump to get to the next one, but none of the distances were a problem for her.

She finally made it to the building directly across the street from the boarding house. In the time she had left and made her way back to where she was now, the woman could have exited the building, but Nyght, having followed the woman for quite some time, could feel she was still inside.

Before she moved to the edge of the building, across from the boarding house, Nyght laid down on her stomach and crawled the rest of the way to where she could watch the building and the woman inside.

She knew she had to kill the woman. Not only because Moon had instructed her to do so, but because it was what she was feeling inside her as well. She did not know who the woman was, but it did not matter. Something inside of the assassin was telling her that she had to end the golden-haired woman's life.

Nyght waited on the roof across the street for so long the sun had left the sky. With that, she was feeling more comfortable. Not just because the sun had taken the light and the heat with it, but because now Nyght could see Moon. Although she did not say anything to Moon, Moon spoke to her, when Moon grew tired of waiting. *"Kill the one."*

Nyght heard the words in her head, and even understood them and agreed with what Moon had asked of her, she would. Just not yet.

She did not speak to Moon about why she was waiting. Moon would not understand. Esteemed-High-Master Wraith had trained her in the art of making a kill. He had told her that what an assassin does is not for the eyes of others. Therefore, when they make a kill, they need to make sure there are no witnesses. That means no one can be about, or if there is someone, they are not breathing when the assassin leaves.

Nyght continued to watch the front of the

building. When she saw light coming from one of the upper rooms, she knew someone had entered it and had lit a candle or lamp. A few breaths later, another light appeared through the window next to the first. Since she did not know the inner outlay of the building, she did not know whether there was one room or if there were two separate rooms. She also did not know which room belonged to the person she was after.

That answer came a few moments later when Nyght saw the curtain to the second window move. Standing at the window, looking out, was the golden-haired woman.

Still, Nyght did not move from where she was. As she waited, she saw the light from the first room go out, but the light from the second room was still shining. There was enough light in the room that when the woman moved around, it cast her shadow onto the curtains. Nyght knew the woman was still in the room, and since she noticed the shadow at the same time the light in the first room went out, she knew the two rooms were separate, and what was more important, the woman she had followed was alone.

Nyght could feel Moon edge into her thoughts although Moon did not say anything to her. She could tell that Moon was just as anxious for her to end the woman's life as she was. Even though she wanted to go across the street and kill the woman, her training as an assassin stopped her. Esteemed-High-Master

Wraith had taught her that the best time to strike is during the hours just before the sun made its first light. People were well into their sleep, and there would be less of a chance of them waking up. Because of that, Nyght waited.

When she looked up to the sky and saw Moon's position, she knew it was going on the fourth mark. She had not seen any movement from inside of the house for some time, and so it was time for her to move.

She stood up and positioned herself at the edge of the building she had been on for the past few marks. She looked over the edge and decided that even though there was some distance to the ground, it would not be too much for her, which meant she would not have to backtrack to where she had entered onto the rooftops or find another way down.

Instead of jumping over the side of the building and straight to the ground, when she stepped off the edge, she turned her body so that she was now facing the wall. As she fell, she grabbed onto the ledge and held herself for a few breaths then let go. By doing this, she reduced the distance to the ground by the height of her body including her arms. Just before she landed, she turned her body in mid-air so that she was facing the building she had been watching. When she landed, she allowed her legs to bend enough to absorb some of the impact with the ground and to reduce it even more, she immediately went into a forward roll, coming up still facing the building. She then ran across the street.

When she reached the building, she ran up to the front door. To her surprise, when she tried to open it, she found it unlocked, which was a very big mistake by whoever was responsible for securing the building at night. If it had been, Nyght would have had to deal with the lock or find another way into the building, and that would have given the woman just a few more moments of life.

Nyght quietly opened the door and stepped inside, then quietly closed the door behind her. She saw the stairs to her right and headed for them. From the outside, she could tell that there was only one level above the one she was currently on. Since she had been watching the room for a good portion of the night, when Nyght reached the top of the stairs she knew exactly where she had to go.

She walked down the hallway, and as she passed one of the rooms, she heard snoring coming from inside. If that did not wake up some of the other residents, then she did not have to worry about them waking up from hearing her. Not that she made a single sound.

After watching the building from the outside, she remembered the location of the golden-haired woman's room, so Nyght walked further down the hall and turned the corner. She saw two doors, but the one farthest away was the one she wanted. When she reached it, she slowly placed her hand on the handle and turned it. Since it did move, but the door would not open, Nyght knew someone secured it from the inside. This was not a problem for the trained assassin.

She reached inside her cloak and into one of the two pockets at the back. She pulled out a small leather case and while holding it in her left hand, she undid the flap that kept the items secured. She then pulled out a very thin piece of metal and slid it between the doorframe and the door. She moved the piece of metal upward until it came to a stop. She knew she had touched the bottom of whatever was keeping the door from opening. Leaving the piece of metal where it was, she pulled out another piece that matched the first. She slid this one between the door and the doorframe like the first, but this time she inserted it just above the first piece, but high enough so she could find the top of the locking mechanism.

Once she had, she put pressure on both pieces of metal, then moved them at the same time in the direction of the door. Since she was able to feel the part move, she knew the mechanism was so simple it was not meant to secure the room from danger. Even though every time she moved the locking bolt, it only moved no more than a hair's width, she would eventually have it far enough in place to where she could open the door.

As she worked the latch, she knew she could have just forced her way into the room by ramming the door, but she was an assassin, and the noise would have brought others, and then she would have to deal with them. As an assassin, she could enter and exit a place, with as little notice as possible, if any at all.

When she felt the two metal pieces slide slightly faster together, she knew the locking bar was past the edge of the doorframe. She pulled the pieces of metal out, and returned them to their case, then replaced the case inside her cloak. When Dart had given it to her, she knew she would find something to store in the pockets.

She then took hold of the handle again, but this time when she turned it, and put the slightest pressure on the door, it opened. Through the small crack, she was able to see the light coming out of the room. There was nothing she could do to dowse the light, so she did not put any thought into it.

She slowly opened the door, and when it was wide enough, she stuck her head inside the room to inspect it. Not only did Nyght see the candle on the nightstand, on the other side of the bed, but the light clearly showed the woman lying there. She was sleeping on her left side, so her back was facing the door, and Nyght.

She stepped into the room and quietly closed the door. Without making a sound, she walked over so that she was standing next to the bed. She moved her right hand to the hilt of her dagger Full at her hip in its sheath but did not draw the blade. She could not.

She had spent the entire day looking for this woman. She had felt hate and anger toward her, even though she did not know who she was. Moon had told her that she was to kill the woman, which was exactly what Nyght had planned on doing. Until she saw the woman lying on the bed, facing away from her.

She was in the same position Esteemed-High-Master Wraith had been sleeping when she had taken his life. Nyght did not have a moment of compassion because of the memory, but she did remember one of her mentor's lessons.

He had told her that an assassin is nothing without honor. Yes, they kill but they only kill those Creator has chosen. Creator does this by having someone else decide who they will kill, and the assassin takes the life assigned to them. To kill in any other way, with the exception of protecting their own lives, is dishonorable, and once an assassin has no honor, they have nothing.

The death of this woman did not come to Nyght in the way an assassin would normally receive it. She had felt something before she had entered the city, but she was the one who had chosen to kill the woman when she had seen her. Even though Moon had told her the woman had to die, Nyght knew Moon had not come to her and given the woman's life to her. So therefore, if she were to kill the woman, she would lose her honor. She was an assassin; her honor was something very important to her.

Hanna had not fallen asleep at all, and she did not know why. Maybe it was because she still felt as if someone was watching her. It was only a few moments ago that she had sensed someone in the house, and the moment the feeling came over her, she remembered that in her rush to follow Elisa up the stairs, she had forgotten to secure the front door.

When she felt the presence coming closer to her door, she knew that everything she thought she had imagined was not some wild fantasy. Someone was after her and she did not know why, or what she was going to do. When she heard her bedchamber door start to open, she froze.

She had her back to the door and kept her eyes on the candle. Now that someone was coming into her room, she knew she should jump up and try to defend herself. Only her body would not listen to her thoughts.

The person was walking over to her bed and had not made a single sound, but Hanna knew exactly when the person was standing behind her, looking down at her body. Hanna did not know if she meant to stop breathing to make it appear as if she was asleep, or had she done it without thinking because of the fear she was feeling. It did not matter because if she did not act soon, she would never breathe again.

The only thing stopping her from moving was because she could tell that the person who entered her room was not moving either. It seemed as if both of them were trying to decide what their next move would be.

Nyght still felt the need to kill this woman, but her training from Esteemed-High-Master Wraith was interfering with her feelings. She did not know whether that was good or bad. There was no contract on the woman with the golden hair, so it meant she had no right to take her life. She also thought that maybe the woman was someone Creator needed to have kill, and that was why Moon was so adamant about ending the woman's life.

Still, Nyght did not move forward. She did not know how long she had stood there looking at the woman, but she knew she had to decide. For the first time in her life, she was confused about what she should do. She did not have Esteemed-High-Master Wraith there to ask him, but she remembered one of his lessons. He had told her that when she is confused and does not know what to do, she should not trust her feelings because they can lead her in the wrong direction. To find the direction you need to go, ask, and you will find the answer.

Nyght was going to do just that. She would ask this woman who she was and find out why she had a need to kill her. Nyght leaned over and extended her right arm out so she could wake the sleeping woman. She did not get the chance.

Hanna knew the moment the woman began to

move closer to her and that she had run out of time. In the last few moments, she had come up with a plan, and with a bit of luck, it might save her life.

She waited until she knew the woman was almost upon her. Hanna then quickly stuck her right hand out and grabbed the candleholder on the nightstand. In one fluid motion, she sat up in her bed, and brought the object around, hoping to strike the intruder on the side of the head. She did not get the chance.

Nyght saw what the woman was doing, but she had moved so quickly that Nyght only had time to bring her right arm up to block the swing and stop the candleholder from hitting her.

With the positions the two women were in, neither of them was able to perform at their best. Nyght was able to block the swing but was only able to use the back of her right hand to stop the woman's attack. When Hanna swung the candleholder around, the back of her right hand led the way, so when the two women encountered each other, it was the backs of their right hands that made contact.

As soon as they made contact, Nyght felt pain. Hot searing pain from the back of her hand all the way through her entire body. It was so bad, she fell backward, grabbing hold of her right hand. Nyght lost her balance and fell to the floor.

As soon as they made contact, Hanna felt pain. Cold numbing pain. Unlike Nyght, who felt as if the sun engulfed her entire body, it was only the back of Hanna's right hand that felt as if she had just fallen into the coldest lake in the highest mountains. Also, since it was only her hand, she had no problem with using her legs to jump out of the bed, run to the door, open it, and run into the hallway.

If she had been thinking properly then she probably would have banged on Elisa's door or any of the guests to seek some help with the intruder. However, Hanna had been feeling uncomfortable for the entire day because she felt someone's eyes on her. Now, after the attack in her own bedchamber, she knew she had been right, which only made the fear in her grow, which made her make the decision that the best thing to do would be to get as far away from the person as she could, so Hanna ran past the rooms upstairs, ran down the stairs, through the kitchen, and out the back door.

The two had only touched one another for a breath, and even though she was still feeling pain, Nyght knew there was something more to this woman, and she had to find out what it was.

She saw the woman jump out of the bed and head out the door, and Nyght was willing to let her get away for a moment. At least until the pain in her body left, but Moon thought differently. *"KILL HER! KILL HER NOW!"*

The way Moon yelled into her thoughts caused her almost as much pain as the woman had. Although she was still unsure about killing the woman, Nyght decided to go after her. Still feeling pain, she rose to her feet and ran out of the room.

She had not been down on the floor for as long as she thought because when she made it to the top of the stairs, Nyght saw the woman had just reached the bottom and ran to her right.

Nyght was quick down the stairs as well and was at the bottom in plenty of time to see the woman run through another door. She followed, and when she entered the next room, she only saw one door the woman could have used and had been in such a hurry to get away, that she did not even bother to close it behind her, so Nyght did not have to stop to open it before she rushed through.

Nyght saw the woman running away, but when she reached the small relief shack, the woman stopped and turned around. This was Nyght's chance to find out who the woman was, and why she had felt so much pain when their hands touched. Since the woman had stopped running, Nyght did as well and walked toward the woman who was apparently frightened.

Hanna did not know what to do. She was so scared that when she ran to the relief shack, she just stopped and turned around. When she did, she saw the woman who had come into her room and caused her hand to hurt. She did not know who she was, or even why she wanted to hurt her. Hanna only knew that she had nothing left in her. Everything in her mind told her she was going to die.

Hanna stood there as the woman moved closer to her. She did not have another candlestick to use as a weapon, but since it did not stop her before, Hanna did not think it would this time.

The woman was just a pace away from her and Hanna believed she had run out of time. She saw a figure come up behind the woman and thought that one of the male guests had come to her rescue. That thought became even stronger when she saw the figure swing something, hitting the woman on the back of the head. Not only knocking her to the ground but unconscious as well.

Hanna looked at the figure in front of her, then at the woman on the ground. She then put her eyes on the person who had saved her and realized it was not one of the men staying in the boarding house. In fact, Hanna did not recognize the man at all. She was not even sure if the man was there to rescue her or do her harm, like the woman lying at her feet. The man moved up to stand directly in front of her, and once again, Hanna was too scared to move.

"Hanna! We have to leave now!" the man said and grabbed her by her left hand. Hanna was still confused about everything that had happened, so she did not take a single step forward. The man turned back to look at her. "Hanna, we have to leave, before she wakes up!"

The man turned to lead her away but once again,

Hanna did not move, but she was able to ask a question, "Who are you?"

The man let go of her hand and moved to where he was standing as close to her as he could so she could see him. "Hanna, it's me, Colton." He turned his head and looked at the woman lying on the ground to his left, then turned back to face Hanna. "We have to go, now." He once again took hold of her left hand, and at least this time, she started running with him. Although she still had no idea what was going on.

THREE

Whether it was by reflex or instinct, as soon as Nyght felt someone touching her, she rolled over, reached down at her sides, and drew both Umbra and Full. As she did, she also rose to her feet. The man who had touched her was now sitting on the ground since he had fallen backward when he saw her move. He had tried to help the woman when he found her lying not too far from the relief shack, but for his help, he was now the one on his back and the woman he had shown concern for was on top of him with two daggers against his throat. Even though the sight of the blades caused him to be worried, the sight of the woman's pale white skin was just as disturbing.

Nyght did not know the man she had forced away from her and it was easy to tell that he was no threat. Realizing she was in no danger, and with her initial surprise gone, she felt the burning pain of the sun which was now in the sky. She quickly rose, placed her daggers back in their sheaths, and ran back toward the house, pulling the hood of her cloak up over her head and the rest of it around her.

Instead of going into the house, she ran down the small path to the left, which took her to the front of the building, where she continued to the street and ran until she found a place where she could stop and figure out what had happened.

She found a small alleyway and walked down it enough to keep her out of the sight of anyone around. By the position of the sun, she could tell that it was about the seventh mark of the day. She remembered making for the house where the woman was around the fourth mark. She was no more than maybe less than a half-mark making her way inside, including when she ran after the woman, which meant she was unconscious and had been lying where the man found her for almost three marks. She found that very disturbing.

She did not know what happened, but she knew who would. *"Father,"* she thought to Moon. She waited a few breaths and when Moon did not reply, she called again, *"Father."* Once again, Moon did not reply.

Nyght looked around the alley and knew she could not stay there, even though she wanted to. Her head ached because someone struck her, she just did not know who the person was or what they used. Another disturbing fact was that for the second time in her life, someone caught her off guard. The only other person who was ever able to take her by surprise was Esteemed-High-Master Wraith when he tested her to be his pupil. This time, whoever the person was, they were not testing her. The thought alone was enough to force herself to ignore the pain in her head and walk out of the alley.

When she was back on the street, she pulled on the hood of her cloak, but it was already as far over her face as it would go. When she was unconscious, the sun had started to rise, and even though it was nowhere near its highest point in the sky, enough of the morning rays were shining down and irritating her skin, so she wanted to keep it off her as much as possible.

While trying to hide deeper inside her cloak, she remembered something else that had happened with her encounter with the golden-haired woman. When she blocked the woman's hand with her own, when they touched, she felt as if her entire body was on fire. She did not know what had happened, which was another disturbing item. She now realized there were too many things she did not know. She remembered one of Esteemed-High-Master Wraith's lessons. Find out everything you can about your target, then you will find out their weakness. That was exactly what Nyght planned on doing.

It took her some time, but she made her way back to the stable where she had left her horse. She was not ready to leave, but since she had not planned on staying this long in the city, she had only paid the stable keeper for one sun-cycle. She was going to be needing the horse, and she did not want the man to do anything with it because she had not paid. If he had, Nyght was sure he would regret it when she met with him.

When she arrived at the stable, she did not see the man but did hear the sound of someone banging on metal. She followed the sound through the stable and came out of the far exit. She saw the man bending over an anvil, working on a horseshoe. He did not have his back to her, but the way he was standing did not allow him to see his customer, and since Nyght always moved, making no sound, he definitely did not hear her. "Where is my horse?" Nyght asked in a not so pleasant manner because when she had walked through the stable, she had not seen it inside.

The man turned and when he saw Nyght, sat the hammer, tongs, and horseshoe on the anvil. He pulled out a cloth from his belt and wiped his hands. "This way," he said, then turned his back toward Nyght and walked away.

Nyght did not know where the man was going to lead her, but as she began to follow him, she placed her hands on the hilts of her daggers inside her cloak.

When she turned the corner the man had gone around, she saw not only him but her horse as well. The stable keeper had turned the horse loose inside a big pen. The horse was running around, but when it saw it had visitors it stopped and faced them.

"He seemed to have a lot of built-up energy, so I put him in there to burn some of it off." The man turned to his right to look at his customer, but still could not see her entire face. "When was the last time you ran him?" When she did not answer, he continued with what he wanted to tell her. "With an animal like him, you need to let it run every so often, so it doesn't get restless. Another thing you can do is breed him. Let him mate with a mare or two and that will calm him down as well."

Nyght stood there looking at the horse. She noticed it was looking back at her. She could tell the stable keeper knew what he was talking about because it was obvious the horse seemed more relaxed compared to when she had started out on her travels. She had no need to run the horse because she had planned the amount of time it would take to arrive where she needed to be. However, now with the extended stay in the city, she was going to have to adjust her time frame, and when she did begin again to fulfill the contract, she might just have the opportunity and the need to run the horse.

While still looking at the horse, Nyght asked the stable keeper a question, "I thought you said if I did not come back for the horse, or pay you for another day, the horse was yours?" Nyght still had her hands on the hilts of her daggers waiting for the man's response.

He turned and looked at the horse. "Yeah, well usually that is true, but there is something about that horse I can't put my finger on. All I know is that if I took it from you, I don't think I would feel right about it."

Nyght wanted to tell him that if he took the horse from her, he would be dead but did not. "I will need to pay for another day." While she had her hands in her cloak, she took hold of her coin purse. She then brought it out, and moved as quickly as she could, because the bit of sun touching her bare hands was causing her discomfort. She emptied some of the coins into her hand, then picked out only one. After she placed the rest of the coins back in the bag and secured the bag to her hip, she extended her hand out to her left to give the man the coin.

When he saw her pale white hand, he was once again hesitant about accepting the coin, but he had seen which one she had chosen to give him and could not turn it down. He extended his hand and Nyght placed the gold coin in his. "This will cover more than one day. I take it you plan to stay for some time then."

Nyght kept her eyes on the horse who was still watching her. "I will be leaving late this evening." She knew the man was wondering why she had given him the gold coin and not some of the copper pieces she had poured out. "For the use of your stables. Feed for the horse. Also, give it a rub down and a brushing."

"I still owe you some coin back."

Nyght did not need coin, she needed something else. "Keep it, in exchange, tell me if a woman with golden hair has come to you for a horse. She might have been with someone else."

The stable keeper was an honest man. He could tell, by the way the woman asked the question, that if she did find the woman with the golden hair then it might not be well for her. Even though the stable keeper felt uncomfortable about helping someone to bring harm to another, he knew his answer would not. "No golden-haired woman has come here."

Nyght believed the man. It would only be by luck if the woman did come to the same stable she had been using but she had to make sure. What she did know was that the golden-haired woman was no longer in the city, because she did not sense what she had felt when she came close to the place yesterday. Leaving only three possibilities. She was only able to sense the woman for the one day. The woman had done something to stop her from sensing her, or she was no longer in the city. Nyght believed it was the last one.

Having finished with the stable keeper, Nyght turned and headed back inside the stable. "I gave your horse a name," the man called to her. She stopped but did not turn around to face him. "You said it didn't have one, and it doesn't seem right, a horse like this, not to have a name. So, if you don't mind, I gave him the name Stygian."

Nyght did not say anything. She just walked back into the stable and through the other exit.

The stable keeper watched the woman leave.

With his job, he had seen many strange and curious types of people paying for his services. Some even pay for information, but he had never said anything to cause problems for someone else. The woman had given him a gold coin and did not try to take it back because the information he provided was nothing she could use. By that act alone it was easy to tell the woman with the pale skin had a great deal of honor.

He turned and took one more look at the horse in the pen. It had gone back to running around, and the stable keeper could not help but admire the beauty of the creature and would love to have it as his own but knew that no one could or would ever own the animal. Not even the woman with the pale skin.

Just in the section of the city she was currently in, Nyght had counted six different stables close to the city gate she had entered through yesterday. She paid two copper pieces to a man appearing to be one of the city's least fortunate and learned that there was a total of four gates to the city. Each one heading in a different direction. She also found out from the man that around the area of every gate, there were stables. More than what she could cover in a day.

When she had arrived at the city and passed through the gate, she had seen the city guards stationed there, and she guessed that the other gates would have them as well. If the woman had left the city, then she would have to have passed through one of them. The guards might have seen her, but with all the people coming and going through the gates, one woman would not have been so apparent to the guards. Even if she did have golden hair.

Nyght also knew that questioning the city guards would bring too much attention to herself. She could find a single guard and threaten his life for any information, but if she knew which guard to threaten then she would already know which gate the woman had gone through.

She walked around the city until she found an inn. She paid for a room, went to it, and fell asleep on the bed. There was nothing else she could do. At least not until the sun went down.

Nyght was once again looking at the house where the golden-haired woman had been. This time she had come out into the city when the sun had gone down and Moon was in the sky. She had called to Moon but received no response.

When she was ready to enter, she walked next to the side of the house and made her way to the back door. Once there, she tried to open it but found it barred. She had a feeling it would be, along with the front door. She caught the man by surprise when she had woken up and pressed her daggers against his throat. Whoever was still in the house, would take extra precautions now.

Nyght had run out of the very door the previous

night, and when she did, she noticed what barred the door now. It was a simple wooden latch across the door allowing it to remain shut. It would be easier to open than the lock on the golden-haired woman's bedchamber.

She pulled out Full and placed the tip of the blade between the door and doorframe. She knew where the latch was situated and when the blade touched the bottom of the wooden latch, she forcefully lifted the dagger, causing the latch to rise with it. When it was high enough, it fell back, out of the way.

She opened the door and stepped inside, once again entering the kitchen. Having been through this way before, Nyght knew where she had to go, so she walked into the next room.

She made sure she moved slowly, to watch for anyone on the ground floor. It was going on the first mark, so most people would be in bed, but it was better to be cautious than caught.

She did not see anyone, and when she reached the stairs, she went to the next floor. When she had been there last night, she heard someone snoring in one of the rooms. It was not the same tonight. Maybe the person was in the room but had not gone to sleep yet. She did not see any lights coming from under the door but that would not tell her whether there was someone in there or not.

Nyght had gone there for information. She figured these rooms were for any guest staying at the boarding house. The room where she had found the golden-haired woman was bigger, so she must have been the one who owned the building. Since she was not there, Nyght had to talk to whoever remained.

She took hold of the door handle to the room to her right, and when she turned it, the door opened inward. Nyght quickly looked inside, and since she had no problem seeing in the dark, she saw that no one was in the room at the moment. Nyght then moved to the door across the hall and tried the handle. The door opened and once again, she saw no one inside. She checked two more rooms, which were also empty.

Nyght walked down the hall, turned the corner, and saw two more doors. She knew which one the golden-haired woman used. It was not the one she was heading for.

When she came to a stop, Nyght saw light coming from the space between the door and the floor. While she had watched the house the previous night, this was the only room with a light burning besides the one the golden-haired woman used.

Nyght had not seen anyone else in the house since she had entered. All the other bedchambers were empty except for this one. Because of this, she could be a little more forceful.

Part of an assassin's training was how to move in stealth. To be in, and out, with no trace of them being there. That pertained to when they were fulfilling a contract. Nyght also learned that sometimes making herself noticed was an advantage.

She kicked open the door and rushed into the room. She saw the woman inside jump out of her bed and run toward the window. Nyght reached her before she was halfway there, grabbed her by the arm, and spun her around so they were facing each other. The main difference between the two was that Nyght had drawn Full and now had the blade against the woman's neck. "Try to scream and you will be dead before the first sound leaves your throat." The woman did not say anything, but Nyght needed to know she had made herself perfectly clear. "Nod if you understand." The woman did but only as much as she could with the blade touching her skin.

Nyght turned around, and bringing the woman with her, walked back to the door and closed it. She then went over to the bed and tossed the woman onto it. With the force she used, the woman bounced on the bed and half laid/half sat on it. She thought it was best if she did not try to move.

Nyght moved over to the nightstand and blew out the candle. She did it so there would be no shadows cast onto the curtains at the window in case someone just happened to walk by, and with the lack of light, Nyght had the advantage since she had no problem seeing in the dark. Of course, since she was an assassin and the woman was only a cook, Nyght had no disadvantage at all.

"What is your name?" Nyght asked but did not receive a reply. She understood that the woman was probably in shock because of what she was going through from the moment her unknown and uninvited guest entered her room, but she did not have time to ask a question more than once. "If you do not answer my questions, then I have no need of you. If I have no need of you, I see no reason in allowing you to continue to breathe." Nyght took a moment to let the woman think about what she had said then asked her question again, "What is your name?"

"Eli...Elisa," she then gave more than what she had been asked, "I am the cook, nothing more."

Nyght figured the person in the room worked at the boarding house. Whether she was related to the golden-haired woman she did not know, but with the apparent age of the woman on the bed, she could have been an older relative. "What is the woman, who slept in the room next to this one, to you?"

"She is my employer. I work for her," Elisa said keeping her eyes on the mattress, not wanting to see what the woman was going to do to her.

"Where is she?" Nyght asked but Elisa did not answer fast enough, "Remember the part about you breathing?" Since she could see the woman was trying to speak, she held back on threatening her anymore, for the moment.

"She is not here. No one is. I am the only one." She regretted saying the last part as soon as she heard it. Now her attacker knew no one else was in the house, but Nyght already knew it.

"What is your employer's name?"

Elisa felt conflicted. She did not want to die but she did not want to bring any harm to Hanna, but when Nyght leaned a bit over her, Elisa answered the question and then some, even though she did not want to. "Hanna, her name is Hanna Gransby. She runs the boarding house she inherited from the previous owners. I have been the cook for two seasons. The guests staying here left this morning after a woman with pale white skin attacked one of them. They were worried she would come back." As soon as she said it, Elisa realized the woman had returned. "It's you. The one who attacked the man this morning."

Nyght did not correct the woman. She had not attacked the man. He had touched her, and she had stopped him from putting his hands on her again. Nyght would let the woman continue to think what she believed had happened. It would keep her wondering if she was going to see the sunrise. "This Hanna has not been back today?" Nyght asked.

"No," Elisa answered quickly.

"Do you know where she is?"

"No."

Nyght had a name. Hanna Gransby, but that did not help her find the woman. If this Hanna had not returned, and if this woman was telling the truth, there was nothing else Nyght could find out from her. She looked at the woman on the bed who was in the same position as when she had landed. "I will be leaving now. If you do not wish for me to return, I suggest that once I am gone, you crawl into your bed and try to get some sleep." Nyght saw the woman nod then turned and walked out of the room. Elisa did exactly what the woman with the pale skin instructed her to do.

She returned to her room at the inn. Not knowing where the woman had gone, and not obtaining any information about the woman from the cook to help find her, Nyght did not know what her next step would be but knew who would.

She sat on her bed, with her legs crossed in front of her and her knees pointing toward the sides. Even though she had her eyes closed, she lifted her head to face the ceiling, *"Father,"* she thought to Moon, but Moon did not respond.

Nyght had not heard from Moon since she had woken after she was attacked. Even if Moon was not in the sky, and was on the other side of the world, she could still speak to Moon and Moon to her. Now, there was nothing but silence.

She called out again, only this time she spoke as to why she believed Moon had not responded to her. *"Father, forgive me, for I have failed you. The woman, this Hanna Gransby escaped. I do not know how I was able to sense her, nor do I know why when I touched her, I felt the pain that I did. I believe someone helped her, but I did not see the person."* Nyght did not know whether Moon was listening to her or not, but she continued. *"You are wiser than I am.*

You are in the sky and see all in your sight. I need your help to make amends for the disgrace I have shown you. Without you Father, I am nothing."

Nyght said what she did because she believed it. What she did not know was that Moon heard her words, but what was more important, her words reached Moon where Moon was weakest, Moon's ego. *"In that, you are correct, my child. You are nothing without me, and if you should fail me again, then I will find another who is worthy of my blessings."*

Nyght was not only pleased to hear Moon speak to her, but she was also thankful. Moon had been with her longer than anyone else had. Moon had taught her how to hunt and fight. Moon had given her not only her daggers but also made her skin the color of Moon. More importantly, Moon had given her a name. *"Forgive me, Father. I am sorry I let the woman escape me. I believe she had help, and even though that does not excuse my failure, I would have killed the woman if I was not interfered with."*

Moon knew Nyght was telling the truth. At least the way she saw it. Moon did not even know what happened when Nyght had been walking toward the woman. One moment Moon was looking down watching her, and then suddenly, Moon saw Nyght lying on the ground. Moon had called out to her, but she did not respond. By the time Moon heard from her, Moon was on the other side of the world and was not able to see her. Moon did not want her to think that Moon was not powerful and wise enough to know what happened, but Moon knew, someone else was involved, and whoever it was, they were powerful enough to hide from Moon. Sun was able to hide things from Moon, but Moon knew that whoever had concealed what had happened with Nyght, must have been more powerful than Moon, and there was only one. Moon did not think that one would take an interest in what Moon did. That one never had before.

Moon knew Nyght was going to need help to find the woman, as well as knowing that Moon needed Nyght to do so. First, Moon had to show Nyght that there was no ill will between them. Even though Moon was not happy with the child's failure, Moon still needed her. *"We will not discuss your failure again. It is in the past but know that I will not accept any more excuses."*

"I understand, Father," Nyght said, thankful that Moon had not given up on her.

"Very well. I will tell you what I know. Perhaps that was my part in your failure," Moon said this to see what Nyght would say.

"No, Father. The woman escaping was my doing. You have no blame in my failure."

Moon was happy with what she had said. Of course, Moon would not take any of the blame. To Moon, Moon did not make mistakes. To Moon, Moon was perfect. Moon was just testing Nyght's devotion to Moon, and of course, Moon was pleased she had passed the test. *"As I said, we will not discuss your failure. As for the woman, she has one purpose in life."*

"And what is that, Father?" Nyght asked.

Moon waited a moment before answering, *"Your death."* Moon felt the concern rise in Nyght.

"But I have never met the woman. Why does she want to take my life?"

"Because you are my child and my warrior. You are the one I have chosen and have blessed. And the one who has chosen her wishes to see your death, because that one wishes to hurt me. And if you were taken from me, I would be hurt."

Nyght heard the care in what Moon had relayed to her. To her, Moon was speaking the truth. To Moon, Moon was only saying what Moon believed would encourage her to seek out the woman.

"Who wishes to hurt you Father, and I will see to their death myself."

Her statement did not move Moon, in fact, Moon felt insulted by the way Nyght thought she could do anything to anyone who would try to hurt Moon. Moon did not let her know. Moon would use her protectiveness to Moon's advantage. *"The one who wishes to hurt me is Sun, and not even you, my child, can stop Sun. But you can stop the one Sun has chosen. Sun chose her when I chose you. Sun has sent her to kill you, to take you from me."*

Nyght understood Moon, but something was still unclear to her. *"Father, then why did this woman run* when I went after her? If she wanted to kill me, why didn't she stand and fight?"

Moon was not sure of the real reason, but Moon did give an answer. *"The chosen one of Sun is not as strong as you are. I have given you all of my blessing. Sun has not. The warrior of Sun is still very vulnerable, very weak. Sun has only touched her in a minute way. That is why you were able to sense her. You felt the small part of Sun given to her. And because she still does not fully have Sun's blessing, she was able to sense you as well. If Sun fully blesses her, then you will not be able to sense her, or be sensed by her."*

"So, I must find her before she receives the blessing of Sun."

"Correct, my child. You must find her and kill her before Sun blesses her, and before she comes for you."

Nyght did not know how she would find the woman. *"I cannot sense her now. Can you Father?"*

Moon could not. When Nyght had come close to the woman, Moon had been watching, waiting to see the end to Sun's warrior. Moon had never known who Sun had chosen, but when Nyght had found her, and Moon entered the sky, Moon was able to see the woman clearly.

Moon could even see the mark on the woman's hand, placed there by Sun. However, as Moon had told Nyght, Moon was not able to see where she went. Moon did not want Nyght to think Moon was not as powerful as Moon thought Moon was. "*Sun has hidden her from me. I am sure Sun has done this so the woman can fully receive the blessing of Sun. Even though I am stronger than Sun, Sun will use her as a weapon.*" Moon did not know why the woman was hidden from Moon, but Nyght did not need to know that. "*But I have my own. I will tell you where to begin your search.*"

"*Where, Father?*" Nyght asked anxiously.

Moon had not been in the sky over the village when Sun had chosen the woman all those seasons ago when she was but a child. Moon did know the day Sun had touched the child. It was the same day, and even though they were on opposite sides of the world, it was at the same moment Moon had first worked through Nyght.

Sun and Moon were exactly opposite. That was the way Moon saw it. The truth was that they were not opposites, they only stayed on opposite sides of the world separated from one another. Even though neither one of them would admit it, Sun and Moon were very much alike. That is why Moon knew when and where Sun had marked the woman all those seasons ago and Moon told Nyght, "*Lorraine.*"

"*Why Lorraine, Father?*"

Moon was not pleased with Nyght in the way she questioned Moon, but Moon did not want her to think Moon was unhappy with her, even though Moon was, due to her failure in killing the chosen of Sun. "*Lorraine is the village where the child had been touched by Sun, a little more than fourteen seasons ago when she was no more than five seasons."*

Nyght could not stop herself from thinking that the woman she was after, the one wanting to kill her, the one she needed to kill, was about the same age as her. She did not know which of the two was older, but what she did know was that the woman named Hanna did not fight as well as she had.

"The woman has not been fully blessed by Sun. She will return to the place where she was first touched, to receive Sun's full blessing." Moon decided this was the perfect time to show how much more Moon loved the one Moon had chosen than Sun did the other. *"I blessed you when you were only fifteen seasons. I wanted you to have my gifts so you would be strong and able to defend yourself. I should have told you about the one Sun had chosen, but I did not believe the two of you would ever meet, and if you did, you would be stronger than her."* Moon did believe what Moon had told her. Moon believed Nyght would be the stronger of the two because Moon believed, Moon was stronger than Sun.

"Thank you, Father. For the gifts and for believing in me. I will not fail you again."

"I know you will not, my daughter," Moon said to end the conversation.

Nyght lowered her head and opened her eyes. It was too late to go out now, the shops would have closed for the night. She would have to wait until morning to purchase what she needed. She would leave the city while the sun was up and would do as much traveling as she could before the sun became too much for her. Until then, Nyght laid down and slept. Dreaming about the next time she came upon the golden-haired woman named Hanna.

The map she obtained from the Guild House did not have the village of Lorraine on it. Either the creation of the map was before the village existed or the village was too small to be of any importance. When the sun had risen and the shops opened, Nyght found a mapmaker shop. After the man working there got over the shock of seeing Nyght and her pale white skin, he was able to locate a map with the village she needed to head for.

It was to the south, about ten sun-cycles at a hard ride. If Hanna was heading there, then she already had over a day's lead on her. If Hanna was in a hurry, then she would rest as little as possible. Nyght would have to ride for longer periods as well to catch up to the woman. Only stopping long enough to rest her horse and take a break from being out in the sun. Even though the sun bothered her at all times while it was in the sky, the buildings in the city kept the sun's rays off her mostly, except when it was directly overhead. While she was traveling, there would be no buildings. Unless woods surrounded the route she took, the sun would bother her greatly while it was in the sky, but since she had to reach Lorraine, and fast, she would have to suffer through it and keep her cloak wrapped as tightly as it could go.

Before she even went to the mapmaker's shop, Nyght found a shop and purchased a pair of gloves that she could wear on her hands. Normally she did not use them because she preferred to feel the metal of her blades while holding them. Since her encounter with Hanna, and the contact they made with each other's hands had caused her pain and suffering, Nyght decided that the gloves would be preferable to the pain.

After what Moon had told her, Nyght now understood why the sun, no, why Sun, affected her so much. Sun had been attacking her all this time, ever since she was a young girl because Sun did not like Moon. They were enemies, and since Sun could not get to Moon, Sun was taking it out on her. Nyght could not stop Sun, but she could stop the one Sun had chosen, especially if she could reach Lorraine before Hanna arrived to receive the blessing of Sun.

Nyght left the mapmaker's shop and walked to where she had her horse stabled. She had not gone back to pay for another day, but with the gold coin she had given the man, it would cover the time she had left the horse.

As she walked, Nyght went over everything she had seen or heard concerning Hanna. She remembered everything Elisa had said, which was not much help. Moon had explained a great deal but there was one thing Moon had not mentioned, which was who had come up behind her and knocked her unconscious. It had to be someone skilled since she had not sensed them behind her. The person had used something to hit her on the back of her head, but when she had woken, she did not remember seeing anything lying around, so they must have taken it with them. More than likely, they used the pommel of a sword or whatever weapon they carried. Nyght also figured they must have been in a hurry to leave and that was the reason they did not take the time to end her life. To Nyght, that was the worst mistake they could have made.

She would have to deal with the unknown assailant as well if that person still traveled with Hanna. Before or after she dealt with Hanna, it did not matter to Nyght. Before, if they interfered with what she had to do. After, if they did not, just to show them that attacking an assassin and leaving them alive was not a wise decision.

When she reached the stable and told the stable keeper she was leaving, the man brought her horse to her. He had already saddled it, and gave her another bag of grain, even though she did not ask for it. He must have figured the gold coin she had given him covered it because he did not ask for payment.

Before she left, he told her that the next time she was in Maridian, and if it was the breeding season, he would pay her to allow him to mate her horse with one of his mares. Nyght could tell that if he could not have her horse, he would settle for one of its offspring. Nyght told him that she was not planning to return, then rode off.

She traveled along the path around the inside of the city wall which people used for riding horses or driving wagons, so they would not clutter the streets with extra traffic.

She reached the southern gate and rode her horse through the portcullis. When she was seven paces away from the city, she stopped and looked out at the view in front of her. She saw some trees off in the distance, but it would be a while before she reached them, and when she did, the road she needed to travel on may not go through the woods.

She could feel the sun overhead, but she did not look up at it. Not just because it would bother her, but also because she now knew that Sun was against Moon, and anything against Moon was against her. Just like Hanna.

Nyght leaned forward a bit, just enough to pat the side of the horse's neck. She then sat back up. "Let's go, Stygian," she said, and without even putting her heels to his sides, the horse took off running, knowing his rider needed him to make great haste.

As the horse ran down the path, Nyght thought about what she would do when she found Hanna. She also thought about how much she liked the name Stygian and the horse it belonged to.

FOUR

They rode through the north gate a full mark after they left the boarding house. Even though they had two horses, Colton and Hanna shared one.

When Colton led Hanna to the entrance of Maridian, the horses, as well as enough supplies to last them for a couple of sun-cycles, had been waiting for them. Colton obtained everything he thought they would need before he had even gone to fetch Hanna. A friend of his from the temple, one who had joined the priesthood at the same time Colton had, stayed with the horses to make sure no one took them or the supplies. As soon as Colton said goodbye to his friend, both he and Hanna left Maridian behind, along with the unknown woman.

Colton was quick to get Hanna moving, although with the way she was acting, as if she was in shock, he did not think she would be able to handle a horse on her own. He also wondered if Hanna even knew how to ride.

When they had known each other before, neither of them had ever ridden a horse. Colton learned while at the priesthood. As for Hanna, he had not seen her for over four seasons and did not know if she had been on a horse during the time they had been apart. He placed her on the back of one of the horses and climbed up behind her. He then took hold of the reins to the second horse and began leading them away. Where to, he had no idea.

After they rode steady for two full marks, Colton had them stop so they could switch horses. They were both riding the same horse and it was tiring out from carrying two people, so they climbed onto the second one to give the first horse a break from the weight. As soon as they had transferred to the other one, Colton had them racing down the road once again.

They had been traveling north since leaving Maridian, but after they switched to the second horse, as soon as Colton saw a road heading toward the east, he changed their direction. He still did not know where he was going, but by changing directions, he was hoping the woman after Hanna would have a more difficult time following them. One thing Colton did know was that Hanna was still not safe. He could feel it in the deepest part of his soul.

After another two full marks of riding, Colton stopped them again, only this time he made sure they had moved far enough into the woods and out of sight from the main road so they would not be seen by anyone passing. With the exception of the short break to change horses, they had ridden for over four full marks, and since he had pushed the horses as far as they could go, they were going to have to rest if they were to carry him and Hanna to wherever he decided.

Once they stopped, Colton jumped off the horse and then guided Hanna down as well. She still seemed to be in shock over everything that had happened, because when she dismounted, she simply fell with his pull. He led her over to a fallen tree and guided her to sit. He then went over to the horse they had ridden last and began to remove the saddle to allow it to rest more comfortably. He left the bridal on so he could tie the reins around a tree so it would not walk off. He gave the horse a pat on the side of its neck then went over to the other horse to take care of it.

When they had transferred to the second horse, he had moved all the supplies they had to the first horse so the one they were riding did not have to bear the burden of their weight and the supplies. He removed the supplies off the horse and took them over to where Hanna was. She was still sitting on the fallen tree, with her hands clasped together in front of her. She was watching Colton work, which he took as a good sign. At least she was aware of what was going on around her, even though she had no idea why.

Colton removed the bag of grain from the back of the horse but did not give any to the horses. He removed the waterskin, poured some into his hand,

and held it to the horse that had been carrying all the supplies. He poured some more water into his palm and allowed the horse to drink again. Once done, Colton went over to the other horse and gave it two handfuls of water as well. They only had one bag of water, and he did not know how far away it was to refill their supply. This was the first time he had been out of Maridian, and even though he had studied about the world while at the priesthood, books did not give him the experience he would need to be out in the world himself.

With the horses taken care of, apart from feeding them, which he would do after they rested a bit, Colton went over to Hanna and offered her some water. He did not pour it into his palm as he did with the horses, he just held the bag out to her, and she took it from him. As she began to drink, Colton saw how much she was taking. "Go easy on it. I am not sure when we will be able to get more." She held the waterskin for a moment longer up to her mouth then brought it down and handed it back to Colton. He took a quick drink from it himself, then replaced the stopper and sat the bag down with the rest of the supplies. He looked down at Hanna and saw that she was staring at him. He gave her a quick smile then turned around and went back over to the horses.

He walked around to the other side of the horses and saw that Hanna was still looking at him. Before he could say anything, she did, "You grew." He was not sure what surprised him more. What she had said or the fact those were the first words she had spoken since he had dragged her from her home.

Hanna was right though. Colton had grown, which might have been the reason she had not recognized him when they were standing behind the boarding house, with him just having knocked the woman unconscious.

The last time she saw him, she was fifteen and he was fourteen. He had come to her and told her he was going to become a priest and then he left. She had not seen him since. Back then he was a bit shorter than she was, and even though Hanna had grown in height in the four seasons they had not seen one another, Colton now stood at least a handbreadth and then some over her.

It appeared to Hanna that not only had he grown taller, but his body and muscles had as well. As he was removing the supplies from the horses and their saddles, Hanna had been watching him, and every time his clothes went taut, because of the way he moved, she could see the outline of his body, and knew Colton was not the person she had known all those seasons ago.

"So have you," Colton said when the silence between them went on long enough. Like Hanna, he had not talked to her in over four seasons. Even though he had no problem with recognizing her, especially with her golden hair, she still looked different to him. On the day he entered the priesthood, she was a fifteen-year-old girl. Now, she was indeed a woman.

Colton noticed something else about his old friend. Something the Hanna of fifteen seasons had in common with the Hanna sitting across the way. Neither one of them smiled. "Are you hungry?" Colton asked as he forced himself to stop staring at Hanna even though she was staring just as hard at him.

He walked over to where he had sat the supplies. He bent over and picked up the bag with the food he had obtained for them. It was only enough to last about three sun-cycles. Five if they skipped a meal, but since they had been on the run before the sun had even risen, he felt they could use something to eat. He also could use it to keep both of them busy, and perhaps, it would remove the awkward silence between them.

He pulled out a loaf of bread and tore a piece of it off. He then handed it to Hanna who took it from him. When she did, she looked up at him, but when their eyes met, she quickly put them back on the bread in her hands. "Thank you," she said and brought the bread up in front of her but waited until Colton had turned to the side to begin eating.

Colton took a piece of bread for himself. One less than half the size of the piece he had given Hanna. It was not just because he wanted to make the food last longer, but also because in the time he had been at the priesthood, he learned that his body did not need to have the amount of food most people would consume. Colton learned a lot when he entered the priesthood.

Instead of sitting next to Hanna on the fallen tree, he walked to where he was halfway between her and the horses. He knelt down on the ground so that he was resting on his knees and his legs were under him. He then bowed his head and said his prayer to thank the Creator for the food he had provided. It was a short prayer and did not take him long, but when he lifted his head, he could tell that Hanna had been watching him. He turned his head and saw that she had not swallowed the piece of bread she had placed in her mouth, and he was not sure if she had stopped because she felt she should wait until he finished his prayer, or because she was surprised he had prayed in the first place. Since neither of those things bothered him, he stood up and began eating the small piece of bread he had. Out of the corner of his eye, he saw Hanna had begun to chew her food again.

Once finished, Colton walked back over to where he had sat their supplies and picked up the bag of feed for the horses. He then went over to the one they had been riding last, pulled a handful of feed out of the bag, and held it in front of the horse so it could eat. As soon as the horse had finished, Colton pulled out another handful and gave it to the horse. He then went to the other horse and gave it two handfuls as well.

Like their food, they had a limited amount of feed for the horses. The only difference was that the horses would have an opportunity to feed on any grass they would come across. Colton knew about some of the wild berries that grew in the woods, but he had only read about them. Since this was the first time he had actually been in the woods, it would take him some time to find any berries and then he would have to determine if they were not harmful to humans. There were a couple types of berries that looked the same, but one was not edible.

Colton turned and looked at Hanna. She was still eating the piece of bread, and even though it was bigger than the one he had eaten, she should have finished by now. He figured she did not know what was happening, and since she had no idea, thinking about it was only causing her more confusion. He felt the same way.

The silence between the two was only growing more uncomfortable. It was Colton who decided it was time for the two to start talking. Just as he did all those seasons ago. Colton did most of the talking and Hanna did the listening. Although he was not sure if she ever really paid attention to what he used to say to her. "I am sorry about Mama and Papa. I know you were close to them."

Hanna stopped chewing her food and looked at Colton. She had put the two elderly people behind her, including their deaths. "It happens," she said to give a response to the subject, and he heard the emptiness in the words.

"I saw you on the day of Mama's funeral. I was assigned to work in the temple during the service."

He took a moment before he continued. "I guess you didn't see me. I wasn't allowed to talk to any of the people attending. But if you had seen me, then I thought you would have said something to me."

Even though Hanna did not want to, she thought back to the day of Mama's funeral. She did not remember much, having her mind on what was going on at the moment, but she was not sure whether she would have recognized Colton or not. She had not even recognized him when he appeared at the back of her house, where he had taken her from. "Who was that woman?" she asked to start with one of the many questions she had.

Colton gave her his answer, "I do not know."

They looked at each other, and Hanna asked her next questions, "What were you doing there? And what did you do to her?"

Colton figured he would answer the second question first. At least it was an easy answer. He walked over to where he had placed their supplies and picked up a wooden staff. It was the first time Hanna had even noticed it, although he had it with the supplies the entire time. Colton walked back over to where he had been standing, between her and the horses. He then began spinning the long wooden staff.

He twirled it out in front of him for a few spins, with both of his hands. After it made a few rotations, more than Hanna could count, he moved the staff over his left shoulder and made it spin around his neck a couple of times. From the moment he began spinning it in front of him, the staff did not come to a halt.

After a couple of spins around his neck, and as it came around to the front of him, Colton allowed the staff to move outward, but before it went farther than his reach, he grabbed hold of it by the very end. He then brought the staff around his left side and made it spin around his back and to the front of him again, grabbing it in the middle to control the flow of the staff. After a few spins around his waist, he brought the staff back in front of him, spun it a couple more times, and then tossed the staff in the air. While there, it spun a couple of times, and so did Colton. He made two complete circles where he was standing, and as the staff came back down, Colton who was in mid-spin himself, and facing away from Hanna, caught the staff as it reached the middle of his back. He then continued to keep the staff in motion, spinning it around his back and to the front of him again, as he spun his body around to face Hanna. Once in position, he spun the staff a few more times in front of him and then brought it down so that it was at his right side, pointing upward. Finished with answering her question about what he had done to the woman, he placed his left hand across his mid-section and bowed at the waist. As he rose, he tossed the staff from his right hand to his left and when it was standing next to him, he raised his right hand and gave his patented salute.

Even with everything she had been through, she could not stop the smile from coming to her. She might not have recognized Colton by his appearance but there was no other person who could, or would, perform his standard bow and salute. She had seen it too many times to ever forget.

Colton saw the smile. It was something he had always tried to get Hanna to do, and most times, he had failed. If all it would take to get her to smile was to do a few basic moves with a wooden staff, he would have learned how to do them when they were younger. As much as he wanted to let her keep smiling, he knew it would not last. He still had to answer her first question.

He walked back over to where the supplies were and sat his staff down. He then looked at Hanna who was watching him. She was no longer smiling, and he was sure she had stopped because of the look on his face. "I do not know who the woman was. All I know is that she was there to kill you." With what he had said, she definitely did not smile. He moved to stand in front of Hanna, looking down at her, but before he could continue with what he was going to say, she spoke.

"You saved me," she said looking directly at his face, which quickly took on a light shade of red. Hanna had seen him do quite a few exploits and had heard from him personally, everything he had done when he was living on the streets, and not once had she ever seen him blush.

"I am not sure I did," Colton said and turned around, not wanting to face Hanna when he told her what he wanted to say. "I knew she was there to kill you. I also know she is going to try again."

Hanna stood up to continue their conversation. "Why does she want to kill me? And how do you know?"

He turned around to face her, and answered both of her questions at once, "I don't know." He saw the confused look she had, but there was something else and he knew what it was, anger.

"What do you mean you don't know?" Hanna shouted and now her face had taken on a light shade of red, but it was not because she was blushing. "You show up just when some woman was trying to kill me. You used that staff of yours to knock her unconscious, so you were prepared to fight her. Then you rush me through the city to one of the gates where you had horses and supplies waiting." Hanna walked around Colton and took a quick look at the horses tied to the trees. She then turned back to face Colton. "You had two horses waiting so you must have been planning on abducting me even before you showed up at my place."

"I did not abduct you," Colton said, with a bit of anger in his own voice, not liking the accusation aimed at him for something he had not done. At least not in the way Hanna had meant it.

"You took me from my home and from the city. You made me ride that horse and now I am sitting in the middle of the woods. If that is not what abduction is, then what do you call it?"

"I call it saving your life!" Colton said, and after two breaths of silence, he turned around, so he was not facing her. He was not angry, and he was sure Hanna was not either. Confused is what they both were. Hanna did not speak, and Colton took a few more breaths, then turned back to look at her. When he was ready to continue, he did so calmly. "I do not know who the woman was. All I know is that she would have killed you if I had not arrived. I also know she will continue to come after you and that is why I had to get you out of the city." He took another breath before he spoke again, "I am sorry for having not been able to tell you what I was doing at the time, but I will not apologize for saving your life." He turned away to get control of his emotions. He still was not angry, he was worried. Even though he had saved Hanna once, he was not sure he would be able to again.

"Thank you for saving my life," Hanna said, in a calmer tone.

Colton turned around to face her. "You're welcome," he said and smiled hoping to get the same response from her, but he figured it would be another hundred seasons before she smiled again. "As I said, I do not know who she was or how I knew you were in danger, but I will tell you what led me to save you." He looked over his shoulder at the fallen tree then back to Hanna, "We should have a seat. This may take some time."

Hanna did not like the sound of that, but since she was not sure what was going on and was just as confused as when she was back at her place, she did as Colton suggested. He moved out of her way for her to sit in the same spot she had been, then he sat down at her right, and began his story.

"Two sun-cycles ago I was in my room at the priesthood. All of a sudden, something came over me. Somehow, I knew you were in danger." He turned his head to the left and saw her looking at him. Since she did not ask a question or say anything, he turned back to look out in front of him and continued. "I didn't know what the danger was, but I knew I not only had to save you, but I had to get you out of the city. I knew we would need horses and supplies, but I didn't have any coin."

"Did you steal them from the priesthood?" Hanna asked and with the speed he turned his head to face her, she knew he had not, and was offended by the question."

"No, I did not steal from the priesthood."

"I just thought that maybe..."

He filled in with what he believed she was thinking. "You thought that the Colton sitting here with you is the same Colton you knew four seasons ago." She nodded to give her answer, but he could tell she was sorry for what she had thought. He turned to face forward, not because what she was thinking offended him, but because he knew the truth, which he told her. "I am not the person I used to be."

"You still do your bow and salute," she said.

"The truth is, I haven't done either of those since I entered the priesthood." She heard the sadness in the words. As if he missed a bit of what he once was. She did not know it, but he did. "We needed supplies, so I went to some of the people I knew when I was living on the streets. The ones I had helped with their bags, the ones I did a few odd jobs for. I even went to the vendor I had helped all those seasons ago when I was only seven." He did not say it to her, but he thought it to himself, *"The one I called Father."*

Thinking about the man, he stood up and moved away from Hanna. When he was a pace away, he turned back to face her. "When I explained to them who I was, and when they realized I was the Colton they knew, they were more than happy to donate to our cause."

"What do you mean by 'our cause'?" Hanna asked then had a follow-up question, "What did you tell them?"

Colton smiled and then answered, "I told them the truth. Or at least what I believe." He could tell she wanted to know if the explanation he had used was the actual truth or the truth told by Colton. "I told them I have been given a mission from the Creator and I asked them to give whatever the Creator put on their heart."

"You lied to them?" Hanna asked after hearing his take on the truth.

He answered her question, "No, like I said I

told them the truth." Colton had never been more serious in his entire life, and Hanna knew it. "I got enough coin to buy the horses. As for the supplies themselves, Father gave them to me. He had wanted to give me more, but I told him I did not want to weigh the horses down because I would need to be moving fast so I took what you see there."

Hanna looked to her left and saw the supplies sitting next to the fallen tree, then looked back at Colton. She knew he was not finished, but she had a question for him. "These people, the ones you have not seen in seasons just gave you coin and supplies with no questions asked. You just told them you were going on some mission for the Creator?" He only nodded so she moved on to her next questions, "So what made you come to my place? Did the Creator tell you to?"

Colton heard the disdain in what she asked which did offend him, but he knew that many people did not believe in the Creator, especially as he did, so he let it go and continued. "As I said, I did not know what danger you were in, only that you were. I also knew I was to get the supplies and horses before I came for you. When I arrived, I knew you were in the back of the house, even though I had not seen you. When I saw that person moving close to you, I knew what the danger was. I didn't even know it was a woman until I saw her lying on the ground."

"Would you have struck her so hard to knock her out if you had known she was a woman?"

It took him less than a breath to answer, "Yes." When he spoke the single word, he could tell Hanna was holding back a smile. Just as she used to when they were younger. "I had to stop her and knocking her unconscious seemed to be the best option. It would give us time to get to the city gate and to the horses, more importantly, to get away from her."

Hanna asked her next question, "If you knew she was going to try and kill me, why didn't you kill her?"

He took a few breaths before he answered, "It was not my desire, nor the will of the Creator."

Hanna had now reached her limit. Some unknown woman, for some unknown reason, had attacked her in her own home. She was in the middle of the woods, and away from the city and the house she had known for the majority of her life. Even though she was angry about all those things, what made her the angriest was that Colton kept on bringing up the Creator. Someone she did not believe in, and even if she did, she would not follow. If the Creator was real and was in control of everything, it would mean it was the Creator who allowed her father, her mother, Mama, and Papa to die, leaving her all alone. If the Creator was in control of everything, then the Creator took everything from her. She stood up and looked Colton directly in his eyes. "We're going back," she said and walked toward him.

Just as she passed him, and after he got over the shock of what she had just said, he turned, grabbed her by her arm, and spun her to face him, "We cannot go back. Don't you understand? That woman wants to kill you. If you go back, she will."

Hanna looked into his eyes, then down at her left arm where he had a hold of her. She pulled out of his grasp. "No, she won't." She turned and headed to the horses, "We can go to the city guard and tell them what happened. They will find her and lock her up. Then I can get back to running the boarding house." When she reached the horses, she did not know what to do with them, but she knew Colton did, so she turned around and saw him staring at her, "Get the saddles and put them on the horses." She spoke to him the same way she would speak to Elisa when she was giving her a task to do.

Colton stayed where he was, "No," he said and crossed his arms in front of him.

She waited a few breaths to see if he would do what she told him to do, but when she was sure he would not, she started walking toward their supplies and the saddles. "Fine, I will do it myself." When she reached the saddles, she bent over to pick one up. She was able to, but the weight was more than she could control, and she stumbled slightly as she turned to head back to the horses. Once she had control of her body, she began walking. She had the saddle out in front of her, and it was obvious she was having trouble carrying it.

Colton had turned as she moved so he could watch her. He was sure of what was to come. When

Hanna reached the nearest horse, she tried to lift the saddle and place it on the horse's back. Since it was heavy, she could not lift it upward, so she swung it out to her right a bit to get some momentum behind her toss. All she ended up doing was throwing the saddle into the side of the horse who was not happy with her lack of skill concerning horses. It pushed its side in Hanna's direction and hit the saddle she had up in front of her. The force from the horse was enough to make her take two steps back and fall on her rear, she had let go of the saddle and it fell with her.

Colton, having watched the entire scene, did the one thing he should not have. He laughed. Hearing that, Hanna turned to look at him, and he saw that she was not pleased with being neither his nor the horse's amusement and to show them both that neither of them would get the best of her, Hanna rose to her feet, turned, and started walking. Planning that if she could not use the horse to get back to Maridian, her legs would do just fine.

"Where are you going?" Colton asked before she was four paces away.

"Home," she said but did not turn around.

Colton realized she was serious, so he ran from where he was and caught up to her. When he reached her, he once again grabbed her by her arm and spun her around to face him. Only as she came to face him, he had to duck, or she would have struck him with the fist she had aimed for his face.

He had no problem in avoiding the clumsy attempt, but he knew if he laughed it was only going to make her angrier, so he restrained himself. Since she was facing him, he decided to try to explain to her what they needed to do. "We cannot go back to Maridian. We have to stay away from there and away from that woman."

"I am going back, and you cannot stop me!" She turned and started walking in the same direction as before. Before she had taken two steps, Colton reached out with his left hand, placed it on her right shoulder, and turned her around to face him. As she spun, Hanna had her left hand up in the air aimed right at his face. Since he was closer to her than before, he only had enough time to lean back and let her hand pass, just missing the tip of his nose. As her hand passed his face, she turned back around and started walking again.

Colton knew three things. One was that he could not let Hanna go back to Maridian. Two, the unknown woman was still going to try to kill her. He had told her about those two items, but it was the third one he was sure Hanna did not know.

He let her get a few paces ahead of him, hoping she would calm down a bit, but before she got too far away, he ran and caught up to her. He then wrapped his arms around her waist, picked her up, and turned her around to face the opposite direction. He then let her go, and of course, since he had stopped her again, she was ready to strike, again.

When he removed his arms from around her, she quickly spun to her right, with her left hand already positioned high enough in the air to attempt for a third time to strike his face.

Since they were so close to each other, and her hand was coming a lot quicker than previously, Colton did not have time to duck or lean away. So instead, he resorted to his training in the priesthood. Just before her hand reached the side of his face, he brought up his right arm, blocking her swing. When the part of her arm below her wrist struck his arm, it felt as if she had just hit a tree. A very solid tree. She quickly brought her arm down and started rubbing the sore area with her opposite hand.

Colton felt bad about what he had done but only a little. He took a quick look at Hanna who was staring at him while she tried to rub feeling back into her wrist. He then stepped around her and as he walked away, he told her the third thing she needed to know, "You were going in the wrong direction." Not wanting to look at the woman who he thought should be a little more grateful for what he had done, rescuing her that is, not hurting her arm; he walked over to the supplies and started going through them. Not looking for anything in particular, just so he could take a few moments for himself, but watched her out of the corner of his eye. If she chose to continue to try to return to the city, he would still be able to see her start walking and would stop her. It was for her own safety.

Hanna did not move from where she was. She stood there looking at Colton, who was kneeling over the supplies and going through them. She was hoping he was preparing to place them back on the horses and then take her back to the city. She had a feeling that was not his plan. "I appreciate what you did, in saving me, but I cannot stay out here in these woods. You can take me back to Maridian, so I can go back to running my boarding house and you can go back to being a priest." She thought that if she reminded him of why he had walked out of her life four seasons ago, it would make him want to return to his. When he stood up and turned to face her, she could see that her words did affect him. Just not the way she wanted them to. There was something about her mentioning him being a priest which brought sadness to his eyes.

They had only held their stare for a moment, but in that time, Hanna thought she knew what had upset him. "When you left the priesthood to save me, you gave up your chance at becoming a priest didn't you?"

Colton did not realize his emotions were so obvious, but if anyone knew him, it would be Hanna. He had spent so much time with her when they were younger, and he had told her everything about himself because he wanted her to know. She did, and even though what she said was true, it was not his truth. If a person was to leave the priesthood before they finished their training in becoming a priest, they could not return. For Colton, he had a different reason why the priesthood would not accept him back.

"I cannot go back to the temple," he said and looked to the ground.

She gave him a moment to get over what he had just told her then asked her question, "Because you left to help me?"

Colton looked up and could tell Hanna was now feeling sorry for not just the way she had acted, but for what she believed was her fault. She did not have to feel sorry for the last one at least. "Do not worry. It was not my helping you that keeps me from returning to finish becoming a priest." He tossed the piece of cloth he had in his hands he had taken from the pile of supplies back with the other items and then sat down on the fallen tree. Once there, he had his head bent, but then looked up at Hanna, "They expelled me from the priesthood."

Hanna remembered the day he had come to her and told her that he was going to join the priesthood. She was not happy with the idea, but Hanna was not happy with a lot of things. She knew when he had told her it was something he wanted to do, more than anything else, he was serious about his decision.

She walked over, forgetting about what he had done in bringing her out into the woods, and even about how her arm was still stinging from when he blocked her swing. She then sat down next to him, waiting for him to tell her his story, in his own time.

"I told you that I was in my room when I felt you were in danger." He stopped and turned his head to look at Hanna who nodded, letting him know she remembered what he had said. He then turned back and continued, "I was there because I was already packing." He looked down at himself, "This robe and one more, the sandals that I am wearing, and my staff are all I brought with me." He looked to his left and saw his staff. He had very few belongings.

"So why did they expel you?"

Colton turned from looking at his staff but did not look at Hanna while he told the rest of his story. "They did not believe I was suitable to be a priest. They thought I was too radical in my views and what I thought about the Creator."

He stopped talking so Hanna had to say something to get him to continue, "What, you don't believe in the Creator?"

He turned and looked at her, "No, the other priests think I believe in the Creator too much."

Hanna was never a spiritual person. It was not that she did not believe in the Creator, it was just that she did not care one way or the other. Even in her limited understanding, she did not see how someone could believe in the Creator "too much." She did not have a chance to ask because Colton began again.

"In the four seasons I was with the priesthood I learned a lot."

"Like how to use that staff of yours?" Hanna asked, interrupting him.

"We were trained on it from the moment we entered the priesthood. It was a way to keep our bodies fit. But it was also what began leading me to what I eventually discovered."

He stopped talking so Hanna asked her question. "And what was that?"

Colton took a deep breath, "That the Creator is a part of everything."

Hanna did not know much about the Creator, but she thought she understood what Colton had just said. "Yes, the Creator is supposed to be in all of us." She still had a bit of cynicism in her words.

Colton turned his head to look at her. "Not just us. He is in everything." He turned his head to look at the things in the area. "The horses, the grass, the trees, the rocks, the ants at your feet." When he said the last one, Hanna looked down and saw the line of ants on the ground, crossing in front of her. She had not noticed them, but apparently, Colton had. "Everything is connected to everything else. Humans are not the only ones the Creator is involved with."

"He was supposed to have made everything," Hanna said to add what little she knew about the Creator.

"But when he did, he placed a bit of himself in every creation. Because he did, everything is the Creator, and the Creator is everything." He stood and walked over to his staff. He picked it up and turned back to face Hanna. "I was researching the history as to why priests were trained in how to use the staff.

The priests at the temple said that it was just a way of keeping their bodies physically fit. I had a hard time believing it, especially since the priest who told me that had never missed a meal in his entire time in the priesthood and could not even see his own toes when he looked down." He was surprised when Hanna smiled. It did not last long, but Colton was happy to see it. "While I was researching, I found a book that told me what I was looking for. It said that priests were trained on how to use the staff because they would use it as a means of defense."

"What would priests need to defend themselves from?" Hanna asked.

"Themselves nothing. Others, from everything." He could tell she did not understand his answer. "The first priests did not stay in temples and preach their sermons behind a pedestal. Yes, they would spread the word of the Creator, but they did it while they traveled across the world."

"And they needed a staff for that?"

"Many of the places they went had a great deal of fighting. The priests went among the people and would use their staffs to protect the innocent and defend the defenseless. When I first brought what I found to the temple's priests, they told me that was during a different time. Now their job was to make sure people knew who the Creator was and what they should do to be good so they will be rewarded when they leave this world."

Hanna took a moment and then gave her opinion,

"Maybe they are right. Maybe the Creator just wants us to be good, but maybe the Creator does not really care what we do. If he did, why does he let so many bad things happen in the world?" Hanna had one last point to add, "Especially to good people."

Colton knew she was referring to what happened to her mother and father, and maybe even Mama and Papa. He knew there will always be those who do not believe in the Creator or even in the way he allows things to happen, good and bad. He still did what he believed the Creator wanted him to do, and it was time Hanna knew it. "I believe it was the Creator who wanted me to save you. I believe he was the one who told me you were in danger and that I had to get you out of the city."

Hanna had allowed him to talk about the Creator, and the priesthood, but now he had once again reminded her of why they were in the woods, and if it was because of the Creator, she was definitely not going to remain. "The Creator did not bring me out here!" she said as she stood up and faced Colton. "You did, and even if I don't know how you knew I was in danger, I am not going to believe the Creator told you to come and save me and told you to drag me into the wilderness."

"I believe he did tell me," Colton said looking directly at Hanna.

Hanna crossed her arms at her chest, "Then what did he sound like?"

Colton could tell she was mocking him and his

beliefs. "The Creator does not speak to us with his voice. He speaks to us in here," he said as he pointed to his chest.

"Maybe it was just a bad piece of meat you ate."

He was doing his best to restrain himself from her heresy. "It was not a piece of bad meat," he said to try to calm himself down.

"Because you do not eat meat? I should have known there was a reason you stole so many apples when you were younger."

"I did not steal apples," he said with more emotion than he had wanted to. "And if I did, I always went back and paid for them."

"So that makes it ok? You stole and then paid, that definitely sounds like a priest of the so-called Creator."

Colton could take what she was saying about himself, but when she spoke against the Creator, he was ready to defend his beliefs. "Do not mock the Creator. It is disrespectful and dangerous as well."

"Dangerous! Dangerous! Some woman tried to kill me, and you want me to be worried about someone who doesn't even exist!"

He took two steps so that he was standing right in front of her. Since he was taller, he had to tilt his head down to look at her. "Do not disrespect the Creator."

She met his glare, and then said what she really thought about the one they were discussing, "To the Pits of Myrkur with the Creator." It was a saying people used to curse someone.

Colton did not appreciate it, but before he could say anything else to her, he heard someone off to his left clear their throat. Both he and Hanna turned to see who had walked into their camp.

Standing at the tail end of one of the horses was a man looking at them. "Sorry to interrupt your conversation, even though I felt it was a good place for the two of you to take a moment, but I was wondering if you could keep it down a bit? You see, me and my mule were off in the distance taking an early morning nap, and your voices were disturbing us." The man stopped talking and smiled at the two young people. He could tell what they were both thinking about asking so he went ahead and answered their unspoken question. "Oh, where are my manners? Let me introduce myself. I am Adoni."

Colton and Hanna forgot about the argument they were having, at least for the moment. Now they were more interested in the man standing alone, in the middle of the woods, smiling at them.

FIVE

As Colton and Hanna stared at the man, Adoni walked between the two horses and started patting them. "I do love horses," he said smiling, but since he was shorter than the horses, Colton and Hanna could not see the expression on his face. They did see when he started moving from between the horses because his legs and feet were in view. When he came back to where they could see him, he spoke, "So what brings the two of you out into the woods discussing a topic you both appear to have strong opinions on?"

Hanna turned and went over to where their supplies were and began rummaging through them. Not in search of anything in particular, but to her, it was better than having to talk to Colton, or the man, about what they had been discussing a moment ago.

"Forgive us, sir," Colton said, turned to look over his shoulder at Hanna then turned back to face their company. "We did not mean to speak so loudly." He put aside the conversation he and Hanna were having, sure that it was not over, but it could wait until they were once again alone. "My name is Colton. This is Hanna," he said waving his hand in her direction.

"Nice to meet the two of you," Adoni said, then stepped forward toward Colton. Which was obviously the more sociable of the two. He extended his hand out.

"And you, good sir," Colton said shaking hands. "I invite you to sit and have a quick bite with us, to make up for our disturbing you."

"We don't have much for ourselves," Hanna said, ensuring there was no mistake to Colton and Adoni that she did not agree with the invitation.

"But what we have we will freely share," Colton said to rebuke Hanna's statement.

"Well, if your supplies are limited then might I suggest you join me at my camp. It is not too far away." Adoni looked up into the sky, then back at Colton, "There is still time before mid-meal, but there is no reason we cannot have a light snack to pass the marks. I have plenty and more than happy to share with you."

"Thank you, sir. It would be a pleasure to join you," Colton said and gave the man a slight bow.

"We need to be leaving," Hanna said.

Colton turned slightly to see her and the look on her face told him that she did not wish to go anywhere with the man. "But he has offered his hospitality, and it would only be proper for us to accept." Colton decided that maybe he needed to say one more thing to let her know she was being disrespectful, "As not to offend his generosity. We were the ones who disturbed his rest." Hanna and Colton held their stare at each other, and she decided it was not worth it, so she put her focus once again on going through their supplies, looking for nothing in particular. Colton turned back to face Adoni, "We would be delighted to join you, sir."

"Outstanding," Adoni said and clapped his hands once to show his excitement. "Just follow me. My camp is not far from here." He then turned and started walking away. "You can leave your supplies and horses here; they will be safe."

Colton watched the man and was going to follow him but realized Hanna was still where she had been, so Colton turned to look at her. "Are you coming?" he asked.

Hanna took another moment to go through the supplies, but could not tolerate Colton staring at her, so she stood up and began walking in the direction Adoni had left. When she passed Colton, it was obvious to him that she went out of her way, not to make eye contact with him. At the moment, he did not care what she was thinking. The man who went out of his way to be polite and generous had offered them his hospitality and it was only proper they accept. Colton knew that he and Hanna still had a lot to discuss and deal with, but right now, what they needed was time to let their anger subside, and once that happened, they would be able to think more clearly. Adoni's arrival had come at the best possible moment.

It did not take them long to reach the camp. Colton had walked behind Hanna, but since he could still sense her anger toward him, the Creator, and the situation they were in, he kept a few paces behind her to give her some space. When he stepped into Adoni's camp just behind her, he was amazed at what he was seeing. Since Hanna had stopped so abruptly it was obvious she did as well.

Adoni was already sitting on a small stool in front of the fire in the center of the camp. On a skillet over the fire, Colton and Hanna could smell the fish cooking and they were close enough to see that there were three of them. Hanging over the skillet was a metal pot, and from the smell coming from it, there was food cooking in it as well. What surprised them both were the two stools sitting next to the fire at the sides of Adoni, one to his left and one to his right. The fish, the pot of food, and especially the two stools made it appear to Hanna and Colton that their host was expecting them. Which they thought could not be, because they had arrived at the campsite just a few breaths after Adoni, and he did not have time to arrange what they were seeing.

"Come, take a seat," Adoni said as he took the skillet by the handle and pulled it enough from the fire and jerked it slightly, but with enough force to cause all three fishes to rise up, flip over, and land on their opposite sides, all at the same time. He then replaced the skillet back over the fire and used the ladle in the pot to stir its contents. "The meal is almost ready but until then we can have a chat. Sometimes cycles of the sun or the moon will pass before I have a chance to talk to anyone besides my mule." At the mention of the word, the mule hee-hawed as if it did not like the comment its owner had made. "Well, it is not like you are the king of conversation," Adoni said to his mule, who just turned its head and looked away.

Colton and Hanna had not even noticed the mule because their focus was on the fire and the food. Now that they saw it, they both noticed it was not wearing a bridal and they wondered why it had not wandered off while its owner had gone to where they were.

Having gotten over the initial sight of the scene before him, Colton stepped around Hanna and moved toward the fire. When he was a few paces away, he turned his head and gave her a look to let her know that she might as well join him and their host. He then turned back to look toward the center of the camp and walked over to the stool to the right of Adoni.

Hanna waited until Colton had already taken his seat before she took her first step to join the two. She did not want to, but she knew she did not have much of a choice. She did not know where she was in the woods, especially concerning where Maridian was located. She needed Colton to take her back home, and it was obvious he was not going to, at least not until he had eaten the meal offered to them. Hanna also thought he might not even afterward.

She walked over and sat down on the stool to the left of Adoni, making sure she gave Colton a glare to let him know that she was not happy with where she was or what was going on. Colton just smiled, because one thing he did know was that Hanna was never happy.

Adoni started the conversation off, "So what brings the two of you out into these woods? Most travelers stay closer to the road."

"It doesn't look as if you did," Hanna said mockingly, and Colton immediately gave her a look to let her know she was being rude.

With the way he replied, Adoni had taken no offense to Hanna's disposition. "Oh, I travel the roads most of the time, but sometimes it is good to get off the path and see where my feet take me." Just then the mule hee-hawed again, "Yes, it is your feet that do most of the walking, but I was stating the fundamentals to our friends. Now if you do not mind, the humans are trying to get to know one another."

The look Hanna and Colton were sharing with each other showed that they were both thinking that maybe their host had spent too much time alone with his mule because he was talking to it as if it was talking to him. Colton did not say anything about what he was thinking because he would not insult the man who was being so gracious to them.

Hanna kept quiet because she did not care about the mule or her host. She just wanted to go home.

"So, what brings you out here?" Adoni asked.

"We are traveling," Colton said.

"To where?" Adoni asked.

Colton did not answer because he did not know, but Hanna spoke what she believed, "We are heading to Maridian." Once again, they held their gaze on each other.

Adoni leaned forward to stir the contents in the pot, and asked his next question, "So where did you come from?"

Once again, Colton did not respond, even though he knew the answer, but Hanna did not hesitate to reply to the question, "Maridian."

While still leaning over the pot, Adoni looked to his left at Hanna then turned his head to the right to look at Colton, then looked back at the pot and stirred it again. "Well, if you are heading to Maridian but you came from Maridian, then it sounds as if the two of you are going in circles." He gave the pot one more stir, then sat back up on his stool. "Going in circles just makes a person's head get cloudy and fuzzy. I've found that picking a destination and heading straight for it is more helpful."

"Sometimes the destination we start out for is not where we end up," Colton said with his eyes locked on the fire, and Hanna knew he was not speaking of any city. He was talking about him becoming a priest.

"Oh, I am not so sure about that," Adoni said to bring Colton out of his own thoughts and to look at his host. "We may not reach our destination when we want to, but that does not mean we will not get there or that we have not already arrived, or we just haven't realized it yet. Or maybe we have to wait for our destination to find us."

Colton looked at Adoni and thought the man had only talked to his mule for so long, he was not used to talking to other people and what he wanted to say was not what he had spoken. Colton turned his head to look at Hanna and when she slightly shook her head, he knew she had not understood what the man had said either.

"Oh, where are my manners," Adoni said and stood up. He walked over to his blanket a couple of paces from the fire and picked up some items that neither Colton nor Hanna could see until he turned around. Adoni came back over to the fire and handed a metal cup to Colton and one to Hanna, holding onto one for himself. Hanna and Colton looked back over to the blanket but did not see any more cups. Their host had just the three. Just enough for the number of people present. "Something to moisten our throats," Adoni said and poured some of the contents of the waterskin he had in his hands into Hanna's cup. He then walked over to offer Colton some.

When he saw his host extend the waterskin, Colton positioned his cup for Adoni to fill. Once the liquid started flowing out, Colton saw that it was not water. "Forgive me, but I do not drink spirits of any kind."

Adoni did not stop pouring until the cup was full. He then went over and sat back down on his own stool, filled his own cup, and then sat the water-skin down to his right. "Well, that is something we have in common because I do not touch the spirits myself." Adoni raised his cup and took a drink, then brought the cup back down, "It is made from wild berries, honey, and water. Trust me, my friend, this will not affect your mind by any means whatsoever."

Colton was not sure whether he believed the man or not. The drink might just be what made his host to be out in the middle of the woods talking to his mule. Since he did not want to offend Adoni, he took a sip of the drink, and the second it touched his tongue, he tasted the sweetness. He tilted the cup a bit to look at its contents then brought it up and took another drink. He looked over to Hanna and it appeared she enjoyed the drink as well.

"Well, I believe our snack is ready," Adoni said, and the mule hee-hawed again. "You had your morning meal and you are not invited to this one," Adoni said looking over to the mule, and Colton had to wonder if he had been smart about emptying the contents of his cup.

Adoni reached down to his left and pulled up a plate, but it was not just one. Two others were under the one on top, and on it, there were three forks. Just enough for everyone sitting around the fire.

With the three plates situated on his left arm, from his hand to the inner side of his elbow, Adoni placed a fish on each of the plates, then a ladle full of the contents from the pot. He then stood, took a step to his right, and handed Hanna a plate, then walked over to Colton and handed him one, then returned to his seat.

With everything that had happened, and even though she had eaten a small piece of bread, the smell of the fish, as well as the potatoes and vegetables from the pot, was too enticing to resist. Before she could take a bite of the fish from the piece she had on her fork, Adoni spoke, "Would you do the honors of saying a prayer for our meal, priest."

Colton looked over and saw that Adoni was talking to him. He also saw Hanna staring as well, only she had her fork almost to her mouth. "I am not a priest, but I will speak the blessing." He waited until Hanna had placed her fork back on her plate. Adoni had already bowed his head and closed his eyes. Hanna did not. Colton lowered his head, closed his eyes, and began. "We thank the Creator for this meal he has provided for us, and we are grateful for all he has blessed us with. Please watch over us, and guide our steps, so we can work toward your will for our lives." He paused then ended his prayer, "To the Creator."

Adoni added his ending to the prayer, "To Creator,"

Hanna just began eating.

It was Adoni who started the conversation again. "So why did you say you weren't a priest?"

He had asked the question to Colton, but Hanna asked her own, "Why do you think he is one?"

Adoni turned to look at her and swallowed the bit of food he had placed in his mouth, "Well, he wears the robes of a priest, and when I came upon your camp, I happened to see the staff laid with your supplies." He then turned to look at Colton. "So why did you say you were not a priest?"

Colton was not ashamed of not having obtained the title of a priest. He was not even ashamed of his expulsion from the priesthood. He was just hesitant about speaking about what had happened because when he had talked to the priests training him, they looked at him as if he was crazy. He decided that since he was the only one with a strong belief in what he had discovered, it was best to keep it to himself.

"Come now, I have been everywhere, and have heard all kinds of craziness, so I think you could give me the opportunity to decide for myself if your reasons are crazy or not."

It amazed Colton at what Adoni had said. It was as if he had been inside of his head. Colton knew that was impossible and the old man must be able to read people. Read them very well. Since he had offered to listen, Colton figured that if Adoni was a bit crazy, since he appeared to carry on conversations with his mule, then he would be able to tell if what

Colton believed in was crazy as well. "I was asked to leave the priesthood because of my beliefs. The priests thought I was too radical and that I would not fit in with being a priest of the Creator." He sat there and waited for Adoni to respond, which he did.

"Well, if they are the ones who taught you then I can see they taught you wrong, so what would they know."

Colton was confused, and since Hanna was as well, she asked, "What do you mean they taught him wrong?"

Both had stopped eating, but Adoni had to wait until he finished the bite of fish he had in his mouth before he replied. Colton and Hanna sat there waiting. "They taught him wrong, is what I mean, and by that, I mean they taught him to call Creator, the Creator."

Both Colton and Hanna thought their assumption about the man not being completely in his right mind was accurate, but Colton spoke, "That is who the Creator is."

Adoni bent over and sat his plate down on the ground in front of him, then sat back up and looked at Colton. "He is not the Creator, he is Creator."

"What is the difference?" Hanna asked, thinking it was a logical question.

Adoni quickly turned his upper body to look at her and it was obvious he was not happy with the question. "What is the difference? What is the difference?" He turned, bent down, and picked up his plate. He then stood and walked over to the fire and dipped more of the vegetables out of the pot onto his plate, mumbling to himself but loud enough so that Hanna and Colton could hear. "These priests today would not know their head from their bottom. They think they know it all and believe that what they have learned and what they teach to others is the truth. How are they to know the truth when they do not even call Creator, Creator? They refer to him as if he is a tool. An object." Before he could say his next complaint, the mule sounded again, "I am not getting myself in an uproar. They are the ones who forgot what their true calling is, and if they kick out one such as this young fellow because they think he is too radical, then they need to have their heads removed from their necks, and the straw that they are using for their brains pulled out and put to good use doing something else." Adoni walked around the fire and over to the mule. He then sat the plate on the ground and the mule began to eat the bit of fish and vegetables offered to him. "These priests today need to get out in the world and out of their temples, then they would know what they are supposed to be doing, and then maybe they would learn just what they are to call the one they claim to follow."

Adoni walked back over, sat down on his stool, picked up the cup at his right, and took a drink. Hanna and Colton thought the man had finished with his outburst but were not sure if they should speak yet. Thankfully, Adoni was ready to speak again, but in a calmer manner. "I suppose I should set you straight young man."

"On what?" Colton asked.

"On what those so-called priests have incorrectly taught you."

"But the Creator is the Creator," Hanna said, and with the speed Adoni used to turn his body on his stool, she thought he was about to start ranting again. The only thing that stopped him was the heehaw from his mule, and when he heard it, he twisted his body to face forward, "You don't get any more. You had enough."

Colton wanted to know what the man was going to say to him, so since Hanna and the mule appeared to agitate the old man more, he spoke to him, "Adoni," Colton waited until the man was looking at him, "What did they teach me incorrectly?"

Adoni took a deep breath, then spoke, "What they taught you to call the one who created everything."

"The Creator," Hanna said, and Colton wished she had remained silent.

"He is not 'The Creator'," Adoni said, aggressively as he stood up from his stool, and looked at Hanna, who actually leaned back on her own stool, almost to the point where she was about to fall off. As Adoni sat back down, she moved forward on her stool, and he spoke again but this time he was much calmer, "He is Creator."

Colton could tell Hanna was about ready to ask

another question and he was sure if she did, Adoni would once again become agitated, so before she could, he took control of the conversation, "Could you please explain it to us?"

Adoni looked over to Colton and smiled, "It is a wise person to ask for knowledge on what they do not know rather than to think they know the knowledge of what they do not know." Even though the statement made some sense to him, Colton did not ask for an explanation to it. He wanted to know what Adoni was going to tell him about the Creator, or as the man had just said, Creator. "What is your name?"

Since he was looking at him, Colton knew he was asking him the question, but he also knew he had told the old man his name already. Nevertheless, so his host would not go on another rant, he answered the question, "Colton."

"And what do others call you?" Adoni asked.

Hanna answered, "Colton."

Adoni turned and looked at her and at least this time he did not have the appearance that she had spoken foolishly. "That is correct," Adoni said then turned back to look at Colton, "So when they see you, or they call out your name to get your attention, they call you Colton. Not 'The Colton.'"

Colton was sure Hanna was about to ask, "What is the difference?" so before she could, he spoke, "So you are saying that the priests have taught me wrong. That the Creator," Colton quickly continued to explain because he saw Adoni's jaw tighten up when he said, "The Creator." "He is Creator. That is his name?"

"Yes, that is what I am saying," Adoni said smiling. The smile then left his face and he turned to look directly ahead of him and down into the fire. "But it is not their fault, at least not completely." He took a deep breath, and Hanna and Colton knew their host had something else to say. "Times are not what they used to be. People used not to think of Creator as someone who was in a temple or wanted them to do good just for a reward. Creator wants them to do good because doing good is the right thing to do, whether they receive a reward for it or not. But long ago, long, long ago, when peace came to this land, the priests began to stop wandering. They built temples and began telling others about Creator. It did not take long for Creator to become 'The Creator.' They made him from the one who created everything, to nothing more than a tool. Something they could use. They use his name like some object. They say, 'Hand me the hammer or I need the bucket.'" Adoni took a deep breath then let it out, and began again, only so quietly, that Hanna and Colton could just barely hear him, "They say 'The Creator' because they want to use him and when they feel they are done, they just toss him away, until they need him again. Then they go to the shelf and pull him off as if he was nothing more than a book, collecting dust from sitting for so long."

They all sat there. Adoni stared into the fire. Colton stared at Adoni, and Hanna stared at the two of them. She was the one to break the silence, "Isn't that what you told me, Colton?" He and Adoni looked at her. Colton's expression was asking her what she meant. "You said that you found something that said just what he said. That priests used to travel the world and help the helpless. Defend the defenseless."

She continued to look at him, and Adoni put his eyes on Colton as well, then asked, "What did you find?"

Colton looked at him then at Hanna, and then went back to eating his meal, "It doesn't matter," he said just before he took a bite of fish. When he had finished with it, he continued, "What I found, no one else believes. They all said it was the old ways and times have changed."

"And so they have; but Creator never does," Adoni said. "He remains the same now as he did when people first called out to him. It is the people who have changed. They chose to believe more in themselves than they do in him, and because of that, they forgot that Creator is the reason they exist."

Colton looked at Adoni, and even though he believed what he had just said, Colton knew he was the only one in the priesthood who did. "A single person's beliefs do not matter if everyone else is telling them they are wrong."

Adoni had a response for that as well, "Maybe

the person just hasn't found the right people to tell their beliefs to."

Colton was almost ready to believe just that, but he knew one person was not enough to make a difference in the entire world. He had spent many nights lying awake in his bed dreaming of the day when he would be a full priest and be able to tell others what he had learned. If the church would not let him teach in their temples, then he would build his own. Now, with his expulsion from the priesthood, he would never have the title of priest. "It doesn't matter what I believe. I am not a priest and never will be."

"Or you are a priest and always have been," Adoni said, which brought a response out of Hanna.

"Colton has definitely not always been a priest."

She said it with a smile, and even though what she had said was at his expense, he was glad it had brought a smile to her face, and he had to smile with her, and agree. "I spent my early seasons on the streets of Maridian. That does not sound like the life of a priest."

"Not to mention he had the entire city believing he was helping them when actually everything he did was to help himself." Once again, Hanna was smiling, and Colton did as well.

"She is telling the truth," Colton said, to agree with her. "I stole sometimes, and even though I did help people, I did it to live and to earn coin."

Hanna wanted to make sure Adoni knew her

opinion of Colton's previous life. "That doesn't sound too much like a priest," she said.

"I said he was a priest, not a saint," Adoni said, and gave Hanna a look, then turned to face Colton. "You might have stolen, but I am quite sure many people who have become priests have stolen a thing or two before they joined the priesthood. I am also sure there are a number of priests who never stole a thing in their entire life until they joined the priesthood and started receiving offerings from their congregation. They steal while being a priest, and you stole before you became one. Who do you think Creator shines his light on between the two?"

Colton thought about what Adoni had said but he still believed he was the only one who thought as he did. Even though Adoni seemed to believe the same way, what would one expelled man from the priesthood and one crazy man with a mule be able to do?

"There is no telling what a person can do when Creator shines his light on them," Adoni said, and Colton felt as if the man had just responded to what he had been thinking to himself. Before he could say anything, Adoni continued, "The priests today are nothing more than fare collectors. They take coin from people who think they will be rewarded based on their good deeds, and how much coin they give."

"But doesn't the Crea..." Before she could finish the sentence, Adoni gave her a hostile look so Hanna stopped and corrected herself before he could say anything, "I mean, doesn't Creator want people to give coin to help others and do good things?"

Adoni relaxed. Not just because she had corrected herself, but for the first time, Hanna had asked a question without any cynicism in it. "Yes, Creator wants people to give some of their coin and help others, but not just so they can make themselves feel good, but so others will. A good deed is not a good deed if the heart that leads the person to do it is filled with pride and self-worth." He looked back into the fire. "As for the coin the priests collect, how much is put to filling the bellies of the hungry, and how much is put into the pockets of the ones who collect it?"

Even though he did not think Adoni had expected a response, Colton gave one, "Very little, if none at all." Adoni looked over to him and nodded. Both of them knew Colton had spoken the truth.

"Are you saying the priests are stealing coin?" Adoni and Colton both looked at Hanna, "Then why doesn't Creator do something about it?"

Even though Adoni could tell that she spoke with a bit of hostility, he did not fault her for it. One reason was because she had said "Creator" and not "The Creator." It might not be much, but even the smallest change in the right direction was an improvement. Another reason he could not fault her for the anger she had spoken with was because he knew that sometimes, if a person's anger was for the right reason, then they would act in the right way.

"Creator does not interfere with the choices an individual makes. That is the gift of free will. But as one with free will…," Adoni turned and looked at Colton, "…what can you do, knowing what the priesthood has become?"

Colton and Adoni stared at each other, but Hanna answered the question. "He can go back to the temple and tell everyone what the priests are doing. How they are taking everyone's coin and keeping it for themselves."

Adoni turned to face Hanna to give his reply, but Colton spoke up first, "That is not the way." Adoni turned and looked at Colton, waiting for him to continue. "You cannot point people to Creator by pointing out the wrong in others. Because all they will see is the wrong of the people and then they will believe in Creator even less or not at all. You have to set an example. People have to see what Creator is truly like, and they have to decide if they will choose to follow that example. They have to choose of their own free will."

Adoni smiled and gave his response, "Spoken like a true priest of Creator." Colton not only returned the smile, but with it, he felt as if he now knew what he was supposed to do. He even felt as if his expulsion from the priesthood was a blessing. If he had stayed, he would have had to change the way he believed. He would have had to start thinking like the other priests. If he did, how long would it take him to begin to believe the way they did? Now that he was out of the priesthood, he was not only free to follow his own beliefs but to live them. Live them for others to see.

"What, is Colton supposed to go off and be this wandering priest for the rest of his life?" Hanna asked, and once again, there was mockery in her question.

"Oh, maybe not for the rest of his life; just long enough to let others know what he has learned so they can pass it on to others," Adoni said.

Adoni might not believe it would take him his entire life, but to Colton, he thought it would, but if it did, then he was alright with it. "How do I begin?" Adoni turned and looked at him. "You seem to know a lot about Creator and what he wants from us. You can tell me how to begin, and you can join me as well."

Adoni laughed, reached down to his left, and picked up a long stick. He then held it out in his right hand and stirred the embers of the fire. "I am too old to be gallivanting around the world showing people what Creator requires of them. No, I am more suited for frying fish and cooking vegetables. And as for how you should begin, I think you already have."

"What do you mean?" Hanna asked.

Adoni turned his head to look at her, "He has left the priesthood." He then turned back to face Colton, "And by your appearance, you seem to fit right in with the first priests of Creator. When they set out on their journey, all they took with them were two sets of robes, a set of sandals, a staff, a horse, and a few supplies."

Hanna looked directly at Colton who was staring at her and then she said what they both were thinking, "That is exactly what Colton has."

"Well then, it seems that he is more of a priest than what he thought he was," Adoni said.

"But how can he survive off of what little he has?" Hanna asked.

"Creator will provide," Colton said, knowing the answer somehow.

"Yes, he always does," Adoni said, as he continued to poke at the embers. "The old priests did not just go around and tell others about Creator. They protected the people as well. Where there was injustice, they would bring justice. Where there was strife, they would bring peace. Where there was hopelessness, they would bring hope."

"And he is going to do that with a wooden stick?" Hanna asked and once again she spoke with disbelief.

"It is not a stick; it is a staff," Adoni said then stood. He then held the stick he had out in front of him so the tip was as far away from his body as it could reach. "A priest's staff is not just a piece of wood. It is a representation of his beliefs. A priest who can wield a staff can go up against anything, knowing Creator is with him as he takes on the most impossible task. Because it is not he, nor the staff, that will bring him through it, but Creator himself."

"Well, he definitely knows how to wield that staff," Hanna said.

Adoni sat back down and laid the stick next to him. "I'm surprised the priesthood even continues with training the new priest with it. I have not seen a full priest carry one in a long time."

"They don't," Colton said. "Not even the priest who taught me to use a staff. They taught by drawings and explaining what they wanted us to do."

"And you learned how to do all you showed me from some drawings and talk?" Hanna asked.

"Well, I sort of practiced a lot on my own. Mostly when no one else was around." When Colton had finished, he looked over at Adoni and saw that the man had a very big smile on his face. "What?" he asked.

"A priest from the beginning to the end," Adoni said. He then stood up, bringing his waterskin with him. He went over to Hanna and filled her cup, which she had extended to him. He then went over and poured some into Colton's cup, noticing that the young man had a lot to consider. Like whether he was going to become a priest or was he already one.

Adoni then walked over and sat back down on his own stool, filled his cup, then placed the waterskin back on the ground at his feet. He swallowed every bit of drink he had. "Ah, that is some good stuff." He then turned and looked at Hanna who went back to eating her food. Even though she had a mouthful of fish, he asked her a question, "So, what is your story?"

She looked at him and then at Colton who was staring back at her. They had been talking the entire time about Colton and had never even mentioned what she had been through just recently. She had a feeling that it was her time to tell Adoni what they were doing in the woods. The only problem was that she was not sure herself.

SIX

anna continued to chew her food, knowing that as soon as she finished Adoni would want an answer as to the reason she was out in the woods with Colton.

"She was attacked by a woman," Colton said since Hanna was not ready to speak.

Adoni turned and looked at him and then turned back to face Hanna, "Well that sounds like something the city guards could help you with, definitely not a reason to be out here with an old man," the mule then sounded again, "Yes, yes, an old man and his mule. I did not forget about you," Adoni said looking at the mule who had turned its head to give its opinion, then it turned its head to go back to staring at the ground. "I think sometimes that mule believes he is the center of everything." Adoni then put his focus back on Hanna, "Now where were we? Oh yes, you were about to tell me about this woman."

Hanna swallowed the bit of food she had in her mouth so there was nothing stopping her from explaining what had happened. Except she did not want to, because if she did, she would have to realize it was not all just a bad dream. She looked at Adoni then looked across to Colton, "I am sure it was a misunderstanding." She then turned back to Adoni, "When we return to Maridian it will be cleared up."

"We cannot go back to Maridian," Colton said to re-emphasize what they had been discussing before their host had appeared. "We need to get as far away as we can, from Maridian and the woman."

Both he and Hanna went quiet. Adoni altered his gaze between them but since they were trying to stare down each other, he decided a third person's outlook on the situation might be helpful. "It is obvious the two of you have come to an impasse. Perhaps I can be of some assistance. If you tell me what you know, then maybe I can shed some light through the cloud passing overhead."

With the look on Hanna's face, Colton knew she was not going to say anything. "I knew Hanna was in danger. When I arrived at her place, I found her outside. There was a woman standing in front of her, even though I did not know it was a woman until after she had fallen to the ground. I knocked her unconscious. I grabbed Hanna and brought her out here. Now she wants to go back to Maridian where I am sure she will still be in danger."

Adoni looked over to Hanna, but she did not add anything to Colton's explanation, so he turned back to continue the discussion with Colton, "How did you know Hanna was in danger?"

Colton looked at Hanna before he answered, "It

was a feeling I had. Something told me that I had to get her out of the city, but even then, she still would not be safe so I must get her as far away as possible. From the way the feeling came over me, I am sure it came from Creator."

Adoni was happy to see that Colton had not reverted to once again calling Creator, "The Creator." To him, it meant the priests' teachings had not interfered with what was in the young man's heart. What Creator had placed there long before he had even entered the priesthood. "What else can you tell me about the woman?" Adoni asked.

Colton took a few breaths to think, "Nothing, it was dark out, and I had come up behind her. I was not able to see her face. When she was lying on the ground unconscious, I was in too much of a hurry to get Hanna out of there to stop and examine her closer."

Adoni and Colton were looking at each other. Until Hanna said two words, "Her skin," then they turned their heads to look at her. She waited a moment before she began to speak again, but both Colton and Adoni could see that she was thinking back to what happened. "It was pale white. I did not see it when she was in my bedchamber. I was lying in bed with my back toward her. When I felt her close to me, I grabbed the candleholder, sat up, and swung it around to hit her. The flame of the candle had gone out, so I was not able to see her then." Hanna stopped speaking for a moment. She remembered what happened next

141

but since she did not want to talk about it, she moved the story to the part where she was outside. "When I ran out the back of the house and turned around to see if she was following me, there was enough light from the moon for me to see her face. It was pale white." She stopped talking again, took her eyes off the fire where she had been staring while telling her story, and looked over to Adoni, "Her skin looked like the color of the moon itself."

Adoni held his gaze on Hanna for a moment then put his eyes back on the fire. "Did you see if she had any weapons?" Since neither of them answered, he turned and looked at Hanna who shook her head to let him know she had not. He then turned and looked at Colton.

"No, I did not see any, but her cloak could have been covering any weapons she had."

Adoni scoffed, "Oh, I am sure she had some," he said then put his eyes back on the fire.

Colton and Hanna exchanged looks. To them, it was apparent he knew something about the mystery woman. Even though Hanna would like nothing more than to forget what happened, her curiosity got the better of her, "Do you know who she is?" she asked Adoni.

He picked up the stick he had sat down and started turning the embers in the fire, "Yes, I know." He did not say anything else.

Colton asked to hear the answer both he and Hanna wanted, "Who is she?"

He continued to stir the embers, but began talking, "She is a descendent of the Elves. She is an assassin, and she is also the warrior of Moon."

Hanna and Colton took their eyes off Adoni and looked at each other, both having more questions about the answer the old man had given them. "Who is Moon?" Hanna asked, referring to the last item Adoni had mentioned, which to her, was not the strangest of his statements.

Adoni turned his head to look at her, "Moon is not a 'Who,' Moon is Moon."

Hanna immediately did not like what she had heard, so she did not speak. Colton had no problem with continuing the conversation. "You mean like the moon in the sky?"

Adoni turned and looked at him, "Not like, is the moon in the sky. Moon is Moon just as Sun is Sun."

"I do not understand," Colton said.

Once again, Adoni admired the man for his admittance of lack of knowledge. "Perhaps I should tell you both the entire story of Sun and Moon." Adoni received a nod from Colton to let him know he would appreciate all he could tell them. Then Adoni turned to look at Hanna who was once again staring into the fire; looking as if her thoughts were far away, maybe even in the past. Since she would hear what he was going to say, he began with his story.

"Creator created the world. He created the great lands, and the great waters, and all the life that dwelt in the two places. He also created two

Guardians to watch over the lands and the waters and all the creatures that made the two places their homes. Creator placed the great lands into the care of Sun, and to Moon, the great waters. Each was responsible for watching over their given domain. It was not long before Sun and Moon became like so many other siblings."

He stopped talking so Colton asked his question, "What is that?"

Adoni turned and looked at him, "They each became jealous of the other and wanted what the other had; believing what Creator had given to the other was better than what they had themselves." Adoni turned back to look at the fire before he continued. "Moon saw all the land and all the plants and animals that lived there. Even though the great waters had their own animals and even their own plants, Moon wanted the ones Sun had. Sun saw how the great waters could move freely. The land could not do that. Even though Sun could shed light on the great waters, Sun's heat could only penetrate so far below the surface of the great waters."

He stopped talking but Colton knew the story was not over. "What happened?" he asked Adoni who continued to look into the fire and continued with the story.

"Sun and Moon fought. Sun used the heat Sun had and burned the waters trying to make them evaporate completely away. Moon controlled the great waters and tried to force it up onto the great lands, hoping to cover it all."

"Since they are both still here, it is obvious they did not succeed," Colton said.

"No, they did not. But they would have if Creator had not separated the two."

He stopped talking again. Hanna had been listening the entire time and wanted to know how the story ended. She wanted to know about Sun and Moon. She needed to know. "What did Creator do?" she asked.

Both Adoni and Colton looked at her, surprised when she spoke. After Adoni smiled at her, he continued. "When Creator created Sun and Moon, he placed them in the sky and they were able to travel freely so they could watch over the domain given to them. But since they continued to battle one another, Creator took his sword and severed the space between them. He separated them in the sky so that they would never be able to be on the same side of Eirene together. Sun on one side of the world, and Moon on the other, and then Creator forbade them to use their powers to harm either the great lands or the great waters." Adoni then turned back to look at the fire. "But even though they were no longer able to be next to each other, their hatred for one another continued, and to this day they are determined to fight." He stopped talking once again.

"What does this have to do with the woman who attacked me?" Hanna asked.

Adoni turned and looked at her, "Since Moon cannot attack Sun directly, Moon blessed the woman. She is Moon's warrior."

"So why does she want to kill Hanna?" Colton asked.

Adoni was still looking at Hanna, but he knew she was not going to answer the question. Since she was not going to tell him, he would. Adoni turned his head to look at Colton. "As the woman who attacked Hanna is the warrior of Moon, it is safe to say that Hanna is the warrior of Sun."

"No, I am not!" She jumped up, turned around, and took a few steps away from her stool, but kept her back toward the other two.

Both Adoni and Colton watched her, but when Colton stood to go to Hanna, Adoni used the stick he was holding to stop him; he nodded to the young man to return to his seat to give Hanna some time alone. Colton did not want to but did as the elderly man had advised. Now seated again, and with Hanna standing away from them, Adoni continued with his story. "Moon and Sun cannot hurt each other, so they each chose their own warrior. Warriors to be given gifts by each of the Guardians to represent a part of them. But as well as the gifts, they also will give their warriors the passion, anger, and hatred Moon and Sun have for each other."

They were all quiet for a moment, and finally, Colton could not keep silent any longer. He had to know. "Hanna?" he said from where he was, and she turned around to look at him. "Is what he said true?"

She looked at Colton and answered, "No. I am no warrior of Sun, and I do not have any hate, or anger toward Moon."

Adoni did not hesitate to let her know what he saw in her. "You have no hate for Moon, but your hate and anger for Sun is more than obvious."

"Sun ruined my life!" she said and not only moved to the stool she was using, but passed it, and went over to Adoni. She bent down and grabbed hold of him by the front of his shirt, which forced him to stand as well. "Sun took everything away from me. That day when I was five, Sun might have stopped those Mountain Raiders, but when the people of my village saw what happened they started calling me Wicked Girl. Then everyone stopped buying my father's crafts. It forced him to take my mother and me to Maridian where those men murdered him. When he died, so did my mother's reason for living. She died from a broken heart." She then shoved Adoni so hard, he fell backward over his stool and onto the ground. He sat there looking up at Hanna who finished what she had to say, "Sun had talked to me for as long as I could remember, and what Sun did on that day was the start of my life becoming nothing more than one lost after another." She turned, walked back over to her own stool, and sat down. "I have had nothing to do with Sun since that day and want nothing to do with Sun now."

Colton sat through the entire scene between Hanna and Adoni. Now that she had stopped talking and was sitting down, he walked over and helped Adoni up, back onto his stool. Once seated, Colton returned to his own stool and took his seat. He still waited a few moments to let tempers fade, and even though she did not want to talk about it, he had to ask, "What happened that day?" From the look she gave him, he knew that like a lot of her past, she was not going to talk about it.

"I take it that was the day that Sun marked you," Adoni said looking at Hanna. He was not even upset about her pushing him to the ground. "Sun marked her as Sun's warrior, but because she did not receive the full blessing of Sun, the warrior of Moon was able to sense her, and found her. If she had Sun's full blessing, the woman who attacked her would not have even been able to sense her at all."

"Then can she hide from this woman if Sun blesses her?" Colton asked, seeing a solution to Hanna's safety.

"I will have nothing to do with Sun!" Hanna said, and with the way she spoke, Colton was sure she was adamant about her decision.

"If Sun blessed her, then yes, the chosen warrior of Moon would not be able to find her." Adoni saw that Hanna was about to repeat what she had said to Colton, so he quickly continued with what he wanted to say, "But if Sun did bless her, then she would have the same hatred and anger the other one has,

only it would be against Moon and Moon's warrior."
He turned and looked at Colton. "I am afraid that at
this point it is all or nothing, and by nothing, I mean
the death of Hanna."

"What do you mean?" Colton asked.

"She was touched by Sun all those seasons ago
and carries the mark with her to this day. If the warrior of Moon gets close enough to Hanna, then she
will be able to sense her and will do everything she
can to find Hanna and kill her. Once touched by a
Guardian, forever touched."

Colton looked from Adoni over to Hanna, "That
mark on the back of your right hand. The one you
have had ever since I have known you. That is where
Sun touched you." As he spoke, Hanna covered the
back of her right hand up with her left. As if being
out of sight would make the problem go away, but
she knew it would not.

"Even before the day you received the mark, you
were part of Sun's plans," Adoni said, and Hanna
turned to look at him. "You cannot hide it from the
one that is after you, and you cannot hide it from
yourself. You are a part of this and will be until the
end."

"What end?" Colton asked with concern in his
words.

Adoni turned and faced him, "To the end of this
woman or to Hanna. Moon and Sun have chosen
them to do battle. To battle each other since Sun
and Moon cannot do battle themselves. They will

use their warriors to continue what they started from the time Creator created them."

Colton looked at Hanna. He was sure his face was showing how much he was worried about what Adoni had said, but Hanna looked as if she was angry "I am not going to fight anyone," Hanna said to let Colton know what her plan was. "I do not care about some battle between Sun and Moon, or about some woman Moon has chosen. I want nothing to do with any of them."

"I am afraid you have no choice," Adoni said and Hanna turned to look at him. "This warrior of Moon has found you, and even though I do not know why she did not kill you when she first came to you, I have no doubt, that the next time you meet her, she will not hesitate to end your life." He had one more thing to say, "And there will be a next time. That I am sure of."

Hanna thought she had a solution of her own, "Then I will talk to her, and I will tell her how foolish it is to let anyone control her, especially just so Moon can watch her kill me. She will understand."

"And if she doesn't?" Colton asked.

Hanna paused for just a moment then answered, "Then I will make her understand. There is no reason for her to kill me because I am not going to try to kill her. I am not a killer. I run a boarding house."

"You may not be a killer, but she is," Adoni said and saw that Hanna did not know what he was speaking of. "I know more about her than you do. I have heard stories of a woman with skin as pale as Moon and black hair as dark as night. Who wears a black cloak all the time to hide from the rays of Sun. A woman who carries not one but two fighting daggers. One black as night and one white as the moon." He took three breaths to let Hanna take in all he had said, then he continued.

"I told you that she is an assassin, as well as being descended from Elves. It is not just the fact that she joined the Assassin's Guild. Even though she would end up a killer even if she had not."

"What is she?" Colton asked, and Adoni turned to look at him.

"The Elves that she is descended from are a caste of killers. That is what Creator blessed them to be, and anyone from their bloodline will be the same. They bring death to death, and they are good at it. She is the warrior of Moon, an assassin, and comes from a caste of the Elves who kill because it is what they do. All three of those things allow her to be a very dangerous opponent." He then turned back to look at Hanna. "One who is not going to stop trying to kill you, because you have a talk with her. Before you speak your first word, she will have taken one of those daggers of hers and placed it in a part of your body, someplace where she can watch your eyes as your life drains from you."

"Then I will take Hanna far away from here, someplace where this woman will not be able to find her."

Adoni looked at Colton, "That might delay the outcome for a while, but this woman now knows of Hanna's existence. She will not stop hunting her until she finds her and ends her life. Moon has not only given the woman the color of her skin and those daggers but also the hatred and anger Moon has for Sun, as well as the determination to do battle." He turned back to look at Hanna, "Nyght is coming for you, that I am sure of."

"What does that mean?" Hanna asked.

"That is the name she goes by. From what I understand, Moon gave it to her on the night the woman received Moon's blessings. Although the spelling is different. Not N-I-G-H-T as in the night, or even K-N-I-G-H-T, as in a man that rides a horse. No, she spells it N-Y-G-H-T. It is spelled the way when all races of the world of Eirene spoke the same language."

"It doesn't matter how she spells her name!" Colton said and stood up from his stool so fast that it fell over behind him, "This woman is going to kill Hanna if we do not do something about it!"

"I am afraid my dear priest," Adoni said in a very calm tone, "there is nothing we can do. Hanna does not wish to be blessed by Sun, and without that blessing, she will not be able to stop her."

"Then I will!" Colton said staring down at Adoni.

"And how will you do that? The woman is a born killer," Adoni said.

"Then we will have her taken into custody for

trying to kill Hanna," Colton said, trying to come up with a solution.

"I would love to see that. Being the person that she is, she would have no problem with anyone who tried to take her into custody. And even if you sent armies against her, which would be what it would take to stop her, she would just retreat, knowing that her enemy outnumbered her, but eventually, she would once again come after Hanna. And she will not stop until Hanna, or she is dead, and we both know you are not up to that task." When Adoni said the last part, Colton's expression changed. He then turned around, placed his stool back in the upright position, and sat back down.

"What does he mean?" Hanna asked, hearing the comment Adoni had made and seeing the reaction of Colton.

"Do not think you are less of a person for it priest," Adoni said to Colton but then explained to Hanna. "A true priest of Creator cannot take a life. No matter what they might do."

Hanna looked from Adoni over to Colton, "Why not?"

Adoni continued with the explanation, "Every living being has a part of Creator in them. A true priest of Creator cannot only sense that part but can feel it. If the priest were to kill someone, when the person dies, the priest would feel their death as well. And being a true priest of Creator, they would not be able to live with themselves for taking a life."

He then turned and looked at Colton, "So to put it simply, a priest that kills someone kills themselves."

They all remained silent for a few breaths, then Hanna spoke. "But you both said the old priests would go around and help others. They would defend the defenseless. Surely when they did, they had to go up against someone they had no choice in taking their life."

Adoni did not have a chance to answer, because Colton did, "A true priest of Creator would die before they took the life of another. The death at the hands of someone else would be less painful than what they would feel by taking a life."

Hanna did not doubt that Colton was speaking the truth. "Did they teach you that at the priesthood?" she asked.

He looked at her and gave his answer, "I just know." It was the way he said it that let her know no one had taught him about what they were discussing.

"It does not matter if Colton will not take the woman's life. She received training to be an assassin and I am not talking about the Assassin's Houses on this side of Eirene. She learned at the Assassin's Guild. The very first Assassin's Guild created. Unlike our priest here, she can take a life without even losing a single bit of sleep."

"Then we have no choice but to run," Colton said to get the subject back on the woman and off him. "You said she came from the other side of Eirene, but she is here now, so I will take Hanna to the other side of the world."

"And when Nyght finds out where you have taken her and follows, then what will you do? Bring her back to this land, and when the warrior of Moon finds out where she is again, and comes looking for her, will you travel across the great waters for a third time? The two of you would be running for the rest of your lives, which will not last long with Nyght seeking you."

Hanna spoke up to give her opinion of the situation, "If we cannot get the city guard to hold her, then we can hire our own assassin to stop her. I have some coin saved up."

"No! I will not be part of taking someone's life," Colton said, and Hanna could tell he would not change his mind.

"It wouldn't matter anyway," Adoni said and the two looked at him. "No assassin will go after one of their own. It is a rule they have and one they follow to the letter."

"Then we have no options," Colton said and began listing all the things they had come up with. "This Nyght will not listen to reason. We cannot run without her pursuing Hanna for the rest of her life. The Assassin's Guild will not go after her, and I will have no part in taking her life."

"Then that leaves us with only one," Hanna said. Both Adoni and Colton looked at her. She took a deep breath and then continued, even though she did not want to even say what she was thinking, "I will ask Sun for help."

"How?" Colton asked.

Hanna looked up into the sky and saw the sun's rays passing through the tops of the trees then looked back down at Colton. "I have not spoken to Sun for many seasons. And once I stopped speaking to Sun, Sun stopped speaking to me. But now I will talk to Sun." She looked over to Adoni, and he nodded once, to agree with what she had decided to do.

Hanna once again looked up to the sky and thought to Sun, *"Sun, do you hear me?"* She waited a few moments then asked again, *"Sun, are you there? Can you hear me?"* Still, Sun did not respond. She lowered her head and looked at Adoni then at Colton. "I don't think Sun hears me."

Adoni chuckled, "Oh, Sun hears you, that I am sure of. Sun is just being a spoiled child!" He said the last part looking up to the sky, and then looked back at Hanna. "It appears that since you abandoned Sun, Sun does not feel a need to help you now."

"How can you be sure Sun knows what is happening with Hanna?"

Adoni turned and looked at Colton, "When Sun is overhead, Sun can see and hear all that is going on in the great lands. No doubt, Sun is sitting up in the sky, basking in arrogance with what our dear Hanna is now facing." Adoni looked over to Hanna. "Of course, Sun's ego is Sun's weak point as well."

"But you said Sun was going to use Hanna to

fight the warrior of Moon. So why won't Sun help her now?"

Adoni looked at Colton, "Oh, I am sure Sun will help her, she just has to do some groveling before Sun will even respond to her calling."

"I am not going to grovel," Hanna said adamantly.

"What could it hurt?" Colton said, but with the look Hanna was giving him, he knew he should not have said what he had.

"There might be another way?" Adoni said and Hanna and Colton stopped staring at each other and turned to face him. "Hanna will need to show Sun that she is committed to what Sun desires. That she will be the warrior of Sun and fight the warrior of Moon."

"And how can she do that?" Colton asked.

Adoni turned and looked at Hanna, "By going to the land where Sun shines the brightest."

"And where is that?" Colton asked.

Adoni kept his eyes on Hanna, "To the great desert to the west of here. Out in the middle of the desert sand, Moon has no control. Even though Moon can see the desert when Moon is in the sky over it, there is no water or the water is so deep and there is so much land, Moon cannot affect a single bit of life." Adoni turned and looked at Colton, "There, Hanna might convince Sun that she has returned and is willing to take on the title of Sun's warrior."

"I did not say I would become Sun's warrior. All I said was that we could ask Sun for help."

Paul W. Gibbs

Adoni turned back to look at her, "The only help Sun will give you, is the help Sun will benefit from. Which is for you to become Sun's warrior. Sun will not help in any other way."

Colton then came up with another plan. "Why doesn't Sun just choose someone else to be the warrior? Somebody who wants the title. Then they can go after this Nyght, and the two of them can do battle."

Adoni looked back at Colton, "That is not possible as long as Hanna still has the mark of Sun from her youth. Sun and Moon can only choose one mortal to be their warrior at a time. And since Sun has already touched Hanna, she is the only one who can receive the blessing of Sun." He then looked at Hanna, "At least as long as she is still alive, and since we are trying to figure out how to keep her that way, then I don't think killing her ourselves is an option." Colton and Hanna did not say it, but they agreed wholeheartedly.

"We need to decide what we are going to do," Colton said and stood, "We are still close to Maridian, and this Nyght might not be too far behind us." He looked over at Hanna, "I suggest we head west and make for the desert. As we travel, we can discuss what we can do once we arrive. If we keep on the move, it will be more difficult for this woman to catch up to us."

"I agree," Adoni said and stood as well. "We make for the desert. It will take at least ten sun-cycles, at a hard ride, to reach it and by the time we get there, I am sure we will come up with a plan to save Hanna." For some reason, Hanna thought Adoni did not have too much faith in the last part of his statement.

Colton faced Adoni to address his concern. "We thank you for your hospitality, sir, but we cannot ask you to join us. It is dangerous enough for us, with an assassin at our backs."

"An assassin that is descended from Elves that kill, as well as an assassin who has been blessed by Moon. So yes, it will be dangerous, but I was heading that way myself so I might as well travel with you." The mule sounded again, and Adoni leaned to his left to look around Colton, "Yes, you are coming as well, you crazy mule. You didn't think I was going to walk there on my own two feet, did you?" He then leaned back up and smiled at Colton, who was really hoping the man would change his mind about joining them. Even though Adoni had been very helpful, not just with what Hanna was facing, but with his doubts about being a priest as well, Colton thought the man was not all there in the head, and maybe the mule was the more sensible of the two. "It is settled then. You two go back to your camp and prepare your belongings. I will pack up my camp and join you at yours. Then together we will all go to the great desert." Adoni turned, grabbed his stool, and went over to his mule to pack.

Colton walked over to Hanna who was now standing as well, took her by her left arm, turned her, and gave her a nudge to start walking, quickly. When they were away from Adoni's camp Hanna asked her question, "Are you in so much of a hurry to get to the desert that you have to pull me through these woods?"

Colton continued to walk, holding onto Hanna's hand to make sure she kept up with him. "I am in a hurry to get on the road and even to the desert. But I am in more of a hurry to leave before our friend we just left joins us. We have horses and he only has that mule of his, and he will only slow us down."

She understood his reasoning, but in her mind, slowing down might be the best thing for her to do. No, she did not want this woman called Nyght to kill her, but she did not want to go and talk to Sun either. Hanna had stopped talking to Sun a long time ago. So long, it all seemed to be a bad dream. A nightmare. It was because of what Sun did that caused her family to have to go to Maridian, where both her mother and father died. Sun was the cause of her problems, and Hanna knew that no matter what Colton thought, or even Adoni, Sun was not going to help her. At least not in a way where she would not have to surrender to what Sun wanted her to be.

As soon as they reached their camp, Colton began gathering their things together. Since the one saddle was still lying next to the horse when Hanna had tried to saddle it to head back to Maridian, Colton started with it. He did have to grab the blanket and place it on the horse because Hanna had not even attempted to do that earlier. Colton figured it was not because she was in a hurry to leave, just that she did not know the blanket went on before the saddle.

As he was tightening up the straps to the saddle, Hanna came over and stood on the other side of the horse. "I don't want to become Sun's warrior."

Colton looked up and into her eyes. He walked around to the side she was on to speak with her, "What if it is the only way you will be able to stop this assassin?"

Hanna gave her answer, "I would rather die."

Colton knew she was serious in what she said. He could only turn and go back to the side of the horse where he had been. Once there, he started working but responded to Hanna's statement. "That is a very selfish thing to say."

"Why?" Hanna asked from the other side of the horse.

"Because Creator gave you life. To want to die shows that you do not have respect or care for those that love you."

Hanna walked around to the side where he was, and even though she was looking at him, he still kept his eyes on what he was doing, "The Creator took all the ones who loved me away. I have no one." She then turned and walked over to where their supplies were.

Colton took another moment to adjust the straps to the saddle even though he finished with them before Hanna finished talking. He just needed more time to deal with what Hanna had said, and to keep his response about how all the ones who loved her were no longer with her, to himself. He also noticed she had gone back to calling Creator, "The Creator." Once again, she was showing her animosity toward Creator, not only for the death of her family, but also for everything that had happened to her. Colton could have told her, Sun was the beginning of her problems, but he was sure she would only say something like, "Then why didn't the Creator stop Sun?" Which Colton had no answer to.

He turned around and headed back over to the second saddle and blanket. He put the second item on top of the first then picked them up, holding them at his waist, "We can head for the desert and if we can come up with a better solution then we will try it, but for now, Sun is the only one that can help us." As he spoke, he kept his eyes off her, but when he finished, and she did not give any type of response, he looked at her and saw her staring at something behind him. He turned around and standing at the edge of the clearing where they had stopped to rest, sat Adoni on top of his mule. Not only had he packed up his supplies and arrived before Colton had a chance to saddle the second horse, but the man had ridden that mule of his through the woods.

When Colton and Hanna had walked through them, they had to push aside branches and go around trees, but somehow Adoni had no problem with bringing his mule through the dense forest. Not only that, but Colton did not even hear the man or mule coming up on them.

"I'm ready when you are," Adoni said, with a great deal of excitement.

It was apparent to Colton, that there was more to Adoni than what Adoni was letting on. Colton did not know what to expect as they traveled to the great desert to try to communicate with Sun, but he was sure it was going to be very interesting.

Hanna saw Adoni enter their camp but did not put any thought into how fast he had arrived. When she had seen him, it only reminded her about what she was about to do. She had spent so much time not thinking about Sun, and now that was all she could do.

She decided she would go to the desert and even talk to Sun, but no matter what, she was determined not to become the warrior of Sun, that she was sure of. At least that was what she was telling herself. What was in her mind and what was in her heart were two different things.

SEVEN

The ride to the desert normally would have taken ten sun-cycles, but with the pace they were moving, they would be lucky to make it in a full cycle of the moon. Colton thought Adoni would have been the one to slow them down because all he had to ride was his mule. The elderly man and his mule were not the problem, Hanna was. She had never ridden a horse before on her own and had trouble controlling it, as well as staying on it.

When they had left Maridian, Colton placed Hanna on his horse with him because she appeared to be in shock with all the things that had happened to her. Even when he stopped to switch horses they rode together, but when they set off for the desert, he wanted her to ride by herself to make it easier on the horses and it would help them move faster. At least that was what he thought.

When he gathered the supplies before he left Maridian, he also brought a change of clothing for Hanna. Since he knew she would be riding a horse, he gave her a shirt and a pair of trousers to wear instead of the dress she had on when he arrived at her house. He also gave her a pair of boots, which she definitely needed since she had run out of her house with nothing on her feet. Even with the change in clothing, it did not help her to ride any better.

The only thing Hanna accomplished without much trouble was when she climbed onto the back of her horse for the first time. She had seen other people performing the task, so it was easy to duplicate. As for using her legs to steady herself while on the horse, she had to learn that on her own. She also had trouble controlling the direction the horse moved in. Either she pulled on the reins too tight, causing the horse to jerk its body, or she did not use enough force and the horse did not change directions when she needed it to. Before the day was over and to make it easier for all of them, Colton rode next to her or in front of her, holding onto the reins of her horse so he could guide it.

Even without the task of leading the horse, Hanna still had trouble when it came to remaining on its back. The first time she fell off was when she was trying to control the horse herself, and she pulled too hard on the reins and the horse turned to its right. It was smart enough to lower its head to avoid the branch to the tree it walked under, so it would not hit him. Hanna was not as smart or she just did not see the branch, but when it struck her upper body, she flipped over the back end of the horse. Colton, who was coming up behind her to get her and her horse back on the correct path, jumped off his own horse to help. By the time he reached her, Hanna was already back on her feet, her pride hurt more than her bottom.

As Colton tried to help her back on her horse, she pushed his hands away and tried to climb back up on her own. She swung her right leg too far over and tumbled off the other side of the horse, which having had enough of her abuse walked away. When it had moved, Colton stood there looking down at Hanna sitting on the ground with her head down. Since she was not looking at him, and he could tell it might be best for him to give her a few moments alone, he walked off in the direction her horse had gone.

When he thought both the horse and Hanna had taken a long enough break, he walked it over to her, and he was sure he felt the horse resisting being led to the woman who had fallen off twice.

When he reached her, Hanna was still sitting on the ground. When he reached down to help her up, Colton thought she would push him away, but she was so tired of everything that had happened, that she rose as he took her by her arm and brought her to her feet. He then positioned her on the horse's left side. She placed her hand on the top of the saddle and her right foot in the stirrup. Colton was about to tell her that she had to use her other foot, but she realized her mistake before he could say anything, and she made the adjustment herself. She then pulled herself up and to make sure she did not repeat the same thing as before, Colton grabbed her left arm before she fell off on the other side.

He waited until he was sure she was sitting as steady as she could then turned toward the horse's head. As he walked by it, he patted it on the side of its neck, as if to apologize for what the woman was putting it through. He then took hold of the reins and guided the horse back to where they needed to be, grabbing his own along the way.

When they reached the path they had been traveling on, Colton guided the horses onto it and took a quick glance at Adoni who had been sitting on his mule watching the entire amusing scene. Adoni only smiled as if to say it was no one's fault, but Colton was sure the mule had shaken its head as if to say, the woman was useless when it came to riding. Colton was ready to agree with the mule.

When they began to travel again, Colton kept a hold of the reins to Hanna's horse, but when he tried to speed all of them up, Hanna told him to slow down because she was about to fall. It was the first words she had spoken since they left their little camp, and with the way she said them, Colton knew she was not happy with the way they were traveling. To avoid another incident with her falling off the horse, Colton reduced their speed to a very, very, slow walk. He thought that if he walked on foot, they would make better time but did not tell Hanna.

By the time the sun had started to set, Hanna

had started to complain about how much her bottom was hurting. Colton took that as a sign that they had traveled enough for the first day. He made sure not to turn around and look in the direction they had come from because he was afraid he would have been able to see the same trees they had left when they entered the road from their camp. He knew they had gone farther than that, but the amusing thought alone kept his spirits up.

When Colton had picked out a spot for them to rest for the night, he quickly dismounted so he would be able to help Hanna. Just as he turned to go over to her, he saw her slide down the side of the horse. She did not do it with any bit of grace or style, but at least she got down on her own. Of course, Colton could not help but think that when it came to horses, the one thing Hanna was good at was getting down from the back of one, even though the correct term was falling.

Just before she stepped away from her horse, Colton saw her give the animal a stare as if to say all of what happened to her was the horse's fault. Colton knew it was not, but he was not going to tell Hanna. All he did was watch her turn and stagger away from the animal, while she rubbed her bottom. Either to stop any pain she was feeling or to get feeling back into that part of her body. Colton turned his head to make sure she did not see him smiling at her discomfort. He felt sorry for her and the horse she was riding because he wanted to be back on the road before the first light of the sun. He just hoped Hanna and the horse were well rested.

Colton took care of his horse and Hanna's, since he thought she and her horse needed some time away from each other. While he did, she leaned against a tree, well out of his way, and well out of the way of her horse. It was obvious to Colton that Hanna had not sat down because of the way her rear was feeling, and once again, he had to make sure he was not facing her as the smile came to his face.

As he began to situate their supplies, he noticed that Adoni and his mule were not around. He did not see any sign of them. The clearing he found appeared to be a site used by other travelers as a resting point because it was wide enough and no trees were in the immediate area. Colton thought he would have been able to see if Adoni had left and which way he would have gone. Colton decided that he either must have been too busy with the horses or watching Hanna when their third companion went off on his own. Since the man was only traveling with them, Colton had no say in what the man did, so he put the thought out of his mind and went back to setting up the camp.

When he finished with the supplies, he pulled out his extra robe and laid it down on the ground in front of the spot where there were already rocks made into a small fire pit. He looked over to where Hanna was and saw her still leaning against the tree, although she positioned herself so her bottom did not connect with it. "You might be more comfortable if you come over here and lie down while I prepare our meal." He made sure he did not say, "sit down" because he knew she would not be able to. He also chose to use his spare robe instead of one of the horse blankets because he wanted to give her a break from anything dealing with horses. He did not wait for her to take him up on his offer; he just went back to setting up camp.

As he was rummaging through their meager supplies, out of the corner of his eye, Colton saw Hanna walk over to the robe he had spread out for her and take a seat. When she did, he saw the expression on her face when her bottom touched the ground, and once again, he had to control himself so he would not laugh. He did see Hanna adjust her position so that she was sitting/lying more on her side instead of her rear. It was obvious she was still feeling pain.

While they were riding, and to make up for the fact they were not moving very fast, Colton had them take their lunch while they walked the horses. They had a bit of bread and some water. Now having stopped for the night, they could take a bit more time to eat their evening meal. It just happened to be bread and water again.

When he reached the fire pit and was about to hand Hanna her portion of food, Adoni stepped back into the clearing. Colton saw that he had the reins of his mule in his left hand, but in his right, tied to a string, Adoni was carrying three fish. Colton looked at the man and thought he had not been gone long enough to catch three fish. Then Colton was wondering just where was the water supply that would even have what the man was carrying. Colton put the thought out of his mind, because since Adoni had the fish, then there had to be a river or stream to catch them. Colton was just thankful they would have something to eat besides bread.

"If you had told me you were going fishing, I would have given you a hand," Colton said as Adoni reached where he and Hanna were.

"Oh, I saw that you were busy and wanted to earn my keep." Adoni let go of the reins to his mule and it walked over to where the two horses were, tied to a tree at the edge of the camp. "But if you want to help, then you can clean them while I prepare the potatoes and carrots." He held the fish out to Colton who took them. "I will get you my skillet." Adoni started walking over to his mule.

"What can I do?" Hanna said, sitting/lying on her side.

Colton looked at her then turned his head to look at Adoni who had already turned to face him and Hanna. Adoni and Colton shared a moment then Colton turned back to face Hanna and told her what both he and Adoni thought she should do. "You just rest. You have had a long day, and we will be leaving early tomorrow. Adoni and I can take care of preparing the meal."

Colton had spoken in a pleasant and comforting

tone. Hanna still did not like it. She adjusted her position and even made a face when her bottom touched the ground, but she was able to stand and walk over to Colton and snatched the fish out of his hand. "I have been cleaning fish since I was two seasons old. I can do some of the work, just as you two can."

Colton could tell that no matter what he said, Hanna was not going to be happy. He wanted to let her take it easy because she had a rough time, but with the anger he saw in her eyes, which came from him trying to be nice, he knew the best thing he could do for both of them was to let Hanna do what she wanted to.

Adoni saved him by moving back over to the two, "Here you go," he said and gave Hanna the skillet and a knife. "I'll get the fire going so I can start boiling the water for the vegetables." He then moved over to the fire pit and pulled out a flint stone from one of his pockets.

Colton walked over to his and Hanna's supplies and picked up the waterskin. When he felt the weight, he noticed they did not have enough water to drink and to boil the water for the vegetables. He looked over to Adoni, who was bending over blowing the flames of the fire to get them to catch the few twigs he had placed in the pit, "How far away is the water where you caught the fish? I will need to fetch some for our meal."

Adoni stood up, "Oh I have plenty in my waterskin." He walked over to his mule, pulled out a waterskin, and started walking back to the fire. When he passed Colton, he handed him the bag. Colton noticed that it was full. He also remembered not seeing the bag before, nor did he ever see Adoni drinking from it. He was sure it was a different color than the bag he had the drink made from berries. He put the thought out of his mind, just thankful he did not have to go and fetch any water. Hanna was not the only one having a long day, and out of all three of them, Adoni seemed to be the only one full of energy.

With the fire going, Adoni made another trip to his mule and brought out a metal frame which he sat over the fire then he hooked the small cooking pot onto it. He pulled three potatoes and four carrots out of the pot, then poured in some water. While he was waiting for it to boil, he began cutting up the vegetables. Colton did not remember seeing him put the vegetables into the pot when he had pulled it out of his pack on his mule. Colton figured he had just not been paying attention.

With Adoni taking care of the vegetables, and Hanna taking care of the fish, Colton had nothing to do to help with the meal, so he decided to brush down the horses. Since Hanna's had the more stressful day, he figured he would start with it. He retrieved the brush from their supplies and walked to the right side of Hanna's horse. He faced it and started brushing its side. Adoni's mule was to his back, and it was only a few moments before the mule turned its head around and nipped Colton on his right shoulder. It did not hurt, but Colton was not happy with the animal, and when he turned to look at the mule, it had already turned its head to look forward.

Colton went back to brushing the horse, but before he had made two strokes, the mule bit him on the shoulder for a second time. "Ok, that is enough of that," Colton said as he turned to look at the mule who was once again facing forward. Colton turned and went back to brushing the horse, but right on cue, the mule bit him on his shoulder for a third time. "Fine then," Colton said and turned completely around and started brushing the mule. It took him about five passes of the brush before he realized that somehow, he knew what the mule had wanted. He stopped on his sixth stroke to think about what had just come to him.

"Something the matter?" Adoni yelled from over by the fire.

When Colton heard the man's voice, he came out of his thoughts. "No, everything is fine," he said looking at Adoni who was smiling. He then went back to working with the pot of vegetables and Colton went back to brushing the mule.

"I am glad you like it," Colton said and realized he had just spoken to the mule, because the mule had spoken to him, saying, *"That feels great."* Colton stopped again because he knew the mule had just passed the thought to him, even though mules cannot talk.

"Don't stop yet. That old codger never brushes

me." Colton began to brush the mule again. *"Oh, that does feel great,"* the mule thought to Colton.

"You should have finished with my coat first. I was the one that had to carry the golden-haired woman. Either she held on too tight with her legs, which caused my sides to hurt, or she did not hold on tight enough, and she would fall off. I have never seen someone with no skills at all for riding," Hanna's horse thought. Even though it had not spoken aloud, Colton was able to hear it.

He turned and looked at the horse behind him. Most people who thought they heard a mule and a horse talking would think they were going crazy. Colton thought that it was wonderful. He knew he had heard the animals and could not resist trying to communicate with them more. "So how are you able to speak?" he asked the mule and horse.

"What did you say?" Hanna yelled at him.

Colton turned his head and saw Hanna looking at him from over by the fire. He had spoken aloud and she must have thought he was talking to her. "Nothing," he said and turned his head and went back to brushing the mule.

"You might not want to speak out loud when you talk to us. People might start thinking that you are crazy, just like Adoni," the mule said.

"You can speak, and I can hear you," Colton thought to the mule.

"Well of course I can. Just because humans call us dumb creatures does not mean we are."

"But how?" Colton asked.

"Don't you know?" the horse on the other side of the one at his back asked.

Colton thought for a moment then gave his answer, knowing it was the right one. *"Creator."*

"That is correct," the mule thought to him.

Colton wanted to continue with the conversation and could only think of one question to ask, *"So do you have a name?"*

"We animals do not use names. At least most of us do not. We identify each other by our scents," the mule thought to Colton.

"Then how do you call out to one another?" Colton asked, wondering how one animal got the attention of another.

"You are thinking like a human," the mule said, and Colton was sure that the comment was an insult to him and the rest of his kind. *"All things are linked through Creator. If I wanted to talk to a fellow creature, I would just pass my thoughts to them. Of course, we have to be within sight of each other, but we have not had a problem communicating since our creation, so I think we are a bit smarter than your kind."*

"Hey," Colton said out loud wanting to defend his kind.

"What are you doing over there?" Hanna yelled at Colton.

He turned his head and looked at her. He did not think it would be wise to tell her he was talking to the mule and horses. "Uh, nothing," he said then went back to brushing the mule.

"See what I mean," the mule thought to him.

"What?" Colton thought to the mule because he did not want to draw Hanna's attention.

The mule was ready to explain, *"You did not tell her that you were talking to us."*

"But you just said that I shouldn't let someone hear me because they would think I was crazy."

"Yes, most humans, but not your mate."

Colton was about to respond verbally but remembered that he did not want Hanna to hear him, especially with what he was about to think, *"She is not my mate."*

"But you want her to be?" the horse he had been riding asked him.

Colton thought about it, then gave his answer, *"It is complicated. She has been through so much, with the death of her parents, and even Mama and Papa. She is afraid to let anyone in. Afraid to love someone and let someone love her."*

"Humans make everything so difficult," the horse Hanna had been riding said. *"You are afraid to tell her how you feel because you already believe she does not want love. All humans want love, even if they do not admit it to themselves."*

Colton took a moment to think about what the horse said, then turned his head to look at Hanna who was now cooking the fish over the fire, "Not all of them," he said out loud but kept his voice low enough so only he, the horses, and the mule heard him.

"Well let me give you a bit of advice," the horse at his back said, Hanna's horse, *"If you do mate with her, be careful, she sure does have a lot of strength in her legs and thighs, so you might want to prepare yourself if she wraps them around you."*

The two horses and the mule started whinnying and hee-hawing, and Colton took it as their way of laughing. He was about to join in but then realized exactly what the horse meant. "Hey!" he said aloud and turned around to face Hanna's horse ready to reprimand it for the inappropriate comment. Before he could say anything, or even think something to the horse, he felt someone grab his arm and force him to turn. Hanna was standing there looking at him.

"What are you doing over here talking to yourself?" she asked while still having her hand on his arm.

He looked at her face and then down at her hand, enjoying the small bit of contact they were sharing. He lifted his eyes to look into hers. "I was just singing to myself. That is all." He then turned around and started brushing the horse in front of him. Out of the corner of his eye, he saw Hanna take a few more moments to stare at him then she turned and went back over to the fire and back to working with the fish.

"See what I mean," the mule said, and Colton turned his head to the right and saw the mule

looking at him, *"You could have told her right then that you have feelings for her, but you chose not to."* The mule turned its head to look forward, *"At least we creatures do not waste time. Life is too short to be waiting for the right moment. Because the right moment never comes, or it has already passed."*

As he continued to brush the horse, he looked over at Hanna who was sitting by the fire. The sun had gone down behind the tree line, so the glow from the flames made her golden hair shine like the sunset itself.

When he first met her, he had always dreamed of the two of them being together. Not just as friends but as husband and wife. He had even been saving up coin so that one day the two of them could have a place of their own. That is after they traveled the world and did everything that was fun to do.

Colton knew it had been a child's dream. On the day he realized he needed to join the priesthood he also realized his childhood dream was never going to come to pass. Priests did not marry, and they definitely did not travel the world in search of fun.

Then the day came when the priests ordered him to leave the priesthood. He had no idea what he was going to do. He did not want to go back to living on the streets, even though he would have no problem picking up right where he left off, but he was no longer a child. When the feeling came over him to save Hanna, he felt as if he would get part of his old life back. He did not know what kind of trouble she was in or what he was going to do. He did know his place was at Hanna's side.

She had never used the word, "friend" to him, and she would probably never use the word "husband." Colton could accept that, as long as she remained safe.

"Are you ok, son?"

Colton came out of his daze and turned his head to the left. There he saw Adoni looking at him. "I'm fine," Colton said, but with the way he forced the two words out of his mouth, he did not think he convinced Adoni that he was.

"Hanna called to you to let you know our meal is ready. When you did not come over, I figured you were enjoying their company over ours."

He was not sure, but with the smile Adoni had, Colton thought that maybe he knew he had been communicating with the horses and the mule. He decided that it was best if he kept his bit of oddity to himself. "I just wanted to finish up here."

"Well, you have been brushing the same spot for quite some time. If you keep at it, you will be down to its skin," Adoni said and laughed. Colton gave a small chuckle as well but did not say anything. "Come on son, it's time you ate and then maybe you should get some rest yourself."

As they walked away, Hanna's horse thought to Colton, *"Be careful of those legs,"* and once again, the two horses and mule started laughing. Colton did not turn around to look at them.

When they reached the fire, Adoni sat back down where he had been, on the other side of the fire, across from Hanna. Colton sat on the stool to Hanna's left. When he was situated, Hanna handed him his plate with a fish and some carrots and potatoes. When he took hold of it, she did not let go, "Are you alright?" she asked.

He looked at her, and replied, "Yes, I'm fine."

He then heard the mule speak into his thoughts, *"What did I tell you about the right moment?"*

Colton did not respond to the question. He just pulled his plate to him and began to eat. He saw Hanna had taken a moment to watch him then she went back to eating her meal. Bewildered by what had happened with the animals, Colton forgot to say his prayer to thank Creator for providing the food.

With what they had been through, Hanna and Colton were happy to eat their meals in silence, but Adoni always enjoyed a conversation with his. "So, Hanna, what are you planning to do when you reach the desert?"

She continued to chew her food, but she looked across the fire at Adoni and then turned her head to look at Colton, who had his fork halfway between his plate and his mouth, waiting for her to respond to the question. She put her eyes back on her plate, "I don't know." She used her fork to poke at the food. "It has been less than a sun-cycle since we came up with the plan to go to the desert. I still have time to think about it on the ride there."

"Oh, my aching sides," Hanna's horse thought, and Colton, hearing him, had to force himself not to laugh with the three animals.

"Well, I am sure you will have made a decision by the time we reach the desert," Adoni said and went back to eating his meal. "So, tell me about the mark on your hand and how it hurt the one who came after you," he said after he had finished swallowing the last bit of food he had placed in his mouth and saw Hanna and Colton were both staring at him. "What?" he asked.

Colton finished chewing his food, then told Adoni why they had been staring at him, "I don't remember either of us saying anything about the mark hurting the woman after Hanna." Colton turned to look at Hanna, "In fact, I did not know myself." He then turned back to look at Adoni wondering how the man knew something about Hanna and what happened to her when he did not.

Adoni smiled at him, "Then how else would I have known about it unless one of you told me."

Colton looked over at Hanna who was looking at him. Hanna turned her head, so she was looking at Adoni. "When my hand touched hers, she fell back in pain. I felt some as well, but not like she did. It gave me the chance to get away." Hanna took another bite of her fish, swallowed it, and then continued, "Why do you think it hurt us both, but her more?"

Adoni stood up, leaned over, and used the ladle to put some more vegetables on his plate; he then walked over to where his mule was and placed the plate on the ground. He came back over and sat back down before he answered Hanna's question. "Moon has blessed her. You have only been touched by Sun. Those two are enemies, so the two of you are as well. If the both of you come in contact with one another, you are going to feel the hatred and anger as well as the power of the two Guardians Creator placed in the sky. It hurt her more, probably because she is more of Moon than you are of Sun."

Colton asked his question. "If Sun blesses Hanna, will she feel the same pain the other woman did?"

"I have no doubt about it. Hanna will have the blessing of Sun, but also the anger and hatred Sun has for Moon."

"I never said I would accept any type of help from Sun let alone being blessed. I am only going to the desert to try to communicate with Sun. I want no part of whatever battle Sun and Moon have going on, and I want no part of this woman called Nyght." With the way she had spoken, both Colton and Adoni knew Hanna did not want to continue with any more questions. It did not take her long to come up with one of her own. "Why doesn't Creator just stop Sun and Moon from fighting?"

Colton had just taken a bite of his food and did not answer the question; he did not know the answer anyway. He did notice how Hanna referred to Creator as Creator and not "The Creator" as she did when it was just the two of them. Colton suspected she did it to show respect for Creator when Adoni was present.

"Creator gives Sun and Moon the same opportunities he gives all of his creations," Adoni said.

"And what is that?" Hanna asked.

"The opportunity for them to choose between right and wrong."

Hanna let out a laugh, "Right and wrong. They are just concepts based on a person's own beliefs." She looked at Adoni sitting across from the fire then to Colton. She could tell he did not like the way the conversation was going, but Hanna did not care. "The two men who killed my father thought they were in the right to take his life. They chose to do wrong because it was not wrong by their standards. So right and wrong are only what someone believes them to be."

"That is because they are choosing their actions based on their own ethics," Adoni said.

"What else do they have to base it on?" Hanna asked.

Colton answered, "On what Creator wishes us to do." He turned and saw Hanna looking at him. "It is like when I chose to enter the priesthood. It was something I felt I had to do because Creator wanted me to. I could have chosen not to, but since I believed it was what Creator wanted me to do, I chose to do it."

"And look how that turned out for you," Hanna said sarcastically. "They kicked you out of the priesthood. So why would Creator want you to join it if you were not going to be able to stay there?"

"Maybe Creator wanted him to join it but did not want him to stay there forever," Adoni said, and Colton was not sure if he was asking a question or making a statement. "Creator might give us choices, but everyone is allowed to make their decisions based on their own beliefs."

"And what if the decision a person makes goes against what Creator wanted them to do?" Hanna asked.

"Then Creator will use their decision for that person and his own best interest," Adoni answered.

"In other words, it doesn't matter what we decide, Creator will always use us," Hanna said.

Colton felt he should say something to calm her down before the conversation got out of hand, "He does not use us as if we are a tool. He uses us to work his will. Even though there are people who do their own thing, some of which goes against Creator's will, he still allows us to have free choice, because he wants us to choose the right path on our own. If he forced us to do his will, then he would be nothing more than some being who is a tyrant, and that is not what Creator is."

Hanna looked down at her plate, and scooped up the last of her food, just before she ate it, she asked one more question, "Are you sure about that?"

Neither Colton nor Adoni replied, even though they knew the answer. Hanna was going to have to decide for herself, just who Creator is to her.

Colton finished his meal and sat his plate down

on the ground to his left then stood, "I am going to go fill the waterskin."

Before he could turn and retrieve his waterskin, Adoni stood up and walked over to where Colton and Hanna's supplies were. He reached the waterskin before Colton did. "Oh, you have had a long tiring ride, so why don't you take it easy, and I will go and fill it up for you." Adoni looked at Colton, "I need to walk off that fine meal anyway." He then turned to look at Hanna, "You did an outstanding job with the fish, my dear." He then walked out of the camp.

Colton watched him leave and even though he wanted to go and see where Adoni was going for the water and where he had caught the fish, he decided he was just too tired and it was not worth it.

Colton walked over to the fire and picked up his plate and Hanna's, which she had sat down to the left of her stool. He then walked over to where the mule was and picked up the plate Adoni had been using. *"The old man is right about one thing, she did do an outstanding job with the fish,"* the mule thought to Colton.

"I'll let her know," he said, and Hanna heard him.

"Let who know what?" Colton looked at her. "Are you talking to that mule?" she asked.

Colton walked back over to the fire. "Just picking up some bad habits from the old man I guess."

"Well stop it. We have enough problems without you going crazy."

Colton wanted to tell her that he was not crazy

but remained silent. He wanted to tell her a lot of things. She was right about one thing; they had enough problems without adding any more. He walked over to the stool Adoni had been using and picked up the old man's waterskin. When he lifted it, he felt the weight and it seemed to be full, even though he knew Adoni had used some of the water to fix the vegetables. He then walked closer to the woods and began pouring some water on the plates to clean them. He made sure he spent some extra time on the plate Adoni had used and allowed his mule to eat from. Colton did not like the fact that he might eat off the plate after the animal, even if he could communicate with it.

"What do you think I should do?" Hanna asked while Colton was still cleaning the plates.

He only stopped for a few breaths to take in the question then went back to his task. "That is your decision to make." He knew it was not what she wanted to hear but it was the truth, and he would never lie to Hanna.

"I want to go back to Maridian."

Colton turned around and looked at her, "That is not an option."

"I thought you said it was my decision to make?"

Colton came back over to the fire and sat on the stool Adoni had been using. "That decision is not yours to make. It was mine, and I am glad I made the right one."

"How do you know it was the right one?"

He did not even have to take time to think about the answer, "Because you are still alive, and if you return, you won't be."

They sat there in silence for a while, and when Hanna spoke, she surprised Colton with what she said, "I miss my mom and dad." Colton did not know how to respond, but Hanna still had more to say. "I miss Mama and Papa. I miss the boarding house. I miss Elisa. I miss cleaning out the pots in the relief shack." Colton was about ready to smile, but he saw that Hanna was not trying to be funny, she was serious. "This is not what I want to do," she said when she took her eyes off the fire and looked at Colton. "I don't want to go to the desert. I don't want to talk to Sun, and I don't want to fight some woman called Nyght, who wants to kill me."

Colton held her stare and gave his reply, "At first, I did not want to join the priesthood, but I did. I did not want to leave the priesthood, but I did. I did not want to take you out of Maridian, but I did. It's not about what we want to do, but what we have to do."

"It doesn't seem as if Creator is giving us much of a choice in anything," Hanna said, and this time she had no sarcasm in her words, only sadness.

Colton stood up and walked over to where she was sitting. He knelt down next to her and they looked into each other's eyes. "By doing what we must do, instead of what we want to do, we are making the choice we are led to, by our hearts. That is where Creator dwells in us and is how we should decide what we should do. Not with our heads."

Hanna was not sure if she believed what he had said, but she was ready to change the subject, "Wouldn't you rather go back to Maridian, and steal some apples?"

Colton looked deeper into her eyes, "If I stole two, I would give you one."

Hanna did not know what she saw in his eyes, or maybe she did, but she did not want to think about it, so she quickly turned her head and put her eyes back on the fire.

Colton was not sure whether his attempt to show a bit of kindness had comforted her or not, so he stood and went back over to his own stool and sat down.

"How long do you think it will take us to get to the desert?" Hanna asked.

Colton kept his eyes looking ahead and answered, "That would depend on how many more times you fall off your horse." After a few breaths, he looked to his right at Hanna. They both started laughing at the same time. It was a sound he could listen to for the rest of his life, and never grow tired of hearing it.

When they finally stopped, Hanna spoke up to defend herself. "It is not my fault. There is something wrong with that horse. I think one of its legs is shorter than the other three." Once again, they started laughing, knowing that what she had said was not the reason she could not stay on a horse.

"What is so amusing that has you both laughing?"

Adoni asked as he came back and saw the two in good spirits.

Colton and Hanna looked at the elderly man, then back at each other, then ended their moment since they were no longer alone. "Just discussing riding techniques. Nothing more," Colton said. He then looked over to Hanna, "We better all turn in. We need to get an early start in the morning."

Hanna nodded, eased off the stool, and stretched out on the robe Colton had placed on the ground for her to use. With her back to the fire, she heard Colton and Adoni both settling down for the night. She placed her arms under her head to give her some support and closed her eyes, but she did not think she would be able to sleep. Too much had happened, and she had some decisions to make.

Just before she fell asleep, she realized the robe she was lying on had Colton's scent on it. She slept peacefully.

EIGHT

The ride from Maridian to Lorraine was ten sun-cycles. Nyght made it in eight. She rode mainly at night to keep out of the sun as much as possible and only stopped when the sun became too uncomfortable to continue. She and her horse Stygian would rest during the day, although it appeared that when she stopped to make camp, her horse was no more tired than when she had started riding the previous evening.

She arrived at Lorraine at the third mark. Moon was in the sky, but Nyght could not see Moon because clouds covered the entire area, but they did not interfere with her being able to see out across the way. She had followed the road and was now looking at the west side of the wall that went around the village. What she did not see was a gate or even any guards walking at the top of the wall. She knew that most small villages, especially ones off in the woods by themselves, usually had sentries on duty, but Lorraine did not.

Something else Nyght noticed was that the road she had been traveling on and brought her to the village did not lead to the front entrance on the side of the village that she was looking at. The dirt road continued to her left so she figured that it would lead her to the village gate, which she knew there had to be one.

Nyght decided to go the rest of the way to the village on foot. She had to find the side of the wall where the front gate would be, and instead of riding up to it, she went on the outskirts of the woods, using them for cover. Just because she did not see any guards did not mean there were not any.

She climbed off Stygian and walked into the woods to her left. When she thought the horse would not be visible to anyone in the village, she tied his reins to a tree and then started making her way through the woods.

She walked at the edge of the tree line in a northeastern direction. When she was able to see the next side of the wall, she also saw the entrance to the village. What she did not see were any gates to keep anyone out. The village was wide open, and from what she could see, there were no guards watching the open space between the village and the woods where she was.

Since it was night, Nyght decided it would be best for her to enter the village before the sun rose. She would be able to make her way inside and find out whatever she could about this Hanna, the warrior of Sun.

As soon as she took a step out of the woods, she

screamed out in pain and quickly retreated back to the tree line. Her foot felt as if it was on fire. The pain was so great she had to place her hand on the nearest tree to hold herself up while she kept her right foot from touching the ground.

"The land has been touched by Sun," Moon thought to her.

Nyght was grinding her teeth to get control and to force herself to accept the pain, as well as her foolishness for having screamed out because she knew she would have alerted anyone in the village to her presence. She was still able to see the front entrance, but what she did not see was anyone coming to investigate the noise she had made. *"Then she has been here and has received Sun's blessing,"* Nyght thought to Moon while trying to bear the pain.

"No. What was done here, took place many seasons ago. It must have been when Sun first touched the woman when she was a child. She was probably no older than you were when I brought you out of the first town where you lived."

Even though Nyght did not remember the name of the town, she did remember that night. The night Moon had focused the power through her and brought the mountains down covering the town.

Her foot was feeling better, so she placed it back on the ground. When it made contact, there was still pain, but she was not going to let it control her. She would accept it and continue with why she had come to Lorraine. "Then the woman is not here," she said aloud but Moon was still able to hear her. "She left the city before I did, and since I did not see her on the road then she would have arrived first. But I do not sense her in the village, and it is smaller than the city where I found her. If she was here, I would be able to sense her." Nyght did not say the next part, and she kept the thought to herself, so Moon would not hear it. Since Sun had touched the land in such a powerful way, then the woman probably did come from this place, but it was many seasons ago, and it was apparent she was not here now. Which means Moon had been wrong in sending her to Lorraine.

Nyght still wanted to get inside the city. Maybe she could find something to lead her to where the woman was. "Can you tell if all the land around the entire village has been touched by Sun?" she asked Moon.

"Only the land leading to the front wall of the village from where you are. There is some land away from the front entrance that has not been touched by Sun. Travel to the eastern side of the village and you will be able to walk to the wall, then follow it to the front entrance."

Nyght had only asked one question, and once Moon had answered it, she knew how she would get to the village. She did not tell Moon that she had already come up with a plan.

She stepped back further into the woods, not only to make sure no one from the village saw her, but to give the land touched by Sun a wide burst. She was able to walk, but every time she put pressure on her right foot, she felt pain. She wanted to remove her boot and examine the damage. Even though her skin did not make direct contact with the land, it felt as if blisters were on the bottom of her foot. She also knew she would have to wait because when she did remove her boot, she might not be able to put it back on if it began to swell. At least with the boot on, it would keep her foot bound until she had a chance to take care of it properly.

When she reached the tree line, opposite the eastern wall of the village, Nyght hesitated before she walked out into the open. Moon had been wrong about the woman coming to Lorraine, Moon could also be wrong about the land in front of her. She was going to have to test it so she moved her right foot forward, the one already injured. She would use it again because it was better to be with one injured foot than two. When she placed it down on the open ground, she only felt the pain she had from when she placed her foot on the land touched by Sun in front of the village. She slowly moved her left foot forward and stepped on the ground but felt no pain.

Nyght looked out across the open land and saw the side of the wall. She still did not see any sentries posted so she began to walk toward the village. Every time she brought her right foot down, she felt pain, and by the time she was halfway to her destination, her foot was numb. Even though her body was trying to force her to limp, to take some weight off her injury, she refused to yield to it.

When she reached the wall, she turned to her right and started walking. When she reached the corner, she turned left and started walking toward the front of the village, making sure she stayed as close to the wall as possible. Moon told her that there was a small part of land on the side with the entrance not touched by Sun, but Moon had not told her how much. When she looked to her right, and even though it was night, she saw what appeared to be a line scorched into the ground running the entire length of the wall. She could also see that it was darker than the land around it. She determined that the land from the wall to the line was probably the part not touched by Sun. There was plenty of space between her and the line, so she did not have to worry about coming in contact with what could harm her.

Nyght even guessed part of what had happened in this village. Sun must have caused the land to burn from the line all the way across the open field to the tree line where she had stepped on. She did not know the reason why, but she knew the woman Hanna, was part of it.

She continued to walk along the wall and when she came to the part where the front gate should be, she looked around the wooden post, into the village. She did not see any guards or any other type of movement. It was after the third mark so if there were any people in the village, they would more than likely be asleep.

Nyght moved around the wood beam and entered the city, keeping her back against the inside of the wall. She looked around and saw some houses. She looked over to her right and saw what looked to be a stable, but a good part of the roof was missing. When she went back to looking at the houses, she realized most of them were showing some type of damage. Some were missing their rooftops; some were even lacking doors. Just like the wall going around the village was missing its front gates. Whatever Lorraine was before, something had happened to cause it to be the way it is now.

Nyght did not see anyone so she decided she would take a more direct approach to one of the buildings. When she reached the front porch, she stepped up onto it, making sure she avoided the multiple holes in the wooden planks. When she made it to the front window, she looked inside and saw nothing. Not because she could not see, but because there was nothing inside. Whoever had lived in the dwelling took everything when they left, or someone came and emptied the place after the owners abandoned it.

Nyght walked to the edge of the porch, looked out over the village, and realized it was exactly like the house, abandoned. Whoever had lived in the village left a while ago. She did not know how many seasons, but the people had been gone long enough that the weather and time had decayed everything left behind. She was able to see the wall where the front gates should have been. Nyght knew that even if the gates had suffered from natural attacks, there would have been some remnants of them. Whatever happened to them, a human had to have some involvement.

Her doubts about finding something to lead her to Hanna were growing. The only thing she would find in Lorraine was crumbling buildings, but she decided to continue her search. Esteemed-High-Master Wraith had taught her that when seeking out something, do not stop just because you see nothing else to seek. There is usually something hiding in the smallest of gaps. She had not thought about her teacher since she had begun searching for this warrior of Sun, so when she did, she felt a tug in her heart. It was from his absence in her life.

As she made her way through the village, she looked inside some of the dwellings she passed. Some she was able to see into without moving closer. Not only were the doors missing, but also parts of the walls had fallen and the interior was visible. Not that there was anything in them to see since the belongings were taken away some time ago.

When she made it to what appeared to be the center of the village, she saw the largest of the buildings. She also saw smoke coming out of the chimney. It appeared that Lorraine had at least one citizen.

As soon as she took her next step closer to the building, she stopped. Not because she felt the pain in her foot. No, this time, something inside her was telling her that she was doing exactly what someone would expect her to do. Moon had not made her feel this way. It was the part of her that knew when there was going to be danger, and that she was about to walk straight into a trap.

While still facing the building, she looked out the corner of her eyes to see if she could see anyone. She did not, but that did not mean someone was not there. *"The fire,"* she thought to herself. Realizing the smoke coming from the chimney was the bait. Someone must have seen her enter the village or even heard her scream when she had walked on the land touched by Sun. It did not matter how they noticed her, Nyght would give them what they wanted which was her going to the building.

She started walking again, and when she reached the steps, she climbed them. The next thing someone would expect of her was to head to the front door, which she did. Just as she was about to take hold of the handle, she heard the twang of the bowstring and turned around so her back was toward the front door. The door now with an arrow sticking in it at the height where the middle of her back was. When she turned, she moved enough out of the way, so the arrow flew past her and into the door instead of her.

As she was looking in the direction where the

arrow had come from, she saw the figure, which she could tell was male, staring back at her. Nyght was sure her dodging the arrow, meant to kill her, was a sight her attacker had never seen before. Nor would he again. "You missed," Nyght said, and the man turned to his right and took off running.

Nyght did not let the injury to her right foot stop her from taking chase. Not only did she want to catch him, because he tried to kill her, but also when she caught him, she would be able to get answers about what happened to this village and maybe even about Hanna.

Nyght did not use the steps to take her to the ground. It was quicker for her to turn to her left and run the length of the front porch. When she reached the end, she jumped over the railing, landed, and took off after the mystery man. If anyone were around to see her, they would not believe she had an injured foot.

The man was quick, but Nyght made sure she kept him in sight. Even when he ran into one of the abandoned houses, she was close enough to see him race out the back exit, which just so happened to be the entire back wall, since there was not one.

As she followed, and while still running, Nyght bent over and grabbed a piece of wood that was a little longer than her own arm. She then increased her speed. The man was fast, but she knew she did not have to catch him, to stop him.

While still running, she pulled her right arm back

and then brought it forward, putting all her force into the throw, releasing the piece of wood she had acquired. She threw it so that when it left her hand, it traveled at a declining angle, and when it reached the running man, the wood struck him in the back of his knees. This caused the piece of wood to tangle up in his legs, which caused him to tumble forward, landing on his stomach and face. Nyght had no problem reaching him before he recovered.

By the time the man had raised up onto his hands, Nyght was at his side. She grabbed a hold of his left shoulder and forced him onto his back. It was easier for him to see the blade of the pale white dagger at his throat. "You should have run to begin with instead of firing your arrow at me," Nyght said and moved her face closer to her captive, "You might have lived then."

With the fear she had put into the man, she had no problem standing up and bringing him with her. She positioned herself so that she was at his back and pressed up against it. She kept her blade at his throat and her face next to his right ear. "Is there anyone else in this village?" Nyght whispered, and to answer, the man nodded three times. Nyght pressed the blade more into the man's skin, "You're lying, because if there was, then a coward like yourself would have had them with you when you tried to kill me."

The man started crying. He thought that if his attacker believed there were others in the village, he would have a better chance at living. Now he was not so sure.

"The building with the fire, is that where you live?" Nyght asked.

Since the man had a blade up against his throat, he thought it would be best if he did not move his head, so he spoke his answer, "Yes."

The chase did not help her foot, and the pain was back and worse than before. She knew that even her self-control would only hold out for so long before her injury forced her to take care of it. It seemed to her that the best place to rest and question her prisoner would be in his own home. She whispered into his ear, "We are going to go back to your place. I am going to be right behind you as we walk. If you try to run away…" she stopped talking and the next thing the man felt was the tip of a second blade at the center of his back. The exact spot where his arrow would have penetrated his captor if she had not moved out of the way. Nyght finished her threat, "…you will not get far." She then shoved the man forward, making sure the blade at his throat caused a slight cut to let some of his blood flow.

The man felt the sting of the wound, and as much as he wanted to reach up with his hand to see how much of his blood he was losing, he kept his arms at his sides so his attacker, which to him sounded like a woman, did not take his movement as a threat. He started walking forward, thinking he should have run instead of trying to kill the person he thought was trying to invade his home. He was not sure if he would see the sun rise. Not that it ever did in Lorraine.

Nyght kept her eyes on the back of the man. He was too much of a coward to turn and attack her; but he might not be too much of a coward to try and run, even if she had threatened him. If he did, she would not kill him, at least not immediately. She needed information, which was the only reason the man was still breathing. The Assassin's Guild had a rule that an assassin could not kill anyone without a reason. Luckily, attempting to kill an assassin was one, so Nyght would be within her rights to take the man's life. As she looked around the village, she decided it probably was not much of a life anyway, and killing the man might just be doing him a favor.

The man was a coward and was too scared to come up with a plan to save his life. He figured he would do as the woman said and hoped she would just let him go. When he climbed the steps to his home, he saw the arrow he had shot at her still embedded in the door. He never even thought about reaching for it and using it as a weapon on his captor, but when he reached for the handle to the door, a small knife flew past his face and became embedded in the door. He still had his hand extended slightly toward the handle, but since he did not want to die, he did not move his arm forward or pull it toward him. Instead, he slowly turned his head to look at the one standing at the bottom of the steps looking at him. Even though he could see her entire form, he could not see what she looked like, because she had kept the hood of her cloak up the entire time. It did not even fall down when she chased him or captured him. He waited for his next instructions.

It was not so much as instructions Nyght wanted to give him but more like advice. "If I were you, I would open the door and leave the arrow. The knife that just missed your head was not one of the ones I had at your throat or your back." Even from where she was, she heard the man make a gulping noise.

To let his captor know he understood, he nodded, and without taking his eyes off the one threatening him, he moved his arm forward, took hold of the door handle, and opened the door. He pushed it hard enough so it swung inward, squeaking as it did. Then he stood there waiting for his next instructions.

Nyght walked up the steps, and as she did, she made sure she did not show any hints to let the man know she suffered from an injury. Even though her foot was now hurting more than it ever had, she did not let it take away the control she had over her captive. When she reached the top step, she stopped and nodded once to the man to let him know he should go inside. He slowly turned his head and walked into his home. Nyght waited until he was a couple of steps ahead of her, then she followed. When she walked past the door, she raised her right hand and pulled her knife out from where it had landed in the door. When she was far enough in, she pushed on the door, closing it behind her; the arrow still embedded on the outside of the door.

They were standing in a small hallway. From the outside, she noticed the building was three levels. The tallest one she had seen in the entire village. She took a couple more steps and saw the man who was facing her back up further to put more distance between him and his uninvited guest. It appeared either he did not want to take his eyes off her, or he did not want a blade in his back, possibly both.

Nyght continued to walk, and with each step she took forward, the man took one backward. When they were out of the small hall, she saw some stairs to her right leading to the levels above. She looked over to her left and saw a room. What she did not see were any types of candles or lanterns. She looked at the man and was trying to decide if maybe he was smarter than he appeared to be. When he discovered that someone was in the village with him, he might have been asleep, which would explain why there were no lights. The smartest thing he had done was not light any. If he had, the light would have possibly shown through the windows to the outside, letting someone know he was in the building. Even with the smoke rising out of the chimney, a person would think that whoever lived there was asleep. She then turned to face the man, "Do you have any candles?" The man did not speak but answered by raising his arm and pointing to the room off to Nyght's left.

She took a step backward and gestured with her head for him to go into the room. When he passed her, he kept his eyes on her, and his back away. The man was too much of a coward to try anything.

He backed up into the room to allow Nyght to step in as well. When she did not say anything, he turned around and went over to a small table. She heard him fumbling with the flint. There was no light in the room, but Nyght had no problem seeing what he was doing, as he worked in the dark. He did not work with skill or speed, but he did eventually light a candle. Once he had a flame on one, he used it to light the other three in the holder. Once they were, he replaced the candle in his hand back in the holder. He then picked up the candleholder and turned to face his guest. When he did, what he saw surprised him and caused him to gasp to let Nyght know. She had pulled back the hood of her cloak and for the first time, the man got a good view of what she really looked like, his eyes focusing on her pale white skin.

Nyght did not show any sign that the surprise of the man affected her in any way, because it had not. In fact, she had timed the removal of her hood, so the effect of her appearance played in her favor. Now the man was even more disturbed about the woman he had tried to kill. Which was the way Nyght wanted it.

She looked around and saw two chairs at the table where the candleholder had been. "Sit," she said, and the man backed up into the table. Now knowing where it was, he kept in contact with it, to lead him to the side where there was a chair. He had to use the table to guide him because he did not take his eyes off the woman with the pale white skin, something he thought was more disturbing than having a dagger at his throat or back.

When he had taken a seat, Nyght walked over to the opposite side of the table and took hold of the back of the second chair. The man had turned his head to follow every movement she made. When she took hold of the chair, she held his stare for a moment to add a bit of fear to him, then pulled the chair across the room and placed it two paces from the man and the table. She wanted to keep some distance between them while she asked her questions; just in case he got a moment of bravery and tried to attack her or tried to escape. It would give her enough time to react to any foolishness he might try.

Nyght decided to help reduce the chance of him thinking he had an advantage. "You can place that on the table." The man knew she was talking about the candleholder, so he did as she instructed and sat it down to his right. With no type of weapon in his hand, Nyght sat down in her chair. Once again, she did not let on that she had an injury, but she was ready to take the pressure off her foot.

"What do you want?" the man asked, staring at his captor.

"I want information; that is all."

"I'll tell you whatever you want."

Nyght now had to make sure the man understood her. "Will you tell me what I want to know, or what you think I want to hear?"

The man slightly shook his head, "Wha...What is the difference."

Nyght raised her right foot and placed it on her left knee. To the man, it would appear she was making herself more comfortable, but what she was really doing was situating her injured foot to relieve some of the pain, at least she hoped it would. "You could tell me what you think I want, believing that the sooner I have my answers the sooner I will leave. Trust me, that will only get me to leave and you..." Nyght paused a moment, "...well when I leave, you won't be better off." The man gulped again. "Now if you tell me what I want to know, I will leave, and you can go back to whatever you were doing in this place all by yourself."

Now that she had explained herself, and the man had a moment to weigh his options, he gave his response, "I will tell you want you want to know."

Nyght smiled, even though her foot was feeling even worse. "Good, we can start with your name."

"Darius. Darius Porter."

Now that she knew his name, she had a bit of control over him. "How long have you lived here, Darius?" She made sure she used it.

"Almost my entire life."

"Almost, Darius?" Nyght said and removed her right foot from off her left knee. Raising it had not helped with the pain, in fact, it made it worse, but since she smiled when she had just spoken, Darius would not have been able to tell.

"I lived here when I was a child. When I was fifteen, I left. I have only been back for six moon-cycles."

Nyght heard every word he had said, and even though none of it referred to the woman named Hanna, she wanted the man to keep talking. With him being concerned about how he would end up when all of this was over, he was not concentrating on what he was saying. By freely giving information, she might hear something she would never have thought about asking. "What happened to this village, Darius?" Nyght asked to get the man to start talking again.

"It died," he said, then went quiet. Nyght gave him a look to let him know he needed to elaborate on what he had said, or else she did not have a need for him. He understood perfectly. "When I came back, the town was like this. Everyone had left."

"So why did you return to an already dead village, Darius?"

He finally realized she used his name a lot. Darius did not like it, but he answered. "I had no other place to go, and I only found out the village had been abandoned when I arrived."

"Since you had no other place to go, you decided to make yourself the ruler of your own little village.

Your subjects may only be a few rats, but you are a ruler nonetheless." It was obvious to Nyght that the man did not see himself like that, but she wanted to mess with his mind to keep him off guard. "Do you know just how your little kingdom came to ruin, Darius?"

"Yeah, I do," he said but did not continue.

"What caused it?" Nyght asked.

Darius took a deep breath, let it out, and answered, "It wasn't a what, it was a who." He paused then spoke the name, "It was the Wicked Girl."

Nyght did not know what he meant, but she had no problem sensing his anger when he said the last two words. It was time to move the conversation to where she needed it to be. Since she did not believe in coincidences, she had a feeling she already knew the answer to her next question, "Would this Wicked Girl, also be called Hanna Gransby?" She knew she had presumed correctly just by the way Darius' jaw tightened up. If the girl was there in the room at that very moment, he would kill her himself. "Why don't you tell me the entire story from the beginning, Darius," and he did.

He told Nyght about the day Hanna had destroyed the Mountain Raiders. How she had caused the sun to rise in the sky and how she set the entire land in front of the village on fire, burning all the invaders. Nyght thought the villagers should have shown more gratitude, because even though she was going to kill the warrior of Sun, it was clear to

Nyght that Hanna had saved the entire village from certain destruction. She did not interrupt the man because she wanted him to continue talking.

He told her that after Hanna and her family had left, something happened to the village. The sun never shined on the village again. Every day clouds blocked out its light. That caused whatever crops the villagers used to feed themselves to die. Soon others started to leave the village of Lorraine, but not Darius' family. They stayed, but when he turned fifteen, he left. His story then covered what he had been doing, and even though Nyght did not care, and was only interested in Lorraine and the woman named Hanna, she allowed him to continue. From his tale, Nyght learned that a boy of fifteen seasons, who had grown up in a small village, was no match for life in the big city. He found that trying to earn a living was not as easy as he thought it would be.

He had left Lorraine because there was nothing for him in the village and he thought he would make it big elsewhere. Once arrested, and had spent time in prison for stealing food, he decided to cut his losses, swallow his pride, and return to Lorraine. When he arrived, he found everyone else had left or died. He had found some graves, but there were no markers to let him know if any of them belonged to his parents. Since he had not been able to make it out in the world on his own, he decided he would try to make it in a dead village.

He also said the front gate and most of the other

buildings were already damaged when he returned. With the clouds always over the village, there was a lot of rain, which caused the buildings and the gate to rot. He did not know what happened to the wood that made up the gate, but he figured someone had used it as firewood.

When he finished with his story, she asked a question she had come up with at the beginning of his tale, "So Darius, aren't you afraid the Mountain Raiders will come back to this place? Maybe not for the likes of you but for the remaining bit of wood they can scavenge." Nyght had read about Mountain Raiders as she was preparing to come to this land. They were just like the Wild Tribes that lived on the side of Eirene where she was from. Men, women, and children that lived in the wilderness, surviving by pillaging small villages and caravans to obtain all they needed to live. Like the Mountain Raiders, the Wild Tribes would take the youngest children to add to their numbers. Nyght had never met any, which was surprising, since she had spent a good portion of her life in the wilderness.

"The Mountain Raiders in this region will not come close to Lorraine. When I was growing up here, the adults figured that the remaining Raiders learned about what happened with all the ones who attacked that day the Wicked Girl killed them, so they stay away because they think this area is cursed." He stopped for a moment then added one more of his opinions, "Which it is."

Nyght doubted what he had said was what really happened. Not about the curse. From what Darius had said, Hanna had killed every single Mountain Raider. There were no survivors to go back to wherever they had come from to let anyone know what had happened. Nyght believed that when none of the Raiders returned to their own lands, the remaining ones decided their warriors had fallen to a mighty army or something. If these Mountain Raiders were like the Wild Tribes, they were only strong when they went up against much weaker opponents. Since the ones that came to Lorraine had not returned home, the remaining ones would have made sure they did not make for the area where they lost so many. Their numbers were not great, so any loss would be very damaging, and the numbers Darius had spoken of were on a large scale. Possibly every male Mountain Raider in the region. They might not have attacked again because there were only women and children left.

Since he had been in Lorraine for six mooncycles, Nyght also knew the answer to her next question, but she had to ask anyway, "In the time you have been back, Darius, have you seen Hanna Gransby, this Wicked Girl?"

Though he once again tightened his jaw, he still answered, "No. She is the reason my life is the way it is. She caused this village to die. If it had survived, I would not have left. I would have been able to stay here, and so would my family and so would others.

We would be a village. But the Wicked Girl cursed us the day she left. That I am sure of."

Nyght wanted to tell the man that he was a fool. She had only seen this Wicked Girl for a brief moment, and even though Sun touched Hanna, Nyght was sure she did not have the power to curse this or any other village. Moon blessed Nyght and she was sure Moon would not have made her weaker than what Sun had done to Hanna. Nyght could not curse anything or anyone, so Darius placed the blame for the way his life turned out on Hanna so that he did not have to take responsibility.

As for the village itself, Nyght did believe the lack of sun had something to do with Sun. Maybe Sun had caused the clouds to remain in the sky blocking out the light, causing the crops to die. Sun might have punished the village for forcing Hanna and her family away. It was only a theory, but it sounded like something Moon would do. Moon did bury an entire town by bringing the mountains down on it to keep the people of the town away from her.

It did not matter to Nyght what happened back then. Hanna was not in Lorraine, but she did not know where she was either. She had come here because Moon had instructed her to. If she had stayed in Maridian a couple more days, she might have been able to find out what gate the woman had used to leave the city. Apparently, it was not the southern one. That left only three other directions, but since it has been over a moon-mark since Hanna Gransby had escaped her, there is no telling where the woman might be. She might have left through one of the other three gates but then changed directions. Her only option now was to head back to Maridian and try to pick up the trail.

As soon as she stood, the weight on her right foot caused her even more pain. She wanted to sit back down in the chair but did not want to show any signs of weakness. Even if Darius, the coward, was the only one in the room. "What is this building, Darius?"

"It belonged to the family that oversaw Lorraine. Since they had built it so well, it is the only building to last all these seasons. But it is even starting to show some damage. I don't even go up to the third level because the floorboards are rotting away."

Nyght did not need the third floor. She only needed one room; one she would choose for herself. "I have tied my horse out in the woods. I am going to retrieve it, then come back and get some rest. I suggest if you wish to stay in the village while I am here, you go find another building to take as your home. If you are here when I get back…" Nyght did not finish what she was going to say. She just turned and walked out of the room and out of the building allowing Darius to figure out how she was going to end her sentence. When she returned, having tied Stygian out to the front of the house, Nyght did not see Darius anywhere around.

As much as she wanted to go to a higher room in

the house, her foot was causing her so much pain, she stayed in the room where she had her conversation with Darius. She removed her boot and saw that her foot was not only swollen but also covered in white blisters. Some already had pus coming out of them. Nyght knew that she would not be going anywhere until her foot healed some. She would have to stay off it, or else risk getting an infection, which would cause her even more problems.

She had never suffered from an injury like the one she has now. All because she stepped on the ground Sun had touched. She remembered the pain she felt when she touched the back of Hanna's hand. The anger Nyght had for Sun and Hanna was growing. She knew she had to heal, or she would only cause herself more harm. When she was ready to travel again, she would find and kill Hanna. That thought alone would be what got her through the time she would not be able to go after the Wicked Girl.

NINE

I t took them half of a moon-cycle to reach the great desert, although they had spotted it off in the distance two sun-cycles ago. When they arrived, it was the sixth mark, the sun had only begun to rise into the sky, the white sand reflected the early morning rays, causing the three travelers to feel the heat. Each of them knew that if they could feel the heat this early, and the sun was barely in the sky, when it rose to its midpoint, the desert would be unbearable.

Hanna had not spoken since the great desert had come into view. Neither Colton nor Adoni interrupted her thoughts, each knowing she was dealing with what she needed to do, what she wanted to do, and what she was going to do.

The three sat on top of their mounts looking out across the barren land before them. "We will need to fill our waterskins before we even begin to start out across that empty space," Colton said, not just to make a point, but to get all three of them to start moving.

"It takes ten sun-cycles to cross the desert,"

Adoni said, and he looked to his right and saw Colton looking at him. Hanna, sitting on her horse on the other side of Colton, was staring ahead. Adoni took a quick look at her then looked back at the desert. "The heat is so strong that the water people carry evaporates within four sun-cycles."

Colton kept his eyes on Adoni for a moment then turned his head to the right to look at Hanna. "Maybe we don't have to cross it. Maybe you can speak to Sun from here."

It was the first words he spoke to her in two sun-cycles, and Hanna wished Colton had remained silent because what he suggested was not going to be possible. She knew what she had to do, but it was Adoni who explained it to Colton.

"Sun will not speak to her from here." Colton turned back to look at Adoni. "She will have to travel at least part way into the desert." Colton gave him a look to ask why. "She has cast Sun away, so Sun will need to see that Hanna is coming to Sun humbly. She will have to prove to Sun that she is worthy even to talk to Sun, so Sun will test her."

"How?" Colton asked.

Adoni turned and looked back at the desert. "By traveling out into that wasteland."

Colton thought he heard a bit of sadness when Adoni said the last word. He did not know why, but it was obvious that Adoni did not like what he was seeing. Colton turned his head to look at the desert and realized he was not happy with having to go out into the burning land either. "We will need to take enough water for us and our mounts. We better find a town or someplace where we can obtain what we need."

For the first time in two sun-cycles, Hanna spoke, "There is no need." She did not turn her head, but she knew Colton was looking at her. She could not hold off any longer. She had to tell him what she had known when the desert first came into view. She turned her head and looked at Colton. "I am going alone." She only held her stare with him long enough to see the look on his face telling her that he was not going to do as she had said. Before he could verbally reprimand her, she turned back to face the desert and told him what she had known before they reached the desert. "Sun will not speak if you are with me. I will go on my own from this point forward." She kept her eyes on the wasteland in front of her.

"You are not going out there by yourself!" Colton said and even though the words came out harshly, it was not because of anger, but the concern he had for Hanna. "If you have to be alone just so Sun will talk to you then Adoni and I will go off somewhere, but only far enough so that we can still see you. Then you can try to talk to Sun."

Hanna did not look at him when she replied, "That will not be good enough for Sun. As Adoni said, I stopped talking and listening to Sun when I was five seasons. Sun does not think I am worthy to speak to Sun any longer, and if I want to, then I have to show Sun that I will do whatever it takes."

"Even if it means you die out there?" This time, Colton's words did have a bit of anger in them.

Hanna continued to look out across the desert. "Sun will not let me die. Sun wants me to be Sun's warrior. Sun wants to use me the same as Moon uses the woman who came after me. But Sun believes I abandoned my calling and now I must show Sun that I am willing to bend to Sun's will."

"That sounds like Sun," Adoni said, and when Colton turned to look at him, Adoni saw that he was not going to let Hanna go out into the desert alone. "This task is not for you or me, my friend. This is between Hanna and Sun, and we cannot be part of it." Adoni spoke with as much compassion as he could to let Colton know that he did not wish Hanna to go off alone either, but it was what she would have to do. Those words convinced Colton that he was not going to be able to change Hanna's mind. Even though he did not like it, he would not be going with her.

Colton turned his head to look out at the desert. "We will still need to get her enough water and supplies to last out there. My one waterskin and the one you have," referring to Adoni's, "will not be enough to last her and her mount." While he was still looking at the white sand, out of the corner of his eye, he saw Hanna dismount from her horse. He turned his head to look at her, "What are you doing?"

Hanna let go of the reins to her horse and stepped closer to its head. The horse nudged her shoulder as if to say it did not think it was a good idea for her to be going out into the desert alone either.

"I will not need water," Hanna said staring out to where she had to go.

Colton jumped down off his horse and rushed to Hanna's side. "You cannot go out into that barren land with no water. You will be dead in less than a sun-cycle. In normal conditions, a human can go a few sun-cycles without water, but out there the heat will take every bit of moisture out of your body in less than half a sun-cycle."

Hanna knew how long a person could live without water, but it did not matter. Even though Sun did not tell her what she had to do, she knew. Sun wanted to test her. Sun wanted to see if she had what it would take to become the warrior of Sun. Hanna still did not know if she would accept the title. On their way to the desert, Hanna spent a great deal of time thinking about what she was going to do.

She wanted to just turn around and go back to Maridian. By now, there was no telling what had happened to the boarding house. She was sure Elisa would be able to run it for a little while, but without Hanna there to watch over it, Elisa would not last long. She was only the cook.

Hanna also knew she could not go back, at least not yet. The woman named Nyght had shown up and taken what little bit of life she had. If she did go back, the assassin would eventually come for her, and when she did, Hanna would not survive their next encounter.

Her only option for the moment was to try to talk to Sun. The fight between Sun and Moon was not Hanna's concern. She had turned away from Sun before her family left their village in search of a better life. Hanna's life had gone in a downward spiral from the day Sun had killed the Mountain Raiders. Now, with everything that has happened, Hanna cannot keep telling herself that it had been nothing more than a dream. She had no choice but to believe that Sun had talked to her when she was a child and had touched her.

While they traveled to the great desert, Hanna thought about what her life would have been like if she had not turned away from Sun. If she had allowed Sun to bless her, then maybe she would have been able to save her father; and if he had lived, then her mother would not have fallen ill because of a broken heart, and eventually died herself.

While Hanna had grown up, especially after both of her parents passed away, even though she convinced herself that everything Sun had done was all in her imagination, she could still blame Sun for the way her life had turned out. Now she had time to think about all that had happened, and she was starting to blame herself. It was her guilt that made her continue toward the great desert.

It was her fault. She was the one who turned

away from Sun, and if she had not, maybe her parents would still be alive. She did not know how her life would have turned out if she had accepted Sun's blessing, and there was no way she could get her parents back. The only thing she could do now was talk to Sun, and hope Sun could make the woman after her go away.

Hanna still did not want any part of Sun, Moon, or even the one called Nyght. She just wanted to run her boarding house, and one day leave the world herself. To her, that was her life now. To continue with the life she has, and to have a future, she was going to have to confront her past.

Hanna walked over to where the grass ended and the desert began. She extended her arm, so it was out in front of her and over the sand. When she felt the heat of the sun, she was not surprised at how it felt, as if she was part of the sun and the sun was part of her. As much as she denied it for the majority of her life, she had always known. She turned around and faced Colton who was still standing by the horses. "You cannot join me. I am thankful for all that you have done." Hanna stopped for a moment, and then added one more thing, "You were always a good person." She then turned back to face the desert. Before she could take her first step, Colton came up behind her and turned her around so they were facing each other.

Colton knew what he wanted to say. He knew what he wanted to tell the woman with the golden hair, but he could not. There were too many complications, not just in his life, but in Hanna's as well. He could not say what he wanted to, so he said what he felt the most in his heart, "Come back to me." She nodded, but he did not know if she meant she would, or she would try.

She turned around and stepped onto the white desert sand; she did not look back.

Adoni gave Colton time to watch Hanna walk away. The young priest needed this, and the old man did not want to interrupt whatever thoughts Colton had. When he was not looking at Colton, he watched Hanna. When they arrived at the edge of the desert, he saw the change in the young woman. As if she would no longer run from her past and was now going to confront it. Adoni also knew Sun was not forgiving.

Hanna had refused Sun's blessing. Sun had chosen her to be Sun's warrior, and she turned her back on it and Sun. Adoni knew she had to be strong to step away from Sun. She did so because she realized that all the whispering Sun had done when she was a young child meant nothing when she began to lose what meant so much to her. First, her village cast her and her family out. Then two men murdered her father, and then her mother died. She blamed Sun and that was what gave her the strength to reject Sun.

Two sun-cycles ago, Adoni saw a change in Hanna. As if she was rethinking all she had done in her life. To her, she had nothing left for anyone to take from her. Maybe she was just tired of the way her life had turned out and wanted to see what she had given up.

Adoni felt sad for the young woman. Not for what she had gone through. Many people lose their parents, it was part of Creator's plan. Now Hanna was going against what she had decided all those seasons ago. She had turned her back on Sun, and Adoni knew it was the wisest decision she could have made. However, the next choice she will have to make might be just as important, and not just for Hanna.

Sun did not care for Hanna, just as Moon did not care for Nyght. The two women were nothing more than pawns in a never-ending battle that would go on until all existence ended.

Hanna said she was going to try to communicate with Sun. Sun wanted more. The only thing was, would Hanna accept what Sun could offer her? Adoni did not say anything to her while they traveled the last two sun-cycles to the desert. Whatever Hanna decided to do, it was her choice, and Adoni would not interfere with her decision.

When Hanna was nothing more than a spot off in the distance, Adoni climbed down off his mule and went over to Colton who had not taken his eyes off the woman who had just walked into the barren wasteland before him. "Come on, son. There is nothing else for us to do. We can make camp and wait for her to return." He turned around to head back to his mule.

"How long will she be out there?" Colton asked.

Adoni turned around and saw Colton was still watching Hanna walk away. He knew the young priest would not leave his spot until she was completely out of his sight, or even longer, but he did answer Colton's question, "As long as it takes." Adoni then walked back over to his mule and took hold of its reins and the reins of the two horses.

He led them away from the desert sand. He did not bother to tell Colton to come along with him. He would in his own time.

Hanna did not look back as she walked across the desert. If she did, she would lose what little bit of courage she had, and she needed it to face the unknown.

When the desert came into sight, two sun-cycles ago, it was not the white sand she took notice of, it was the light reflecting off it. Before they had even reached the desert, she could feel the heat of the sun's rays casting down onto the land. Between the light and the heat, Hanna felt Sun's presence, not just on the outside, but inside her as well.

When she took the first step and placed her foot on the desert sand, Hanna felt a power she had not felt since she was five seasons old. The sun shined down from the sky onto the white sand. The white sand reflected the light back upward. Because of this, the power of Sun was coming from the sky and the land itself. Hanna was walking through it all.

As Sun rose higher in the sky, Hanna continued to walk. She had not looked upward for a number of seasons, and she still did not. She knew when Sun was directly overhead. Sun's heat was bearing down on her, and the sand all around was reflecting the heat back up to the sky. The power of Sun surrounded Hanna. She could feel it on her skin. She could feel it through the soles of her boots. She could feel it through her clothes. She could feel it on the inside. As much as she did not want to admit it to herself, it felt good. As if she had found something she had misplaced a long time ago.

It did not matter how long she walked or how high Sun rose in the sky; the heat did not bother her. In fact, she was beginning to welcome it. A part of her even wanted to remove her clothes so her body could feel the full effects of Sun so she could feel the power surrounding her, but did not, and continued to walk across the desert.

Hanna had not taken any water when she left Colton. Sun did not tell her not to, it was something she felt she needed to do. After half a sun-cycle, Hanna did not even feel a bit of thirst come on her. She then realized that in her entire life, she had never succumbed to the lack of water from being out in the sun. Yes, she would drink water but not because she required it due to thirst. Her body needed liquids to survive, but not because she suffered from the sun's heat.

Hanna continued to walk across the desert until

the last bit of Sun's light left the sky. When it did, she stopped and laid down in the sand. When the sun left the sky and the moon rose, Hanna felt different. She felt cold. She had no problem with being without a horse or even water, but as the moon rose higher in the sky, Hanna wished she had a blanket. Not like the one Colton had placed on the back of the horse before he saddled it, but the blanket she had back in her room at the boarding house. The one she used in the cold season to keep warm at night. Hanna wanted it more than anything else at the moment.

She rested in the sand, waiting for the sun to rise again. She thought about continuing to walk just to warm herself but decided she would wait until Sun came back to the sky. Then she would be able to feel the warmth. The warmth and the power of Sun.

She pulled her legs up to her body, with her arms pulled tight against her chest to try to keep what little heat she had. Through the night she was able to get some sleep, but it was restless, and she woke more times than she could even count. To her, it was as if the moon was trying to stop her from doing what she had come to do. As if Moon was taking every bit of warmth out of her, trying to freeze her to death. When her eyes did close on their own from being so exhausted, she was not sure if she would wake up again.

When the sun's rays broke over the horizon, Hanna immediately looked to the east. She had not seen the light but felt it. Not just on her skin but in her as well, and for some reason, she felt as if she had won her first battle. It was not one against Sun but against Moon. She thought that if Moon could, Moon would have killed her last night. Since she had survived the attack by the woman called Nyght, Moon's warrior, then Moon was coming after her personally.

Hanna did not know it, but Moon was not able to see her or even knew where she was. When Sun left the sky, and Moon rose over the desert, Moon did what Moon always did. Sun was Guardian over all land, and even though the desert was not what it was originally, it still fell into the realm of Sun. The white sand reflected Sun's power back into the sky as long as Sun was visible. When Sun left, Moon dispersed all that power, forcing the desert to become cold. It did not matter how many times Sun heated the desert or Moon banished the heat. Sun would rise and heat the desert again, and again, and again. It was a never-ending battle between Sun and Moon, one which has been going on since the two came into existence and would continue until one or both of them were no more. They would continue to battle one another, neither of them winning.

That is why they needed their warriors. They were human, and they could die. Whichever one killed the other, the one who created the survivor would be the victor of all the battles Sun and Moon had ever had, from the beginning of their creation.

Each of them wanted to claim the position of being the grander of the two.

As soon as the light touched the sand and Hanna, she began to walk again, deeper into the desert. Sun had just barely breached the horizon, but already the heat was rising. Hanna did not mind, in fact after the coldness she felt at night, she welcomed it.

She continued this routine for four sun-cycles. When night came and the moon was in the sky, Hanna would lie on the sand and try to stay as warm as possible waiting for the sun to rise again. When the sun was in the sky, she walked across the desert. Not once did she even think about a single drop of water. Not once did she become thirsty.

At the midpoint of the fifth sun-cycle, Hanna stopped walking. Somehow, she knew all around her, on every side was the power of Sun. She had come to the middle of the desert.

It had been a long time since Hanna had looked up into the sky. Even when she was hanging the linen out on the roof at the boarding house, Hanna made sure she never looked up at the sun. Now, she had no choice.

She tilted her head upward, and even though the sun was shining brighter in the desert, the glare from it did not bother her eyes in the least. In fact, without even thinking about it, she closed her eyes. Not to hide them from the sun, but to bask in its warmth.

It had been many seasons since Sun had talked

to her, and even longer since she had talked to Sun, but she knew she was the one who would have to speak first.

Hanna opened her eyes and looked at Sun, "I am here," she said. She could talk to Sun just by thinking of what she wanted to say, but she spoke the words aloud to emphasize to Sun that she wanted to talk. Sun did not respond.

Hanna continued to look up into the sky, but turned in a circle to continue with what she had come to say, "This is what you wanted, is it not? You wanted me to come to you. Like some lost child running to their parent. You wanted me broken so I had no choice but to come back to you, so you can force me to do what you want." Still, Sun did not respond to her.

She stopped moving and continued to look up in the sky. "I know you want me to be some warrior for you, to fight this warrior of Moon. Moon's warrior attacked me. I got away and now I am here. Not to surrender myself to you, but to ask you to stop all of this. Stop this battle with Moon and tell Moon to stop the one coming after me. All of it is pointless. No one can win this battle. No one." Still, Sun did not respond.

Hanna held her gaze upward for a moment longer, then lowered her head and put her eyes down on the desert sand, "What do you want from me?" she asked humbly. She did not know it, but that was what Sun was waiting for.

"I wanted you to become what you were supposed to be. I wanted you to destroy the one Moon has blessed. I wanted you to become my warrior."

Hanna heard the words in her mind. It had been a long time since Sun had spoken to her, but since they were communicating with one another again, she knew her life was going to change forever. She could no longer tell herself it was a dream. "You took everything away from me," she said with her eyes still on the sand.

"I took nothing from you. You turned your back on me. You left me and all I had for you."

Hanna looked up at Sun, "After that day, the people of our village forced me and my family to leave. They would not have anything to do with us, and my father had to take my mother and me to another city just so he could provide for us. Both he and my mother died." Hanna did not receive any sympathy from Sun, not for what happened to her or for any other reason.

"Humans die. It is the way of life. It was not I who killed your father, but two men. It was not I, who killed your mother. She could not accept what happened to your father and fell to her own despair."

"But if you had not done what you did that day, then my family and I would not have had to leave the village."

"If I had not done what I did, you and your family would have been dead. I saved them and you. And as for the village of Lorraine, I punished them for forcing you to leave."

For the first time, in a long time, Hanna thought to Sun, *"What do you mean?"*

"When your family left, I had Cloud keep a portion of Cloud over the village of Lorraine. I did not allow my light to shine down on the village, and even now, it does not. Their crops died, as well as whatever fools remained when they realized that I would not return. Lorraine is no more."

Hanna did not say or think of anything to Sun. She thought about the town of Lorraine. About how they had treated, not only her but also her family, as if they were outcasts. She almost felt sorry for the people of the village, but then she remembered what they had started calling her after the Mountain Raiders had come and Sun destroyed them all. They had called her "Wicked Girl." Hanna remembered the name and realized that she did not miss the village at all, nor did she feel sorry for its people.

She then started thinking about what Sun had said. About how if Sun had not stopped the Mountain Raiders, then they would have killed her and her parents. They would have died long before they did. She started thinking that maybe she had been wrong in blaming Sun and even herself for what had happened to her parents. Had it not been for Sun, she would not have had the time she did have with her mother and father. Even though it was not as long as she would have liked, it was longer than what she would have had if Sun had not been there.

She had held onto her anger at Sun for a very long time. So long, that she was not going to let it go after just the few words the two of them shared. She still had more to say to Sun, *"What can you do about the one who is after me? This warrior of Moon. The one called Nyght."*

"That is why you seek me now. Because you cannot defend yourself against Moon's warrior. You turned your back on me, so why should I help you now?"

Hanna did not have to wait to think about her answer, *"Because this Nyght belongs to Moon. You can stop her. Or are you not as powerful as you think you are?"* Hanna thought of what she was doing before she had even stepped onto the desert sand. Adoni said that the biggest weakness that both Sun and Moon have is their egos. If she could attack that weakness, then maybe Sun would deal with Moon and the woman after her.

"My power is greater than you can imagine, you impudent child."

Hanna could feel the anger in her mind. Even though it caused her head to ache, she knew she was getting to Sun. *"Then put an end to all of this. Put an end to this woman called Nyght and put an end to this battle between you and Moon. It has been going on since the beginning of both of your existence and neither of you can win."*

"I will win!" Sun said, and Hanna had no problem with hearing the conceitedness in the statement.

To her, it was obvious that if there had not been a winner between Sun and Moon by now then there never would be. *"The warrior of Moon will find you and kill you. That I am sure of because it is why she was created."*

Hanna knew Sun was telling the truth. There was no doubt in her mind that the woman called Nyght would find her again. *"Does that mean you cannot stop her? Even with all the power you have."* Once again, Hanna attacked Sun's ego.

"Even though I am more powerful than Moon, Moon is still strong enough to make a weapon to use in our battle. A weapon to end your life. And even though I cannot sense the warrior, others, such as Cloud, Wind, and Ocean can; and they have informed me that the one Moon has chosen, and has blessed, has embraced what Moon has given her. She has accepted what she is and is willing to do what is necessary to be victorious in the battle between Moon and I."

Hanna thought she would be able to attack Sun's ego again. *"And if she wins then you lose to Moon. You will be the one seen as being weak."* Her plan did not work.

"It will not be I who is proven weak. It will be you. When the child of Moon destroys you, I will simply choose another to become my warrior. One who will accept my blessings. One who will destroy the warrior of Moon. The one called Nyght."

Hanna had run out of options. She was hoping

Sun would do something to stop the woman coming after her. She thought she could use Sun's ego to her advantage but even that had failed. Sun was ready to cast her aside and replace her as if she was nothing, and to Sun she was exactly that. That was why the next words she thought to Sun hurt her deeply, *"I will become your warrior."*

Sun took a moment before responding to Hanna. Sun had not lied. When Sun told her that after Moon's warrior killed her, Sun would choose another, Sun had meant it. As long as Hanna lived, Sun could not claim another. As soon as she was no more, Sun could choose a warrior, and the next time, Sun would choose someone who deserved the blessing of Sun. *"I have no need for you any longer. Leave and accept the fate you have brought on yourself."*

Hanna did not leave, in fact, she believed she could still use Sun's ego to gain what she needed, even if it was not what she wanted. *"Is that what you want? For the warrior of Moon to kill me. What would others say when she does? What would Cloud say? What would Wind say? I'll tell you. They will say the chosen of Moon destroyed the chosen of Sun because she was weak. She was weak because Sun is weak. It doesn't matter that after I am dead and you choose another because Moon would have been the one to win the battle and that is what others will believe."*

Sun did not like what Hanna had said. Sun did not like it, because it was the truth. Sun and Moon had chosen a warrior for one reason, and one reason only. To see which of them was truly the strongest. Neither Sun nor Moon could die so the only way for one of them to win was to have a mortal fight in their place. The one who survives would be the victor and whoever had created them was ultimately the victor as well, because they created the weapon. When a battle is over, no one remembers the sword or the spear or the bow and arrow used, but the one who wielded the weapon. Sun wanted to be the victor, but would not allow Hanna to think she had convinced Sun. *"You have been away for too many seasons. You do not have the time to become what you should have been."*

Once again, Hanna used Sun's ego to her advantage. *"But you can make me into what I need to be. It is true that I am weak. Even more so since I turned my back on you. And now I see the error of my ways. I should have stayed with you, so you could make me into the great warrior of Sun."*

Sun adored the words she was saying but was not ready to accept her defeat just yet. *"And if I choose to give you my blessing, what can you offer me?"*

It only took Hanna two breaths to think of the answer, *"I offer you the end to this battle between you and your enemy. And with that, all will see, and know, who is the greatest. Not just Moon, but any who think they might outshine mighty Sun."*

Sun adored the words she had spoken, and Sun

could not wait any longer. This was what Sun wanted, from the moment Sun had chosen Hanna. For her to become the warrior Sun needed her to be. Now she had come to Sun, begging for just that. *"Very well, my child. I accept your submission and will bless you."*

"It is an honor, mighty Sun," Hanna thought as she bowed her head.

"Remove your garments, so my light can embrace all that you are."

Hanna did not question what Sun instructed her to do. She removed her clothing, even her boots. Once finished, she was standing in the middle of the desert naked, with the rays of Sun touching her skin, but those were the normal rays. For what she had to become, Sun had to shine brighter than she had ever seen.

"I grant you my blessing, my child," Sun said then shined the brightest light ever onto Hanna's body. The white sand around her took in the light as well and passed it to the sand beneath her feet. She stood there in the brilliant light, light so hot, that the sand at the edge of the light began to heat and turn to glass. It did not affect Hanna, at least not in a normal way. *"Look at your skin, my child,"* Sun thought to her when Sun's light had finished the transformation.

When the light had first touched her skin, Hanna had closed her eyes. Not because it had bothered them, but so that all of her skin could feel the power

Sun was passing to her. She opened her eyes and did as Sun had instructed. She saw her skin was now completely red. Not a dark red. A light red. The color of someone's skin after they spent too much time in the sun. Their skin changed color because the sun had damaged it. Hanna's skin was the color of Sun. The reddish hue of the sun while shining over the land.

She looked at the back of her right hand, for the mark she had since she was a child. She did not see it. She realized that it was not gone, it was still there, but now the rest of her skin had become the same color as the mark, so it was no longer a different shade. Her entire body was the same, including the bottoms of her feet.

The only thing that had not changed was the color of her hair. It was still golden because even that color was a representation of Sun. Even though her eyes were not red, they did take on a golden tint to match her hair.

"Look down and accept my next gift to you, my child."

Once again, Hanna did as Sun commanded. She bent down and picked up the two items at her feet. She then stood back up and looked at them. In her right hand, she held a dagger the same color as her skin. She looked at the one in her left hand and saw that it was the same color as her hair. The one she held in her right was red, and the left was golden. The ends of the hilts were in the shape of orbs. On the outer edges of the orbs, five spurs extended outward. They were no longer than the tip of her smallest finger. Hanna knew that the orbs and the spurs were small replicas of Sun.

"The weapons I have given you are made from material that has fallen into myself. My power has forged them for you. The one you hold in your right is Blaze. When you call upon its power, it will wrap your body in flames so hot no one will be able to touch you.

"Blaze," Hanna said to speak the name of the dagger.

"The other is named Flare. When you call upon its power, it will bring forth a light so bright it will blind any who looks upon it. It will shine as bright as I."

"Flare," Hanna said to say the name of the dagger.

"And now." Hanna had just heard the words when she felt a pain rush into her head. It was so powerful she fell to her knees, using her hands while holding onto the daggers to stop herself from falling the rest of the way to the ground.

It did not last long and as soon as it was over, Hanna could tell that she was different. "What did you do to me?" she asked aloud.

"I have existed before the first of the sentient beings who walk this world. I have seen all five of the species: Elves, Dwarfs, Gnomes, Trolls, and humans all battle one another and even their own kind. I

have seen wars fought, with great numbers, and I have seen single combatants fight to the end. All I have seen I have passed on to you."

Hanna knew Sun was telling her the truth. She had so much knowledge. She knew what to do when it came to fighting in every situation imaginable. She knew how to fight a single opponent and even multiple ones. She knew when it was safe to remain in a fight and when retreat was her best option for survival. Even though she had never taken up a weapon in her life, she knew how to use the daggers in her hands.

Something else Sun had given her, even though Sun did not tell her about it, Hanna could sense it in her. The hate and resentment Sun had for Moon. Not just toward Moon, but also toward the one called Nyght, Moon's warrior. She did not like those feelings. She never hated anyone in her life, and she knew what she was feeling now was not coming from her, but from Sun. She would not be able to get rid of those feelings, but since she knew they were there and where they came from, she would be able to control them, and that was the key to her survival, control.

Hanna did not want to surrender herself to Sun, but she had very little choice if she wanted to survive when Moon's warrior came for her. She had to allow Sun to bless her if she was going to put an end to all that was happening with Sun, Moon, and even Nyght. She might have allowed Sun to bless her, but she would never allow Sun to control her. Only Sun did not need to know that.

"Rise, my child."

Hanna stood, not because Sun commanded her to, but because what Sun wanted, at the moment, was what she wanted. She also decided that it would be in her best interest to play once again upon Sun's ego. *"Thank you for these blessings. I am sure that with what you have given me, I will be able to stop Moon's warrior and show both Moon and you who is the strongest."*

What she had said worked, because Sun's pride grew, if that was even possible. *"I am sure you will not fail me, but I have one last gift for you."*

It had been ten sun-cycles since Hanna had walked out into the desert. Not a day had gone by that Adoni did not have to convince Colton to trust in Hanna and let her come back on her own.

Colton sat in their camp looking out across the white sand. Even though they were a few paces from where the sand of the desert started, they could still feel the heat as the wind brought it over to them. That did not stop Colton from keeping his eyes directly on the same path he had watched Hanna walk away. Because he continuously watched, the moment the smallest image appeared in the desert, he stood up and ran to the edge of the sand.

He had moved so fast that his motion startled Adoni, and it took him a moment to realize what had caused the young man to jump up in the first place. When he saw the small speck off in the distance, he joined Colton at the beginning of the desert. There, they both waited.

It still took time for Hanna to reach the two positioned at the edge of the desert from when they first spotted her. Even before she did, Colton had no problem seeing the way she looked. He did not know how, but he knew the redness of her skin would not go away over time. Although she looked as if her skin had suffered from the sun, he knew it was not the sun that had caused her skin to turn to the light shade of red, Sun was the one who had changed her. He also saw that she carried a dagger in each of her hands, although she had not left with any items.

When she reached the edge of the desert, she stopped in front of Colton but did not say anything, so he spoke, "What happened to you Hanna?"

She looked at him and gave her answer, "My name is Daie." Her new name explained it all.

TEN

Daie stepped around Colton and headed for the small camp. She walked over to where Colton had placed the saddles, grabbed one of them, took one of the blankets, and went over to the horse she had been riding. She then began to saddle the animal, as if she had been doing it her entire life.

As she continued to prepare her horse, Colton came up behind her. "Do you want to talk about it?"

While working with the saddle, and not looking at him, she gave her answer, "There is nothing to talk about. I did what I had to do." She walked around to the other side of her horse to finish securing the straps of the saddle. They were perfect, even though this was the first time she had ever saddled a horse. She then walked back over to where the supplies were and picked up the horse's bridle. She went back over to the horse and placed it on him. "Get your horse ready," she said to Colton who was still staring at her.

"Where are we going?" he asked.

Daie pulled the reins up over the horse's head

and rested them on the saddle, then turned around and faced Colton, "We are going back to Maridian." She saw the look he was giving her. "That is where we last saw Nyght."

"Why do you want to go back?" Colton asked. He had taken her out of Maridian to save her life and he was not in a hurry to take her back so she could end it.

"Since that is where we last saw her, she might be waiting for me to return."

"All the more reason not to go back," Colton said adamantly, hoping she would see his point.

She looked at him for a few breaths then turned around to face her horse, "I have to go back. I have to find her."

Colton walked over to her, placed his hand on her shoulder, then turned her so that she was facing him, "Hanna," he did not continue because he saw the look in her eyes, which for the first time Colton noticed were the same color as her hair.

"That is not my name any longer," she said when the silence had lasted too long. "My name is Daie."

"As in Nyght and Daie?" Colton asked, even though he knew the answer.

Hanna stepped around him and walked a pace away. "Sun gave me the name. Sun wanted something to show that I belong to Sun."

"And do you?" Colton asked and Daie turned around to face him. "Do you belong to Sun? Is that what you want?"

Daie did not have to think about her answer. "We do not always get what we want. You of all people should know that."

Colton stepped over to her. "Me not becoming a priest is not the same as what you have done. You were supposed to talk to Sun and see if there was some way to stop this woman who is after you."

"And there is," Daie said to let him know the solution to their problem. "I am the way to stop her. No one else can." They stood there looking at each other, and when it became too uncomfortable for Daie, she walked around him and went back over to her horse.

Colton turned as she walked past him so that he could look at her, "You've changed," he said, and she turned around to face him. "And I am not just talking about your appearance. And what is that about anyway?"

Daie looked down as she raised her arms up to see them. She then lowered them and looked at Colton. "I have been blessed by Sun. Sun gave me the knowledge I need and the skills to stop Nyght."

"Including those daggers?" Colton asked as he looked down at her boots where she had placed them while she was taking care of the horses.

"Those as well," she said and turned back to the horse. She took hold of the saddle, and then pulled herself up onto its back, positioning herself as if she had been riding for her entire life. "I am heading back to Maridian. You can come with me or stay here. It is your choice." Having finished what she wanted to say, Daie kicked the side of her horse and it took off running. As Colton watched her ride away, he noticed that she was having no problem staying on the horse, as well as controlling it with ease, considering the speed it was moving.

He walked over to where his saddle and supplies were and began preparing to leave. He would have to pack everything up and take it with him because Daie had not taken anything but her daggers. He grabbed his horse's blanket and saddle and lifted them up. Before he started moving toward his horse, he looked around. It was just then that he noticed Adoni was nowhere to be seen. Both he and his mule were gone, and Colton could not remember when they had left.

By the time Colton had caught up to Daie, she had already reduced the speed of her horse to a slow trot to allow it to rest after the hard run she had put it through. Colton had to run his horse just as hard to catch up to her, so he was ready to go at a slower pace as well.

"How are you going to find her when we get to Maridian?" Colton asked when he brought his horse up alongside hers.

"I will find her. Since we are now both blessed, neither of us will be able to sense the other, but I will search all of Maridian."

"But you are not sure if she is even there."

Daie turned her head to the left to look at him then put her eyes back on the way they were traveling. "No. I am not. But it is the last place we know she was, so it will be the first place we start looking for her."

Colton looked up into the sky at the sun, then back at Daie, "Sun cannot tell you where she is?"

"No. She is blocked from Sun, as I am blocked from Moon, by Sun. I will have to find her, or she will have to find me."

"And that is when you are going to kill her?" Colton asked and did not take his eye off Daie, waiting for an answer.

She did not turn to look at him, "It is my task to stop her. To put an end to the battle between Sun and Moon. Once and for all."

Colton did not like what she had said. To him, it sounded as if there were only two possible outcomes for what was going to happen when they found the woman called Nyght. Either she would be dead, or Hanna would.

Colton could not help but think of her as Hanna. She has gone by the name ever since he has known her. When he thought about it, he was probably the person who had known her for the longest. Her parents were dead, and so were Mama and Papa. If it was up to Hanna, she probably would not have even let him get to know her, but thanks to his persistence, Colton never gave up on Hanna, and he was not about to start now. "Do you really think you can kill her?" he asked and she turned to look at him.

"It does not matter what I think," she said and turned back around.

Colton did not understand her reply because she had not answered his question. Whatever happened to her out in the desert, Hanna, the Hanna he had known, did not come back. He had a feeling his Hanna was still in there somewhere, and he would do what he could to bring her back.

They rode in silence until the sun had almost left the sky. Colton thought she would want to continue riding well into the night, but Daie was the one who decided they should make camp.

When they found a place to rest for the night, Daie dismounted from her horse with more ease than she ever had. Whatever Sun had done to her, she definitely knew how to not only ride a horse but maintain it as well, because when she dismounted, she immediately began to undo the saddle and take care of her horse's needs before her own.

With the horses settled, Daie began to start going through their supplies. "We will need to obtain some more food." She then lifted the waterskin. "There is enough water to last you a few sun-cycles so you should be ok."

"What about you?" Colton asked.

"I need very little water. I have the blessing of Sun, and there is no water on the sun, so I do not need it as much as I used to."

Colton was not sure whether he liked what she had said or not. It sounded as if she was more a part of Sun than she was Hanna, and that disturbed him greatly.

"I will start a fire," Daie said and began to gather some of the sticks and twigs in the area. She looked around and saw that there were not many. "See if you can find some more wood for the fire."

Colton looked around and saw that there was not a lot to choose from, but it would do. "We should have enough to last the night." He looked over at Daie who was staring at him, "What is it?"

Daie walked over to the middle of their camp where they would start the fire, "I will need to keep the fire going and make it bigger than what we have before."

"Why?" Colton asked.

"Because!" Daie yelled as she forcefully tossed the bit of wood she had in her hands onto the ground. She had startled Colton with the way she replied and took a few breaths before she spoke again, "I am sorry." She then turned from him and bent down to gather up the wood. Out of the corner of her eye, she saw Colton walk off into the forest, knowing that he was going to look for more wood. Daie began building the fire, moving as fast as she could.

Colton walked away from Hanna because she had never yelled at him before. Yes, there were times when she would voice her opinion about something he had said or did, but never with the harshness he had just heard.

The sun had not left the sky yet so there was still enough light to see the ground. When he found a branch, he picked it up and held it in his arms. When he thought he had enough, he continued to look for more. Hanna, or Daie, did not want to run out of wood while they camped. To him, they would only need the fire to cook their meal, and since all they had were some potatoes, there was no need for a big fire, but he continued to search for kindling. Not just because Daie had told him to, but to keep him from having to return to camp right away. He wanted some time to himself.

When his arms were full, and he could not carry any more, he turned around and looked behind him. If Daie had started the fire, either the trees were blocking its view, or he had gone too far into the woods. Either way, he thought he had gone far enough.

He dropped the wood he had collected and then sat down on the ground. He crossed his legs in front of him, and placed his hands together, interlocking his fingers. He rested his arms on his knees at his sides. Then he prayed. "Creator, I seek your wisdom. I did as you wanted me to. I rescued Hanna and took her out of Maridian. I even found out what was happening with her. A warrior of Moon, a woman named Nyght is after her. A man," Colton paused to change what he was going to say, "a very strange man told us everything he knew about the woman, and Moon and Sun." Colton paused again because he was coming to the part which bothered him the most. "Creator, she has been blessed by Sun, just like the woman Moon has blessed. Although I do not believe either of them have been blessed for their benefit." He stopped to gather his thoughts together.

"Creator, I think that both this Nyght and Hanna," He paused again to change what he had said, "this Nyght and Daie, are nothing more than tools. Both Sun and Moon are using them for their own purposes. And if one of them were to kill the other, neither Sun nor Moon would care about the person's life. Only to the point where the weapon they have chosen has lost to the other."

Colton took a deep breath to prepare himself for what he really wanted to ask. "Creator, you are the one who made both Sun and Moon. Adoni said you were the one who separated the two. You placed them on opposite sides of the world. Creator, you created everything. Even Sun and Moon, so I come to you to ask you to stop this battle. Between Sun and Moon, but especially between Nyght and Daie. Between Nyght and Hanna."

Colton tilted his head down, and held it there for a moment, then looked upward. "Creator, I do not want to see Hanna killed by this woman, but most of all, I do not want to see Hanna kill Nyght. Yes, she has suffered a lot, but we all have, and I know Hanna, my Hanna would not want to kill anyone." Colton lowered his head. "But now that she has taken the name Daie, the name Sun gave her, I believe she is more inclined to do what Sun wants than what she would do herself."

Colton raised his head and looked back up at the sky. "Creator, if you choose not to stop this battle, then I understand it is your will, but tell me what I am supposed to do. I saved Hanna but I feel that bringing her out here and taking her to the desert has only put her life in greater peril. I do not believe her dying at the hands of Nyght would be the worst that befalls her."

Colton rose to his feet but continued to look up to the sky, "Creator, tell me what to do!" he yelled.

He stood there in the middle of the woods, waiting for an answer, a word from Creator, which he did receive, *"Be there for her."*

Colton did not hear the words with his ears or even in his mind. He heard them in his heart, and he knew that the simple phrase Creator had spoken to him was not going to be an easy thing to do. He would be there for Hanna, but while he was there with her, he might have to watch her die, or worse, watch her take the life of someone else.

"I will Creator," Colton said and began to pick up the firewood he had collected, and then started making his way back to camp. As he walked, he had to wonder just who would be waiting for him, Hanna or Daie.

By the time he reached the camp, the sun had left the sky. That was not what caused him to be surprised. It was when he saw Hanna curled up by the fire, lying on her side with her legs pulled up to her chest, as far as she could get them. She was so close to the fire that if she were to move any closer, she would be in the flames themselves.

"Hanna!" Colton screamed and rushed over to her, tossing the wood he had brought back with him to the side. When he reached her, he bent down and took hold of her left arm, the one she had not been lying on. As soon as he touched it, he could feel the coldness. As if all the warmth had left her body. "Hanna, what is the matter? What happened?" He heard her teeth chattering as she tried to speak, but she was only able to whisper.

"Sun has left, Moon is here."

Colton did not understand what she had said. He looked up into the sky and saw the moon. It had barely risen. He then looked back down at Hanna, then over to the fire, and realized why she was so adamant about needing more wood.

He jumped up and ran over to where the sticks he had brought back landed when he tossed them. Even though he tried to grab every bit, in his rush to get back to Hanna, he dropped more than half of what he collected. Since he did not need it all at the moment, he used what he had been able to hold on to.

He started breaking the sticks in half and placing them on the fire. It would take a moment for the wood to catch, but as he turned his head to look at Hanna, he thought it was not fast enough.

The wood was catching fire, and the flames were

starting to grow. He then turned and took hold of Hanna, moving her into a sitting position, directly in front of the fire. She was so close that she had to move her feet back or her boots would start to burn.

When Colton had raised her up, he once again felt the coldness of her body. The sleeves of the shirt she wore went all the way to her wrists. She had on trousers and boots, but when he brushed up against her legs, Colton could feel the cold coming through the cloth.

He left her side and ran over to where he had placed the saddles. He grabbed both blankets used for the horses and ran back to Hanna. Even though they might smell like horses, they should help keep her warm. At least he hoped they would, so he wrapped them around her.

When he had finished wrapping her, he stood up and realized he was sweating from what he was doing. Here Hanna was freezing, and he was perspiring so much he wanted to find a cold stream and jump in it to cool off.

With the fire bigger, it appeared she had warmed up some, but she was still shaking from being cold. Colton went back over to their supplies and pulled out his spare robe. He then went back over to Hanna and wrapped his robe around her, making sure it was tight against her, along with the blankets, against her body, which he could still feel trembling.

He stood back up and saw that Hanna appeared to be warming up even more, for which he was thankful. He walked over to where he had dropped the rest of the kindling and collected it. He then took it back over to the fire and began breaking the bigger pieces in half but did not place them in the fire. He sat the pieces next to it, so they would be nearby when they needed to add more. He looked at the stack he had made, then at Hanna, "I'll get you some more," he said, and she nodded to let him know it was a good idea. For a second time, Colton went off into the forest to collect firewood. When he returned this time, he had double the amount he had before.

They sat in front of the fire. Daie watching the flames, and Colton watching her. They had both passed on their evening meal, neither of them in the mood to eat. Daie's teeth had been chattering so much that she probably would not have been able to chew properly, and Colton would not have been able to eat because he was worrying too much about her.

"Thank you," Daie said after they had sat for quite a few marks.

Colton wanted to say there was no need for her to thank him or even say you're welcome, but he decided on something else. "What happened to you?" She turned her head to look at him, and he remembered he had asked her that same question when she came out of the desert. He thought he would explain what he was most concerned about. "Why did you become so cold? Is it something Sun did to you?"

She turned back to look at the fire, and to help her warm herself up even more, she extended her hands to feel the flames on her palms. If she moved any closer, her hands would be in the fire. "Sun did not do this to me," she said to begin her answer, and since she was talking, Colton did not interrupt her. For the first time, she had spoken about what Sun had done. "When Sun left the sky, Sun's heat went as well."

"So, Sun did do this to you?" Colton asked and it was obvious to her he was not happy with the thought.

"It is not so much that Sun took the heat, but that Moon brought the night. When Moon is in the sky, Moon takes as much of Sun's heat and warmth that Moon can. Moon cannot take all of it because Sun shines down on the land and stores heat in it. But at night, Moon makes the sky dark, and the heat leaves the land. At least until Sun returns." Hanna reached over to the pile of firewood, picked up a couple of sticks, and tossed them into the fire. "When Moon is in the sky, I am weaker. When Sun returns, I will once again feel the heat of Sun."

"Until the night returns," Colton said, and Hanna nodded to let him know he was correct. He then realized that when Hanna had walked out into the desert, she had not taken anything with her to start a fire. "When you were out there in the desert, and Moon entered the sky, you did not have anything to keep you warm, so every night you felt the coldness."

"Yes," she said to let him know he was correct, then paused a moment to warm herself more by the fire. She then continued to tell Colton what happened in the desert at night. "When Sun left the sky, Moon pulled all the heat from the land. Every night I felt as if I would not see Sun rise again." She pulled her arms back under her blanket remembering the coldness she felt in the desert at night.

Colton asked her a question to hear the rest of the story, "What did you do to make sure you saw Sun rise again after you went to sleep?"

Daie continued to stare into the flames, and answered his question, "After Sun blessed me, I did not go to sleep. I stayed awake and forced myself to suffer through the cold."

When Colton heard her response, what bothered him most was that he had not been there to help her. He then realized her tale was no stranger than his own. She talked to Sun, he could talk to animals, and now he could even talk to the plants and trees. Something he had discovered while Hanna was out in the desert. She had told him something about herself, but he decided he would keep his own secret for just a little bit longer. He did not want Hanna to think he was crazy. "We better get some sleep," he said, stood up, and looked at Hanna. "Do you need to sleep?" He asked because he had no idea if she needed to any longer.

"Yes, I still need to sleep," she said, and with the

blankets and Colton's robe around her, she laid down next to the fire. Any further and she would be in it.

He moved closer and placed a couple more pieces of wood on the fire. He did not need much sleep so he decided he would stay up a little longer and make sure the fire did not die down. He even thought about staying up the rest of the night just in case Hanna needed him. He could get some sleep when they were once again riding.

"Good night, Hanna," Colton said.

She waited a moment then spoke, "That is not who I am; I am Daie."

Colton did not like the way she said those last three words.

Colton stayed awake the entire night and made sure the fire kept burning. As soon as the sun came over the horizon, Daie sat up and threw off the blankets and his robe. "Good morning," he said but she did not return the greeting. She stood up and walked off behind him. He turned his body around enough to see where she was going. He thought that maybe she needed to take care of her morning needs, which seemed more likely as he saw her stop walking and remove her clothes. He quickly turned his head and realized that if she had planned to relieve herself, she would have walked further into the woods. Of course, maybe Daie did not feel she needed to put some distance between them.

His curiosity got the better of him, and he turned

his head to look over his right shoulder. He saw Daie was still standing, and since he knew women sat to relieve themselves, he thought she was doing something else. He saw her stretch her arms up to the sky, with her fingers pointing up as well. As she stood there, Colton realized what she was doing. She was bathing in the sun. It had risen into the sky, and now, after the cold night she had suffered through, she had the chance to feel the heat of Sun on her skin. Colton did not like the idea that she took so much comfort from Sun, as if she depended on Sun for her survival.

Colton did not know how long she was going to stand there bathing in the sun, naked. He did know that if he did not take his eyes off her, she would turn around and see him staring. He forced himself to turn away, which was not easy for him to do.

It was obvious she did not need the fire any longer, so he removed some of the wood to allow the flames to lower. He then stood and walked over to their supplies. He pulled out a couple of potatoes and the small cooking pot he had. He poured some water into the pot so he could boil the potatoes for their breakfast.

He walked back over to the fire and sat up the small stand to hang the pot. He then hung the pot on the small hook and placed the potatoes inside. It was not going to be much of a morning meal, but it would put something in their stomachs. Luckily, while they were waiting for Hanna to return from the desert, Adoni had given Colton a few of his potatoes.

While he was watching the water boil, Daie came back over to the fire, already dressed, and sat down in her spot, "Good morning," she said to return the greeting he had given her.

"How are you feeling?" he asked.

"I am fine."

He waited a few breaths before he said what he wanted to, "But you won't be when the sun goes down again." Daie did not reply to his statement, because there was no need to. They both knew that when night came, she would feel the warmth leave her as Sun left the sky. "We will stop earlier tonight to build the fire sooner. I will gather more wood after I get the fire going for you tonight, so we will be more prepared."

She stared at him for a moment, then spoke, "Thank you." Colton did not reply. He just continued to watch the potatoes boil. "Where did Adoni go?"

It had been almost an entire day, and she had just now mentioned their missing traveling companion. Colton did not know how to take that. Maybe she just had so much on her mind, that she had overlooked his disappearance, or maybe she just decided it was time to ask about the elderly man. The truth was that Colton did not know where Adoni had gone. "He was with me when you returned."

"I remember seeing him," Daie said to agree with him.

"As we were discussing what you wanted to do, he left, although I don't remember seeing him leave." To Colton, it appeared that Daie had nothing else to say about Adoni. He was not there. Although Colton was starting to miss the fish Adoni always seemed to be able to catch. He decided he would change the topic of conversation, "Are you still planning on going back to Maridian?"

She looked at him and nodded. "You do not think it is the best place to start searching for Nyght?"

Colton was quick with his reply, "I don't think we should be searching for her at all. There is no reason to go looking for trouble."

"It is not trouble I am looking for," Daie said.

"Then what is it?"

"And end to it all."

Colton did not like the sound of what she had said. To him, it seemed to be final. He believed that the only thing to come out of the two women meeting would be the death of one.

The potatoes finished and they did not speak as they ate. When they were through, they packed up their supplies. Colton made sure he took the last of the kindling so he would be able to start the fire as soon as they stopped for the night.

They traveled during the day, and before the sun left the sky, they stopped, made camp, and the first thing Colton did was build a fire for Daie. When the sun rose in the morning, Daie would bask in its morning light, while Colton went off to find what he could for breakfast and to keep his mind, and eyes, off Daie.

On most days, it was any wild berries he could come across, but on the third day when he made it back to camp, he saw Daie using the small knife they used to cut up potatoes. When he walked over to where she was working, Colton saw what she was doing. "You killed a rabbit."

Daie looked up at him, then put her focus back on the rabbit. "I am getting tired of berries; and since that is all you seem to be able to bring back, I figured I should go out and see if I can catch us something."

Colton stood there looking at her. She seemed as if she had no problem with what she was doing. She was preparing the rabbit for cooking as if she had done it her entire life. "Did Sun give you the knowledge on how to fix a rabbit for eating?"

As she cut up the meat and placed it in the pot, she answered, "My father taught me when we lived in Lorraine. Papa would bring some home for Mama to fix. He bought them fresh, so Mama had to skin and prepare them, and I helped. After a couple of seasons watching, I started cleaning the rabbits myself."

"Oh, I thought that maybe it was another blessing from Sun."

Daie put the rest of the meat in the pot for it to cook. "Sun taught me how to find and kill them. Sun has seen many hunters over the many seasons Sun has existed, and Sun passed the knowledge on to me."

Colton wondered just what else Sun had passed on to her but did not say anything.

Daie stood up, took the unused parts of the rabbits over to the edge of their camp, and tossed them into the woods. She then came back and poured some of the water out of the waterskin onto her hands to wash off the blood. Colton saw the blood on her hands, which did not seem to bother her at all, and he thought it was because she had worked with animals when she was at the boarding house. At least that was what he told himself.

It took a while for the rabbit meat to cook, so they got a late start traveling. When they stopped again, Colton made sure he had the fire going before he went off to find more kindling to last the night. During his walk through the woods, he spotted a small stream, and he was very thankful. Their water supply was low, and even though Daie did not drink much, he required some every day, but since he had not known when they would be able to refill their supply, he had rationed what he had.

When he reached the edge of the stream, he knelt down, cupped his hands together, and pulled some water up to his mouth. Just as he was about to submerge his hands to take another drink, something caught his eye. When he was sure of what he saw, he could not stop the smile from appearing on his face.

Daie was sitting by the fire with the two horse blankets and Colton's spare robe already around her even though the sun was still in the sky. She discovered that if she wrapped herself up before the night came, the garments kept her body heat confined within them and she was able to stand the night a little better. Although she still needed the fire.

She heard Colton coming up behind her. "Were you able to find more wood?" she asked without turning around. She knew it was him because she recognized his footsteps. Something she had not been able to do before she had received the blessing of Sun.

"And something else," Colton said. Daie turned around and not only did she see him holding a pile of kindling under one arm, but in his other hand, he was holding four fish out in front of him to make sure she saw what else he had brought back. She also saw the smile he had on his face. "You aren't the only one who can get us something besides wild berries." Colton had meant it to be funny and even though he smiled at his own remark, Daie just nodded and turned back to face the fire.

Having failed at bringing a smile to her face, Colton walked over to the fire and sat the kindling next to it. He then went to his supplies and removed the small skillet he had. It was not as big as the one Adoni used; with it, they could cook three fish at a time. With this skillet, he would be lucky if two of the fish would fit in it together.

He went back over to the fire and sat down to the left of Daie. They had taken the same positions whenever they made camp. Colton never sat next to her directly, in fact, the only time they had even made any type of contact was on the first night when he had helped her to sit up by the fire. Colton did not expect to get any closer to Hanna, and especially Daie. Physically or any other way.

He may not have known how to fix and cook a rabbit, but Adoni had taught him how to cook fish. As he was preparing them, Daie asked the question he was afraid she would. "How were you able to catch them? You did not have any fishing line or lure."

Colton did not take his eyes off the fish while he continued to work with them. Daie told him Sun had shown her how to catch a rabbit just by waiting and grabbing the animal at the right moment. He was amazed at what she said, but his way of catching the fish was even more peculiar than her way of hunting, which is why he kept it to himself. "I just happen to find them in this stream I came across. They weren't very fast, so I was able to reach in and grab them." Since she did not ask any further questions, he took it that she believed him.

Colton had not lied to her; he just did not tell her the entire story. The truth was that he did just find them. The part he left out was that when he had spotted them, the four fish were out in the middle of the stream. It was not until he said a prayer to Creator, asking for assistance in catching the fish. The fish then came up to the edge of the water and stopped. All he had to do was reach into the stream and grab them.

Colton was not ashamed of what he was learning. That was not the reason he kept what he was doing from Hanna. About talking to animals. Not just horses, but others as well. Birds were all through the woods, and he could hear them talking to him. He heard the trees and flowers as well. He even heard the fish when they told him they would be honored to give their life for him to live. Even though he had never had a conversation with the food he was about to eat, Colton knew the fish understood that their death was a part of their life. It was one of the reasons Creator had created them, and they felt no fear of dying, serving their purpose. He did not tell any of this to Hanna, because she seemed more on following Sun than Creator. She had more things to be concerned with than what he could do because he was a priest of Creator. That he was sure of.

They made it to Maridian in nine sun-cycles. They had traveled in a southeast direction from the desert, so it reduced the amount of time it took to reach the city than it did for them to make it to the desert. Of course, the fact that Daie did not have a problem with falling off her horse any longer helped a lot as well.

"Do you want to go back to the boarding house and check on it?" Colton asked.

Daie kept her eyes forward and answered his

question, "No, that is no longer my life." She then kicked her horse for it to take off running toward the city. Colton was not sure what she had meant, but it did not matter, so he tapped his horse's sides to catch up to her.

When they reached the city gate, the guards and all the people watched as the two passed into the city. They were not so much looking at Colton, but the woman with him. The one with the long golden hair and red skin. To some, the woman even seemed familiar, but they could not think of who she was. Since they had never seen a woman with skin like hers, they took it as if it was just their imagination, not realizing that it was not long ago that a woman with hair just like this one, had operated a boarding house within the city itself.

When they had passed through the gate and entered the city, Daie stopped her horse. "We will meet back here in two sun-marks," she said to Colton, he did not like the idea of them separating. "See what you can do about getting us some supplies for the road."

"We could get what we need from the boarding house," Colton said, trying to convince her where they should go. It was not so much that Colton wanted to go back to where Hanna had lived, but he thought that they would be able to get their supplies and get out of the city all the sooner.

For her response to what he had said, she rode off, guiding her horse through the crowded streets, as if she had been doing it her entire life.

Colton had a feeling that like him, Daie knew Nyght was not in the city. He did not know why, but there just seemed to be an absence of something. As if the combined hatred shared by the two women was not present.

Two sun-marks later, Colton was waiting for Hanna close to the west gate where they had entered. He went to some of his old acquaintances and was able to obtain some coin and provisions. Neither would last long but he figured they could do some more hunting to resupply their food storages.

It was passing the thirteenth mark and Hanna had not returned yet. Colton was starting to think that maybe he was wrong and Nyght was in the city and Daie had come across her. He did not know how that made him feel. Worried, that Hanna might die at the hands of the one after her, but also saddened because she might be the one who does the killing.

Just as he was about to go into the city to look for her, he turned around and saw Daie walking toward him. "Are you ready?" she asked when she reached him.

"I was able to get us some food and some grain for the horses. And..." he started his next sentence but stopped, turned around, went over to his horse, and pulled something off the saddle. He then brought it over to Daie and unfolded it. "This is for you."

Daie looked at the cloak he was holding. It was a

golden color. The same color as her hair. She could tell by the look of it, that it was thick and well-padded. It was not a cloak worn in the hotter season, but one used in the cold season or by someone living in the colder regions to the north. Even from just seeing the item, she knew that when she wore it, it would reach to the bottoms of her boots. "Where did you get it?" she asked.

"At my father's shop," Colton said, referring to the man he had called "Father" when he was younger and trying to coerce people into buying the man's wares. "I went to see him and spotted this. I asked him how much he wanted for it and he said I could have it. He had just received it the other day, but no one seemed to be interested in it. It is thick and should help keep you warm at night." Done with telling her about the cloak, he held it out for her to take.

She did but seemed hesitant about accepting the gift. "Thank you," she said but kept all emotion out of her voice. She turned around to go over to her horse to put the cloak up on her saddle. Since Sun was in the sky, she would not need it.

"Where did you get that?" Colton asked when he saw what was on her back.

She looked over her shoulder and saw that he was looking at what she had strapped to her back. It was a holster that held her two daggers. With them in their sheaths, the hilts of the weapons extended up past her shoulders and positioned so that she could draw them with speed. "I found it in a weapons shop. I went in to see if I could find something to hold my daggers. The man who owned the shop showed me the holster. He said he had it for quite a few seasons but there are not many people who carry two fighting daggers at once."

Colton did not say it, but he knew at least one other woman who did. "How much did he charge you for it?" he asked.

"Nothing," Daie said, and she saw the surprised look on his face. "The man said that he had it for so long, he doubts he would ever sell it, so he gave it to me for free."

"For free?" Colton asked questioningly. He above all people knew that very few things in life were free.

"The man thought I would have a good use for it and by me using my daggers I would do great things. He said that for payment, I was to tell people where I acquired the holster, and he would earn the coin for it from the customers I send his way."

She stopped talking and Colton could tell she was thinking about something. "What is it?" he asked.

"Nothing, just that the man who ran the shop reminded me of Adoni."

Colton looked at her curiously, but since she did not continue with how she received the holster, he let it go as well. "If you are ready, we can leave now," he said.

"Are you in that much of a hurry to get back on the road or just to get me out of the city?" Colton did not answer, because he was sure it was a bit of both. Daie turned and climbed up on her horse; he did as well.

"So where are we going?" he asked.

She looked at him and then at the gate leading out of the city. "North," she said then kicked her horse and it took off running. Colton was quick enough this time that he was riding through the gate right behind her.

The holster for her daggers was not the only thing Daie received in the city.

ELEVEN

I t took two moon-marks to reach the town of Sundridge, and when Daie and Colton arrived, they went straight to the tavern called The Last Stop. They did not know how the establishment had come by the name because there were other villages and towns north of the village, which would nullify the tavern's claim. As for Daie and Colton, it was the last stop for this part of their journey.

When they had left Maridian, they had exited by the west gate but changed their direction to head north. Not only did Daie know the way they needed to go, but she knew the name of the village, as well as the names of the two people she was after.

When she had received Sun's blessing, Sun could not tell her where Nyght was located because she was under the concealment of Moon. Sun would have to have others search for Nyght and once found, Sun would inform her. Until then, Sun wanted Daie to become more efficient with the gifts Sun had given her. Sun knew exactly what to start her with. Even though Sun had given her the hate and anger Sun had toward Moon and Nyght, there were two others Daie despised even more, and Sun was ready to use that to bring her even closer to what Sun needed her to be.

Daie returned to Maridian hoping Nyght was there so she could end the conflict immediately, but she had another reason to go back to Maridian as well. Which was to get the names of the two men who had killed her father twelve seasons ago.

Dillon Polk and his brother Hale. They had worked at the same place as her father, and when he began taking coin out of their pockets because his wares were in more demand, they killed him and took what coin he had at the time. It was not much, but they were not after the coin he had; they were after the coin he would have made if he was alive. The only problem was that after the brothers had committed the murder, they decided it was best if they went to another city to get a fresh start.

They did not have much success, so when their carpentry skills failed them, they began to rely on the only other talent they had which was killing. They might not make as much from the killings that they did as carpenters, but they did not have to work as hard. It is easier to destroy something than it is to create, and the easy path was what they had chosen.

They traveled from city to city, and when they found someone, they thought was weaker than they were and had some coin on them, the brothers would take the opportunity to relieve the person of their coin and their life. The brothers did not want any witnesses and they made sure there never was.

After they committed a few killings in one place, they would move to another. When they had left Maridian all those seasons ago, they went east. Then they made their way south and the cities there. They then headed west, and eventually, their travels took them to the town of Sundridge. Where they had already made two killings and were spending their coin in the tavern called The Last Stop. An ironic name for the two murderers.

At the time of her father's death, Daie, who was then only Hanna, might have heard the names of his attackers, but after so many seasons, she had not known what they were. Even though Sun was still in the sky at the time of her father's death, and saw the incident, Sun had not paid much attention to the point to know who the killers were. Sun took very little interest in the lives of humans, but Sun had no problem finding where they were once Daie had the names and was ready to find the two men. Sun could see everything Sun was over when Sun was in the sky, so when Sun was over the town of Sundridge, Sun saw the two men Daie was after. Sun told Daie where they were, and she and Colton had now arrived.

Colton was not sure how he felt about what they were planning to do. When Daie said that she was going after the men who killed her father, he thought she was not going to let them live. She told him that there were still certificates of capture for the two men for her father's death, and she would find them and turn them over to the local authority. She also explained that if they resisted capture and it led to their deaths, then that was on them. Colton had a feeling she was hoping they would resist.

Now sitting on their horses outside of The Last Stop, Colton stared at Daie, the name he had come to call her. She was staring at the door to the tavern. "Are we going inside, or do we wait until they come out?" he asked.

"We're going in," she said then climbed down from her horse with ease and determination.

Colton climbed down off his horse as well, and standing at its side, he pulled out the staff he had secured in its holder so when he was riding he did not have to carry it. He then walked around to stand at the front of his horse where Daie was still watching the tavern. "We're going to take them alive remember," he said. Daie turned to look at him but did not say anything. She just turned and walked toward the entrance. Colton made sure he was right behind her.

As she stepped inside, Daie did not know what was more irritating to her sense of smell. The smoke coming from all the lit pipes and smoking rolls, the stench of whatever passed for a drink in the establishment, or the smell of the patrons. Daie was ready to give it to the last.

Once she was through the entrance, the only person she saw looking at her was the one behind the counter serving drinks to the patrons. He might have been the owner, so he was watching the entrance to see whose coin he would be receiving. When he saw Daie, with her red skin and golden hair, it looked as if coin would be the least of his problems. Unless he was thinking about how much it was going to cost him when the woman, and the man who had entered behind her, started causing trouble. It was obvious to the man behind the counter, the two new arrivals had not come to drink.

He had been the owner of The Last Stop for over forty seasons, and he had no problem with determining who came to his place to drink and who came for other reasons. It was the other reasons which caused him to lose a good portion of his coin in repairs. To reduce the amount of cost, the man started clearing the counter of any unused glasses. One less broken glass would be one more coin he could keep in his pockets.

Hanna had never known what the two men who had killed her father looked like. Daie on the other hand did not have that problem. It was not because of their pictures on the certificates of capture she had, it was because once Sun had found them, Sun passed their images to Daie, so when she scanned the crowd, it was easy for her to spot the two brothers.

She stepped away from the entrance and headed over to the counter where the two men were. She noticed the man behind the counter had moved to the far-left end. Probably the safest place for him to be, while he still was able to keep an eye on his stock behind the counter. When a brawl broke out in his place, more than one patron tried to use the fighting of other patrons as a diversion while they tried to obtain a free bottle or two, or three.

As she approached the counter, Daie did everything she could to hold back her anger. A part of her wanted to kill the two brothers, but she fought that part and was even thankful Colton was with her as a voice of reason. If he had not been, the two men would already be dead.

The brothers were standing at the bar facing each other. Dillon was on the left. He had long brown hair and was taller than his brother. Hale, the one on the right had short brown hair and even though he was facing his brother, Daie could see the scar on the left side of his face, running from his hairline all the way down his left cheek. The scar had not been in his picture on the certificate of capture, so he must have received it after he left Maridian. Her father's employer had given the city guard a description of the two men. Since the picture had no scar, her father's employer must not have known about it.

Before Daie reached the two men, they turned their attention to the red-skinned woman coming toward them. Both were smiling.

"Well, you are an interesting looking woman," Dillon said, drank the last of whatever liquid he had in his glass, then sat it on the bar behind him.

"How much?" Hale asked and Daie had an idea of what he was referring to.

"One hundred silver, each," Daie said, and the two men started laughing.

When they finished, Dillon spoke first, "Missy, I don't care how striking you look, I doubt very much, a turn in the bed with you is worth one hundred silver."

"Each," Hale said, and the two brothers started laughing again.

Daie figured that when Hale had asked how much, he was referring to her pleasing them in their beds. It was time to let them know just what she meant by one hundred silver each. She reached behind her and pulled out the two certificates of capture she had placed in the top of her trousers. While keeping her eyes on the two brothers, she unfolded the certificates and placed one in each of her hands so they could see what was on them. When Dillon looked at the one in her left hand, and Hale at the one in her right, they realized she was not what they had thought she was. Especially when they noticed what was written under their pictures. The words "**Wanted for Murder**," and below that was the reward for their capture, "**100 Silver**," each.

Daie dropped the parchment in her right hand because she needed it free to catch the glass Hale had been holding but decided to use it to throw at the woman who had come for him and his brother. As soon as she grabbed the small glass out of the air, she immediately threw it back at Hale's head, who was not as fast as she was and was not able to catch or dodge the flying object. It hit him on the head which forced him to turn his body toward the counter.

Dillon had seen his brother toss the glass and was going to use the attack to his advantage. He thought the woman with the red skin and the golden hair would have to turn away from the flying object or it would strike her. Then with his opponent distracted, he would have the chance to take her down. Dillon did not think she would be able to not only snatch the glass out of the air but also return the item back to his brother who now had broken glass on the side of his face. Along with what would eventually be another scar.

The older brother did rush toward the woman who had come for him and his brother, but Dillon did not think the woman would be fast enough to raise her leg just as he reached her, causing him to run into her foot, positioned at the height of his midsection. The impact not only knocked the air out of his lungs, but it forced him to fall back to the bar.

Daie looked at the two brothers. One was trying to stop the blood from running down his face where the shards of glass had cut him, and the other was holding his stomach, either trying to catch his breath or stop the pain from the rib she had broken.

While keeping her eyes on the two men, Daie bent over and picked up the certificate of capture she had dropped to intercept the flying glass and placed both of them at her back. She then stood back up. "You're wanted for the murder of Hann Gransby." As soon as she said the name, the two brothers turned their heads to look at each other. It was obvious they knew whom she had mentioned because it was the name of the first person they had ever killed, although he was not the last. Daie took a step closer to the two men, "He was my father." If the mention of the name had stirred something in them, the mention of the word "father," made them realize the woman was not there just for the coin. She was there for revenge.

"Uh, Daie."

She heard Colton behind her but did not take her eyes off the two brothers.

"Uh, Daie!" Colton said again, only this time with more urgency.

She turned around and saw Colton standing a pace away with his back toward her. She knew immediately why he was not facing her as well as why he had wanted to get her attention. It was because a good majority of The Last Stop patrons decided they wanted to be part of what was going on at the bar. Daie did not believe they had any concern for the two men she and Colton had come in after, it was more likely the patrons just wanted something to do, and she and Colton had given them the opportunity to do so.

Colton was the person of reason. Perhaps the

only one in the entire place, and that included Daie. "We are only here for these two men," Colton said to let all who were watching him and Daie know their intentions. "They are wanted for murder, and we have certificates of capture for them. Everyone else is free to go about their business." As soon as he said those words, Colton knew the patrons had decided the two new arrivals were their business. Colton took a quick look over his right shoulder to see what Daie was going to say or do. It was obvious from the smile on her face she had nothing to say to the additional patrons. What she was going to do was also obvious to him.

Daie raised her hands, reached over her shoulders, and drew her two daggers. She smiled, turned to face the two brothers, and said, "Let's begin." The patrons took that as their cue, and they all rushed the two newcomers.

With the onrush of the other patrons, the two brothers regained some of their courage. Daie noticed that each of them was now holding a knife in their right hand. They must have drawn them while she was facing the other way. Their weapons were nowhere close to the length or beauty of her own daggers, but she could not help but think that those two knives might have been the ones they used to kill her father. If they were not, the men wielding them had killed him.

The two brothers were nothing more than thugs with weapons. They used surprise to attack and kill their victims. Now moving closer to the red-skinned woman, they had lost their element of surprise, and even if they had not, Daie was not going to be a victim.

Dillon, the man on her left came in first, but Daie knew he was only a diversion. To let the two men think their plan would work, she put her attention on the man who had reached her first. When he did, he thrust his knife at the left side of her body causing her to move to her right. He took that opportunity to move to his right. As he had wanted, this made the woman turn so that she was facing him completely. It would allow his brother to come up behind her and end the fight before it had hardly begun.

Daie knew the man was coming up behind her, but she did not want him to know she did. To play along with their ruse, she extended the dagger in her right hand outward at the man in front. He jumped back, not only to get out of the reach of the blade but also to try to draw the woman along with him. As she moved forward, the man's brother came up behind her.

Instead of taking the last step to engage the man in front of her, as soon as the man jumped backward, Daie turned around and forced the blade in her left hand out and to her left. The smaller brother had been so close to her, he did not have time to get out of the way of the blade as it sliced across his left side. He quickly tried to protect his injury with his hands, so Daie raised her right leg up and kicked the man in his midsection. He bent forward, and with the cut she had given him, he fell to the floor. She was not sure whether he was out of the fight or not, but she knew the other brother was coming up behind her.

Colton did not want to be part of a tavern brawl. He had no problem with the old priests' ways, defending the defenseless, but he was pretty sure the people coming toward him were not part of that group. A couple of them had pulled out swords, and a couple had knives. Those that did not have any actual type of weapon, made do by using a bottle of drink, and even a couple had broken up some stools to use the legs as clubs. Before they reached him, Colton decided to give diplomacy one more try. "Please, good people, I do not want to hurt any of you." Apparently, the patrons did not understand diplomacy, because when he finished his statement, it appeared to be the signal for everyone to start running toward him.

The numbers were against him. He did a quick count and came up with fifteen patrons taking part in the fight. The only benefit of the numbers was that the room, having tables and chairs, caused the crowd to get in each other's way. By the time the first attackers reached him, there were only three people directly in front of him.

Colton twirled his staff out in front of him, and at the speed he made the staff move, it caused the patrons to stop and rethink just what they were doing.

Three of the attackers decided they had some other place to be. It was obvious to them that the man knew how to use the weapon. Since the patrons in the rear of the crowd did not have a good view of what the man had done with the staff, they pushed the people in front of them which in turn pushed the people in front of them. This went on until the three people at the front of the crowd closest to Colton moved forward, and since they did not want the twirling staff to come in contact with any part of their bodies, they raised their weapons to defend themselves. Colton had no choice but to do the same.

He had never been in a fight. Even when he lived on the streets of Maridian, Colton always made sure that whatever he was going to get himself into, he would be able to talk his way out of it, or simply run away. Not because he was a coward, but because running was the best option for survival. In this place, talking had failed, and running was not an option since the patrons were between him and the exit. For the first time in his life, Colton had to fight, to survive.

The man at the far left of the three people was the first to get close to him, just in reach of his staff. The man had a knife in his right hand, and when it was at the proper distance, Colton stopped the twirling of his staff and brought the end of it down, directly on the man's wrist. The strike from the hard wooden staff caused the man to drop the knife, and as he looked down at his empty hand, Colton shoved his staff outward, causing the end of his staff to strike the man's chest. He did it with enough force to not only knock the air out of the man but also caused him to fall back into the patron behind him, which caused both men to take out the third man in line.

When he pushed the man, he had extended his staff out, so he had a hold of it by the end closest to him. He pulled it back and swung it over his head in a circular motion, and right back around causing it to land on the side of the face of the man at the far right. The force of the blow was not strong enough to kill him, Colton made sure of that, but the man would not be eating any solid food for quite some time.

The man who had been standing in the middle of the three had no problem hearing the man's jawbone break, or it could have been the man's teeth. Either way, the man decided he was not brave enough, or drunk enough, to take on the man with the staff, and since he had already bent down to avoid the swinging staff, he chose to fall to the floor and crawl away on his hands and knees.

Colton saw the man leaving, but that did not make him believe he had won a major victory. The first man was out of the battle because he had a broken wrist. The next man he had struck had a broken jaw. The men who had fallen because of the first man were back on their feet, and now the remaining nine patrons were coming for him.

Colton decided that there was no need to wait until they arrived. He twirled his staff in front of him and once again, it caused the crowd to stop moving and wait to see what he was going to do. Colton stopped the twirling staff so that it was out in front of him, horizontally to the ground. He then rushed forward to take the fight to the patrons.

While at the priesthood, Colton had read how the old priests had never initiated a fight. They were men of peace and only resorted to violence when the occasion called for it. Colton believed this one did.

Daie quickly turned to face the older brother. To her, it looked as if his heart was not in the fight. It might be because with his brother injured, he would have to take her on all by himself, and as with most cowards, they needed someone to fight alongside them, or they would lose their nerve.

The younger brother was at her back but down on the floor, even with his injury he was able to yell to his older brother, "Kill that whore, Dillon!" It was all the encouragement the older brother needed.

He came forward and swiped his knife out in front of him. Daie had no problem with avoiding the attack by forcing her midsection in a little. She also noticed that the man had no skill when it came to fighting.

Normally, the two brothers would sneak up on their victims. With the way they took them out, they did not rely on skill, and when Daie realized just how clumsy the man moved, she could not help but wonder if the killings they committed, were successful due to luck instead of skill. The thought made her want to kill them even more. Because these men had killed her father, and if they had not worked together, neither of them would have been able to take him away from her.

As his arm passed in front of her, Daie used the blade in her right hand to cut the back of the man's upper right arm. It was not enough to hurt him badly, even though it did draw blood. The cut did not even force the man to drop the knife. Daie did not want the fight to end too soon. She wanted it to last a bit longer, so she could hurt the man. Even to the point he had hurt her father, which was to the point of death.

Colton rushed forward, forcing the patrons close to him to think he might just be out of his mind. What man would come rushing toward a group of people outnumbering him?

The pause they took was enough for Colton to take advantage of the situation. When he reached the group, he tossed his staff into the air. The patrons' eyes followed the moving object, which gave Colton the time to forcefully extend his arms, his palms facing outward. He struck the chests of two of the patrons, and with the force behind his blows, it caused the men to stumble backward. Since none of their fellow attackers tried to help them, they fell to the floor, holding their chests. They decided the floor was the best place for them to remain until the fight ended. Since the other patrons around had also been watching the staff take to the air, they were only able to see the end results of what the man with the staff had done.

As the men fell backward, Colton reached up and grabbed hold of his staff, which was already coming back down. He placed his hands four handbreadths apart, in the proper position to push the staff forward, allowing the staff to strike another two patrons in their noses. They went stumbling backward as well, and after the strike from the hard wooden staff and with the force the man used, blood came spilling out of their noses. They were out of the fight as well. The number of his attackers was now down to five.

After seeing most of the attackers were out of the fight, three more decided it was time for them to leave. Out of the fifteen, only two patrons remained, but they were the ones with swords.

The younger brother was still kneeling on the floor. Daie knew she had only grazed his side, and he should have recovered from when she knocked the air out of him, but he still did not join the fight.

The older brother, with his back toward the bar, was facing Daie. He still had his knife in his right hand but seemed a lot more hesitant to use it. In fact, he was waiting for the woman with the red skin to make the next move, but all she did was stand there looking at him, smiling. Dillon did not like that smile and knew exactly how to remove it. "Are you going to plead for your life, like your daddy did, when I stabbed him?" She was no longer smiling. He saw Daie look at the knife he was holding. "Yeah, that's right," he raised his hand so his knife was at the height of his chest. "I used this to kill him. And yeah, I remember him. He thought he was the best carpenter around. Well, being the best only got him killed. We left him there in the middle of the street." He knew what he was saying was getting to her. "What's the matter missy? You miss your dead daddy?" Even though he was not good at fighting or killing, Dillon knew that when someone gets angry, they make mistakes, and in a fight, a mistake can be deadly. He did not know that his opponent did not make mistakes.

She took two steps forward, leading with the dagger in her left hand. She thrust it out, toward the man's stomach and if he had not turned so that his right side was facing her, he would have felt the blade. Even though he had dodged the attack, Dillon regretted having taunted the woman. She had moved so fast that it was by pure luck he avoided the attack.

When he turned, he not only stepped backward, to Daie's left, he stumbled over his own feet and fell to the floor. Daie did not hesitate to straddle him and place the blade she held in her left hand across his throat. The man thought he was about to die. Until he saw that his brother, whom he thought was out of the fight, was not as bad off as he pretended to be and was coming up behind the woman.

Hale had been faking how serious his injury was, waiting for the best moment to rejoin the fight. Now that the woman was on top of his brother with a dagger at his throat, Hale knew this would be his best chance to end not just the fight, but the woman's life as well.

Instead of trying to sneak up on her, he thought it was best for him and his brother, who he thought was about to die, to rush to his rescue. As he reached the woman, he leveled his knife so when he took the last step to her it would enter into her back. It did not make it.

Daie had the man pinned on the ground and was doing everything she could to not end his life. He had killed her father and deserved to die. No one would blame her.

"Kill him. He killed your father. It is not revenge; it is justice," Sun thought to her.

Just as she was about to rake the blade across the man's throat, she sensed someone coming toward her. Without even thinking about it, and while she kept the blade in her left hand against Dillon's throat, she turned her body enough to see behind her. Before she even got sight of the man, she extended the dagger in her right hand, causing it to go into the younger brother's right shoulder. While she stabbed him, she flipped the dagger she had in her left hand, so the tip of the blade was pointing toward the floor, and just as the blade in her right hand entered the younger brother, the blade in her left hand entered the older one. The two did not know it, but they would have the same scar, in the exact same place for the rest of their lives. One more thing they had in common was that when the blades entered them, they both screamed out at the same time.

Colton looked at the two men and decided the one on the left was the more efficient one. It was the way he held himself and his sword. Colton would take care of him first. He brought the right end of his staff over in front of him and the man did exactly what he should have done. He brought his sword up to block the movement of his opponent. As soon as the two weapons made contact, Colton reversed the motion of his staff and brought the right end down while bringing the left end up and across his opponent's sword. He had enough power and speed in his move, to force the sword and the man's arm down to the floor where Colton used his staff to hold it there. He then brought the left end of the staff straight up, and since the man had to bend over at his waist to keep a hold of his sword, his head was directly in line with the end of the staff, which came up and struck him under his chin. The man fell back, dropping his sword so he could use both hands to stop the blood from pouring out of his mouth because he had bit down on his tongue.

The last man saw what had happened and knew

that if he did not commit to his attack, he would end up like the others taken out by the man with the staff and dressed in a robe. It was at that moment the patron realized that the robe looked like something a priest of the Creator would wear, but quickly brushed the thought away when he saw his opportunity arise.

The man with the staff had turned his body slightly away when he had brought his staff up and struck his opponent. The last patron saw that he would have a quick moment to thrust his own sword into the man with the staff, so he rushed forward.

Out of the corner of his right eye, Colton saw the last man coming straight for him, sword leading the way. He spun to his left bringing his staff with him while at the same time he crouched down. When he was facing the last attacker, his staff struck the man in the legs, and Colton swept him off his feet. The man landed on his back and Colton did not hesitate to rise and move to stand over him.

The man had the air knocked out of him, but Colton knew he was far from being out of the fight, especially since he still had a hold of his sword. Colton had eliminated all the other patrons who had attacked him and was ready to end the encounter but did not want this one man to try anything else when he turned his back on him. To make sure he would not, Colton hit him in the middle of his forehead with the staff, knocking him unconscious.

Just as he had finished with the last attacker,

Colton heard the screams of two different men off to his right. The thought of what Daie might have done rushed into his mind, but when he turned to look in the direction the screams had come from, he saw that even though her daggers were in the two men, they were both still alive, something for which he was very thankful.

The men who had killed her father were not up for any more of the fight. She looked at the one to her right then turned and looked at the one lying on the floor. Both of them were scowling because of the daggers embedded in their shoulders. She decided to help them by removing what was causing them so much pain. When she pulled out her daggers, both men screamed again, and the one who had been standing fell to the floor and up against the bar. The one already on the floor rolled so that he was facing the bar, with his wounded shoulder off the floor. The removal of the blades had hurt just as much as when they had entered.

Daie stood up and looked at her daggers. She saw that there was no blood on them, so she twirled them three times in her hands, then quickly and effortlessly returned them to the holster on her back. She then turned around and looked at Colton who was staring at her. Even though he did not say anything about her allowing the two men to live, the smile on his face told her he approved of what she had done. Daie was not sure she did.

They had killed her father, and they deserved

to die as well. The hatred she felt for the two men was not just hers. It was also the hatred Sun had for Moon, and Daie was not going to let Sun affect her to where she did not know whether it was her will or the will of Sun she was acting upon.

With the two brothers out of the fight, Daie walked toward Colton who was making his way to her. When they reached each other, she looked around and saw what he had done. Even though she was fighting two men herself, she was able to catch glimpses of Colton's fight. She did not say it to him, but she was impressed. He had taken down fifteen attackers with just a wooden staff. After seeing him in action, Daie had to wonder if Colton really was a priest. She began to hear a few of the participants of the fight groan as they either woke up or decided it was okay for them to move without receiving another beating from the man with the staff. She realized that even though they were not in the same condition before the fight began, and two had blood coming out of their noses and one had a bloody mouth, all of them were alive. Colton had not gone for a single kill, even though the numbers were against him. Exactly what a priest would do.

She had to do everything she could to stop herself from killing just two men. The moment before she had allowed her blades to enter into their shoulders, Daie had to force herself to alter her attack, because she had almost put her blades directly into their hearts. Almost.

"Are you alright?" Colton finally asked.

Daie looked at him, then turned around to look at the two brothers behind her, each of them holding their shoulders. She then turned back to face Colton, "I'm fine," she said then stepped around him and made her way to the entrance, stepping around and over some of Colton's attackers.

Colton waited until she had left then turned to face the two they had come in for. Both of them looked as if they were ready to call it a day. "Get up on your feet," Colton said but neither of them looked as if they were going to do what he wanted. Colton knew what to say to get them moving. "If you don't get to your feet, I will call my friend back in here and she is not as gentle as I am."

The two brothers looked around the tavern and saw a lot of the people who had stepped up to join the fight were now either lying down on the floor or sitting in a chair, either nursing their wounds or trying to get enough of their senses back to leave. Both thought that if the man who had taken care of all of them was the gentle one, then what would the woman do if she came back? The two brothers looked at each other, and then awkwardly rose to their feet.

"Good choice," Colton said then stepped to the side to allow the two captives to lead the way.

Once the woman and her friend had taken the ones they were after out of the tavern, the owner rose up from behind the bar. He saw some of his

tables turned over and there were a couple of broken chairs. He looked at his supply of drink behind
the counter and saw that not only were all the bot-
tles accounted for, but not even one had suffered
any damage. He then looked back out across the
floor and decided the fight that had just taken place
had been the least destructive in the time he had
owned the tavern. "Drinks are on the house," the
tavern keeper said, and the patrons well enough to
walk made their way to the bar. Needing something
to dull the pain they were feeling.

Daie was already on her horse by the time Colton
came out with the two brothers. They stopped walking and Colton stepped around them and climbed
onto his horse. When he was ready, he motioned
with his head to the right to let the men know which
direction they should go. The two men moved out
into the street and started walking, with Daie and
Colton riding behind them.

It was not long after they had walked down the
street a bit that Hale thought about making a run
for it. "Just try it," Daie said, seeing that the younger
brother was getting a bit twitchy. He looked over his
shoulder at her. "Before you get a pace away, you
will have both of my daggers in your back." He did
not say it, but he believed her and turned back to
look at where he was walking. His idea of running
never advancing past the planning stage.

"Stop here," Colton said when they reached
the building they had been heading for. The two

brothers stopped, and Colton and Daie climbed off their horses. The two brothers did not look at them but knew that they were to enter the building they had come to.

They entered first and right behind them were Daie and Colton. The brothers moved to the left side of the room while Colton stood in front of the door they entered through and Daie moved to stand in front of the desk where another man was standing behind. She pulled out the certificates of capture, unfolded them, and tossed them down on the desk for the man to see. "These two are wanted for murder in Maridian."

The constable of the town guard looked down at the parchments and then looked at the two men who were standing to the right side of the room. They looked enough like the pictures, and he was ready to believe they were the ones the certificates were for. He would have to check their names, which were also on the parchment, but he had a feeling the two were the ones wanted for the murder. Not only in Maridian, but even in Sundridge.

There had been two killings just over the last half moon-cycle, and the two men standing over to the side of the room had been on the list of suspects. There was no evidence, but the murders happened not too long after the two had come to the town. The constable figured that this woman, the woman with the red skin and golden hair, had just solved the crime he and his fellow guards had not been able to.

The man behind the desk looked over to his left and nodded to two of his men who took it as their cue to take the two captives to the back and lock them up. He would have to get them medical treatment, since they were bleeding all over the floor, but he would do that after he had a nice long talk with them. Men in pain seem to be freer with information and he was going to use that to his advantage. The constable did not like conflict in his quiet town, and the murders that had taken place had caused a lot of it.

The constable looked back to the woman standing on the other side of his desk. "I will have to get verification on who those two are, and it will take some time before I can pay you the reward for their capture."

Daie looked directly into the constable's eyes, "Keep it, I did not do it for the coin." She did not have to say it, but the constable knew the reason she had brought the two men in was personal.

Daie turned around and was about to leave but something to her right caught her eye. She walked over and looked at what was hanging on the wall. When she had studied the parchments long enough, she asked the constable her question, "Which one of these is the most dangerous?" She was referring to the images on the certificates of capture posted on the wall.

The constable came from around his desk and over to Daie, "Well, the reward for Wallace Payton is the highest. It is at one thousand silver." The constable turned his head and saw the woman with the red skin looking at him, and he could tell that he had not given her the answer to the question she asked. He turned back to look at the certificates, "If you want the most dangerous, then I would say that would be, Rashad Menlo. He and his band of thugs have been terrorizing good folks for the last three seasons. Of course, they move around so much that I would not have any idea where you would start looking for them." Daie pulled the certificate of capture off the wall, turned, and walked out of the building.

"Thank you," Colton said to let the constable know they appreciated his help, just before he followed Daie.

When he walked outside, Daie had already climbed onto her horse. At least she had not ridden off and waited until Colton was on his horse beside her. "So where are we going?" he asked since it was obvious she was once again deciding the direction they would be traveling.

"Sun said that Rashad Menlo is to the southwest." She turned her horse and started riding out of town to go and find the next person she could challenge and test her skills. She hoped this Rashad Menlo was something more than the Polk brothers. She had not sought them out to hone her fighting skills; something she would do until she could find Nyght. She went after the two men because she wanted justice for her father. A part of her still felt that she would only see justice after the two men who had killed him were dead themselves, but she would settle for what she had done. "For you father," she said to herself, just before she rode out of Sundridge.

TWELVE

Daie and Colton arrived at the small village of Pineview, one moon-mark after they had left Sundridge. Their supplies were running low, and even though Daie had become efficient at hunting and Colton at fishing, they still needed to replenish their stock.

In their time spent in the wilderness, Daie had caught a few rabbits and two beavers and was going to trade their furs for the supplies they needed. Colton did not mention the fact about how if they had waited to receive the payment for taking in the Polk brothers, they would have had enough coin to cover their expenses, but he knew Daie had not gone after the two men for the reward.

There were still two marks before the sun would set, so they had planned to trade the furs for supplies and hopefully enough coin to allow them to pay for a room somewhere in the village for the night. Even if they had to sleep in someone's barn, it would be a change from sleeping in the woods. Colton did not have a problem with it, he liked being outside with nature, it was part of Creator, but even with the cloak she wore, when the sun left the sky, Daie always felt cold.

They rode their horses up to the small building with the sign, General Store, hanging on the outside of the building. They dismounted and Daie removed the furs she had stored on the back of her saddle. She stepped up onto the small porch but just as she was about to open the door to go inside, she realized that Colton was not with her. She turned around and saw him standing next to his horse, with his back toward her. He was looking at something, or more like, for something, because he moved his gaze from the left to the right, viewing the area. Daie walked to the edge of the porch. "What is it?" she asked.

Colton took one more look at the village and then turned around to look at Daie, but when he did, he turned his head to look over his left shoulder back at the buildings behind him. "I don't know," he said and continued with his scrutiny, even though he did not see anything.

Daie looked at him for another few breaths then looked out at the village herself. She did not see anything unusual and did not sense any type of danger. "I'm going inside," she said to Colton, but he did not turn to join her or even look her way. She decided that he could just wait outside while she took care of obtaining their supplies, so she turned around and headed inside the small shop.

When she entered, she saw an elderly woman behind the counter working with some type of cloth.

When the woman looked up and saw Daie, she held her stare a little too long, letting Daie know that the color of her skin once again made people take a longer look at her. Too long for her comfort.

Daie walked over to the counter and placed the furs on top of it. "Do you trade for fur?" she asked to get to the reason she was there.

The woman looked at her, and then at the furs on the counter, then back to Daie. "We do, but my husband is the one who deals with the trappers. He's in the back. If you wait a moment I will go and get him." Daie nodded to let the woman know she would wait.

The woman walked through the door behind her, and it was not long before she returned with her husband. As soon as Daie saw the two of them together, she could not help but compare them to Mama and Papa, the two people who had raised her after her parents had died and passed the boarding house to her when they had passed away themselves. The man and woman she was looking at now reminded her of them.

"What do you have?" the man asked as he came over to stand at the counter and immediately picked up the pile of furs Daie had brought in.

"Five rabbits and two beaver pelts," Daie said but she really did not have to because the man had already started looking through the stack of furs and it was obvious he had been doing the task for most of his life and could tell what the furs were just by sight. "I just need a few supplies and any coin to make up the difference from the trade."

The man took a more thorough look at the pelts separating the rabbits from the beaver. He then slid the rabbit furs across the counter to Daie. "I'll give you ten copper for the two beaver skins, but there isn't much call for rabbit furs around here."

Daie, when she was Hanna, ran a boarding house for a long time, so she knew about doing business. Maybe not about trading furs or things of that nature, but having dealt with others, she knew when there was no hope in increasing the coin she would receive for the beaver skins or convincing the man to take the rabbit furs. She also knew that what he was offering was not enough to purchase the supplies she needed and definitely not enough to pay for a room for just one night.

Before she could take back the furs, thinking she might be able to find some other place to trade them, but knowing that with the size of the village there was not much hope, the door to the shop opened. She turned around and saw Colton had finally decided to join her. He walked up to the counter and the wife of the man moved down a bit to see to her new customer. "May I help you, priest?"

"I am not sure," Colton said as he reached the counter. Daie noticed he did not say that he was not a priest. "I am with her," he said and took a quick look at Daie standing at his right, then looked at the old man who was looking back at him. Colton then looked at the woman to continue his conversation, "Can you tell me if there is something..." Colton took a breath to phrase what he wanted to say the best way he could, "...not right about your village?" By the look on the woman's face, Colton knew that his concern was warranted, which she confirmed even more when the elderly woman turned to her husband who had turned to look at his wife. The stare they shared told Colton something was going on in the village and he wanted to find out what it was, "Tell me what you know," he said, and the elderly couple looked at him.

The elderly man then looked at his wife, "Dear, why don't you fetch the priest," he stopped talking and looked at the woman with the red skin, "and his friend something to eat and drink." He then put his eyes back on the priest, "While you eat, I will tell you what is going on in Pineview. Maybe you can help, priest. Creator knows we need it."

Colton turned his head to look at Daie. She had turned to look at him, and they both knew that whatever the shopkeeper was going to tell them must be something dreadful. They could tell because of the fear they sensed in the words the man spoke.

The woman brought them two bowls of stew. It had some type of meat with vegetables, and it might have even been good, but as soon as the shopkeeper started telling the story, both Daie and Colton slowed down eating their meal.

The shopkeeper told them about how the

sickness started about two moon-marks ago. At first, it was just one child who fell ill, but soon it was two, then three, then six, and then every child in the village became ill and stayed not only at home but also in their beds. Not one of them had enough strength even to feed themselves. The village did not have a true healer. Just an elderly woman who had been taking care of people since she was a young woman herself, but she had no success in helping the children.

In the middle of the story, the shopkeeper stopped talking and both Daie and Colton knew that whatever he was going to say next was not going to be pleasant. "It was three sun-cycles ago that the first child who fell ill died in her sleep." Colton and Daie stopped eating their stew altogether.

The shopkeeper told them that everyone in the village knew it would not be long before one of the other children succumbed to the sickness, and soon all of them would. Pineview would become a village of adults only because the children would be dead.

The man stopped talking but Colton could tell there was something else he wanted to say, "What is it?" Colton asked.

The shopkeeper turned to look at his wife standing next to him, and he placed his hand on hers. The elderly man then turned back to look at Colton and Daie, "Our grandson lives in the village." He did not have to say anything else.

Colton had sat his bowl of stew on the counter

a while ago, so he did not have to before he turned around to force himself to remain calm. The thought of children not only becoming ill but also dying was very upsetting to him, but he knew there was something more to the story. He turned back around to look at the elderly couple. "Now tell me what everyone is not saying."

The man and his wife looked at each other. The woman nodded to her husband to let him know that he should do as the priest asked. The shopkeeper turned back to look at Colton. "One night, a mother to one of the children was lying next to her son in his bed. She had fallen asleep, but when she woke, she saw something." The shopkeeper stopped talking again.

This time, Daie asked a question, "What did she see?"

The shopkeeper took a deep breath, "She was not sure. She believed she had imagined it, but she said she thought she saw someone," he paused to change his word, "something, leave through the window. The child's mother jumped up out of the bed, but when she ran to the window, she did not see anyone. The window was on the second level of their home and there was no way someone could have climbed up to it or even jumped to the ground below without hurting themselves."

Colton had his doubts about what the man had just said. He just did not have anything to prove it, and he was not going to find it there in the shop.

"Take me to your grandson." The elderly couple did not look as if they were going to do what he asked. Colton did not have time to wait for them to think about it. He stepped up to the counter, and if it had not been there, he would have moved to stand within a handbreadth of them, "Now!" With the way he spoke, the elderly couple knew that he was serious, and they immediately started heading to the end of the counter where they could come to the side Colton and Daie were standing on.

When they did, Colton turned to follow them but stopped when he felt Daie place her hand on his arm. He turned his head to look at her.

"What is it?" she asked.

He waited for two breaths before he answered, "Nothing good," he said, then turned and headed off after the shopkeeper and his wife who were already out the door.

Daie stayed behind for just a moment then followed. She had no idea what was going on, but she had never seen Colton act so seriously before in all the time she had known him. Not only that, but she could sense something else about him. He was worried, even more than when he had taken her out of Maridian.

They arrived at the house of the shopkeeper's son, his wife, and their son. When they reached the door, Colton rushed past the shopkeeper and walked inside without even stopping to knock. Daie was sure that if someone had secured the door, denying him admittance, he would have kicked it in so he would not have to wait for someone to grant him entrance.

"Who are..." the man in the house started to say, but saw that the stranger who had just burst into his home was with his own parents, "Father, Mother, what are you doing here, and who is this?"

Colton did not give the shopkeeper a chance to answer, "Where is your son?"

The man looked behind him which was all Colton needed to know on where to go. "You can't just come in..." The man started to say but stopped when his father took hold of his arm. The younger man turned his head to look at him.

"Son, let him go. He is here to help."

With the look he gave his father, he asked what was going on. His father's look told his son that the man might be the only one who can save the child. The man looked at his parents and decided he would trust their judgment.

Colton did not exactly know where the boy was, but something was leading him. It was a darkness Colton was feeling, and as he made his way through the house, the darkness led him to the room with the sick boy and his mother.

When she saw the unknown man burst into the room, she was about to yell for her husband, but she sensed that the man in the robes of a priest was not a threat to her or her son. She knew what she was feeling was correct when he spoke, "I am here to help." She nodded once to let the man know he could enter, and she would not get in his way.

By the time he walked over to the bed, the room was filled with the child's parents and grandparents. Colton stood looking down at the child whose skin was pale white. The first thing he thought of was the way Daie had described the woman who had attacked her, but he knew the boy's color was not due to any blessing of Moon.

"Can you help him?" the boy's mother asked, and Colton knew she was not just asking, she was pleading with him.

Colton did not answer because he did not want to give her any false hope. He needed to know what was going on in the village before he came to any conclusion. One thing he did know was that the illness the children were suffering from was nothing natural. In fact, it was just the opposite.

Colton sat down on the bed next to the boy whose entire body was under a blanket except for his head. Colton reached out and placed his hand over the child's forehead. Before he even brought his hand down to touch the boy, an image flashed in his mind. Colton immediately closed his eyes. Not because he was in any pain, but because he wanted to force the image to remain in his thoughts for as long as possible.

The image was of a creature. Something in the area, but not in the village itself. Colton could tell, because the darkness he had felt in the room was weaker than what he felt from the image in his thoughts. If the creature was in the village, then he was sure he would have sensed it and not just the darkness it left behind when it had been in the room as well as in the village.

Colton made his mind travel to the image. He did not know where the creature was, but he was able to get a clear view of it. It was of a woman, or what used to be a woman. She still had skin on her bones, but pulled so tight that it looked as if she had no flesh at all. Her hands ended in sharp black claws. Colton was sure they had once been her fingernails but what they were now was something that was not part of anything human. The dress she wore was black and tattered.

The creature, sensing that someone was spying on it, shrieked, and moved toward Colton. Even though they were only looking at each other through his mind, Colton had a good view of her rotten teeth and her empty eye sockets. Then the creature pushed him away, and his mind went flying over the distance and back to the room where his body was. The force was so strong, he fell off the side of the bed and onto the floor.

Daie pushed everyone aside to get to him, and when she did, she helped Colton to his feet. "What happened?" she asked, but he only gave her a quick and worried look, and then looked at the boy in the bed. "What is it?" she asked to get some kind of answer.

He turned and looked at her, "It is a lych." He turned and looked at the parents and grandparents of the child, "It has come to your village to feed on the children. When it has finished with them, it will start on the adults. Once it has taken the lives of everyone, it will move on."

The boy's father took his wife in his arms, and the shopkeeper did the same. All of them were more terrified than they had been before. They had not known what had caused the children to fall ill, but now that they did, it did not help. "What do we do priest?" the shopkeeper's wife asked.

Colton looked at her and gave his answer, "Nothing." The look on the parents' faces told him they were about to say that there had to be something they could do, so Colton explained, "I will deal with it." He then stepped through the group of people and walked out of the room, faster than he had entered. Daie and the others were right behind him, all but the boy's mother who stayed with her son.

When they reached the first floor of the house, Colton went over to the fireplace, and even though there was a fire in it, he extended his hand and pulled out a piece of burnt wood. He did not even realize that the heat had not bothered his hand.

He then walked over to the front entrance and with the door closed he began drawing. Once he finished, he stepped back and looked at what he had done. It was three circles, each one intersecting the other two. It was the symbol of Creator. With the way the three circles crossed one another, there were seven parts to the image. The three individual circles represented Birth, Life, and Death. They were the circles that represent the existence of every living being and creature Creator had created. The next inner parts of the drawing represented, Male, Female, and Child. What Creator made to bring life to the world. Elves, Dwarfs, and even Trolls and Gnomes, as well as humans. The innermost part of the drawing was just one section that represented Creator himself. He was the one part that was part of everything. Birth, Life, and Death. Male, Female, and Child. Creator was at the center of every living being and creature in existence.

Colton turned around and saw everyone looking at him. He did not have time to explain so he only said what he had to, to get everyone to start moving. He went over to the sick boy's father, lifted the man's hand, and placed the chard piece of wood in it. "You need to draw that image on every door, and window in this house. Make sure you only draw it on the inside." The man did not move or look as if he was going to do as Colton had instructed, "Go! Now! Or your son will die!" The man took off to do as instructed.

Colton then turned to look at the shopkeeper's wife, took her by her arm, and pulled her over to the door where he had drawn the Crest of Creator. "Did you see how I drew that?" he asked as he pointed to the back of the door but kept his eyes on the elderly woman. She nodded her head to answer the question. "Do you think you can draw it?" Once again, she nodded. "I need you to go to everyone in this village. Go to the ones who have a child first. Tell the parents, they need to draw that symbol on every door and window of their house, on the inside only. Then tell them that they are to stay in their homes and not to come out until the sun is up." She did not give any sign that she understood what she needed to do. "Do you understand?" he asked, and she nodded. "Then go and be quick."

The elderly woman went to the door and opened it but before she stepped through, she turned back to ask one question, "What if they will not listen to me?"

Colton gave her the answer he was sure would get them to do as she instructs, "Tell them, death is coming for their children."

The woman gave him one terrifying look, then rushed out the door.

Colton went to the shopkeeper. "Take me to the place where the children go for their studies." The shopkeeper nodded and unlike his son and his wife, he did not hesitate to do what the priest asked of him.

He led Colton and Daie to a building down the street. The building was small and empty, but Colton knew that did not matter. What was there before had poisoned the place with its darkness. Colton turned to look at the shopkeeper standing on his right. "Go find your wife; help her to pass the word to everyone in the village on what they need to do. Then get her and yourself back to your son's house and stay there until the sun comes up."

The man nodded and turned around to do as instructed, but stopped to ask the priest one last question, "Can you stop it?"

Colton turned around to look at the man and gave his honest answer, "I will try." The shopkeeper knew that he could not ask for more, and then took off down the street to find his wife.

Colton turned back to look at the building. As he walked closer to it, he could feel the foulness grow stronger. When he placed his foot on the front porch, an image of the creature flashed in his mind. He closed his eyes to force it away and walked to the door. When he opened it, the foulness in the building struck him, and he felt sick to his stomach. "Creator, watch over us," he said as a prayer for protection. He then stepped inside.

He saw the benches on both sides of the room. There were six on the left and six on the right with an aisle down the middle of the room. It led to the front of the small classroom, where there was a small podium. He could feel the foulness coming from it, even from where he was standing.

He walked down the aisle and moved closer to the front of the classroom. When he came to the podium he reached out, but before his hand made contact, he pulled it back. He did not want to feel the foulness the creature would have left behind.

"Why did you want to come here?" Daie asked behind him.

Colton turned and saw her standing in the doorway. He then went back to looking at the podium, "This is where she started." He turned around and walked toward Daie but continued with his explanation. "She started draining the children while they came to this place for their lessons."

"This lych?" Daie asked.

"Yes."

"What is it?"

Colton came to stand in front of Daie before he answered her question, "It is a creature made by Defiler."

Daie did not believe much in Creator, and with what she did believe, she did not put much faith into, but even she knew of the Defiler, what Colton and others called the enemy of Creator. Defiler had only one agenda, which was to take everything Creator made and corrupt it. To turn what Creator had made naturally into something unnatural. To take life and make it into un-life. To defile everything Creator created and loved.

"What does this lych want?" Daie asked.

"The life of every person in this village. It came here and took on the form of the schoolteacher. Killing her of course, and then using the school as a place to begin to drain the children. She would have started by taking a bit from each child while they were here. It would not have been long before the children became too weak to leave their homes. Then the creature would visit the children at night to continue feeding from them."

"Why at night?"

Colton turned and looked at the podium. "The creature's power is limited while the sun is up. It would only be able to do so much damage while the children were here for their lessons. When they took to their beds, the creature would come at night because it was safer for it. It cannot stand the light of the sun. And even though it will not kill the creature it will weaken it greatly."

"And that is what you are going to do, kill it?" Daie asked.

Colton turned back to look at her, "That is what I am going to try."

Colton made a gesture with his head to let her know it was time for them to leave the school. Colton wanted to get out of the building tainted by the lych, and since it was a creature of Defiler, and he was a priest of Creator, it was affecting him more than it affected Daie.

"If the sun weakens it, then maybe we should wait until the sun rises to hunt the creature down," Daie suggested once they were outside.

Colton who had walked a pace ahead of her to get away from the building turned around to face Daie, "Even though the sun cannot kill it, a lych can only be killed when it is in its true form. And it will not show it while the sun is in the sky. At night, it will cast away the false appearance, it will be stronger in its true form, which means at night is the only chance we have of stopping it."

Daie nodded to let him know she understood, but she had one more point to discuss with him, "I did not know the priesthood taught their priests about these things."

Colton looked at her for two breaths then replied, "They didn't. I just know." He did not know how else to say it. He did not learn about the creature at the priesthood. He had not even read about them himself. When he had touched the boy and saw the creature in his mind, everything he needed to know about it came to him. He knew what it was, as well as what it was doing in the village, and that killing the creature would be possible, but very dangerous.

It would take a lot to destroy the creature and Colton had to wonder if he would be able to. If he could not, it would kill everyone in the village, and since he revealed its presence, there was no longer a need to remain hidden. It would now attack in the open. It would kill the children and then the adults. Colton did not tell the shopkeeper and his family that part. They had enough to worry about and preparations to take care of. Colton would deal with the creature. That was what a priest of Creator was for.

Colton was waiting between two buildings when he heard the first sound the creature was making. It wailed as it moved closer to the village. He knew it was making the noise to let all its attended victims know that it was coming for them and that they did not have much time left. It wailed in anger because its discovery forced the creature to move faster than it wanted to. The lych was a creature of Defiler, and it wanted to make the people of the village suffer as their children's life drained from them bit by bit, until the child's death finally came. Since the priest had forced it out of hiding, the creature would kill everyone this night, and then move on to the next village or town it could find, to continue with its path of death.

Colton stayed between the buildings even when he could sense the presence of the creature within the village. It had stopped its wailing, then all of a sudden it took it up again. Colton knew why. It only took the creature one more attempt to figure out it would not be able to get into any of the dwellings where the people of Pineview were hiding.

It was time for Colton to confront the creature, so he said a small prayer to Creator to give him the strength to destroy what had come to the village to defile what Creator had given life.

He stepped out from where he was, and into the street. The lych could sense him. He was a priest of Creator, and that alone would cause the creature of Defiler to want to end his life. The lych's thirst to end the lives of those it had already touched had become stronger and that was why it had tried to get into the homes, so it could feed and gain even more strength. Then it would have dealt with the priest. Since the Crest of Creator had stopped it from entering a single dwelling, the only thing it could take its anger out on was the priest.

"You cannot get into any of these dwellings!" Colton yelled down the street to the lych. "You will have to settle for me!" With the last statement, the creature who had already turned to look at him, started coming toward him. It did not walk or run, in fact, its feet did not even touch the ground, it was floating above it. As if its own foulness did not want to touch the ground Creator had created.

Colton saw the lych coming toward him but he did not move. He waited until it was in the right position. When it was about thirty paces from him, Colton brought up his staff so that it was out in front of him, angled from his left shoulder down to his right hip. When it was twenty paces away, he started running toward the creature that was coming toward him. As soon as he was in motion, Daie came out from where she was and started running toward the creature as well, only from behind it.

They had decided that the best plan was to attack it from two sides. With the creature between them, Colton and Daie ran to meet the lych. When they were about five paces away from it, they raised their weapons ready to strike down the creature. They only got as close as four paces, when the lych stopped where it was, turned its body so that it was facing the side of the street then forcefully extended out its arms. Colton and Daie both went flying backward, almost to the spot where they had started their run on the lych to begin with. When they landed, the force of the lych's power was so strong they each rolled on the ground a few times before they came to a stop.

Daie was up on her feet in no time, and even though the landing had been rough, she had not let go of her daggers and was once again moving toward the creature. Only now, she was angry.

The lych looked at the priest lying down the street, and as much as it wanted to go over and drain the life out of the human, it sensed the one coming up behind it. The creature turned, and when it saw the human coming toward it, it wailed as if to let the woman know she was coming to her death. The lych had powers that could do more than just toss a person around, but the lych loved to touch its victim. The physical contact allowed it to enjoy the meal all the more.

When Daie reached the creature, she thrust out the dagger in her left hand, but the creature turned its body to dodge the blade. Since it had moved to her right, she then thrust her dagger in her right hand out, but the creature turned its body again to avoid the attack. Only this time as it turned, it extended its own arm and grabbed hold of her right wrist before she could pull it back. As soon as the lych touched her skin, it wailed again. Only this time it did so because it had felt pain.

It had not sensed what the woman was, but now it knew. She had the blessing of Sun. Sun was one of the first creations and Sun's loyalty was to Creator, the enemy of Defiler, and of the lych, which knew the sun could hurt it. The lych did not hesitate to change its tactics, and even though it wanted to physically touch its victim, it did not want this woman of Sun to do it any harm, so it relied on the same action it had before. It let go of the woman's arm and used its mental power to push her away.

Daie flew backward and landed against a wooden post attached to one of the buildings. The post was solid and when her back slammed into it, she fell to the ground. This time she only lifted her head to look at the creature. Even with the force behind the attack, she did not suffer from an injury that she could not handle, but she stayed down a bit longer because she could not stop the small laugh that came out of her mouth. She raised her head higher, looking at the lych, and told it what she thought was amusing, "If you touch me, it hurts, doesn't it?" And with that, she was back on her feet running toward the lych.

Her plan was to grab hold of the thing and not let go. What she would do afterward, she had no idea. Daie did not even get close to the creature, because it thrust both of its hands out toward her again and this time, when she went flying backward, she missed the wooden post but only because she went flying past it, and not just into the building's door, but through it as well. This time she did not get back up immediately.

By the time he shook away the feeling of his head spinning, which it was, Colton had time to see Daie go flying backward and into one of the buildings. As much as he wanted to run to her to see if she was hurt, he knew that stopping the creature was his main concern. He just had to hope Daie was still alive.

The creature turned to face him. He figured that since he was a priest of Creator, it wanted to end his life before it went after Daie. Colton did not know that the lych did not want anything to do with the woman blessed by Sun.

Colton decided that since the last time he had tried to run to the creature had failed, he would allow it to come to him, which it had chosen to do anyway. When he was tossed to the ground, he had been able to hold onto his staff, so he brought it up once again at an angle in front of him. When the creature floated over to him, he just barely had time to block the hand that had gone directly for his throat. When his staff encountered the creature's wrist, it pulled it back, hurt from the contact with the weapon used by the priest of Creator.

The pain it felt was worse than when it had touched the woman. The lych now realized its enemies had more help than it had expected. The woman could cause the creature problems, but the priest was even more dangerous. The woman might have

Sun's blessing, but the priest had something the creature could never defeat, faith. Faith in Creator. The lych decided it would be best to take care of both humans in a less hands-on approach.

Colton now knew his staff could harm the creature, so he thrust it outward believing the lych would move to either the left or right to dodge the attack. He was wrong. The creature did not move to either side, instead, it rose up in the air and over his head. Colton was so surprised at what it had done, that he missed the opportunity to attack the creature while it was above him. He did have sense enough to turn around to make sure the creature did not attack him from behind, but the creature already knew how it was going to deal with the priest. It brought its hands up in front of it, palms facing outward, and once again, Colton went flying backward. All the way to the part of the street, where off to his right, was the building Daie went flying into.

The force from the creature tossed her not just through the door, but also into the counter as well as through it. When she was able to raise her head, she realized she was back in the shop where she had entered to trade the furs. Only this time, she was there for another reason.

Daie now understood how powerful the creature was. She knew it was going to make sure she did not get close to it. That meant she could not hurt it by taking hold of the creature, nor could she get close enough to attack it with her daggers. She came up with another solution. The sun weakened the creature. She was the warrior of Sun, and even though it was night, Sun was with her.

As she rose to her feet, she looked through the opening where the door used to be. Colton had just landed on the ground, and it was evident he had not fallen on his own.

She ran out of the building and over to Colton who was on his feet before she reached him. "I have a plan," she said when he looked at her.

"Well, mine didn't work so what is yours?"

She looked down the street and saw the lych floating from the left to the right of the street, as if it was waiting for them to come to it. She turned back to look at Colton, who was once again looking at her, "Do you think you can catapult me into the air with that staff of yours?"

Colton looked at his staff, and then back at Daie, smiled and said, "I am sure of it."

Daie nodded, then turned and moved a few paces behind Colton. When she was in position, he adjusted his hold on his staff so that his left hand was holding the very end, and his right was toward the middle. He then twisted his body and arms so that the staff was at his right side stretched out behind him, with the far end of it on the ground.

"Once I'm in the air, close your eyes," Daie said to him but he did not reply. He trusted her.

The lych moved back and forth across the street. It wanted to attack the two humans but knew that it could not get close to them or it would feel pain. They were not moving toward it, and its hunger, anger, and resentment of the two humans and the ones they belonged to, forced it to make a move. The lych was evil. Evil cannot resist being evil. Evil cannot resist doing what it desires to do. Evil cannot go against its nature to destroy what is good. Since they were not coming to it, it would go to them.

Colton saw the lych start moving toward him, but he did not move. He did not even turn around to look behind him to see if Daie was ready. He would know when it was time. In fact, he did not wait until Daie was in the air to close his eyes. He closed them as he saw the lych coming toward them both. As he closed his eyes, he took a deep breath and then let it out. He did not take another one. He waited. He heard the lych's wail as it came closer. Still, he waited.

Daie waited until the lych was ten paces away, she then started running forward. She wanted to be at the exact point over the creature, but it was not her position she was judging her movements on, it was Colton and his staff. She would trust in him, so when she reached him, her next step forward placed her right foot on the edge of his staff, she then brought her left foot forward, landing on the staff as well.

As soon as he felt the added weight, he knew Daie was in position. He heard the lych wailing but to add to his own strength he let out his own scream and brought the far end of his staff and Daie up over his head. He did all of this with his eyes closed.

She waited until she was over Colton before she raised her left hand with her dagger high over her head and called for its power by speaking its name, "Flare!" When she did, the entire area exploded with a light as bright as the sun. The sun would not kill the creature, but it would weaken it, enough to allow Colton to put an end to its existence. When she landed, she still had her blade stretched to the sky, and even though she did not turn around, she knew the outcome.

When Colton felt the extra weight leave his staff, he did not stop it from continuing forward. He brought it down and out in front of him. As it stretched out and came down, he spoke one command, "By Creator be gone." He only said it in a whisper, but it did not matter. It was not how loud the words were spoken, but the faith behind them.

As the staff came down, it struck the top of the lych's head. Only it did not stop, it continued downward. Through its neck, through its upper body, and only stopped when the end Daie had used to take to the air touched the ground.

Colton had seen the bright light even though his eyes were closed. Daie had told him what the golden color dagger could do, so he knew where the light had come from. He waited until it had vanished completely before he opened his eyes. When he did, he saw Daie standing five paces away, facing him.

They both looked down at the same time, and all they saw left of the lych was the tattered dress it had been wearing. The creature was gone, forever.

They stayed in the village for one more sun-cycle. The children were still feeling the effects of the lych, but Colton had tossed a small stone into the village well where the citizens drew their water. Of course, he said a prayer over the stone before he tossed it in and told the villagers to let the children drink the water, and within a moon-mark, they would be back to normal.

The villagers had invited them to stay longer but Colton explained to them that they had to be on their way because they had business elsewhere. When they left the village of Pineview, they had enough supplies to last them for quite some time, given to them at no cost. Daie even still had the furs she had come to the village with.

Before they left, and just to be on the safe side, Colton had Daie use her dagger Blaze to burn down the school the lych had defiled. When they left Pineview, nothing remained of Defiler.

THIRTEEN

Nyght secured the saddle on Stygian and then climbed up onto the back of her horse. The sun had just gone down and she did not want to waste any time leaving Lorraine. She had been stuck in the village for over two moon-cycles to allow her foot to heal. Even though it was still sore, the blisters had all disappeared and she was sure the remainder of her healing could occur while she traveled.

Once ready, she turned Stygian to start heading to the front gates of the village. As she passed one of the homes, out of the corner of her eye, she saw Darius standing on the front porch watching her. She did not look at him.

When she had first decided to remain in Lorraine to heal, Darius, the only other person in the entire village, had come to where she was staying to talk with her. It did not take him long to realize that she was not the type of person who wanted to sit and chat with anyone, so he decided it was best to just let the woman have her privacy.

While she was healing, the only times she did

leave the house where she was staying, was when she needed to use the relief shack. She had made herself a wooden crutch to help her walk and to keep pressure off her wounded foot, so she was able to move around but limited her movements to only when she needed to.

She had no problem with obtaining water. Since the village was under the cover of clouds constantly, the rain fell every three sun-cycles. Nyght would hang her waterskin outside when the rain came, and the bag's magical properties kept the water she collected fresh until it rained again.

Even though the clouds blocked out the sun, the sky went from black to gray when the sun was in the sky. Although she never saw it or Moon during her entire stay.

As for food, the supplies she had brought with her had run out after eight sun-cycles, so she had to rely on what was available. There might have been only herself and one other person in the village, but there were plenty of rats, and she had no problem relying on them to keep her fed.

She had also run out of feed for her horse, but it took care of itself. One day, just before the sky turned gray, Nyght went out to check on Stygian and saw that he was not where she had left him tied up. At first, she thought Darius had been foolish enough to steal her mount and run away, but when she found him, he was working in his backyard taking care of what appeared to be a rabbit. She figured that if he had taken Stygian, he would not have remained in the village and she did not feel the need to ask him about her horse.

Nyght limped back to her own house and went inside to get some rest. If her horse was gone, there was nothing she could do about it.

Just before the sky turned from gray to black, Nyght had just woken. She was about to get up anyway, but when she heard the noise outside, she jumped up as fast as she could. She even forgot she had a wounded foot, and accidentally put too much pressure on her injury causing her to feel pain. She took a moment to allow it to pass, then grabbed her crutch and headed outside.

She saw Stygian and walked over to him, and when he brushed his nose against her shoulder, she could not help but raise her hand and give the animal a couple of gentle strokes. She also could not deny the comfort she was feeling because the animal had not only returned but was unharmed. Having her horse back, she led him over to the small barn where she kept him. She placed him in one of the empty stalls and made sure she secured it.

When the sky was about to turn gray again, Nyght headed for the barn, but before she made it, she saw Stygian. He was now walking through the street, and it appeared he was heading for the city's gate. Even though she had to use a crutch to support herself, she knew that if she hurried, she would be able to catch the horse and bring it back to the barn. Before she took a step, she looked at the barn and remembered that she had made sure the gate to the stall was secure. She then turned and looked at Stygian walking away from her. Just in time to see the horse turn to the right, around the corner of a house, and out of her sight.

Nyght wanted to see just how intelligent the horse was, so instead of going after it, she went back inside to rest.

Just before the sky turned from gray to black, she once again heard her horse neighing outside. Even though she wanted to hurry to go and check on it, this time she remembered she had an injured foot and made sure she grabbed her crutch to give her the support she needed.

When she stepped out onto the porch, Stygian was standing in front of the house. She walked down the steps and extended her right arm and hand out. Stygian lifted his head so his nose touched her hand. Nyght could not help but smile.

She gave the horse's nose a couple of rubs then turned around to go back into the house. Before she went inside, she turned back around to look at Stygian. "Go on back to the barn. We won't be leaving tonight either."

Without hesitation, Stygian turned and headed to the barn. Once inside, Nyght wanted to go and see if he had also gone into the stall and locked the door to it as well. She just chuckled to herself, turned, and went inside the house where she was staying. It was time for her to catch some rats for dinner, and Stygian seemed to have no problem taking care of himself.

With her thoughts back on the present, she rode toward the edge of the village and she could see the opening to the front gate. She could also see a figure coming toward Lorraine, and since she had just passed Darius a moment ago, she was sure the unknown visitor was not him. Besides, the person coming to the village was riding their own mount.

Nyght passed through the opening to the entrance of Lorraine and moved Stygian to stop just before the line etched into the ground running the length of the village wall. Just from looking at the line, and the ground on the other side of it, she felt her right foot throb as if it alone remembered the pain she had felt when she stepped onto the land touched by Sun.

Not wanting to think any more about her injury, she put her eyes back on the approaching figure. Whoever it was, the land did not have the same effect on the rider or the animal as it did on her. As the person closed the distance between them, Nyght was able to see that the rider was male, and the mount he was riding was not much of one, because it was a mule, and neither the man nor the mule appeared to be any threat to her. She still did not cross the line as the man approached. Nyght was curious as to why the man and his mule were heading toward a village long abandoned.

The mule came to a stop on the other side of the line. If the man was a threat, she would not be able to cross the line to attack him, or else she would suffer more pain from the land touched by Sun. Nyght could throw one of her daggers, ending the man's life, but then she would not be able to retrieve it. The only other option she had would be to use her knife. It may not be a gift from Moon, but she still had an attachment to it, so she decided she would wait and see if the man would do anything to cause her to have to defend herself. She was not worried; she was sure she could deal with the man and the mule.

Even though she was curious about the man, being a person who spoke as little as possible, Nyght was going to let him have the first opportunity to speak. She was surprised at what he said.

"The woman you are after is heading for Kenshaw." She was about to ask what he was talking about, but did not have the chance before the man continued, "She goes by the name Daie, which is not so surprising since she is the warrior of Sun." Nyght still did not have a chance to say anything, because the mule made a sound and the man took his focus off of her and looked at the mule's head, "Quiet, I am not talking to you," the man said then looked back at Nyght. "Kenshaw is that way, about eight sun-cycles at a hard ride." To show her the direction, he pointed to his right and a little behind him. Nyght turned her head and looked at the direction the man had given her. It was to the northwest.

She turned her head to say something to the man but saw that in the brief moment she had taken her eyes off him, he had already turned his mule around and was halfway across the land touched by Sun. She gave him one more look then turned her head back to the direction the man had pointed. She then pulled on the reins and pointed Stygian toward her left.

Noticing the anxiousness in his rider, Stygian did not wait for the signal to start moving, making sure he stayed on the side of the line where his rider would be safe. Before he was even to the edge of the city wall, Stygian was at full speed, and soon he and his rider were heading away from the village. He understood that Kenshaw was eight sun-cycles away at a hard ride. Stygian was sure he could make it in six.

Just before Adoni entered the tree line, he looked up into the sky. He did not see Moon. Not because it was too early, but because Cloud was covering the sky over the village of Lorraine. "Enough," Adoni said and put his eyes forward. Then both he and his mule entered the woods.

Before Darius even woke, he could feel something bothering his eyes. He sat up in his bed, the bed he had surrendered to the woman who had come to his village when he surrendered his house to her as well. When he realized what he was seeing, the thought of the woman, her horse, and everything that had happened in the past two moon-cycles disappeared from his thoughts.

He rushed out of the room, down the stairs, and out the front door. Once outside, he not only ran off the porch but also jumped over the three steps to the ground. When he was standing in front of the house, Darius looked up to the sky while turning around in a circle. He had to stop because he was getting dizzy, and he raised his right hand to his forehead, above his eyes.

He had not seen the sun since he had been back in Lorraine. Lorraine had not seen the sun since he was a child. Now the sun was back.

Darius squinted his eyes so he could continue to look at the sky. He only held his stare for so long because he felt he was about to go blind from the glare, and he did not want that.

He lowered his head, took a few moments to bask in the sun, and then headed back to the house, the one once belonging to the family in charge of Lorraine when people lived in the village. Darius started wondering if since the sun had returned would people come back as well.

He also thought about how they would need someone to lead them, and since he was already staying in the house of the previous leader, then it would only be fitting for him to take the job.

FOURTEEN

They made camp before Sun had left the sky. Daie was sitting by the fire with her cloak around her. The night chill bothered her still, but with the cloak, she was able to tolerate it a lot easier.

Colton had collected enough firewood to last them through the night, and now he was preparing their evening meal. Since they still had supplies left from what they received in Pineview, they did not need to go hunting. Even if their supplies did start to run low, they had just passed through Kenshaw and they could always go back and purchase any items they needed since Daie received some coin for all the furs she had.

When they reached the city, they did not even stay the night. They arrived early in the morning and only remained long enough to talk to the head of the city guard to find out the location of Rashad Menlo or at least the area in which he was last known to be. The head constable had no problem telling them about the outlaw and his band of thieves.

Rashad Menlo was thought to have fifty men

with him. A number equal to the number of guards Kenshaw had in its ranks. Apparently, the city had spent enough funds on trying to bring in the outlaws, but every time the guards went out to put an end to the man's antics, the ones who did make it back did not have the enthusiasm to make another attempt at Rashad Menlo's capture.

The constable also informed Daie and Colton that before the bandit came to the area, the number of guards Kenshaw employed was over eighty. The number had lessened greatly because of either death at the attempted capture of Rashad Menlo, or the guards injured taking on the bandit decided they preferred another line of work and had quit, even though their contracts were not up. A live man could do a lot more with his remaining seasons than a dead one.

The way the story, or now the legend, of Rashad Menlo went was that he was a general who had served in some army on the other side of the world. Why he had come to the area no one knew, but he was very good, not only at robbing any caravans traveling through the region but also had enough men who were skilled at defending themselves against any attempt at their capture.

The group of thieves lived in the woods a sun-cycle's ride from the city. Even though the city guards and the city officials knew the general area of where the bandit had set up his base of operations, the city officials did not wish to put any more coin into his capture, and the city guard did not want to lose any more men.

There were other cities in the region where Rashad Menlo and his men would attack caravans traveling the area, but like Kenshaw, they had put too much time, effort, and coin into the man's capture and had nothing to show for it.

The officials from five different cities had a meeting to discuss the problem and came up with a plan to send a letter to the realm's ruling family. They had sent the letter by way of a personal carrier but had not heard a reply about whether they would receive assistance in the matter. The officials made it clear in their letter that the only way to stop Rashad Menlo was if the emperor were to send a large garrison to remove the bandit and the men following him.

With the information they received, Daie and Colton headed out of Kenshaw a sun-mark after they arrived. They did not know it, but the guards present while they had been talking to the constable started taking bets on whether or not the two would return. As well as the number of limbs they would be missing. Even though Rashad Menlo and his men had no problem killing people, they always made sure a few of their attackers survived to return to whatever city they had come from, but with a hand or a foot less than what they had come to him with. Rashad Menlo wanted to make sure his name would become something of a legend, and it already had.

Colton walked over to the other side of the fire

where Daie was sitting. She had her arms inside her cloak but when he handed the plate to her, she pulled her right arm out to take it and then brought it as close to her as she could to stay hidden inside her cloak as much as possible while she ate.

Colton went back over and took his seat. He fixed his own plate of vegetables, dried meat, and bread then began to eat his meal. As he took a bite and chewed his food, he looked over the flames and saw Daie sitting there. Eating but not saying a word. It seemed to him that the more time they spent together, the more she drew away from him. She had said very little to him after they had dealt with the men who killed her father, and the most she did talk was when they were in the town of Pineview. Colton figured the only reason she had spoken more was because they had run into the situation with the lych. They had to battle the creature, and Daie talked when they were discussing what they had to do, but once they had finished the task, and were back on the road, she once again said very little.

Colton wanted Daie to let him know what she was thinking about, but even more importantly, he wanted Hanna back. He decided to bring up what he had been wanting to discuss with her, ever since they had captured the two men who had killed her father. "His name was Hann," he said and kept his eyes on Daie.

When she heard the name, she looked up and saw Colton staring at her. She knew he wanted to talk about it, but she did not, so she lowered her eyes and went back to eating her meal.

Colton was not going to let it end that way. The more she refused to talk about her past, the more she would become Daie. The more she would become like Sun. Full of hate and anger, and that was not how he wanted her to be. He just did not know if he could stop it, but he had to try.

"I never knew his name," Colton said referring to her father. He had died before he had meant Hanna, and after he had asked about her father, she had only said that he was no longer with her, and with the way she said it, he knew it was a subject she did not want to discuss. Now he was not going to give her the option. "I know your mother's name was Anna." As soon as he said it, Daie stopped eating her meal and gave him a look to let him know he needed to end the conversation. Colton was not going to. "His name was Hann, and hers was Anna. That was why they chose to call you Hanna. They gave you your name from both of theirs," Colton stopped talking to give Daie a chance to respond. She did, by going back to eating her meal.

Colton took a few moments to take a couple bites of his food and to allow Daie some time with her thoughts, ones he knew were of her parents. When he felt the silence had gone on long enough, he continued with what he wanted to say. "You know that they are still with you?" Not only did she stop eating, but she also raised her head so fast he thought she was going to throw her plate across the fire at him. To his surprise, she did not, so he felt it was safe to continue. "In here," he said and pointed to his chest.

Before she could tell him what she wanted to say about what he had just said, she heard a noise come from her left. She turned to look in the direction and so did Colton. The man they had tied to the tree had woken from his slumber. One he fell into when Colton knocked him unconscious when he slammed his staff into the back of the man's head.

Daie turned back to look over the fire at Colton and saw he was looking at her. The conversation he wanted to have was not going to take place, because they now had someone else they needed to talk with. She placed her plate down, stood up, and started making her way over to the tied-up man.

Colton stood as well to join her, but unlike Daie, he was going to make sure their conversation continued when they had more time.

They reached the man tied to the tree. They had secured him so that he was standing. His arms stretched out behind him against the sides of the tree. His captors used a piece of rope to secure his hands. They did not even come close to touching each other, since the tree was so wide, but that also made sure he could not use one hand to get the other free.

They had tied his legs at his knees, as well as his ankles. Unknown to his captors, he had woken up long before he had made any noise to get the attention of the ones who had captured him. He had tried to free himself, but since there was no slack in the ropes, it did not permit the slightest bit of movement. Whichever one had secured him, knew what they were doing. When he discovered he was not going anywhere on his own, he tried to speak, but since they had also gagged him, it only came out as a muffled moan. It was enough to get their attention because the two were coming over to him.

Even though he did not run, Colton quickened his pace to make sure he was the first one to the man. Not that he did not trust Daie to ask the right questions, he just felt it would be easier to get the answers they needed while the man was still breathing; since Daie felt an almost dead man could answer just as easily.

Colton reached around to the back of the man's neck and untied the gag. As soon as it was clear, the man made a motion with his mouth to show that all the moisture had left. Even though Colton had not known the man would be thirsty, he was sure he would want something to drink and had brought their waterskin when he had walked away from the fire.

Without even asking if he wanted something to drink, Colton lifted the waterskin high enough so the man could take a drink. Colton held the bag for him and only lowered it when he felt the man release his hold on the bag. When he had brought the bag down, Colton was about ready to say something, but before he could, the man spat the water he had not swallowed into Colton's face.

He had shown the man compassion, and for his effort, he received a face full of water. The only good thing that came out of what the man had done was the quick chuckle Daie had allowed to escape. Colton was almost ready to let the man spit water at him again but decided the laugh was just not worth it.

He did not turn to look at Daie. Colton put the cap back on the waterskin and let it drop to his feet, then looked at the man tied to the tree who was smiling at the bit of rebellion he had performed. "We are not going to hurt you," Colton said, thinking that a gentler approach would get them what they needed. "If you answer our questions, then we will let you leave and you can go about your business, as long it is someplace other than the immediate region." Colton had told the man the truth. He was a sentry to Rashad Menlo's band of thieves. Colton had gotten close enough to him to knock him unconscious, then he traveled for two sun-marks back to the camp Daie and him had made. Colton went alone because he felt he would have a better chance to spy on the bandit's camp by himself. He also thought that going by himself would keep Daie from running into the camp and trying to kill everyone without a plan.

Now that they had captured the man, Colton and

Daie had discussed what information they would try to obtain from him. Not that they had any guarantee he would give any, but it was worth a try.

"How many men does Rashad Menlo have?" Colton asked, and for an answer, he received a glob of spit in his eye. The first thought that came to him was how he missed the water in his face. The next thought was that if he had not been a priest of Creator, the man tied to the tree would have suffered greatly. Unfortunately, he might still.

Colton wiped the spit away and when he put both his eyes back on the man, he saw him smiling. He had a feeling he would not be smiling for long. "I thought I would show you compassion, even though our morals might be different from one another." Colton turned his head and looked over his left shoulder at Daie, then back to the man. "I am sorry you could not do it my way." He turned and walked toward Daie, who was now moving toward the man.

The man tied to the tree did not like the smile the woman walking toward him had on her face. He did not have any water in his mouth to spit on her, and either he had used up the last of his saliva, or he knew that if he tried to assault this woman as he had the man, he might not ever be able to breathe again, let alone be able to spit.

Daie was not even two handbreadths away from the man. She looked directly into his eyes, and when she was sure she had his attention, she reached over her shoulder with her left hand and pulled out her dagger Flare. She moved so fast that the man was only able to tell what she was holding when he felt the blade up against his throat. Not only was he trying to get a look at it, but he was also regretting not answering the question when the man had asked him.

"How many men does Rashad Menlo have?" Daie asked the same question Colton had a moment ago.

"One hundred," the man said looking Daie in the eye.

"He's lying," Colton said. She did not look toward him, but the man adjusted his eyes so he could see the man who had just figured out he had not told the truth. The man's gaze asked the question and Colton answered, "I am a priest of Creator. I can tell when someone like you is lying."

Daie did not know whether Colton was telling the truth or not, but she was going to believe him over this man without a second thought. To let their captive know that she did not take his lying to her lightly, she pressed the blade of her dagger harder against his throat. Now the back of his head was against the tree, and it was clear to him, that if the blade came any closer, the tree would be a perfect fixture to allow her to cut into him.

"How many men does Rashad Menlo have?" Daie asked again.

The man answered in less than a breath, not that he was going to try to breathe, not with a dagger at his throat. "Fifty, fifty men."

"He's still lying," Colton said, and this time both Daie and the man looked at him. The man thought he would be able to tell another lie because they would think he was too scared to lie again. He also did not believe the man could actually tell if he was lying, but since the priest had caught onto the second lie, the man was starting to believe him.

When Daie and Colton exchanged looks, all he did was nod his head to let her know that the man was still not telling the truth. Daie turned her head back to look at the man, but before her eyes were looking into his, she had already raised up her right hand, reached over her shoulder, and brought out her second dagger Blaze. Since her first blade was at the man's throat, she decided to place the other dagger somewhere that might convince the man he only had one more chance to answer the question truthfully.

When the man felt the dagger firmly up against his crotch, he did not hesitate to give the honest answer before his captor asked the question again, "Twenty, twenty, twenty, twenty..." The man continued to say the same word until he felt more pressure from the lower blade which he took as he was supposed to stop talking.

While still holding her blades at their current positions, she turned her head to look at Colton standing behind her. Her eyes asked the same question he was thinking, so Colton asked the man. "How is he able to stop the city guards with only twenty men?"

Daie turned back to look at the man who did not hesitate to answer. "He pays off some of the guards to give him reports on when any of the cities are preparing to send out their men. He sets traps for them, in areas long before they reach the camp. He then surrounds the group of soldiers and takes them out with archers. Before the guards even get a chance to organize themselves from the ambush, we are already upon them."

Daie turned her head to look at Colton, who nodded to let her know their captor was telling the truth. "He just uses bribery and surprise to take care of anyone who comes after him," she said to sum up what the man had said.

"Apparently that is all he needs," Colton said to remind her that Rashad Menlo, has been terrorizing the region for three seasons. "More than likely he is a master of strategy. If the guards he paid off could tell him how many were coming after him, and when and where, then he would have time to prepare the field to his advantage." Colton paused for a moment to think and then spoke again. "Still, Rashad Menlo and twenty men will not be easy to stop with just the two of us."

"You were not so bad back in Sundridge. You took care of fifteen men all by yourself. You can take care of the twenty and I will take care of Rashad Menlo."

Even though she did not smile when she said it, Colton was pretty sure she was joking, at least he thought she was. "Those fifteen men in Sundridge were nothing but tavern patrons and had been drinking. Only two of them had swords and they did not even seem as if they were proficient with them. Rashad Menlo and his band of thieves have not only survived but also thrived in this region. They are a lot more adept at defending themselves."

"Yes, we are," the man said without either of his captors asking for his opinion. For his comment, and to let him know he should remain silent, Daie put a little more pressure on both of her daggers. The man could not decide which one he was more worried about, especially since the woman with the blades had not even turned her head to look at him before she made the slight adjustment to lessen his comfort level.

"Then what should we do?" Daie asked because all she could come up with was to rush into the camp and reach Rashad Menlo before he or any of his men could do either of them any harm. A part of her, a big part, wanted to do exactly that to see just what she was capable of.

Colton turned around and walked away. Daie, sensing the questioning of their captive had come to an end, at least for the moment, removed her blades from the vicinity of the man's body and turned her back to him. As she removed the blades, the man took a deep breath, since he had been afraid to when the dagger was at his throat. Now that he could breathe regularly, he had a question for the woman, "So, your father's name was Hann?"

Without turning her head, she lifted up her left arm and jammed her elbow behind her and into the man's face. She struck him hard enough for his head to slam into the tree. Once again, the man was unconscious.

Colton walked to the other side of the camp. He did not do so to get away from Daie or their captive, but to give himself time to think. Daie would have preferred to go in with weapons drawn, but he would not allow that to happen. When he felt Daie come and stand at his side to his right, he let her know what concerned him most. "We are not going to kill any of them." He did not phrase it as a question, but he did turn to her for a response.

"There are twenty of them and this Rashad Menlo. If the stories about him are true, then there is not much of a chance that a few of them won't end up dead."

Colton had no problem in hearing how she only counted their enemies as being the ones to end up dead, and neither her nor himself. The group of thieves might be their enemies, but they were still alive, which meant they were part of Creator, and he would not take their life or allow Daie to either. "No one will be killed. We are all creations of Creator, and all entitled to the life he has given us."

"And what about the lives Rashad Menlo has taken? We're they not also made by Creator?" Daie asked.

He knew what she was asking but he only had

one answer, one he was sure she would not understand, "Creator is the one to decide who will live and who will die, and as a priest of Creator, I will protect all life, even those who may not deserve it."

Colton turned back around and as he headed back toward the fire, he saw the man tied to the tree had his head bent down so that his chin was almost against his chest. Even though he knew the man was not dead, he knew he had not fallen asleep on his own.

"You had no problem killing that lych," Daie said, and he turned around to face her. "What is the difference? Did not that creature deserve to live even though it was killing others?"

"There is a big difference between someone who is alive and something that has been defiled and no longer is a part of life itself. I did not kill it, because it was not alive in the first place." From the look she gave him, she understood what he had said. He still could tell that she was all for attacking Rashad Menlo, and his band of thieves, and whatever happens to them, happens. Colton was not going to allow that. "I think I have a plan."

Daie looked at him and waited for what he was going to say, when he did, she thought that what he told her was not even possible, but he proved to her, that unlike the man tied to the tree, he did not lie.

They situated themselves at the edge of the camp of Rashad Menlo.

When their captive had once again woken, Daie and Colton questioned him even further about the precise location of the camp and about the sentries concerning their routine when they were on duty. The man gave up the information very eagerly since the second round of questioning had both of Daie's daggers at his groin.

With what the man had told them, they had no problem with making their way to the camp and past the sentries. They were still about forty paces away, but they were able to see the tents placed throughout the camp.

The only problem they did have was that they had to make their trip during the night to be in position when the sun came up. Even though Daie wore her cloak, the night still bothered her, and by the time they reached the camp, she was shivering so loud she had to force her teeth together to stop them from making any noise.

They had no choice in the time they had chosen to travel. They needed to be ready when the sun was about to rise because that would be the earliest Daie would be at her full strength. It was her idea to attack at the first light of the sun because that was the time when soldiers were just waking up and were a bit more unprepared. Colton liked the idea because it gave him time to do what he had planned.

They stayed lying on their stomachs as they watched the camp. They saw a couple of people moving around, but it was easy to tell that there were not many early risers. Only the ones that either had the task of preparing the morning meal or had to relieve themselves were up. Still, Colton and Daie waited.

When the first light of the sun broke the horizon and shined through the trees, Daie took hold of Colton's left hand with her right and gave it a squeeze. As much as he wanted the gesture to mean something more, he knew she was only giving him the signal to begin his part of the plan.

Colton closed his eyes and gave the command. He did not say it aloud, not only because he did not need to, but because the ones he was talking to were not close enough to hear any words, but they were close enough to come when he called.

As they waited, Daie was starting to believe that what he had planned had not worked, even though he had shown her what he could do. She turned her head away from the camp to look at him lying to her right. He had not turned to look at her, and she was about to ask him what was going on. That was when she felt it.

Lying on the ground, she could feel the vibration on her stomach. It was a rumbling, and as much as she wanted to sit up and look, she knew that any movement on her part might alert their presence to someone in the camp if they were looking in their direction, so she stayed there lying on the ground, next to Colton. Lying there looking at him, and even though he was still looking ahead, she could see that he was smiling. It was one of those smiles he had when he was younger, telling her about some adventure of his. The smile brought back memories for her, and she could not help but smile herself.

Out of the corner of his left eye, he saw Daie looking at him, and to his surprise, she was smiling. He wanted to turn to her and say how beautiful she looked, but the anticipation of what was going to happen was just too strong, and he did not want to miss what he had planned.

As the vibrations on the ground grew, so did the sound coming their way. It was so loud that neither Colton nor Daie had any problem in knowing when they would arrive. Not only did the noise grow louder, but over it, they heard one of the sentries posted out in the woods shout out, "Get up! Get up!" The man continued to scream as he entered from the woods on the left side of the camp. Colton and Daie knew that was the direction they needed to be watching, so both of them kept their eyes focused on it.

As the man ran back into the camp, others came out of their tents to find out why the sentry had come running back instead of sounding the horn he had, which was the procedure if their camp was under attack. Even though neither Daie nor Colton could hear the conversation, it was obvious the ones who came out to talk to the sentry did not believe what he was reporting.

It did not take them long to stop their discussion

and put their focus on the area of the woods the sentry had come from. It was only a few moments later when they realized the sentry had not been drinking as they thought he had been, in fact, the sentry had been telling the truth.

Colton and Daie adjusted their positions so they were still lying on their stomachs but had their heads raised up enough to see what had entered the camp. The people of Kenshaw and the surrounding cities wanted the emperor to send an army to take care of Rashad Menlo and his band of thieves. They never arrived, so Colton brought his own, and every single soldier was an animal that lived in the woods, and there were a lot of them.

Colton told Daie his plan, and his secret, about being able to talk to animals and that they could talk to him. She gave him a look like she did when they were just children to let him know that whatever he had said was about as idiotic as the time he asked her if she wanted to go and see a skeleton of a dog.

To convince her, he talked to their horses and had them lift up whichever leg he asked them to. Daie was still not convinced because she thought he could have trained them to do those tricks. To persuade her even further, Colton called to the birds in the trees around their camp. Before she knew it, birds were flying out of their nest and not only landing on the ground at his feet, or flying around his head, but landing on his shoulders as well. Even though he thought she was starting to believe him,

Colton called to the bugs in the area as well, and it did not take them long before they came crawling out of the woods, and out of the ground to answer the call from the priest of Creator. Animals need to be in view of one another to talk to each other, Colton could call out to the animals of Creator even if he did not see them, they could hear him, and he could hear them.

It had been a long time since any creature of nature had heard a call from a human belonging to Creator, and even though the animals, birds, and insects that had answered the call had not been around since the last time one went out, they knew what the call was when they heard it. Animals are not like humans. Not even the Elves or Dwarves, who were more in tune with nature than humans, or even Gnomes or Trolls, were closer to Creator than animals were. Their entire existence consisted of what Creator had made them for, and that was to do as instructed by Creator or by one who could call to them. Like the man they had all come to.

The number of animals that came to his call was so great that there was no way to count them. The ants alone were in the millions, and that was only from a few anthills. The birds flew through the sky so quickly that at times they looked as if they were one gigantic creature. There were so many rabbits it appeared the entire ground was nothing but one big giant piece of fur. The herd of deer that came bounding through, moved so fast that by the time one passed, another was right behind it, and two more to the side of it.

The only creatures whose numbers were small enough to know precisely how many there were, were the four big brown bears who had come to Colton's call. They were the only ones in the region because bears like to have a lot of territory for themselves and for any cubs the females would be raising, which there were two of them with one of the female bears.

All the creatures worked together for the benefit of Creator and the one who called them. The foxes did not attack the rabbits. The birds did not eat the insects, and the bears, well they did not attack any of the other animals, which at any other time were fair game. The animals did not come to fight each other. They came there to remove the humans who had been in their woods for too long; and remove them they did.

The animals rushed through the camp, and since there were so many of them, the men did not know what to do. Anyone who had not been awake when the sentry came back was wide awake now, but they had no idea how to handle the stampede of animals. Some of the men grabbed their weapons and attempted to stop any animal they could. If one human raised a sword or arrow, a group of animals fell on the attacker and made sure they removed the weapon from them.

Colton had informed the animals that they

needed to make sure of two things. One was that they were to protect each other at all times, and the second was that they were not to kill any of the humans in the camp. Most of the animals were happy to go along with what he wanted. The four bears let Colton know that if a human was to "accidentally fall" into their mouth, there was nothing they could do about it. After the statement brought a round of laughs from the other animals, Colton stressed the importance of how no humans were to come to any harm that would lead to their deaths. The bears conceded to his wishes, although they were not happy about it.

As the animals tore through the camp, men, as well as tents, went flying. Rashad Menlo and his band might have been able to plan an attack on a group of men they knew were coming, but with the army of animals coming down so fast on them, they had no idea what to do.

Some of the men had immediately started running out of the camp, knowing that the stampede could not be stopped. Others ran because they believed that with so many animals running through the forest, it could only mean that the woods themselves were on fire and the animals were a sign to get away. What they did not know was that there was no fire.

By the time the army of animals had passed his line of sight, Colton did not see a single tent or person standing. There were a couple of men lying on the ground, but Colton was glad to see that they were moving, even if they were not on their feet. He knew the animals did not kill like humans or any of the other races. Animals only kill for the need of survival. Mostly for food or defense against an enemy. Even when an animal dies because of a battle with its own kind for mating rights, it is part of their nature, and the death is an honorable one. Animals did not kill because they could. Not like the sentient beings in the world.

With the animal stampede over, Colton decided to let Daie know they could now search for Rashad Menlo. When he turned his head to his left, he noticed that like the animals, Daie was no longer there.

Daie had asked her captive at their campsite for a description of Rashad Menlo. He had given them enough of one so she would have no problem in picking him out of a crowd. The captured sentry said that Rashad Menlo never left his tent without wearing his purple turban. Rashad Menlo was completely lacking any hair on his head, and it was the one thing he was self-conscious about. Although no one ever brought up the sensitive subject in his presence.

In all the commotion with the stampeding animals, Daie was still able to see the purple turban through all the dust and debris the animals had stirred up. She saw the man they had come for exit the far side of the camp, and when she saw Colton occupied with watching his little army, she silently crawled away and circled the camp to get to Rashad Menlo.

She ran through the running animals, not one striking her as she made her way around the camp. Just to be safe, Colton had told all the animals not to harm him or Daie as well as any of the other humans. He did not tell her, but they would never cause him any harm, as for the one who followed Sun, they had some doubts about if they could do as he instructed. Even though the animals were part of the land, and part of what Sun was to watch over, the animals did not think too highly of Sun. Each of them had their own Guardian, the First of their kind, who they followed, and Creator. When it came to Sun, every creature thought Sun was very egotistical, so the woman blessed by Sun was probably as well.

Colton told them that she was his friend and to do it for him. Since he asked, and he was a priest of Creator they would obey, so when she ran through the stampede, the creatures swerved to make sure they did not run into her.

When she made it to the other side of the camp, Daie took off in the direction she had seen the purple turban go. It was not long before she had a couple of surprises of her own. The first was that she had no problem catching up to the man Rashad Menlo. The second surprise was the reason she caught up to him so quickly.

When she reached him, she bowled into him,

causing both of them to tumble to the ground. When she landed, she did a quick forward roll, came back up on her feet, and turned to face the man she had knocked down. When she was facing him, he was just rising to his feet. When he was standing at his full height, he stood four handbreadths, if not less, than she did. If she were to stand directly in front of him, he would have just barely reached her chest.

Rashad Menlo saw the woman who had caused him to fall, and since he did not know her, he had no doubt she had something to do with what happened at his camp. Before he said anything, he realized he had lost his turban when he fell to the ground. He spun around, looked for his headdress, and saw it a few steps behind him. He quickly ran over, picked it up, and placed it back on his head. Now that the woman had seen him without it, she had to die.

Rashad Menlo turned around and as he did, he pulled out the curved sword he had on his left side in its scabbard. When he was facing the woman again, he was so surprised to see her standing directly in front of him he forgot that he had planned to end her life. He did not know it, but he never had a chance, and before he could get his wits about him, the woman punched forward with her right fist, hitting him directly in his nose. The force behind the blow sent him stumbling backward. His short legs tangled up with each other, and since he was unconscious as soon as the punch connected with him, he ended up spinning around, fell to the ground, and rolled three times before his body came to a stop. Once again, he had lost his turban.

Daie walked over to the unconscious man and looked down at him. She had heard so much talk about Rashad Menlo she thought he would be a challenge to her. Someone she could practice her skills on to prepare her for when she met up with the woman called Nyght. The man lying at her feet was not even a challenge for his own feet, which he had lost to as well.

She heard someone coming closer to her, and when she looked, she saw Colton. He had stopped a few paces away, and the look he was giving her was clear. He wanted to know if she had killed the man at her feet.

She did not give him an answer. She just stepped over the unconscious man and walked toward Colton. "Not much to the legend of Rashad Menlo," she said as she passed him and headed back the way she had come.

Colton walked over to the man and saw that although he was lying face down on the ground, he was still breathing. After tilting his head to get a better view of the man, he realized that Rashad Menlo was a lot shorter than he would have imagined.

When they brought their captive back to Kenshaw, they also brought the only other man they were able to capture from his band of thieves. The one they had tied to the tree.

The constable and the other guards had never seen Rashad Menlo, and when they looked at the man standing before them, the constable was ready to argue that the short man could not be the criminal who had been terrorizing Kenshaw and the surrounding cities. Being a man who valued his pride and his own legend, even more so than his own freedom, Rashad Menlo began telling everything he had done since he had been in the region. With his own confession and that of the man brought in with him, the constable had no choice but to believe that the short bald man was the one who had caused so much turmoil for the past three seasons.

Daie and Colton made sure that Rashad Menlo explained how he had paid some of the city guards, and the constable was very eager to hear that part of the story. It just so happened that when he looked around his office, two of his men had suddenly disappeared and he had a good idea why.

With the confession, the constable told Daie and Colton they would receive the reward for Rashad Menlo's capture and the one they brought in with him, in three sun-cycles. This time Daie had no problem with waiting around for the payment. At least it was something she could receive since she did not have the chance to test her skills against the legendary Rashad Menlo.

Daie and Colton took a room at one of the inns in the city. Since they did not have much coin, the constable arranged for their stay, with the cost of the room taken out of their reward when they received it.

It was a small room with two beds. In the middle of the night, Daie sat up, awakened from her sleep. "Colton!"

He heard Daie say his name, and he could tell she had something important to tell him. Not just because she woke him up and it was not even close to morning, but because of the way she called to him. He raised up enough in his bed and supported his body with his right elbow. "What's the matter?"

Daie waited three breaths then answered, "She's coming." She said the two words with eager anticipation. Colton knew whom Daie was referring to.

FIFTEEN

Colton could not hear Sun, but when Daie told him what Sun had told her to do, he had to agree with Sun, which in itself said how much danger Daie was about to enter into.

Sun was the one who had told her that the warrior of Moon was almost at the outer lands of Kenshaw, although Sun had not sensed her coming. Moon protected Nyght so Sun was not able to see her even if Sun was in the sky above. There were others Sun could talk with, and even though they did not have any allegiance to Sun, they had none to Moon either. Cloud had told Wind that the warrior of Moon was heading toward Kenshaw. Cloud had kept a watchful eye on the woman from the time she entered Lorraine. When she had almost reached the borders of Kenshaw, Cloud told Wind so Wind could tell Sun, and by the time Sun received the information, Nyght was almost to the city.

Sun told Daie to flee because Sun believed she was not ready to take on the warrior of Moon. Sun knew that Moon's warrior had been fighting for almost her entire life, while Daie had only Sun's blessing for a little over two moon-cycles. Sun wanted her to have more time to prepare herself before she took on her rival. Even though the woman would arrive in the city of Kenshaw not long after Sun had risen into the sky, and Daie would be stronger, Sun did not believe Daie could defeat the warrior of Moon, and if Daie did fall to her, it would show everyone, especially Moon, that Sun was not as strong as Moon. Something Sun would not allow to happen, so Sun wanted her to leave before the warrior of Moon arrived.

Colton agreed with Sun, and as hard as he tried to convince Daie to leave immediately, she refused to listen to him. He wanted her to leave for the same reason Sun wanted her to, but he also had another, which he did not tell her. Colton worried about her defeat at the hands of Nyght, but what he was more worried about was that Daie would win. He knew that if she killed Nyght, he would never see Hanna again.

Daie ignored the warnings from Sun and Colton. She wanted to put an end to the conflict, once and for all. She understood that the woman she was going to face was not only someone blessed by Moon, but she also remembered what Adoni had told her. The woman called Nyght, was an assassin, as well as a descendent from a line of Elves born to kill. Daie did not forget that for the majority of her life, all she had done was work at and run a boarding house. The biggest thing she had ever killed were any flies in the establishment. In the time since she received Sun's blessing, she still had not killed a living being. Not even the lych back in Pineview. Colton was the one who ended its life, all she did was help.

No matter how hard Colton or Sun tried to convince her, Daie was set on seeing this rivalry between Sun and Moon, and Nyght and herself, come to an end. She was going to leave the city of Kenshaw but instead of going in the opposite direction Nyght was coming from, she was going to head straight to her.

Before they left, Daie told Sun what she needed, and even though Sun was reluctant to help, Sun could not deny the thrill and anticipation of the fight between the two women. To make sure Sun would help her with what she had planned, she told Sun that before Sun was to the midpoint in the sky, this day, all would see how great Sun is. With that statement, how could Sun resist the warrior Sun had chosen?

When they rode out of the east gate of Kenshaw, it was still dark, and Moon was still in the sky. Daie had to keep her cloak wrapped tightly around her because the cold of night was bothering her and there were still three sun-marks before Sun would even shine the first light of the morning. As she rode, she kept her thoughts to one thing, that she would end this. She also made sure Sun knew what she was thinking, because more than anything, she wanted Sun to realize that after today, the battle between Sun and Moon would be over.

As she rode, Sun grew more and more confident that Daie would defeat the warrior of Moon, and when it happened, Moon would have no choice but to admit who was the strongest of the two. Sun's anticipation and excitement grew as Daie rode on. Even though Sun had wanted her to flee, by the time the two women met, Sun would be in the sky and Daie would be stronger than the warrior of Moon. Sun would be there to see the fall of Moon's chosen, as well as the fall of Moon.

Stygian brought Nyght to the outer lands of Kenshaw six sun-cycles after they left Lorraine. It was just before she had entered the boundaries when Moon passed on to her the message from Wind. Moon wanted her to flee immediately because it was too dangerous for her to confront the warrior of Sun at this time.

Nyght did not turn Stygian to head in another direction, nor did she slow him down. She continued to ride for Kenshaw.

Wind had passed the message Daie had given to Sun to Moon. Sun believed Sun was too grand to talk to Moon. Whether Sun knew it or not, Moon felt the same way toward Sun. Because of the way they felt toward each other, Sun commanded Wind to tell Moon to tell the warrior of Moon what Daie wanted.

Wind did. Not because Wind had any fear of Sun, or any loyalty, but because Wind, like Cloud, has watched the battle between Sun and Moon go on for as long as their creation by Creator. Wind and Cloud wanted to see the upcoming battle between the two Guardians end, and they were not the only ones. Land and Ocean wanted the bickering between the two Guardians to cease, as well as the Firsts of the animals. Created by Creator, and even though they might fight among themselves at times, the Firsts did not squabble like two spoiled children which was what the Firsts of the animals felt Sun and Moon were.

The Firsts of the animals did not care which of the chosen of Sun and Moon won in the end, as long as one lost and one won, then all of creation would know which Guardian was the strongest of the two. The Firsts wanted the battle of the Guardians to come to an end, which had been going on for as long as they could remember.

Out of all the Firsts, Rat was the only one who wanted to see Sun's chosen to be the one left standing. Rat still had not forgotten how many of Rat's children died at the hands of Moon's warrior, and Rat wanted to have some justice for his poor children. Rat did not want anything to do with Sun either, especially since Rat, and Rat's children, were creatures of the night, but for this upcoming battle, it would please Rat greatly to see Moon humbled by the death of Moon's chosen.

Wind gave Moon the message from Sun, and when Moon saw that Nyght would not turn away, Moon told her what the warrior of Sun had planned for the meeting between the two of them. Nyght could not help but smile when Moon had finished, and even though she knew she was going to kill the one called Daie, Nyght had to admire the woman for the tactic she had come up with. What the warrior of Sun wanted was the same as she did, which was why she had not altered her course, in fact, Stygian increased his speed, sensing his rider wanted to reach their destination as soon as possible.

Moon did not like that Nyght would be at a disadvantage. When Sun was in the sky, Sun's warrior would have the advantage. Moon wanted Nyght to stay away from the one called Daie until Moon was high in the sky. Then Nyght would have the advantage, and she would be able to kill Sun's warrior. Then all would know that Moon was the strongest. If Nyght took on the warrior of Sun, when Sun was in the sky, she might fall to the chosen of Sun, and then for the rest of Moon's existence, which was going to be for many seasons, all creatures would see Moon as the weaker of the two.

Nyght understood Moon's concern. Moon had not only blessed her but had been with her, her entire life. Nyght had cherished the moments she had spent with Esteemed-High-Master Wraith, and if there was ever a human that she would have given the title of father to, it would have been him. To Nyght, Moon was her father, and she would not fail Moon. She would show Moon that she was the strongest of the two warriors and she would end the life of the one called Daie.

Nyght was going to meet Daie, but she did not want Moon to think that she could not defeat the warrior of Sun. She believed that with what Moon had blessed her with, it did not matter whether Sun was in the sky or not. To Nyght, Moon was the strongest between Moon and Sun, and because of that, she was stronger than the one Sun had blessed. Moon decided Nyght was correct. Moon was the one who had blessed Nyght, and since Moon believed Moon was stronger than Sun, then Nyght was stronger than Daie. As she rode toward the city of Kenshaw, Moon decided that Moon's warrior would no doubt be the victor. Moon was pleased.

Daie and Colton arrived two marks before the sun came into the sky. Wind had found the area Daie wanted for the meeting between her and Nyght, and Sun led them to it. Now they were standing at the edge of the woods looking at the open space down the hill. It was off from the road leading back to Kenshaw, but Daie made sure Sun passed the location to Moon, and Moon's chosen. Of course, it was Wind who gave the message to Moon, but Moon did let Nyght know where the two would meet.

"I still don't think this is a good idea," Colton said and turned his head to his left to look at Daie who was looking down the hill to the land below. "You have not had enough time to gain any experience in fighting."

"I took down the Polk brothers," Daie said, not taking her eyes off the view at the bottom of the hill.

Colton was quick to give his overview of the incident she had brought up. "They were a couple of carpenters who took up killing because they had no choice. From what we found out about them they were nothing but thugs who jumped their victims from the shadows." Colton turned and looked down the hill, "This Nyght is a trained assassin. She is part of a caste of Elves created to kill, and she has the blessing of Moon."

Daie turned and looked at Colton, "And what am I?"

He turned his head to face her. He wanted to say that she was the golden-haired woman he had known as Hanna, and fallen in love with, but that would not convince her to change her mind about what she was about to do. "You run a boarding house, and the worst thing you had to fight was the stench of cleaning the bins out of the relief shack."

Daie held back the smile she felt coming to her and turned back to look down the hill. "Not anymore," she said, then turned around to walk to where their horses were. As soon as she took a step, and positioned herself so that she was facing Colton's back, she raised her right hand and pulled out her dagger Blaze from behind her back. Just as he was turning around to continue the discussion on what he did not want her to do, she struck. With a tight grip on the hilt of her blade, she punched him in the face with her fist. He fell to the ground unconscious.

She returned her blade to its holster, bent down, took hold of him under his arms, and dragged him back to where their horses were. She leaned him up against a tree, with his back to it. She then went over to his own supplies and pulled out the rope they had used to tie up the man when they went after Rashad Menlo. She then tied his hands behind him and the tree, so when he regained consciousness, he would not interfere with her battle against Nyght.

When she finished securing his hands, she went around to the other side of the tree and knelt in front of Colton. Even though his head was tilted downward, she was still able to see his face enough to realize that even though he had changed physically during the seasons he was at the priesthood, the same features he had when he was a young boy living on the streets of Maridian were still there; only covered by his new devotion to Creator. She did not fault him for that, and if what she had planned worked, then she would come back, untie him, and tell him that even though she had never called him one, he was the only friend she ever had, and that meant a lot to her.

She almost even leaned closer to him to give him a kiss, but instead, she touched the side of his face with her palm, held it there for a breath then stood and turned around.

She walked to the edge of the woods and looked

down the hill. She then looked up into the sky and saw that Sun was about ready to shine over the horizon. Even though they had left Kenshaw by the east gate and had been facing the direction Sun would rise into the sky, when they made their way to the area they were in now, east was now to her right. That was where she saw the first light of Sun pushing away the dark of night. She then put her eyes back on the land below, the place where she would meet Nyght.

She started walking down the hill. Not even looking back at the man she had left behind. The man she was hoping to see again.

When she came to the edge of the woods, Stygian stopped without even a command from his rider. The horse knew she would want to take a moment to see where she was about to enter.

Moon had given her the directions to lead her to where she was and Nyght looked down the hill. What she saw was a small glade. Green grass covered the ground, and it was clear to her that very few humans, if any at all, came to the area. The grass looked as if not a living creature had touched it in a long time except by any animals who made the glade their home. Although, at the moment, there was not a single creature present. They had all left the area to escape the upcoming encounter between the two warriors. They knew the anger and hatred Sun had for Moon and Moon for Sun and did not want to be in the middle of the battle that was about to take place.

Nyght looked to her left and saw the sun's first light was just about to cross the horizon. With Sun in the sky, she would not be as strong as she was at night. She then looked to her right, and what she saw made her cast her doubts away. She then looked out across the glade to the hill on the opposite side. Nyght saw the figure making its way into the glade below. There was no doubt, it was the warrior of Sun, because no one else would be there to meet Nyght. No one but the woman called Daie.

Nyght climbed off the back of Stygian and took a step forward to stand at his neck. He snorted and moved his head to touch her shoulder. She lifted her hand and patted the side of his neck, "Wait for me here; I will be back as soon as I end this." She then started down the hill to make her way to the bottom of the glade. The same as Daie was doing on the opposite side.

Stygian did as his rider had said. He would stay, but he was not sure if the one he brought would return. He was not sure if even Creator knew how the battle between the two warriors would end.

When Nyght was close to the bottom of the hill she saw the woman on the other side coming toward her removing her cloak and dropping it behind her. Nyght knew that when the sun rose high enough, its light would affect her, but she also knew she could not show her enemy any weakness. Nyght figured that the woman knew the sun affected her, but since Nyght wanted to show her that she was not afraid of either her or Sun, Nyght reached up and undid the clasp holding her cloak around her neck. Once free, it fell to the ground behind her as she continued to walk to meet the woman.

When they reached the bottom of their respective hills, they continued until they were in the center of the glade, standing three paces away from one another. Nyght looked to her left and saw the woman across from her follow her gaze. When she had looked at the first light of the sun, Nyght could feel the pain in her eyes, but she held her stare for a few more breaths before she turned away and put her focus back on her enemy, who had turned her head as well and was now facing Nyght.

When they were once again looking at each other, Daie turned her head to her left, but out of the corner of her eye, she noticed that the woman standing across from her had turned as well to look in the same direction. When Daie saw the moon up in the sky, she could feel the warmth leave her body, and her eyes started to hurt just from the brief glimpse. She held her stare for a few more breaths before she turned away and put her focus back on the woman, who was now looking at her as well.

Sun was just entering the sky to Daie's right, and Moon was leaving the sky to her left but had not gone down yet. During this part of the season, there were many mornings when Sun and Moon would be in the sky at the same time, just on opposite sides of the world. Daie knew this, which was why she wanted to face the warrior of Moon, at this precise moment. When both Sun and Moon were in the sky at the same time, the two Guardians could see the outcome they had been wanting for so long.

When Nyght had turned to look at Moon, the pain she had felt from looking at Sun had left. Moon was still in the sky, and as long as Moon was, Nyght would have some protection. Nyght also knew that with Moon in the sky, the woman known as Daie would suffer as well, but with Sun in the sky, she would have the same amount of protection as Nyght had from Moon. Once again, it pleased Nyght with what the woman she was facing had arranged. In fact, she would not want it any other way.

Nyght had planned on going after Daie at night when Moon was in the sky. If she had, she would have the advantage, but it was better than going after her enemy when Sun was in the sky because Daie would be the stronger of the two. Arranging to meet when both Sun and Moon were in the sky, the two combatants were even. Neither of them the strongest nor the weakest. To Nyght this was the way a true warrior could tell who was the greater. Her respect for the one called Daie grew. It was too bad she would have to end her life.

They stood there looking at each other not speaking a single word. There was no need to. They both knew why they were there, and what they had come to do.

At the same time, they drew their daggers. Daie reached up and pulled hers out of her holsters from behind her back, as Nyght reached down, and drew hers from the sheaths at her sides. With blades in hand, they rushed forward to meet each other.

Sun and Moon were both in the sky and even though they did not speak to one another, they both spoke the same words to their warriors as the two moved forward, *"Kill her!"*

SIXTEEN

When the two women were less than a pace away from each other, they immediately, not only began their attacks but their defense as well. They would use one of their blades to thrust forward toward their opponent, while with their other blade, they would defend themselves from the attack coming at them.

If Daie extended the blade in her right hand to attempt to attack Nyght, she would simultaneously have to use the blade in her left hand to defend against the blade coming from her opponent as an attack. Nyght had to fight the same way. With whatever blade she chose to attack with, she had to use the opposite one to guard against the blade coming at her. With every move they made, their opponent would execute the proper countermove, deflecting the attack.

Daie thrust her right blade higher, attempting to make a hit on Nyght's face, close to her eyes. Before the blade made contact, Nyght brought up the blade in her left hand, with the tip pointing upward, across in front of her, deflecting Daie's blade aside. As Daie had executed the attack, Nyght had thrust the blade in her right hand out, attempting to cut into Daie's midsection. The attack failed as well, because Daie swooped the blade in her left hand toward her left, and out in front of her, deflecting the attacking blade of Nyght.

After numerous attempts at attacking, and the same number of successful counterstrikes by both combatants, without saying a word to the other, each woman jumped backward a pace to put distance between themselves and their opponent. They did not do this because the battle was over, they did this to let the other know that they each saw they had made no progress in ending the fight.

Nyght looked at Daie and saw that she was in the same pose as herself. Daggers slightly out in front of her and slightly to her sides, with the blades pointing upward. In the brief exchange of attacks, her respect for the warrior of Sun had increased. Her opponent had been able to block every attack the assassin had attempted, and even though her opponent's attacks were not successful, Nyght knew that the woman she was staring at was an equal when it came to their fighting skills. Even though Nyght respected her, she was still going to end the woman's life. "Second Position?" Nyght asked.

Daie nodded, "Second Position," she said to agree to the woman's proposal.

At the same time, the two women twirled the blades they had in their right hand so that after three spins, the tips were facing downward, while the blades in their left hands were still pointing toward the sky. Neither of the two women had actual training in how to use their fighting daggers. The knowledge came from what Sun had passed on to Daie, and what Moon had passed on to Nyght. They each had knowledge of everything Sun and Moon had seen since battles in the world began.

They each knew the fighting stances for their weapons. First Position was when a person held their two blades with the tips pointing upward. Since neither Daie nor Nyght had been able to break through the defense of the other, the suggestion Nyght had given would require them to adjust their attack methods as well as their defense.

With their new hold on their blades, the two women once again moved forward to end the fight between them and between Sun and Moon.

The fighting technique of First Position allowed the wielder to attack with forward, thrusting moves. With Second Position, they could still use the same tactic with the blade in their left hand, but since the one in their right, was now facing downward, the attack came as a sweeping motion. It would come across their opponent at a downward or upward slash at the body, or at an angle from either shoulder or an angle starting at the hip. The slashing movement would put their opponent off balance and was harder to block, so the person would have to dodge more from the downward-facing blade while at the same time avoiding the attack from the other.

When the two women closed the distance between them, neither opponent hesitated. Each one slashed the blade in their right hand causing the other to have to dodge the weapon while thrusting the other blade outward. The strategy behind Second Position was to force the opponent to move their body in a certain direction to allow the blade in the left hand to make the killing strike. It was a very good tactic, and if the two women had been fighting someone else, it might have worked. Since Daie and Nyght were of equal skill, neither one was not only able to dodge the downward-facing blade, but as they moved, they were able to either attack with the blade in their left hand or block the attack the other had made.

They also had to rely on their speed at adjusting their feet to move their bodies out of the way of the attack from their opponent. Their skill was so great that as they moved and spun, it appeared as if they were dancing. Each woman stepped in the correct way, at the correct moment, to put their opponent in the position to succumb to an attack, while at the same time, their skills were so great, that they positioned themselves to defend themselves from the attack coming at them. When they had first begun their fight, they performed two moves, attack and defend. Now with a third, they had to attack, defend, and dodge.

If they needed to block the dagger from their opponent's left hand, then they would slash out with the dagger in their right to defend. As they slashed out with their right, their opponent blocked with their left. With every attack they threw at the other, they forced their opponent to have to dodge, which in turn allowed the other to attack with their own blade, causing the other to defend.

It went on that way for a number of attempts, each trying to end the confrontation. They would each attack, defend, and dodge. It was a continuous cycle and after each one of them had attempted fifty attacks, neither one had come close to ending their opponent's life.

Since they had not been able to put an end to the fight with the first change in maneuvers, it was time to make an adjustment, and it was Daie who suggested they try something else. "Third Position!" she yelled as she dodged another slash that would have cut her throat if she had not moved precisely at the right moment.

Within a blink of an eye, the two women once again adjusted the holds on their daggers. They flipped the blades so that the one they held in their right hand had its tip pointing upward, while the blade in their left hand was facing downward. This is Third Position.

Most people would think the Second and Third Positions were the same, only with the blades in the opposite direction as before. Both Nyght and Daie knew that was not true. They had something else in common that they did not even know until they had witnessed each other fighting. They were both right-handed.

If Nyght had wanted to have the advantage, and if Daie was left-handed, when she first called out for the change in positions, she would have called for Third Position, where a right-handed person was using their more powerful hand with the thrusting dagger. When she called for Second Position, she did so to see if her opponent had any flaws in using her weaker hand to execute the main attack. Nyght had no problem with using her right or her left. After they had adjusted to Second Position, she saw that her opponent had none either.

Now both women were thrusting forward with their stronger hands, even though there was not much of a difference from their left, their fighting would take on a completely new level. They would still attack, defend, and dodge, but with their stronger hand, their attacks would come faster and fiercer, and they did.

Their attacks increased with speed, and because of that, they had to increase their defense, as well as their dodging. It was the dodging that made it appear that the two women were performing a dance of great beauty. In a way, they were.

They moved their bodies at greater speeds, which caused them to turn their bodies in ways where there were times their backs were toward their opponent. Not once, even when their eyes were off their opponent and their blades, did neither Daie nor Nyght miss a block, or a chance to attack. However, neither one of them scored a hit either. Each opponent met an attack with the proper defense, and with every dodge, they made the perfect attack, which their opponent blocked with the perfect counterstrike. It was apparent to both women they were once again at a standstill. Their fight was a never-ending cycle, with neither one of them gaining the advantage.

After about another fifty attempts to end the battle, simultaneously, the two women stopped their attacks and defense, moved apart, and stared at each other. Neither one of them even breathing hard, even though their battle had gone on for some time. Sun had risen higher in the sky and Moon had lowered more; both of these facts observed by Daie and Nyght.

Nyght had to start wondering if that was the plan her opponent had the entire time. If Daie had lured her there in hopes she would outlast her. If so, then Nyght would have to put an end to not only the fight, but the woman standing before her, and she would have to do it before Moon was out of the sky completely or her opponent would have the advantage. Nyght knew she had to end the battle soon, which she believed she would. She was the warrior of Moon and she was stronger. All she had to do was rely on what Moon had blessed her with and she would end the woman's life.

Daie saw Sun had risen and Moon was now lower in the sky. She knew she had to end the battle soon; before Moon left the sky.

They had been looking at each other while both were in their own thoughts. Each knowing what they had to do. When they had both paused long enough, they spoke at the same time and said the same exact phrase, "Fourth Position." Without hesitation, the two women twirled the blade they had in their right hand so that it was once again pointing downward. The same as the blade in their left. This is Fourth Position. There is no Fifth.

Colton had watched the battle below from the very first attack each of the women had made. He had regained consciousness not long after Daie had started down the hill, and with some help from a couple of rabbits in the area, he was able to free himself after his two little friends had chewed through the ropes his hands were bound with.

As soon as he was on his feet, he rushed to the edge of the woods and looked down to the glade below. He did not follow Daie. As he watched her make her way to the bottom of the hill, Colton saw the woman who had come after Daie. Nyght was walking down the hill on the opposite side of the glade. Colton moved his eyes to look at the center of the glade where the two women would meet. He knew this was what had to happen, and he was not a part of it.

Every bit of him had feelings for Daie, no, for Hanna, and he wanted to rush down and fight by her side or grab hold of her and force her to flee from the battle, but there was no running for her or for the one called Nyght. This fight had to happen, or else it would never end. Just like the battle between Sun and Moon.

"Are you not going to her?"

Colton looked down to his right and saw the two rabbits who had helped him get free. It was the one closest to his foot that had asked the question. He put his focus back on Daie, "This is her battle. I am not a part of it."

The other rabbit gave its opinion of what was going to happen, *"I think the one belonging to Moon will win."* This caused the other rabbit to weigh in on the upcoming battle.

"No way, the one belonging to Sun has the advantage, and as soon as Moon leaves the sky, she will kill the pale-skin warrior." The rabbit then looked up at the priest of Creator, and asked one more question, *"Will your mate kill the other?"*

Colton did not say it out loud, nor thought it to the little rabbit, but his answer was simply, *"I hope not."*

He watched the fight take place and now he saw that they had stepped back again, and they both had their blades facing downward. Somehow, Colton knew it would be over soon.

The two combatants, knowing the end was near, rushed forward. When they reached the other, their blades slashed out with every bit of anger and hate they had for their opponent. The same anger and hate Sun and Moon shared.

Fourth Position was different from the first three. Not just because of the way the wielder held their daggers, but also because of how the new hold would change the way the combatants fought one another. As in the Second and Third Positions, the attack from the blades came in a slashing manner. In fact, the same movements used in the Fourth position were the same as in the Second and Third. The only difference was that there was no dodging. The combatants stood still with their feet shoulder width apart; this gave them the stability they needed. With their feet firmly planted on the ground, they used their midsection, not to attack or to defend, but to add power into each movement they made with their arms.

Their legs remained perfectly still, but when they swung either of their arms across their opponent's body, or downward at their opponent's head or shoulders, or upward from their opponent's waist, they used their hips to force more power into their attacks, causing their strikes to become more powerful. Fourth Position was about power. Both Sun and Moon had seen mortals use Fourth Position, and they had seen them cut through a full-size tree or a very large boulder with just one swing of their blade.

The first three positions allowed the fighters to have mobility, but with it, they had to use more of their strength to move their entire body. With Fourth Position, the lower part of their body did not move at all, and their midsection only moved enough to add power to their upper body. Very few fighters who knew this position used it, because it required them to leave their backs vulnerable. When it came to a battle where the person's opponent was directly in front of them, the Fourth Position was perfect, because the power of a single slash of a blade could remove a person's head from their shoulders or separate their upper body from their lower, which was what Daie and Nyght were attempting to do.

The sound of their blades traveled a great distance away. Only Colton, the two rabbits with him, and Stygian, who was also watching the two warriors and any other animals in the area witnessing the battle knew what was making the ringing sound. It was the two women's blades striking the blades of their opponent.

They started with their attacks so that their blades were attempting to slice the mid-section of their opponent. With the way they were holding their weapons, when one of them sliced with a blade, they could quickly reverse the direction that it had been traveling to either attempt another attack or if necessary, block their opponent. Out of the four blades, only Daie and Nyght knew whether the move they had just executed was an attack on their opponent or used to defend themselves.

Not even Sun nor Moon could see every move their warriors made, and usually, they saw everything while they were in the sky.

Nyght and Daie continued to fight. When neither one of them was making any headway with attacking their opponent's midsection, they adjusted their attacks higher to aim for the upper body. Each attempting to slice the chest or throat of their opponent. With every move one made, the other had no problem with executing the perfect countermove. Blades swept outward, downward, and upward, and with every attempt, their opponent blocked the attack with their own countermove, while at the same time making an attack themselves. It was a never-ending cycle, and no one was moving any closer to ending the other's life, which would have ended the battle.

Nyght continued to attack and defend. She was so skilled she did not even have to think about which move or countermove she needed to make. Her body knew what it had to do, which allowed her to contemplate what she was witnessing.

Her opponent was able to match her move for move. They had been through all four fighting positions without either of them drawing a single drop of blood from their opponent. Not even the slightest cut had come to the two combatants. Nyght knew that if she did not end the battle soon, she would be the one with the disadvantage when Moon left the sky. Even though she had faith in her skills, she would either have to retreat from the fight and go after the woman when Sun was not in the sky, and Moon was, or she would risk her own life. Nyght did not like either of those options, so she decided she would end the fight before Moon left the sky. She just did not know how.

Daie continued to attack and defend. She was so skilled she did not even have to think about which move or countermove she needed to make. Her body knew what it had to do, which allowed her to contemplate what she was witnessing.

Her opponent was able to match her move for move. They had been through all four fighting positions without either of them drawing a single drop of blood from their opponent. Not even the slightest cut had come to either of them. Daie knew that if she did not end the battle soon, she would be the one with the advantage when Moon left the sky. Daie wanted Moon to see the outcome, so she had to end the fight before Moon left the sky, and she knew how.

Daie flipped her daggers in her hands so that the blades were now pointing upward, coming out of Fourth Position, and back into First Position. Just as Daie thought she would, Nyght saw what she had done and performed the same move. Now both women had their blades pointing upward.

The next thing Daie did was to lean backward

while bringing her legs up and over, causing her to flip back. She did this twice, and when she was midway through her second turn, she saw that her opponent had made the same exact move. When they had ended their rotations, they were facing each other.

Nyght looked at her opponent wondering what she was planning next. Since Daie had interrupted their fight, she thought Sun's warrior was going to suggest something else to test their skills, so Nyght waited.

Daie stared at her opponent for three breaths then made the move to end the battle. She flung her daggers downward at her sides. When they came to a stop, the blades were halfway into the ground. Throughout the entire battle, the two opponents matched each other attack for attack, defense for defense, and move for move. With what Daie had just done, Nyght could not follow. In fact, she had no idea what her opponent was doing.

"It's over," Daie said, but before Nyght could reply, Daie looked up to the sky, turned around in a circle, and screamed as loud as she could. "IT...IS... OVER!" When she was facing Nyght once again, Daie repeated what she had just said, but only in a calmer tone, "It's over."

Nyght did not know what the woman was attempting to do, but she was not going to let her guard down and was ready to continue with the fight. "Pick up your blades," Nyght said and took a step closer to Daie, "It is not over until I kill you." She said it in a way to let the warrior of Sun know that they would continue with their battle.

Daie did not take a step closer, nor did she pick up her blades. "You cannot kill me no more than I can kill you." Once again, Daie turned around in a circle and yelled to the sky, "IT...IS...OVER!"

Nyght thought that the fight had been too much for the woman and she had lost her mind. All she was doing was yelling into the air. That was until Nyght realized to whom Daie had been speaking. Not to the air, but to Sun and Moon. Nyght looked up to the sky and took a quick look at Sun, then at Moon. When she heard Daie start to speak, Nyght put her focus back on the woman.

"Don't you see? It is pointless to continue this fight. You cannot kill me, and I cannot kill you."

Nyght did not agree with what her opponent had said. "I can kill you, and I will."

"How?" Daie asked, and the surprised look on Nyght's face told her that she had not come up with a way to defeat her while they were fighting. "We are evenly matched. For every attack I make you block, and for every attack you make, I can block it as well. You attack I defend. I attack you defend. You defend I attack. I defend you attack." Daie took a step toward Nyght, but the woman was so intrigued by what she was hearing, that the assassin did not even move. "Don't you see? You and I fighting each other is the same as Sun and Moon fighting for all this time."

Daie looked up to the sky, to speak directly to Sun and Moon. "Neither one of you will ever win the battle you have waged for so long because the both of you are evenly matched." Daie lowered her head, once again looking at Nyght. "Just as we are."

Nyght still did not believe what she was hearing. She believed she was the stronger one and that she could defeat the woman standing before her. "Moon and Sun cannot die, that is why they blessed us. So that one of us can take the life of the other, and then everyone will know who is stronger."

"Neither of them are stronger and neither of them are weaker. They are that way because it was the way they were created." Daie took another step closer to Nyght, "Just as we are the way we are because they created us to be just like them."

Nyght believed she could kill her opponent. "One of us has to be the stronger and I will show you that it is me."

Daie could hear the doubt in the statement. "I know who you are." As soon as she made the comment, Nyght gave her a look to let her know that she had no idea who she was, but Daie continued, "You were trained as an assassin. You are even descended from a caste of Elves created for one purpose and that is to kill." Daie took another step toward Nyght. "Do you know what I did for my entire life?" Nyght shook her head to let Daie know she did not have the answer. "I worked in a boarding house. I cleaned out relief shacks. Hung up linen. Cleaned floors and cooked meals." She paused a moment to let Nyght take in her list of accomplishments. "I have never even picked up a weapon in my entire life, but today, I was able to bring our fight to a standstill. Not because of what I was, but because of what Sun made me into." She took one more step closer to Nyght, "The same as Moon did to you. We are evenly matched just like Sun and Moon and that is why neither of us can win in a fight against the other and why they have been fighting for all of their existence."

"Kill her!" Sun said to Daie as Moon said the same words to Nyght.

Daie looked up into the sky at Sun and Moon then back at Nyght. "Let me guess, Moon just told you to kill me." Nyght nodded to let her know Moon had, but she also gave Daie a look to ask how she had known. "Because Sun just said the same to me."

Nyght lowered her blades so they were at her sides. She was going over everything the woman had said. The problem she was having was she actually believed her. She then thought about how she was an assassin, trained to kill. Her ancestors were Elves who brought death to others. She raised her blades ready to start fighting again. "I will kill you, Wicked Girl." Nyght thought that if she used the name the man back in Lorraine used when he spoke of Hanna Gransby, it would anger Daie, and she would resume their battle. It did not work.

Daie remembered the name the people in the village had called her. It was too long ago, and too many things had happened in her life for a name spoken by people she could not even remember for it to upset her.

Daie smiled, but she did not do it because she thought what the woman had said was amusing; she thought that it was pathetic. Not the name "Wicked Girl," but the part about how she would kill her. "No, you won't, nor can you," Daie spoke with a caring and concerned voice. "Maybe, if you only had the skills of your ancestors or your training as an assassin, then we would not be evenly matched, and maybe our fight would have a definite victor. But Moon made you into what you are, and Sun made me into what I am. And like them, we have the same strengths, and therefore, no matter how long or how many times we battle, neither of us would win." Daie knew she was finally getting through to the woman when she saw Nyght once again lower her blades. Daie still had more to tell her, more about herself.

"Sun has wanted to control me ever since I was a child, and in a way, I have allowed Sun to do so. Because of what I believed Sun did to me and my family, I chose to wrap my heart so tight that I would not let anyone in. I thought that I was like that because of Sun but I was wrong. I was like that because I allowed myself to be that way, so in a way I allowed Sun to still control me. I am not going to allow Sun to control the rest of my life." She paused for a moment then continued, "Are you going to let Moon control you?" Nyght did not respond so Daie continued. "I chose to accept the blessing of Sun because I did not know what else to do. I thought that I had nothing to lose, and I didn't. I had already lost everything. My mother, my father, Mama, and Papa; and for a while, I thought I lost the only friend I ever had. But he came back to me. He came back to me because he cares. Do you have someone like that? Someone who cares for you? A mother, a father, a friend? Not someone who is with you because they want something from you, but someone who is there for you and asks nothing of you." Just then Nyght looked directly at Daie, and she knew that what she said had reached the warrior of Moon. Daie had someone who cared for her, Nyght did not have that, or at least she did not know if anyone cared for her. Daie had one final statement to make, "You have to decide who controls your life, as well as your actions. Will it be Moon? As for me... I do."

Daie then turned around and started walking back in the direction she came from to enter the glade. As she passed her blades, she did not even stop, she just bent down, picked them up, and returned them to the holsters at her back. She knew the woman called Nyght could attack her while her back was toward her, but she also knew the woman had other things on her mind. When she reached her cloak, she picked it up as well and continued to walk away.

Nyght watched as Daie walked back up the hill. Just before she arrived at the top where a man was waiting for her, Nyght turned around and started going back the way she had entered the glade, returning her blades to their sheaths at her sides.

As she walked, Moon yelled into her thoughts, *"You have failed me. I made you into who you are. I was the one who brought you out of that hovel of a town you were born in. If it was not for me, you would have ended up on your back for the rest of your life as a whore and I command you to kill the warrior of Sun!"*

Nyght waited until Moon had stopped talking to her, then she spoke to Moon, "Do not speak to me again." When she reached her cloak, she picked it up, wrapped it around her body and pulled the hood up over her head, then continued up the hill.

Nyght made her way back to Stygian and patted him once on the side of his head. He took a quick nip at her hand, not as a sign of aggression, but to let her know he was glad she had returned. She then climbed up onto his back and took one more look at the opposite hill. She could no longer see the woman called Daie because she too had entered back into the woods. Nyght was not sure what had happened down in the glade, but one thing she knew was that she did not want to set eyes on the red-skinned woman with the golden hair anytime soon, if ever.

Stygian turned around and started walking, without any command from his rider. He knew she needed to leave the area and find someplace where she could think about who she was, and how she was just humbled.

Moon had left the sky. Moon's warrior had left

the field as well. Sun's warrior had also walked away. The only one still looking at where the two women had battled was Sun. Sun did not bother to try to talk to Daie. Sun knew she would not listen. Sun was also regretting the day Sun had chosen the girl, but Sun was not ready to end the battle with Moon. No, Sun had already come up with another plan.

SEVENTEEN

When Daie reached the top of the hill, she saw Colton staring at her. She did not speak to him; she just walked past him and went over to where their horses were and untied the reins to hers from around the tree. "What made you decide not to take her life?" Colton asked when he turned around to face Daie.

She dropped the reins, moved to stand at the tail end of her horse, and looked at Colton. "I never planned on killing her." She saw the confused look on his face. "I said I was going to stop her, and I did," she said, then she smiled.

Colton, who was still confused, turned his head and looked back down the hill, even though there was no one there. He then turned back to face Daie. He had not been close enough to the fight to hear what the two women had said, although he had no problem hearing Daie when she yelled up into the sky. "What did you say to her?" he asked, wanting to know how she had stopped the woman from killing her.

"I told her the truth. That what she was doing, what Moon wanted her to do, and what Sun wanted from me, was useless. Sun and Moon's fight has been going on for their entire existence, and the same would happen if she and I listened to them. It would be a never-ending battle, one with no winner."

If it were not for the fact that he had seen the two women walk away from each other, and that Daie was standing in front of him, he never would have believed what she had just said and what she had done. "So, you never even thought about killing her? Not once?"

"No," Daie said while smiling.

"And all that 'I am going to stop her' talk you were doing, what was that for?"

Her smile grew wider, and then she answered, "I needed to make sure Sun did not realize what I was planning. So, when you asked me what I was going to do, I pulled on the hate I had for Nyght and gave you my answer." She stopped smiling and adjusted her gaze to look to the right of Colton, "That was Sun's hate though."

"So, you don't hate the woman who tried to kill you?" Colton asked.

She put her eyes back on him, "How can I hate her when I don't even know who she is." She then looked to the right of Colton again, as if looking at Nyght, "She doesn't even know herself, and I feel sorry for her."

"Why?"

She looked back at Colton and then walked over to where he was. She was so close that there was not even a handbreadth between them, "Because she is all alone." She looked up into his eyes. "But I have you." She lifted herself up on her toes, put her arms around his neck, and kissed him on the lips. Even though he did not kiss her back, because he was too shocked at what she was doing, she did not stop until she was ready.

When she finally pulled back, he looked at her and asked, "How long have you wanted to do that?"

She smiled and said, "Since the day I met you on the roof and you tossed me the apple." Her smile grew wider as did his eyes. She gave him a moment to think about what she had said then turned around and walked back to her horse. She picked up the reins and prepared to climb up.

"Are you going back to Maridian now?" Colton asked to find out what she was planning on doing because whatever it was, he was going to be there with her.

She climbed up on her horse and turned it around to face him. "No," she said firmly and continued to explain her answer. "Maridian is where Hanna lived. I am not the woman I used to be."

"Then what are *we* going to do?" Colton asked, making sure she heard the "*we*" which was something that he was happy about.

"Right now, *we* are going to go back to Kenshaw and collect our reward for bringing in Rashad Menlo, then *we* are going to go and round up the rest of his band of thieves. Hopefully, there is a reward on them as well, but if not, at least they won't be bothering anyone else after *we* take care of them." She smiled.

"And then?" Colton asked because he was still curious as to what she was planning with her life as well as his, since he was going to be by her side.

Daie turned her horse so that it and her were facing away from Colton, to answer his question, she turned her head and looked at him over her right shoulder. "We'll see." She gave him another smile, then turned around, kicked her horse, and started riding away.

Colton had spent his entire childhood trying to get her to smile, but he never thought he would see a smile like the one he had, just before she rode off. Not only was it beautiful, but it was seductive, and he started wondering just what she meant by "We'll see."

He went over, took the reins to his own horse, and climbed up. *"Remember, watch out for her legs,"* the horse thought to him, and Colton could not help but smile, and then nudge his horse for it to follow Daie.

Since she was a few paces in front of him, he watched as she sat in her saddle, riding as if she was a new person. She had said that she was not the woman she used to be. When they were younger, and living in Maridian, Colton always believed that if he could just get Hanna out of the city, she would see that there was more to life than what she was used to, and he was correct. He would respect her request and call her by the name Daie, but to him, she would always be Hanna.

The two women had left the glade some time ago, but while the sun was still in the sky, another visitor walked over to the area where Nyght and Daie had ended the battle between Sun and Moon. Behind him came Mule.

Adoni looked up into the sky at Sun, who was about to descend just as Moon was about to rise. Adoni waited just before Sun was out of the sky, and Moon was just rising, so he could talk to them together. "Now that your two warriors have ended their battle, I expect you both to learn from them and do the same."

Sun was the one to answer, *"I will destroy the warrior I have created; I will burn her out of existence. I gave her life, and I will take it away. Then I will choose another. Next time, my warrior will not fail me, and all will see that I am greater than Moon."*

Adoni was tired of the battle between the two Guardians he had created. He had more important matters to see to, and after all this time, Sun and Moon were still acting like spoiled children. His children. Adoni looked directly into Sun. Besides Daie, he was the only one who could, and he made sure Sun saw him; only not as the persona he uses to walk the world of Eirene; no, he made sure Sun saw him as Creator. Sun cringed at the full sight of the one who created Sun.

Creator reached out and took hold of Sun. Something he had never done before, but sometimes a father needs to use a firm hand when dealing with his children. *"It is over. From this moment on, you and Moon will no longer battle one another. After all this time, you still have not realized that the fight between the two of you is pointless. Neither of you are stronger because I made you each for a specific purpose and gave you the strength to fulfill that purpose."* Even though Sun did not breathe, with the hold Creator had on Sun, Sun felt the life leaving Sun's form. Since it was Creator, there was nothing Sun could do but listen to Creator's final command. *"I also forbid you to do any harm to the one you made your warrior."* Creator turned his head completely around to face the opposite direction so he could see Moon. *"That goes for you as well."* He then let go of Sun and forced his power to the level where he could take on the form of Adoni once again. The form he preferred.

Having regained control of his anger, Adoni looked back at Sun, "Do I make myself clear?" he asked.

Sun knew Creator was waiting for a response, *"Yes, Creator,"* Sun said as Sun went down out of the sky.

Now in the form of Adoni, he had to turn his body around to look at Moon who was in the sky behind him.

Moon knew Creator was waiting for a response. *"Yes, Father,"* Moon said, and remained quiet, not wanting to anger Creator any further.

Adoni could not help but smile when he heard Moon's response. Moon had always called him Creator, but for the first time in Moon's existence, Moon called him Father.

Adoni turned and faced the direction Moon's warrior had left the glade. Apparently, her influence on Moon was just as great as Moon's influence on her. If not more.

"Can we go now?" Adoni turned and looked at Mule. *"I am ready to leave this place."*

Adoni did not even respond to the one hundredth and tenth complaint Mule had, just today. Mule was the offspring of Horse and Donkey. Therefore, Adoni, or Creator, had not created Mule. He was a Second-generation creation, and since Mule was a mixture of two of Creator's First, like all Seconds, many of Creator's creations did not accept Mule. To others, Mule was an oddity. Creator loved him for what Mule was, and just because Mule might be different, and was something that was not meant to be, it did not mean Mule did not have a purpose. Thinking that, Adoni looked back in the direction Nyght had left, and then he looked in the opposite direction, where Daie had gone. Along with Colton, Creator's First new priest.

"I am getting hungry," Mule said to Adoni, and this time, he could not hold back his retort.

"You don't even need to eat, so how can you be hungry."

"You are the one who has me carrying you all

over Eirene, and since you made me take this physical form, just because you have as well, this form needs to eat."

Very few of Creator's creations would dare talk to him as Mule does. Maybe that is why Creator chose Mule to be his traveling companion while he walked the world of Eirene. As much as Mule wanted to leave the physical world, Creator, no Adoni still had much to prepare for, and not much time to do so.

He walked over and stood next to Mule and looked at the two birds sitting on the back of Mule. They were both black and almost looked the same, except the one on the left was bigger than the one on the right. They were not the same species even though they were cousins. They were both First. "Raven, Crow, it is time," Adoni said, and the two birds cawed as they flew off the back of Mule and took to the air. Heading south, they had a great distance to go.

Now that the space was free of birds, Adoni climbed up onto Mule. *"Where are we going now?"* Mule asked.

Adoni smiled and gave his reply, "Oh, I think we need to check on Moon's warrior and see how she is doing."

"Why must we do that?" Mule asked.

Adoni did not reply. Sometimes Creator does not answer all the questions presented to him.

Moon was in the sky, but Nyght did not look up. Nor did she answer Moon when Moon called to her. She had a lot on her mind, and with all the questions she was asking herself, she could not find the answers she was looking for.

She sat next to the small fire she had made and was staring into the flames. Not even in them could she see what the point of her existence was and the fire itself only reminded her of the hearth back in the room of Esteemed-High-Master Wraith's quarters, and she wished he was there with her. Maybe he could shed some light on the confusion she had inside of her. If she could talk to him, or even someone else, maybe they would be able to tell her what she wanted to know.

She looked up from the flames as soon as she heard the noise coming from the trees. She did not reach for her blades at her sides because she knew that if it was someone who was going to try to harm her, she would not have a problem ending the person's life. She ended the thought with, *"Unless it was Daie."*

When the man entered her camp, it took her a moment before she recognized him. When she did, she had to wonder why he was there.

"Ah, it is good to see you again," Adoni said as he walked over to the fire and sat down next to it, opposite Nyght.

She had watched the old man, but since she did not think that he was any kind of threat, she did not try to stop him from coming over to the fire, even though she did not want the company. She then remembered how she had just thought about wanting to talk to someone.

She looked over the flames and saw the old man watching her. He had his arms stretched out in front of him, with his palms facing the fire, appearing as if he was trying to warm himself, even though there was no chill in the night air.

"Where's your mule?" Nyght asked, recognizing the man as the one who told her where to find the warrior of Sun when she was in Lorraine.

Adoni turned his head and looked over his right shoulder then back at Nyght, "Oh, I think he is off somewhere eating." He then looked over to the horse standing a couple of paces away. Of course, he knew it was Stygian. One of Horse's immediate children, therefore, Stygian was actually a prince in Horse's hierarchy, but Adoni was not there to check on Stygian. He could take care of himself, and since Adoni had asked Stygian to join the woman sitting across from him in her travels, his presence was no surprise.

"You look like someone with a lot of questions and no answers." Adoni said, and when he saw the look Nyght was giving him because he had read her perfectly, he added, "I am a man who has seen a lot and done just as much. I might be able to clear the fog surrounding your path."

"My path," Nyght said and chuckled. "That is

the problem, isn't it?" she asked, as much to herself than to her guest.

Even though she had not asked for his opinion, he decided that she might benefit from it. That was why he had come to her. "Most people think that their problems are a result of their past."

"Are they not?" Nyght asked, looking at the man across the fire.

"Some, yes." Since she remained silent, he continued. "It does not matter what we were. Whether we came from a caste of Elves, the Assassin's Guild, or were even blessed by Moon." Nyght was so shocked at what he had said, all she could do was sit there and listen as he continued to talk. "You can ask the questions 'Who am I?' and 'Where did I come from?' but those are not the important ones. The more important question is, 'Where am I going from this moment forward?'"

They held their stare for a few breaths longer and then he stood, turned around, and started heading back the way he had come. Before he made it to the trees, Nyght asked her question, "Who are you?"

He turned his head and looked over his shoulder, "My name is Adoni." He then turned back, "I hope to see you again, Nyght."

Just then, Stygian neighed loudly. It startled Nyght and she turned to look at her horse. When she saw that he was in no danger, she turned back to face the direction Adoni had been, only he was already out of sight.

She put her eyes back on the fire. She tried to remember when she had ever told the man her name, but could not come up with the answer, so she moved on to her next question, which she said out loud to hear it herself. "Where am I going from this moment forward?"

Nyght had a lot to think about.